Literat... ...of ...
Design & Communications. Before becoming a full-time
author, Saskia's writing experience included being a health and
beauty editor on women's magazines, a ghost writer for the BBC
and HarperCollins, copywriting and script editing. Saskia lives
in south London with her partner and four children.

**Visit Saskia Sarginson online:**

www.saskiasarginson.co.uk
www.facebook.com/saskiasarginsonbooks
@saskiasarginson

Without You
The Other Me
The Stranger
How It Ends

SASKIA SARGINSON

# how it ends

piatkus

PIATKUS

First published in Great Britain in 2018 by Piatkus
This paperback edition published in 2019 by Piatkus

1 3 5 7 9 10 8 6 4 2

Copyright © 2018 by Saskia Sarginson

The moral right of the author has been asserted.

A CIP catalogue record for this book
is available from the British Library.

ISBN 978-0-349-41998-5

Typeset in Goudy by M Rules
Printed and bound in Great Britain by
Clays Ltd, Elcograf S.p.A.

Papers used by Piatkus are from well-managed forests
and other responsible sources.

Piatkus
An imprint of
Little, Brown Book Group
Carmelite House
50 Victoria Embankment
London EC4Y 0DZ

An Hachette UK Company
www.hachette.co.uk

www.littlebrown.co.uk

For Ana

# PROLOGUE

Ruby doesn't know how the book came into her possession. Perhaps he brought it to her on one of his visits, along with armfuls of tulips and boxes of chocolates. She shows it to her visitors – the woman with the mop in her hand, the girl who blushes when she speaks – 'Look,' Ruby says, pointing to the name on the cover. 'My son. Christopher Delaney.'

It has letters picked out in scarlet, in a raised font, which is pleasing to run her finger over, like Braille, or a secret message. It takes her breath away to know that her child is the author of this novel. She reads and rereads his name, his beloved name.

She opens the book and his words are waiting for her. But it hurts her head to concentrate on such small writing. Squinting at close-packed sentences, the letters break apart, swarming into ants that crawl onto her fingers, marching up her sleeves, tiny mouths ready to bite. She looks away, shutting the book. It doesn't matter. It doesn't spoil the joy she feels from holding it. She likes to keep it with her, carrying it from room to room, and when it's time for bed, she slips it under her pillow or cradles it to her breast.

She misses proper darkness. They won't let her cover the opening in the door where faces watch. She keeps her eyes closed and listens to the flickering hiss of lights in the corridor and feet going by; she recognises the quick click, click of someone who's in charge, and the slow roll and halt of someone who isn't.

By the time the screams begin, the muffled, echoing screams, Ruby hopes for night meds to knock her out like a blow to the head. As she falls asleep, she presses her nose into the pages, inhaling the papery scent of Christopher's words. And it feels as though she's taking him into her lungs too, holding him inside the hidden rooms of her body. As a child, his breath smelt of apples, mint, and cinnamon chewing gum. Hedy's did, too.

Hedy. Her name is a hole to fall down.

When will he come again? She needs to see him, to touch him and make sure that he's real. She used to pat him dry after his bath, rubbing cream into the sores on his skin. She was a loving mother. Yes, she was. She must not remember the cage. She must not. It makes her cry, and if she cries they will come with the wires and the straps, and that will never do, because she's good now, isn't she? She has privileges, like keeping a novel on the cabinet beside her bed. Like spending the afternoon in the garden when it's warm. None of them suspect that while she sits on the wooden bench with her eyes closed, fingers linked, her face tilted to catch the breeze, she's decoding the humming of bees in the roses, tuning in to the whispering of her name over and over: *Ruby, Ruby, Ruby*. Todd's voice, telling her that he'll be here soon to bring her home, back to Iowa. Across the ocean. Back to the two children playing in the yard, blond heads together under the burning sun.

2

# PART ONE

The Base

# ONE

## 1957

This is Hedy Delaney's first stay in a hotel. She was hoping for bell boys in swanky uniforms serving lobster from little trolleys covered in white cloths. She's never eaten lobster, and to be truthful she's not sure she likes the idea; it's what it stands for that counts: the exotic and unknown. Instead, she's sitting on a bed with a view of an air-conditioning box, cooped up with the rest of her family. She wants to let out her frustration in a good long howl from the pit of her belly. But you can't scream in New York City, not unless you're getting mugged. The cops would come and beat down the door. Her parents might even be hauled off to jail. Instead, she channels her agitation into picking at the sticking plasters on the backs of her arms, peeling them away with the edges of her nails.

She's twelve, the age that most girls in her class are getting training bras and joining Future Home Makers of America. Hedy's lanky frame gives no hint that she'll develop curves that will need constraining, and she lacks any desire to learn to hem curtains or make meatloaf. The fact that she's named after Hedy Lamarr by her father is a small cruelty that only Hedy's mother dwells on. Hedy hasn't any use for film stars. Baseball players are more her thing. The Yankees her favourite team. On this particular evening, she guesses she's within batting distance of their stadium, although she'll never get to see Yogi Berra pitch, or Joe Collins make a catch, because she's trapped in this room, and tomorrow she'll be leaving the United States to go to a place where nobody's heard of baseball.

Hedy cranes around further to examine the back of her swollen arm, the difficulty of it making her squint as she tears away a second Band-Aid, darkened with a smear of blood. Her parents are huddled in the corner, locked into a whispered discussion. They never once glance in Hedy's direction. Everyone is ignoring her. Even Chris. He hasn't stopped scribbling in his notebook since they left home. Anyone would think his made-up words were more important than whatever his sister might have to say. Now he's burrowed under a blanket on the put-up bed, asleep. How can he sleep with this ache in his arm?

She picks up his notebook and flicks through to the last pages. But he hasn't been writing another of his stories. Her brother has drawn himself. She touches the pencil sketch and frowns. It's a good likeness. He's included every detail of the Milwaukee Brace he has to wear for twenty-three hours out of each day. Chris has severe scoliosis. The brace is supposed to correct his crooked spine, force his poor twisted bones back into the right places. Mom says that he will be cured by it, so keeping him strapped into the contraption is actually being cruel to be kind. When Mom says words like 'actually', Hedy remembers that her mother is English.

Hedy stares at her brother's self-portrait. He's depicted the buckles and straps on the heavy leather corset that encases him from the tops of his thighs up to his waist. For extra discomfort it has a two-inch-wide metal upright running from the corset up the middle of his chest, where it joins a metal collar that is fixed around his throat. Two more bars press at his back, either side of his spine. Then there is the chin pad, held up by a thin metal bar attached to the collar. The chin pad forces his head upwards, so that like a frightened horse, he must always have his head raised, his eyes rolling with the effort of seeing anything beneath his eye line.

She turns the page. Here is another drawing. This time Chris has drawn a boy smiling inside a big puffy space suit. His head is enclosed inside a glass bubble; through it, he looks out at stars twinkling around him. His body floats through space, free-wheeling across planets, higher than the moon. The sketch doesn't surprise her; her brother is passionate about outer space, science-fiction stories, and especially the idea of aliens. This is who he wants to be, a space explorer, not the kid in the brace with the weird spine. She sighs and shuts the notebook. She goes along with his fantasy of creatures from other planets and space travel because she knows his imagination lets him escape real life, helps him forget his pain.

Thinking of how it must feel to be stuck in the brace makes her itch with claustrophobia. She tugs at the neckline of her shirt. There's no air in here; the window is sealed. Their bags and suitcases are piled around them. The rest of their possessions, nailed into boxes like dead bodies, have been sent ahead on a boat. She smells the hot dogs they had for supper, bought from a sidewalk vendor, ketchup and mustard dripping over their fingers as they perched on the bed to eat, Mom fussing about the mess, reminding them to use the paper napkins she'd handed out and not drop crumbs on the sheets. The hot dogs had been a treat. Like the earlier, hurried trip up the Empire State building. But now the memory of fried onion and rubbery pink makes her queasy. She thinks of home, their yard with the Stars and Stripes flying out front. She wonders if their stuff is floating somewhere over the Atlantic Ocean, or maybe it's already on dry land, at the new house, waiting for them. She wonders what it will be like. She hopes it has a bedroom each for her and Chris, a winding staircase leading to a spooky attic, and a big garden with plenty of room to pitch a fast ball. She glances at her parents. They have their faces close, talking quietly. Dad's got mustard on his shirt.

When Dad broke the news, months ago, Hedy jumped on and off the sofa and hung onto his arms, both her and Chris asking him questions. Would they eat fish and chips out of newspaper? Really? Would the British people understand their accent, would they have to go to school, would they take the Buick? 'Sure we'll take her, Princess,' Dad laughed, swinging Hedy from his biceps. 'No way I'd leave her behind. You guys will love England. The base even has its own movie house.' And would he be flying bombers again? He shook his head. 'My flying days are over. Your dad's been promoted, kids. There's important work on the ground.' He tapped the side of his nose. 'Got to keep those Reds at bay.' At dinner, he let them sip from his beer and laughed when a stream of froth shot out of Chris's nostrils. Dad kept laughing while Chris spat the rest on his plate. Hedy waited for Mom to leap up and start cleaning the mess. But she sat chewing her lip, blind to it all. 'Come on, Ruby, you're like death at a wedding feast,' Dad said, 'you're spoiling the fun.'

Normally, Dad can get Mom to laugh with a kiss or a joke, or he'll grab her in a tango embrace and dip her backwards until her head nearly touches the floor, and after he sets her upright she'll slap his arms and tell him off for making her dizzy, pink-cheeked and giggling. Not this time. After Hedy and Chris were in bed, it started.

'What about Christopher?' Mom asked.

'What about him?' Dad. Low and tired-sounding. 'There are doctors in England.'

'They won't be as good as here. Nothing's as good as America. Going back to England means giving up so much. The kids don't understand. They think it'll be fun.'

A long sigh from Dad. 'You knew we'd get posted again, baby. We don't get to pick, like some holiday. We'll be staying on an American base. It'll have all the amenities you're used to here. And besides, this is a promotion for me – it could lead to something big, for all of us.'

Hedy, her ear pressed against the door, was puzzled. Why wouldn't Mom want to go back? She must have gotten to like Iowa better than her childhood home. She hardly talked about Grandpa, or her brother, or the life she had before she married Dad. England was tiny, hardly bigger than a single state, so although Hedy was hazy as to exactly where her unknown relatives lived, it didn't matter, because wherever it was, Hedy realised she'd meet them at last. Maybe there would be an aunt too, she thought, cousins even.

Outside, the city of New York shoves itself up against the glass, full of show-off noise and flashing lights and too many walls. It makes Hedy's neck ache from looking up. There's no room for the sky. She manoeuvres her arm carefully. It throbs as if she's stuck it inside a hornet's nest. Nobody said *anything*

9

about having to have inoculations. Chris twitches under the blanket. He's not asleep after all. He's crying.

She climbs in next to him, lying on her good side. He is stuck on his back like a beetle. She rubs his shoulder in consoling circles. 'Do you want me to read to you? I've got *David Starr, Space Ranger* in my bag.'

'No,' he whispers, his voice choked with tears. 'Not now.'

'Least we won't catch diphtheria or polio,' she says. 'Think about nice things. Like ice-cream. Tomorrow, we're going in an airplane.'

Hedy is ten minutes older than her brother. He needs looking after. Not that he's stupid or anything. He's the cleverest person she knows. His main problem – apart from the obvious one – is that he seems to lack an instinct for self-preservation, always leaving himself open to teasing and disappointments.

Hedy puts her head on the pillow. She slips her arm around his waist, avoiding the leather girdle of his hips, trying to hug the rigid line of his body, pressing her nose into the curve of his neck. She begins to hum, blocking out Mom and Dad's angry whispers. Chris wipes his nose, sniffs and wriggles. 'You're making me hot.'

'Keep still, loser. Squeeze up. This bed's too small.'

He smiles. She can't see his face, but she feels his smile, feels it as a softening somewhere inside her chest. He gives a shuddering sigh, and then grows heavy against her. She listens to him slipping away into sleep: breathing deepening, the slight asthmatic click of his lungs. Chris is allergic to everything. Milk. Nuts. Pollen. Cat's fur. It has taken Hedy a while to forgive him for this. She's always wanted a cat.

Ruby stands, shoulders hunched, biting her lip.

'Hey,' Todd says gently, taking a final drag on his cigarette and stubbing it out in the overflowing ashtray on the side table. 'Give me a smile, baby. We've got a big day tomorrow. Come here.' He holds out his arms.

Ruby closes her eyes inside his embrace, leaning her cheek against his shirt. She's already said her piece about not wanting to go back to England. And now it's too late to make a fuss; nothing can reverse the events unfolding around them. She's being an idiot. Todd wants this posting badly. It's a promotion for him, and it's churlish of her to take the shine off it. She softens her body, allowing herself the relief of being properly held. 'I'm sorry,' she whispers into his shoulder. 'If you want to know the truth, I'm a little afraid of flying. Silly,' she gives a short laugh, 'with me married to a pilot.'

He smiles, as she knew he would, and begins to reassure her earnestly about how safe commercial flight is. She lets him. She can't untangle the complications of her real fears, let alone explain them. Her main concern is for Christopher. They're leaving the hospital in Iowa with all its up-to-date equipment and knowledge, and she worries about keeping him safe in England, where people haven't recovered from the war yet, and there'll be hardship and poverty. She imagines a muttering crowd of resentful locals, faces pressed against a perimeter fence, looking hungrily at the privileged Yanks in their midst. It feels strange to be going back to a place that she ran from, that she thought she'd never see again. She's certain that being in East Anglia, so close to the farm where she grew up, will remind her of her childhood: all the unhappiness, dirt and drudgery that she's tried to forget. She doesn't want to be that girl again. She could never get rid of the filth under her nails, inside the cracks in her skin. There'd been no love in that house, no kindness, no forgiveness. All she did was dream of escape. But her brother can't reclaim her now, she reminds herself. She'll get on that plane tomorrow in her new blue suit, nylons sleek against her showered skin; she'll make Todd proud. She might be going back, but she's a different person now. A married woman. An American.

Ruby rubs her finger over the oily yellow stain on Todd's collar. It'll need a hot wash to get it out. She brushes her lips against his chin before she detaches herself and goes over to the put-up bed, where her children lie entwined like babes in the wood, milky-skinned, blue-veined, easily bruised; an identical rash of freckles appearing every summer. Viking blood. Her side of the family is full of tall people, heavy with bone, eyes pale as water.

Hedy's and Christopher's hair mingles on the pillow, the same flaxen shade. Ruby leans down, touching her son's forehead, smoothing it with her fingertip. They'll have to find an English doctor that understands his condition. His parted lips tremble with each intake of air. His skin is flushed, his pale lashes darkened and spiky with tears. He sobs more than a boy should, his eyes welling up if he sees roadkill, or if she and Todd argue, or if any living creature is cruel to another. Watching him, she's filled with a familiar fear, and a fierce need to protect him from life's innumerable hurts. Ruby suspects that there was a mix-up at conception, that the little cells that bestow male and female attributes somehow got confused between which twin was which and ended up in the wrong babies. She doesn't know if Todd shares her suspicions, because it's not the sort of thing a man would admit out loud about his only son.

The room is alive with the sleeping breath of her children, the open-mouthed snoring of her husband. But Ruby, her face

12

slick with Pond's cold cream, spiky curlers skewered in place, can't sleep. Outside the window, New York is restless too. The room pulses with lights flickering through the drawn curtains. She hears unknown voices, sounds of passing traffic, and the snap and clip of heels rising relentlessly from the sidewalk below. Where are they going, all these strangers? What mysterious needs and desires have set them pacing the city till the early hours?

She thinks of her little house in Sioux City, the ranch-style porch lost in shadows, the rooms standing empty, stripped of the furniture she painted herself, and the curtains she ran up on her machine like a modern pioneer. At night, the only sound was Pete next door reversing his Chevrolet into the drive, or the cry of a coyote. Orleans Avenue was a place where everyone knew their neighbours, and strangers were a rarity. So it had seemed like a mirage when a whole crowd passed by her house weeks before, most of them in cars, but some travelling on foot like refugees, carrying cases done up with straps, pushing prams loaded with bric-a-brac: the inhabitants of downtown forced to evacuate before the dam broke. The water came, just as predicted, tearing down telephone wires, washing away whole houses, cars, dogs. They said it was the March snows that had caused the Missouri to rise so high. There had been pictures of the disaster on the news, but Ruby had seen it for herself, standing in her own front yard, looking into the valley. Drowned trees holding up supplicating branches. Birds wheeling in circles above. It was biblical, as if she was witnessing the words of the Old Testament come to life; and inside her head she could hear her father: *Come into the ark, you and all your household, because I have seen that you are righteous before me.*

It was after the water that the smell appeared. A dank, oily rotting. A stench of sulphur, like eggs gone bad. In her bed at night, Ruby shut the window against it, bunched her nightdress in front of her nose. It reminded her of Norfolk, of the farm: the slop of mud in the yard, compost heap breathing out ripe fumes, pig blood seeping into damp straw. Orleans Avenue was tainted by it. The bright, clean street with its neat flower beds, newly cut edges and sawdust-scented fences was blanketed in a dark pall, as if something ancient had been woken and was crawling out of the carcasses of buildings and the mouths of animal corpses, the smell rising from the stranded city like a curse.

She'd told herself then that the flood was a sign that it was right to leave Iowa. After all, they'd be living on an American air base in England. She wouldn't visit Norfolk. Her brother wouldn't even know that she was back. She supposes he'll be running the farm singlehandedly now their father's dead, although how he manages she doesn't know. There'll be two headstones in St Andrew's churchyard, both parents buried next to each other, lichen already spotting the newer stone, weeds sprouting from damp grass.

Hedy imagined the first thing she'd see would be Buckingham Palace with the guards out front in bearskin hats, and then maybe red double-decker buses like the ones in films. She expected the sidewalks would be a moving canopy of umbrellas under a deluge of rain. She knows about English rain. Dad told her how he'd spent the war knee-deep in mud, clothes stinking of mildew. He couldn't get warm in his tin hut, not even in his fur-lined flying jacket with electrically heated long johns underneath. He couldn't get warm until he met Mom and love lit a fire inside him.

Hedy feels cheated by those stories. It's dry here. Not a

drop of water, the ground gritty with dirt. They'd landed at a poky airfield that could have been anywhere. There'd been no palace with the new queen on a balcony waving to the crowds. No union flags and bunting like she'd seen on the television programme about the coronation, when Elizabeth II rode in a golden coach. It had been raining then. Black umbrellas everywhere, glistening.

They stand at a bus stop on a country lane. The proportions of road, field, hedge, even sky, are smaller; the colours of nature faded, as if the place is worn out from being so old. Her family blink in the early-morning light; they have sour breath and sleep-crumpled hair, including Mom, whose usual lacquered curls have dropped into fuzzy clumps. Hedy kicks one of the bags at her feet. There should be something to mark the occasion. They're in England. But it feels as if they're lost.

They've hardly got on board before the bus lurches forwards with a grinding of gears, and Dad, stowing bags, swears loudly as he clings onto the back of a seat to stop himself falling. People turn and look. Hedy hears, 'Yanks.' And another voice says, 'Overpaid and overfed,' and there's a burst of laughter.

'They were happy to see us a few years ago,' Dad says, his voice rising. 'Place would be run by jackboots if it wasn't for us.'

Two men in the seat in front of Hedy keep screwing their heads round to gaze at Chris. Hedy wants to punch them, but Mom gives her restraining looks. Everyone on the bus is rude, and they smell like they haven't washed for weeks; there's a reek of raw onion and dirty feet. Worse than that is their ingratitude: Dad saved them from the Germans, and now he's going to protect them from the Russians. Hedy gives them all hard stares, wanting to ask these English passengers if they think getting the A-bomb dropped on them will be any fun, but Mom gives her another warning look as she leans across the aisle to wipe Chris's cheeks with a hanky she's just licked. Chris sits motionless and uncomplaining, letting her scrub at him with her spit. Sometimes his good nature makes him so meek that Hedy wants to stick a pin in him. She keeps her eyes on the other passengers. The women have red faces and bare, mottled legs; none of them wear nylons. Black socks droop around their ankles. The men's faces are bearded and dirty-looking, just like the pictures on her bubblegum cards from The Children's Crusade against Communism. One woman holds a box on her lap. A rustling comes through the cardboard sides, claws scratching to get out.

Hedy stares as the woman gets off, carting the box with her along the grassy verge, her coat flapping at bare legs.

'What's she got in there?' Hedy leans close to the grubby window so that she can follow the woman's progress. 'A puppy maybe? Mom?' Hedy jogs her mother's elbow. 'What's in the box?'

'The box? I don't know,' Mom says, blinking at Hedy. 'Rabbits?'

'Rabbits?'

'Yes. To eat, I expect.'

'To eat!'

'Food is still in short supply there, Hedy. Even now, meat's hard to come by. It's not like America.'

Back in Iowa, the girl next door kept two Dwarf rabbits in a cage in the yard, and Hedy had been allowed to hold one. She'd thought it would be solid and round in her arms like a hairy baby. But under its cloud of fur, the creature was a complication of narrow angles. She could feel the breakable hoop of its ribs and the curve of its spine. A stuttering tick, tick,

tick of fear had come beating straight from its heart into her palms, until she couldn't bear it, the responsibility, and she'd put the animal back onto the newspaper in the hutch, wiping her sweating hands on her jeans. Hedy won't eat rabbit. She would rather starve.

A stocky man in military uniform is waiting at the bus stand in town. He and Dad pummel each other's shoulders with fists, smiling as if they've won a prize.

'You remember Hank, don't you honey?'

Mom nods, 'It's good to see you, Hank. It's been a long time.'

'He's Major Pulaski now.'

'Come on. That's not important between friends. Not while we're off base.' Hank takes Mom's hand, keeps it prisoner in both of his. 'Ruby, you haven't changed a bit. Just as lovely.'

Hedy and Chris exchange eye rolls. It's odd to hear another man give Mom compliments. They glance at Dad, but he's all smiles. Hank ruffles the children's hair and offers them sticks of Juicy Fruit. They unwrap dusty strips from silver foil, placing them on their tongues. He opens the back door of a Cadillac for them, and Dad helps Chris in before Hedy and Mom slide in after him. Then Dad gets in the front passenger seat.

'Good of you to come,' Dad's saying. 'We appreciate it. And I certainly appreciate this opportunity.' As the car rolls along, Hank and Dad don't stop nattering. Hank keeps glancing in the rear-view mirror, winking at Hedy. She wonders if he has a twitch, some disorder left over from the war, like Dad's knee where the bullet went in.

Hedy looks out of her window. They're travelling through a town, driving past brick terraces, overtaking a man leading a horse and cart piled up with rags. She chews until the gum has lost the taste of home, and her jaw aches. She spits it out, wrapping the ball in the saved foil, and puts it in her pocket. The roads here are different, houses rise straight up from the sidewalks. Weeds grow everywhere, sprouting from piles of rubble, spilling out of broken walls, pushing up behind tumbledown fences. Small boys grub about in the gutters, their shaven heads pale; they shout as the car rolls past, but Hedy can't hear the words. Then the town is behind them, and they're driving along narrow roads through fields of earth, between untidy hedges.

Ruby looks at the back of Hank's head. He'd been a skinny creature with plenty of hair when she'd seen him last, lost inside his flying jacket; small enough to curl into the ball turret under the belly of the B-17, although that job was taken by a gunner. Hank had sat beside Todd in the cockpit. Ten young men crammed into a flying metal bucket: somehow they'd all survived their missions flying thousands of feet above the angry earth, winging past death time and time again, grazing its cheek with their own as if they were gods spinning across clouds inside a chariot of fire, lucky charms held between clenched teeth. It's a shock to see Hank again, an ordinary man at the wheel of a car.

As co-pilot, he had been Todd's chief assistant and understudy. The two men had hardly spent a moment apart: eating meals together in the mess, sleeping in the same freezing barracks, then cramming themselves into the tiny cockpit at the controls of the Fortress, fighting for their lives. Todd always said his crew were like brothers, but Hank was his closest buddy. She wonders if Todd minds having their positions reversed. He's working for Hank now. But Todd isn't the kind to be

18

threatened by another's success, and whatever lofty position the braid on Hank's jacket stands for, he's a pen pusher, creeping towards middle age with lines on his neck, his body thickened by the years. She doesn't notice Todd ageing. It's a trick of the mind, of love she supposes, to keep seeing the person as they were, not seeing the daily deteriorations. She looks down at her hands in her lap, examining oval nails in Love That Pink. *Not a whisper pink, a whistle pink.* The clump and pucker of scar tissue across the palm of the left hand won't ever go away, even though at night she smothers herself up to the wrists in hand cream from Paris.

Suddenly her face is hot, her breath trapped in her lungs. She unbuttons the neck of her blouse and presses her cheek against the cool of the window. Hedy and Christopher have fallen asleep. He lolls against his sister. Ruby moves his head across to rest against her own breast, tucks the precious, damp weight of him under the hollow of her shoulder. Hedy startles, as if the loss of her twin has triggered an alarm, sleepy eyelids fluttering open.

'Look.' Ruby leans over, points at two huge black birds landing heavily on a branch, ragged wings closing. 'Crows,' she murmurs. 'Once one attacked my father, stabbed the back of his head. Drew blood.'

Or perhaps she doesn't speak it aloud, only thinks it.

They're driving between tall, narrow trunks. Pine trees. Light and shadow flash on and off, flickering across their faces like a home movie. Hedy gnaws her nails. The black birds on the branch look right at her with their oily gaze, singling her out. She cranes in her seat, staring at the receding road.

Dad keeps talking to Hank. Names of planes and squadrons

and buddies drift over the front seat. 'Remember the first time they dropped us? Never even heard of Norfolk.'

'Mudville Heights.'

'Freezing our balls off under corrugated iron.'

'Accommodation's a tad better. But don't go getting your hopes up. Military likes to stint on luxury. Even for brass hats.'

Dad laughs. The two men light more cigarettes, and roll down the front windows, so that smoke comes rushing in with the sharp sting of pine, making Hedy's eyes water.

'Is there local support for the base?' Dad asks. 'Some passengers on the bus made a cheap crack when they heard my accent.'

'Oh, there's some jealousy. It's understandable. Poor sods are effectively still on rations.' He laughs. 'The Brits round here are kinda like hillbillies; they haven't joined the modern world yet. But we're completely separate from the surrounding community – and best to keep it that way. The base is full of all the home comforts you could want.'

Mom leans forwards and touches Hank's shoulder. 'So you're saying that we shouldn't go out of the base?'

Hank glances at her in the rear-view mirror. 'There's nothing to see, anyway – only forest and a few cottages – I'd keep inside the perimeter fence to be on the safe side. If you want adventure, there's bigger towns nearby. But take your car. You're having the Buick shipped, right?' he asks Dad.

'Did you hear what Hank said?' Mom hisses to Hedy and Chris. 'Don't leave the base without me or Dad.'

Hedy makes a noise in her throat. Chris is blinking at the flashing trees, transfixed, his thumb in his mouth. Hedy grabs his wrist. Thumb-sucking twelve-year-olds are something to be scolded or mocked, depending which parent gets to him first.

Chris glances at the slippery curve of his thumb in surprise, as if he hadn't realised what he'd been doing.

'Here we are,' Dad says over his shoulder; he sounds excited.

The pines have given way to rolls of razor wire. A tall perimeter fence. A sign that reads Blackheath US Airbase. A sentry with a gun at his hip salutes as the car rolls through the gates.

# TWO

Hank parks outside a bungalow. There's a narrow path to the front door, and a strip of lawn bordered with the flimsy beginnings of laurel hedge. Identical bungalows line either side of the street. On this side, the back gardens butt up against a tall perimeter fence, chain-link mesh pegged into the ground with thick, concrete uprights, a roll of razor wire at the top. Just the other side of the fence is the pine forest, an impenetrable wall of thickening darkness that surrounds the base on three sides. Squinting up at her new house, Ruby sees the tops of pines sticking up above the roof like a row of Christmas trees waiting to be decorated. Hank clears his throat, jangles a set of house keys. 'This is it, folks.'

They cram into the tiny hall after him, squashed together between doorways. Ruby stares around her at the yellowing wallpaper. She has a strong desire to get back on the plane to Sioux City.

'What do you think?' Todd asks.

'It's great, honey,' she says.

It'll look different with their own furniture, she tells herself. She'll sew ruffles onto curtains, put rugs on the floor, arrange cushions on the sofa. She's made every temporary accommodation they've ever stayed in look homely. Todd wraps his arms around her, giving her a squeeze that jams the air in her lungs. 'New home, new start,' he says, kissing her hair. He lets go, catching up with Hank, pulling open a door and disappearing inside.

Hedy wrinkles her nose. 'What's that smell?'

Ruby spots a brownish stain trickling down a skirting board. She glances around, as if the offending tom cat might be crouched in a corner, and sniffs again, wondering if there's damp as well. The place is no better than a prefab thrown up in a hurry, but there'll be the usual army rules: no pictures hung on the walls; no shelves; no painting the walls a prettier colour. Peering into another room, she's relieved to find that the removal firm has already been. Boxes dumped in a pile. Todd is there and he gives her a triumphant grin, gesturing towards the boxes as if he's conjured them himself.

Hank is calling. 'Come see the kitchen.'

'Where are the stairs?' Hedy is asking. 'I thought in England we'd have stairs.'

Christopher has opened a bedroom door. 'Can this room be mine? Do we get one each?' He has bruises under his eyes.

'Yes, sweetheart,' Ruby says. 'You can have that one.'

She wants to pull him into her arms and kiss his pain away, but the metal brace doesn't make proper hugging possible, and she knows it would embarrass him in front of the men. She stops beside Hank at the threshold of a tiny kitchen. There's a green cabinet with frosted panels and a wooden draining board. A line of mould darkens the edges of a small white sink and the window above. Below the sink there's a storage space half hidden with drooping curtains.

Hank shrugs apologetically. 'Told you not to expect luxury.'

'Where do we plug our refrigerator in?' she asks, looking at Todd, who opens his palms as if to say, don't ask me, and gives her a hurt, what-do-I-know-of-domestic-details frown.

'You have a meat safe, and an ice box,' Hank explains. 'The ice man comes around once a week.'

'I don't want an ice box,' Ruby frowns.

'Can't use American equipment here. Sorry. The Brits have the wrong plugs. Didn't anyone tell you?'

Ruby shakes her head. 'There must be something we can do to make ours work.' She stares at the place where the socket should be. 'It has thermostatic temperature control, snap-release ice cubes, adjustable shelves ...'

She's talking to herself. Hank and Todd have disappeared, taking the children with them.

'Coming, hon?' Todd calls from the hall.

Ruby doesn't move. Sparks burst under her eyelids, her blood swimming wildly away from her brain. Dizziness overwhelms her. It's got worse since she upped her dose of pills after Todd told her about the new posting. She stands still and focuses on her breath. In and out. Food helps. A mouthful of biscuit. An apple. But there's nothing in the house to eat yet. The cupboards are bare. She'll have to do a shop at the commissary, rustle up some supper on the small cooker.

Those early months in America she'd been in a state of stunned disbelief. She couldn't eat enough, fast enough. Hunched over, cramming in anything her fork could reach. But then she'd begun to take the blessings of her new homeland for granted: its casual abundance of sugar and butter, cars big as boats, clothes made from generous swags of fabric, the smiling faces of her neighbours looking up over their barbecues, flipping over one slice of cow after another.

'How bout I'll show you the movie theatre first? Or we could go visit the commissary?' Hank is asking. 'You kids think you deserve a treat? We have all the candy you can name. Who wants a Kool-Aid?'

'The movie theatre!' Christopher shouts. He loves films, especially anything with aliens in it. He watched *The Forbidden Planet* twice before they left the States. But of course, Hedy has to contradict him, demanding a Kool-Aid. A strawberry one. The buzz of Todd's voice, jokey-stern, rises above the children's squabbling.

Ruby wants the noise to stop. There's a bruise throbbing just under her skull. The door slams, and she lets out a hiss. The sound of laughter disappears. She fumbles with the window catch, shoving the glass open. She watches them moving away along the deserted street. Todd's giving Hedy a piggyback, but Christopher's trailing behind, limping. She shouldn't have let him go. She should have made him rest. But where? Nothing's ready. There are boxes to unpack. So much to do. She watches the little group turn the corner, and it's as if they've been erased; she feels abandoned.

A gust of wind plucks at the branches of a silver birch over the road. She imagines the breeze will be flavoured with lavender fields and the brine of Norfolk mud flats. Ruby can sense her brother at the farm, see him turning towards her. He's like a dog latching onto the spoor of rabbit. He stops in the yard, and his eyes narrow under the seagull-curling sky, nose raised to sniff her out, feeling her arrival, her sudden and puzzling proximity after all these years.

'Well, well,' he says. 'Look what the cat dragged in. All glammed up. Think you're too good for us now?'

The howl of a jet makes her flinch. The windows in the bungalow rattle: a hurricane blowing through. The vision of her brother disappears. She ducks her head, expecting the belly of the plane to smash through the chimney. As the whoosh of the slipstream disappears, her ears are ringing. She rubs them with the flats of her palms, aware of another sound. A knocking at the front door.

A woman stands on the doorstep. Ruby notices the casserole dish held between the woman's manicured hands. Her gaze moves to take in pearl buttons on the woman's yellow cashmere jumper, a matching cardigan slung about the shoulders like a *Vogue* model, hair bottle-bright in chestnut red.

Ruby touches her own hair, smoothing it across her cheek, pressing it down. She remembers that she hasn't looked in a mirror since they landed. And that was another lifetime ago.

'Betty.' The woman's fuchsia lips stretch into a smile. 'Betty Lansens from number five, Lincoln Avenue. Did anyone tell you yet that all the streets on the base are named for American presidents? I'm the welcoming committee. Thought you could do with something hot to eat. I'm guessing you haven't had a chance to get provisions yet.'

Ruby takes the proffered dish.

'Scalloped chicken supreme.'

'Thanks.' Ruby wishes the woman would go away; she can't invite her into an empty house, and she's been caught with her hair straggly, wearing slept-in clothes. Her breath probably smells. 'I would invite you in, but . . .'

Betty flaps her hands. 'Goodness, no! I know you've got a

26

whole lot to sort out and you must be dead beat after that trip.'
She narrows her eyes. 'Did I hear an English accent?'

'Oh.' Ruby nods. 'I thought maybe I'd lost it – I've been living
in the States since my kids were born.'

'Well – you know what they say, you can take the girl out
of the country ...' Betty smiles. 'Now, you be sure to come
and knock on my door when you're good and ready. Did I say
I was at number five? I'll show you around, introduce you to
the gang. The only address that matters, after the commissary,
is the Wives' Club. Bridge afternoons, a reading circle, coffee
klatsches, sewing group, blood drives; we have something for
everyone!' To Ruby's relief Betty turns as if she's about to go,
but then she swings around. 'How many kids?'

'Two.' Ruby says. 'Twins. Boy and girl.'

'Cute. Age?'

'Twelve.'

'Same as my boy, Scott. I'll send him around tomorrow to
say hi. They'll be in the same class. Don't worry, Uncle Sam
will take care of you. We have everything you need right here.
You don't have to set foot outside the base. Not unless ...' she
raises her eyebrows. 'Of course, silly me, I guess you have people
to visit? I mean, being English and everything.'

No, Ruby wants to assure her. I'm going to stay right here,
inside the perimeter fence, inside this bungalow, inside the
arms of my husband if I can. But the words don't come.
Another jet screams overhead. Staring up, Ruby thinks she
sees the pilot's face in the cockpit. He's so close she can make
out the oxygen mask over his mouth. Her body stiffens, hands
covering her ears.

Betty smiles. 'You get used to it. Took me a few weeks. Now I
hardly register them – hard to believe, I know!' She shades her

27

eyes to stare after the shiny speck high in the sky. 'Six hundred miles per hour,' she murmurs. 'Makes you proud, right? Guess those Reds better watch out.'

Ruby shuts the door. She knows it's a cowardly thought, one she'd never admit to Todd, but the only good thing about coming to England is that if the commies drop the atomic bomb, they'll be dropping it on America, not here. Her children will be safe. The thought of that bright explosion and the devastation it brings makes her chest hurt. She watched the footage on TV after Hiroshima. It had been filmed from the bomber's window, looking down on the city. Even in black and white, she could see the fury of the blast; the commentator said it was heat travelling at the speed of light. The big fluffy coil of smoke rising into the sky looked like giant candyfloss. It must have been an inferno on the ground. The commentator didn't talk about that, just the vaporised buildings, as if a whole city and its people had been magicked into thin air.

She supposes the main threat here will be from espionage. The base, with its top-secret Cold War work, will be a target for undercover Reds. She noticed a sign with eagle eyes on it as they drove through the base: *Report any suspicious persons to the Military Police.* She thinks of Julius and Ethel Rosenberg, executed for transmitting atomic bomb secrets to the Soviet Union. For all she knows there could be spies planning to get to Todd right now. Well, good luck to them, she says under her breath. Her husband is the bravest, most patriotic man she knows. There's no bribery or threat invented that could crack him.

Christopher waits for his mother to undress him. She peels his jumper over his head, scratchy wool catching on his eyelashes.

28

He keeps his arms in the air for her to tug off his T-shirt. His body is exhausted, every bone hurting. The worst bit was the plane, sitting in the same position for hours.

Mom kneels to pull down his Levis, easing them over the girdle and straps. He leans on her shoulders so that she can take off his socks, one at a time. Then she stands right behind him, close enough for him to hear the breath leaving her mouth and feel the slow bloom of its warmth on his skin. Normally she smells of perfume and hair lacquer, but today he inhales the sour, stale smell of unwashed skin and airplane. She undoes the thumb screw, opening the circle of metal around his neck, taking away the chin pad. There's nothing to hold his head up anymore. His skull wobbles. Mom's fingers have moved to his waist, working at the buckles. She makes a little grunt of effort as she hauls the corset in tighter to release them. Leather straps fall away, and the corset, brown and tight as a conker, peels apart.

There's a feeling of lightness as the weight shifts from his hips, cold air reaching his hot, clammy skin. His bruised ribs expand to fill his lungs. He gasps with shock. Without the support of the corset, his spine feels as though it's collapsing, as if the bones are flipping apart, tumbling down one after the other like a line of dominoes tripped by a casual thumb.

But his bones hold. He doesn't collapse. He's shivering. Mom has run him a hot bath. She sits on the closed lavatory seat as she used to at home in Sioux City. He would like to have some privacy, but she's frightened he'll slip, and he doesn't want to scare her, or hurt her feelings by asking to be left alone. She keeps her head down, busy re-darning the tiny holes in his clothes that the brace makes. At least he's allowed to wash himself. In the bath, his sore limbs come to life. He bends forwards, hunching and releasing his shoulders to reach the soap.

He raises his leg, touches his bony feet, examines his unfamiliar toenails. He wallows, slipping from one hip to the other, as water slops onto the floor.

The brace waits in the corner of his new bedroom among the packing cases. They're in England, and everything is different. But the cage is the same. It's a prison with three bars, and there's no avoiding his return to it. But for this brief hour, Christopher will stretch out the minutes, imagining he's had a day of running and climbing. Under the distortion of water, nobody could even tell what's wrong with him.

After his bath, Mom oils his back and tends to the welts left by the steel uprights, sores caused by the rub of leather under his chin, around his ribs and thighs. Christopher submits because he has no choice. He's gotten used to separating his body from his mind; he can leave his flesh and bones behind to be poked and squeezed while his mind disappears inside a story. Ever since the prognosis in Iowa, ever since the first fitting, when they'd stripped him naked and hung his head from a halter, stretching him long with pulleys weighted with sand bags, when they'd wrapped him in muddy bandages and left him strung up to dry, ever since then, his body has stopped belonging to him. It belongs to doctors, to Mom, to the cage. To the eight long years before they promised to set him free.

'You see, I told you it was going to be great, didn't I?' Todd breathes into Ruby's neck as his fingers close around her left nipple, tweaking playfully, before sliding towards her belly. 'You've made a friend already. And the kids will settle down so fast, it'll be like we always lived here.'

'Yes,' Ruby says, because she wants it to be true, and she's too exhausted to disagree. It feels as though she's been awake for three days straight.

'I'm going to be doing important work here, hon. This will make all the difference to my career. To our lives. This place is a mini United States – you can pretend we never left. Right? All those other wives to keep you company. We're gonna be happy here, baby. I know it.'

He wraps her in a bear hug, his stubble tickling her ear. Ruby looks over his shoulder at the full moon, watching it float above the tops of the trees that line the back garden. They have no curtains yet. 'Nobody to look in,' Todd had said as he'd undressed in front of the black square of glass. Tomorrow she'll unpack her sewing machine, get their old curtains out to alter.

They kiss, his mouth fuggy with beer and the remains of the chicken supreme he finished off standing in the kitchen in his boxer shorts. Desire tugs at the pit of her belly. Ruby holds her breath, wraps her arms around his neck, lifts her pelvis to meet his. It's only in these moments, when he moves deeper into her centre, that she knows she's alive, can feel the muscle of her heart throb. Her whole body humming with tiny sensations. Their chests stick and unstick with a sucking noise, the bed-springs twang, and with a grunt Todd begins to thrust eagerly, urgently, until with a shudder he shouts a strangled exultation and collapses across her, flattening her breasts, his hip bone hard on her bladder.

'I love you, honey.'

'Love you, too,' she whispers.

'Coming here, this could be the best thing that ever happened to us. You'll see.' He rolls away, fumbling on the cardboard packing case next to the bed for a smoke.

Ruby goes into the little bathroom and snaps on the bare bulb. She pees sitting on the lavatory, while she runs a couple of inches of lukewarm water in the bath. The boiler creaks and gurgles. She squats in the pale tub, her feet magnified, and checks that her diaphragm is still in place. She can't risk getting pregnant again. She dries herself, puts her turquoise baby-doll nightie back on, adjusting the lace ruffles around her neck, patting at folds of nylon. Squinting into the mirror above the basin, she twists her hair into rollers and fastens a net around them. She unscrews the lid from her pill bottle and tips a tablet into her palm, throws her head back, swallowing with a practised dry gulp. She switches off the light, and standing in the dark, she performs the last part of her routine, slathering her hands in cold cream, a waxy layer that turns her skin ghostly.

Moonlight moves through their bedroom, shows up the packing cases and the bed in monochrome shapes. She climbs in beside the dark lump that is Todd. The mattress creaks as she rolls towards him and he clamps a heavy arm around her waist, shifts her close, spooning her, but already his breathing is slow and deep. She listens for his snore. He's haunted by the war, by the horrors of battle after battle fought in the air, but she knows he misses the adrenaline, too. He was used to being a hero; bravery and sacrifice his second nature. For him, the peacetime world is a greyer place. She's hoping this new job will give him back a sense of real purpose.

She closes her eyelids, but however much her eyes burn with tiredness, she can't sleep. High above, a jet screams through the clouds. One of theirs on a night mission, she guesses. Inside her head, she unfolds a favourite memory, worn from use. It's the memory she revisits most, the one that always gives her comfort.

It's not hard to re-imagine herself there, waiting for him at the farmhouse kitchen window. She remembers exactly what she was wearing: her best floral dress and a navy cardigan, mended at one elbow. As Todd veered into view, cycling over the rutted track into the yard, the three farm collies gathered around him, barking.

'Where did you get that bicycle?' She laughed, shooing the dogs away. 'You must have stolen it.'

'Cost me two hundred and fifty dollars from the Red Cross.' Todd grinned, nodding at the basket on her arm. 'I'm hungry. Hop up.' He patted the crossbar in front of him.

Somewhere behind her, through the slats of the barn, she could feel Ernest watching from the shadows, feel the weight of his disapproval and jealousy. But she refused to let him spoil her day. Ruby climbed on, sitting side saddle, thin metal under her bottom; Todd's arms were around her and she leant back against his chest. Late summer, and the fields were dusty and yellow, blackberries out on the bushes, dark globs of sweetness among the thorns. They wobbled along the tracks towards Poacher's Copse, Ruby balancing the picnic basket on her lap, bare legs swinging out of the way of the hissing wheels.

They kicked off their shoes and settled in the long grass at the top of the only hill for miles, a bottle of ginger beer to share, a hunk of dark bread and a bit of green ham, two raspberry tarts. Todd had a portable radio with him and he tuned into the American Armed Forces Radio music programme. Glenn Miller Band's 'Little Brown Jug' came on after they'd finished eating, and Todd pulled her up to dance, Ruby turning under his arm, daisies and buttercups crushed underfoot. As the music changed to some romantic melody, they swayed close, holding each other. Ruby's heart stilled, her breathing slowing as she closed her eyes. Overhead the Eighth Air Force was assembling, squadron after squadron, creating a steady rumbling drone. The sun was a red glow on the horizon.

He dropped a kiss in her hair, his mouth moving to her ear. 'Marry me,' he whispered. 'Live with me in the States. Let's have lots of kids and live happily ever after.'

'Yes,' Ruby murmurs now, aloud into the darkness. 'Yes.' An echo of the same answer she'd given then, her feet bare in the grass, her breath caught in her chest.

Such a small word. It unlocked the future for her, changed everything.

Her existence on the farm had been a horrible mistake. She never belonged with Father and Ernest. She never belonged to Norfolk and the mud and the hardship. She'd been born for better things.

Todd is breathing deeply beside her, and she finds his fingers under the covers and threads her own inside them. This is where she belongs – where she's always belonged, even before she knew it. In his sleep, he squeezes her hand. A feeling of optimism comes: Chris's spine will grow straight inside the brace. Todd will do his job to keep them safe. The bomb won't drop. Ruby folds her arms across her chest, careful not to get grease on her nightdress. Through the window, she watches the line of pine trees behind the garden fence; spiky branches towering over the bungalow like a black fringe, an ever-hovering wave trembling on the brink of falling.

# THREE

'Doorbell!' Mommy sings out from the kitchen. 'Can one of you get it?'

She's been cleaning for hours on her knees in front of the oven, vinegar and newspaper balled in her fist. Damp washing hangs from a rack over the sink, drips plopping into the basin; the room heavy with the scent of soapy wool. Hedy has locked herself in the bathroom. Occasional muffled splashing noises and the murmur of the radio drift under the door. Dad went off to work early.

So there is only one person available to answer the door.

'The bell!' Mommy yells again.

Christopher goes into the hall and unlocks the latch.

Every day he trawls the dictionary for words. It's not like collecting stamps or butterflies. Words are alive, full of power and promise. He memorises them till they slide off his buttery tongue, stitches them into his stories and poems, loving how the syllables clack together like a runaway train, whispery consonants that come from ancient languages, single words that sound like magic spells.

But looking at the boy on the step, Christopher can't remember anything. Not even hello. It's not just the way the boy's nut-brown hair curls onto his forehead, the elongated shape of his mouth, the small chip in his front tooth. It's his ease, as if he's shrugged his skin on and wears it like an old coat. He knows himself. He is utterly familiar with himself. How do you do that, Christopher wants to ask. What's the trick?

They stand on either side of the threshold, just the squeaky sounds of polishing and scrubbing coming from the kitchen, until the boy yawns and scratches his chin.

'You one of the twins?' He shifts a piece of gum inside his mouth. 'Where's the other half?'

Christopher twists with difficulty inside the iron bars of the brace, so he can turn towards the back of the house while keeping his eyes on the boy. 'Hedy?' He calls in the direction of the bathroom. He coughs. 'Hedy?' he tries again. A bit louder. 'There's someone here . . .'

'Scott,' the boy says.

'Scott,' Christopher repeats.

He's in awe. Awe is a good word, he thinks. Short but dense with meaning. Admiration, fear and reverence are packed inside it.

He's thankful that he put his scarf on this morning. Tied it up underneath his jaw to cover his chin pad. Although he can't kid himself that he looks normal. The brace makes a weird shape under his jumper. His chin pokes up at a crazy angle, as if he's continually staring with rigid intent towards the sky.

'You must be Betty's son?' Mommy's voice in Christopher's ear. 'Have you invited Scott in for a lemonade?' The tip of one finger, covered in rubbery yellow, prods his shoulder.

'Nah.' Scott slumps against the door frame, as if the world is exhausting, and the idea of lemonade even more so. 'I'm here to show them around. Mom sent me.'

'That's kind.' Mommy takes a deep breath. 'Don't go too far though, will you? Not out of the base.' Anxiety tightens her voice, making her English accent stronger. Christopher is embarrassed. This boy on the doorstep, with the glow of ripe wheat on his skin, blood-red lips and milk-fed flesh, is like an advert for everything that's best about America.

Christopher wants him to know that they too are proper Americans.

'Jeez,' he murmurs, hoping Scott will understand that he's not a baby, it's just that all mothers worry too much.

'Right then. I'll get Hedy ...' Mommy says. But there's no need. She appears in the hall, wet hair plastered to her skull, her blouse un-tucked, a pair of slacks pulled on in a hurry. A strong smell of lavender bath salts accompanies her.

'Hi,' she says.

Mommy frowns at Hedy. 'Are you going out like that?'

She doesn't approve of Hedy in pants, wants her in dresses with frills and lace ankle socks. But she won't make a fuss in front of company, and Hedy knows it.

'Scott's going to show us around the base,' Christopher says to Hedy, without tearing his attention away from the boy's face. Scott's gaze is like sunlight the way it slips across surfaces, dazzling before it disappears.

They're heading towards Main Street, taking their pace from Scott's stroll. Christopher puts his hands into his pockets, wishing he could hunch his shoulders the way Scott does. He drops behind the other two, ashamed of his clockwork walk. It's busier today, more like a real town. A miniature version of Sioux City. There are men in uniform, women with shopping baskets on

37

their arms. American cars pass slowly, a blue Cadillac, a black Pontiac. Scott pauses outside the commissary. The window display is full of red and white tins of Frank's and different kinds of Campbell's soup. Bunting dangles above, drooping triangles of tiny Stars and Stripes.

They press their noses up against the glass, three misty circles spreading and contracting. Christopher's stomach rumbles. He's hungry all the time. Mommy says it's because he's growing. At night, his body hurts, and it's a different kind of hurt from the usual one. Even inside the leather and metal he knows his limbs are adding more onto themselves.

'What if I told you to bag something in there?' Scott stares through the window. 'Would you?'

'Bag something?' Hedy stares at him, hands on hips. 'Steal?'

'Don't flip your wig – I'm just saying, it's like an initiation,' he explains. He examines his thumbnail. 'Know what that is?'

'Of course,' Hedy scowls at him. 'Course we know what an initiation is.'

'I'm not talking big stuff. Candy. Maybe a Milky Bar.'

'Initiation into what?'

'My gang.'

'Really?' Hedy stands back, looking him up and down, head on one side as if she's considering giving him a job. Christopher holds his breath. Hedy is cool. He hopes Scott thinks he's cool too, by association.

'Yeah. We don't just let anyone in. We've got rules. Of course, if you're too sissy . . . ' Scott scuffs his shoe against the kerb.

'I think it's kind of stupid. But I don't really care. I'll steal a candy bar if you want. Doesn't bother me one way or another.'

'What about him?' Scott turns his blistering gaze on Christopher, who manages a blink.

'Not him,' Hedy says. 'I'll do it for both of us. I won't come if you don't let Chris in.'

'You don't make the rules.' Scott shakes his head. 'I do.'

'Fine. I don't care about your stupid gang anyway.'

Scott gives her and Christopher long assessing stares, then he nods. 'OK. If you take something bigger than a candy bar, then I'll let you both in. Not now, though. Later, when it's quieter.'

Christopher keeps his face immobile. Shame and relief batter inside, all mixed up. They move on, walking further down Main Street, further away from the commissary.

Scott stops, nodding at Christopher. 'Buddy, your lace is undone.'

Hedy's down on her knees. Christopher feels her fingers tugging, his boot getting tighter. Scott watches with a frown. He makes a kissing noise, but it's not a love sound; it's a sound of disapproval. 'Can't he tie his own laces?'

Hedy stands up. 'Mind your own business.' She yawns. 'This place is boring. Haven't you got anything else to show us?'

Scott walks on. 'So how come you're twins, if one of you's a girl? Thought you had to be the same.'

'We're not identical,' Hedy tells him.

'We're fraternal.' The word comes to Christopher in a rush. 'It means brotherly. So it's not a ... a literal meaning, not when it's applied to twins. Then it just means we came from separate eggs.'

Scott jerks his chin. 'Is he all right?'

'What do you mean?' Hedy glares.

'Talks funny.' Scott raises one eyebrow. 'And why does he walk like that? What's up with his neck? He dumb or something? Some kind of spaz?'

It's as though Scott throws a brake on time. Christopher feels the bite of metal at his back. He stumbles, the sidewalk jerking to a halt beneath him. Above his chin pad, above the squishy, concealing scarf, he knows his face has turned scarlet.

Hedy laughs as if Scott is the idiot. 'He's not *dumb*. Matter of fact, he's a genius. Comes top in every spellathon. He's writing a book. A real novel.'

'A novel?'

'Yeah,' Hedy says with passion, 'like *The Chrysalids*. But better. I know because I've read both.'

Scott blinks. His eyes are guarded, suddenly shifty. Christopher can't bear the fault-line of uncertainty running through Scott's expression. He wants to say something – anything – to make Scott powerful again. But his mind's empty, his failure terrible. He stares into the middle distance.

Then Scott shrugs, an easy roll of his shoulders casting off inadequacy. Books mean nothing to him. Christopher breathes again. The world rights itself.

They saunter on past a low building with a playground in the front. A couple of swings hang empty. 'School,' Scott informs them, without breaking stride. 'For the genius.' He gives Christopher's arm a brief punch.

Christopher touches his arm, wondering if there'll be a bruise. Does this mean Scott likes him, after all?

Scott points out the movie house, the Post Office, the medical building. There are basketball courts, too. Four boys are playing; one has the ball and is dodging the others, battling for position – his hand keeps the ball trotting around him like an excited dog, before he leaps for the hoop and dunks it. The boys, all panting heavily, turn to stare. They give Scott nods, watching for his reaction. He ignores them.

A roar overhead. Scott tilts his head, cupped hand holding back the sun. 'Gonna fly one of those one day.'

'A jet?'

'B-47. Stratojet. Bomber.'

'Where's it going?' Christopher asks, staring after the pale speck.

'Are you for real?' Scott gives Christopher a suspicious glance. 'You don't ask those kinds of questions.'

'But the war with Russia hasn't started.'

'Don't you know anything? It's happening all right, just it's invisible at the moment. They're preparing, see. Both sides getting ready for the fight. We got to practise manoeuvres for the day we do get to kill the Soviets,' Scott says. 'Boom!' He claps his hands together. 'We're gonna blow those suckers to smithereens. They might have a bomb. But we got bigger, better ones.'

They're close to the part of the base that's out of bounds. A double chain-link fence separates it, razor wire snarling in twisted hoops. There's a tall guard tower by the entrance, a man with a rifle staring down. Beyond the fence are huge grassy humps.

'Those are the bunkers. Can't see them from the air, because of the grass. Military personnel only have access. Don't ever think you can sneak inside, you'll be shot,' Scott warns. 'There's a War Op room under the ground somewhere in there called The Pit where they plan how to beat the Reds. There's the control tower, runways, aircraft hangars.' He waves his hand towards the glinting expanse of asphalt, grounded planes nosing blindly. The arc of his hand takes in concrete bunkers and landing lights. Jeeps full of men in blue or grey. There's a smell of burning rubber. A constant howl of engines.

Christopher doesn't like it. The noise. The smell. The soldier

41

with the gun eyeballing them. A scrabbling fear makes his heart bump against his ribs. He thinks of the Red Menace, the bomb that can come at any time, without warning, splitting the sky apart with its dazzle, smashing buildings and burning people up in a howling gale of blistering destruction. 'Duck and cover,' they told them at school. But he can't drop onto all fours and crawl under a table. If the bomb comes, he'll be fried where he stands. All they'll find afterwards is a bunch of ash inside the metal bars of his brace.

He turns, looking instead at the perimeter fence and the dark press of trees behind. Tangles of branches block out the light, hold their own thick silence. 'What's over there? Behind the trees.'

Scott purses his lips. 'Nothing. Just more trees.'

'So it's big, the forest?'

'Yeah. I guess.' He looks at Hedy. 'Want to get a Dr Pepper?'

'Buy or steal?' she asks in a deadpan voice.

Scott gives a snorting laugh.

They're strolling away, back to the high street. Hedy doesn't glance behind to check that her brother's following. Christopher expects they just presume he's traipsing along on their heels. He takes a wild guess that they'll be talking about baseball, or some other sport that he knows nothing about. Every boy he's ever met is an expert on baseball leagues and the World Series, Hedy's favourite subject. Christopher turns in the opposite direction, along the perimeter fence, trailing his fingers across the mesh, bump, bump, sending a quiet vibration ringing along the whole expanse of intersecting wires. The smell of pine needles and moss is clean; not clean like the mean bite of detergent, he thinks, but a good, friendly smell. He likes the other smell too, the darker one layered underneath the bright green: brown-coloured, damp mulch, rotting leaves and fungus. The pull of the earth.

Ruby and Betty are on their way to the Officers' Wives' Club. Their heels synchronise along the sidewalk, clipping past identical bungalows. The buildings seem uninhabited, except for a child's sudden cry. Ruby turns her head towards the noise, longing to hold one of her own children on her lap – as they were when they were younger and compliant – comforting them in the safety of her kitchen, and not attending a meeting with strangers who will expect her to perform, to entertain, to be the token English wife.

A roar splits the sky, flushing some starlings out of a tree in a rush of wings. Betty doesn't break stride or glance up. She's wearing a pink wool suit and matching pillbox hat. The pink works with her red hair in a way Ruby would never have imagined or dared. She thinks that Betty looks like Lucille Ball, although Ruby doubts that Betty would ever get caught vacuuming in her pyjamas or hitting her husband over the head with a pillow. Despite her cheerleader smile, Betty isn't the kind of woman to make a fool of herself.

Ruby's regretting her new rubberised girdle. Not because it leaves tiny raised bumps all over her skin – Todd thought at first she'd contracted a rash, then hooted with laughter when she'd explained – but because she's living in her own private sauna. Sweat prickles under her arms. She hopes she won't stain her blouse. Best not to take her jacket off, just in case.

'Thanks for sending Scott round,' Ruby says. 'It was nice of him to take the time.'

'Yeah, he's a good kid.' Betty stops outside a door and pushes. 'This is it.'

Ruby freezes, wishes she could run. But Betty has linked her arm through her own. And then they're inside the Club, which is nothing more than a hut really, with gingham tablecloths on a couple of trestle tables and a big map of the United States on the wall. The high-pitched chatter and clink of spoons against china pauses as women turn to examine her with razor scrutiny. The once-over is executed in a matter of seconds, but Ruby is aware of a continuing prickle of interest following her across the room. She clings too close to Betty, nearly stepping on her heels. Inside her head, she's humming the *I Love Lucy* theme tune. She prays that her stockings haven't got a run, that her cheeks don't look as hot as they feel.

A short, round woman is marching over, hand outstretched.

'CO's wife,' Betty hisses in Ruby's ear. And then, 'Gloria, let me introduce you to our newest recruit, Ruby. Captain Delaney's wife. Ruby, this is Gloria Anderson, the colonel's wife.'

Gloria's handshake is firm. Ruby wishes she'd had time to prepare something to say. She tries to look the woman in the eye. Gloria's dark gaze is not unkind, but beady and all-seeing.

'I hear you're English. You must be feeling right at home.'

Ruby swallows, forcing moisture into her mouth. 'Actually, I'd gotten so used to Iowa. I feel a little homesick for the States, to be truthful.'

Gloria stiffens. 'My goodness! No time for moping. Our boys need us to be home-makers. They need us to stay cheerful. There's plenty for them to worry about already. What a time we live in: Soviet spies in our own government, atomic power in the hands of our enemies! They don't need to worry about us as well.' She gives Ruby a firm pat on the arm. 'It's up to us to put a smile on their faces. We'll keep you busy, won't we Betty? No time to be bored on this base.'

'Oh, I didn't mean ...'

But Gloria has moved on, purposeful strides taking her to another group, ready to issue the next piece of advice, the next command. Like the Queen, Ruby thinks. Sure of a deferential welcome.

'Don't worry about it,' Betty smiles. 'She's a little, how do you English call it? Brisk? Or is it brusque?'

Someone has put a cup of coffee into her hand, and Ruby balances the saucer, sipping at the scalding liquid. She can hardly feel the handle through her glove. She worries about not being able to grip properly, imagines the cup slithering out of her grasp, the slap and shatter as it hits the floor, the appalled silence. In sideways glances, she notices that some women have naked hands. But Betty and Gloria have kept their spotless white gloves on, and she doesn't want to do the wrong thing.

'Sandy Kelly.' A thin, freckled woman puts out her hand, also encased in a white glove. 'I hear that Major Pulaski is a friend of yours?'

'A friend of my husband's,' Ruby says. 'They were stationed together in Norfolk in the war. They were in the same crew, pilot and co-pilot flying a B-17.'

'Major Pulaski's one of the few unmarried officers on the base,' Sandy says. 'Wish I could fix that sweet man up with a date. He needs a wife to look after him.'

'Sandy's a frustrated matchmaker,' Betty says with a wink. 'In this goldfish bowl of a base there's not much scope for her talents.'

A familiar ringing pain has started up behind Ruby's forehead. She thinks of the bottle of pills in her handbag. She tipped them onto the bed this morning, counted them out in groups of four. She has enough for the rest of the month.

'Is the medical centre any good?' she asks Betty in a low voice. 'I have to get a prescription. Something for my nerves. I don't know if my usual medication is available here.'

Betty leans in closer. 'You talking about peace pills?'

Ruby frowns, not understanding.

'Miltown.' She laughs at Ruby's expression. 'Honey, quite a few of the women in this room are taking it. We all need a little help sometimes.' She gestures around her. 'It's enough to shatter anyone's nerves wondering if this is the day we'll be blown sky-high. Sweetie, it's our husbands' job to keep us safe. But our job is to help them do that, and of course, we need to help them up the ladder too. How else are they going to make it to the top, if not for us shouting instructions?' She nudges Ruby, winking. 'We need to keep our marbles, right? What's a few pills between friends? I'd go crazy without mine.'

Relief makes Ruby gulp her coffee. She reaches for a biscuit and crams it into her mouth. Chocolatey crumbs stick to her gloves, her jacket. She takes a deep breath, brushes herself down with quick flicks, dabs at her mouth with a napkin and steps away from the evidence. 'Excuse me,' she murmurs.

She finds the Ladies', moving through the room at a steady pace, careful not to do anything to give away the need inside her. She tries the door. It's vacant. She shuts herself into the small room, slides the lock, and sits on the closed seat to rifle through her bag. Another 400 mg to celebrate. She tips her head and swallows, traces the movement of the pill as it's forced down her neck by ripples of muscle and into her chest, where it seems to press onto her heart. A guided missile. Then it's gone, lost inside her digestive system, already dissolving and working its magic, allowing her to unbolt the door and walk out of there into the milling crowd of women with a smile on her face.

# FOUR

When they get to the red doors of the commissary, Hedy turns to Scott. 'Stay here.' She holds up a hand for emphasis. 'I'll only be a minute.'

His look of affronted surprise makes her laugh. Serve him right for being mean to Chris, and for being such a know-it-all. Inside the shop, thinking about how she stole Scott's thunder keeps a grin on her face as she roams up and down the aisles, past displays of apples and oranges, crates full of bock and Budweiser and stacks of Spam. Possibilities flood her vision. Her heart bangs in her chest and she feels the echo in her limbs, so that her body is alive with the drumming. Two housewives loiter in front of her chatting in low voices, shopping baskets on their arms. Their uninterested gaze slides over her. At the end of the aisle is the check-out till. There's a queue of customers keeping the shop assistant busy. Hedy can hear the ring and bang of the till, the rustle of products being packed into brown paper bags.

She takes a packet of Hostess cream-filled cupcakes off

the shelf and pretends to read the back, frowning as if she's considering buying it, except she can't see a thing, her eyes blurred by nerves. When the writing snaps into focus she realises that this is a special offer package with three colour baseball cards inside. She would like the baseball cards. Her fingers tighten around the packet. It's too bulky. Regretfully, she slides it back.

A bald man in an apron is standing right next to her. She jumps.

'Can I help you?' He talks slowly and clearly, unused to children probably, or a bit deaf.

'No. Thank you.' She makes herself look as she imagines an innocent person would, opening her eyes wide.

He hovers for a moment as if expecting her to say something else. When she remains silent, he walks away, sliding a careful hand over the single stripe of hair licking his scalp. He pauses to talk to the two women. They have their backs turned. Hedy is forgotten. One of the women laughs. Hedy needs to get this over with. She picks up a six-pack of Snickers and slips it under the waistband of her pants. Lucky she's so skinny. She flips her blouse over for cover and feels a moment of elation; it was easy! She resists the urge to bolt. The packet of Snickers crackles against her skin with every step, but she knows it's too soft for anyone but her to hear.

Outside, Scott is waiting, hands in his pockets, frowning. She retrieves the packet and thrusts it towards him. 'When you get a craving for chocolate and peanuts,' she sings the theme song, 'Snickers is the bar for you.'

'You're the one who's nuts,' he says, wrapping his jacket around it quickly.

Hedy can tell he's impressed. But already the thrilling

glow of success is fading, and she looks around. 'Where's Chris?'

'How should I know?'

'Wasn't he with you while I was in the com?'

'Haven't seen him since we were at the airfield.'

The realisation is a cold wind. Everything torn away by its icy whip. She presses her hands over her mouth. Then she's hurrying down the street, leaving Scott and the commissary behind. Impatience and guilt rise and fall inside her, making her sick. She'd been so keen to prove something to Scott, something about how he couldn't boss her around, something about her being as daredevil as him, and none of it mattered. Now she's lost Chris. She swallows, trying not to panic. She needs to retrace her steps. He'll be loitering as usual. She keeps thinking she sees him, but it's always another boy, or a bush, or a shadow.

She walks quicker. Scott has caught up and sulks at her side, unconcerned, chewing and snapping his gum. They reach the spot where the three of them had stood looking at the airfield. She blinks up at the guard in the tower, his steely gaze, the rifle in his hand. 'I could ask him – he must have seen us.'

'He's not allowed to talk to you,' Scott says. 'You could be a spy.'

'That's stupid!' Hedy stares around her. Scrubby ground, prickly gorse bushes, clumps of purple heather. Crouching metal buildings. Wire fences.

'Maybe he split – went back to your place?'

'Maybe.'

If not, Hedy thinks, I will never forgive myself. And with a flash of understanding: Mom won't either.

'Want one?' Scott has opened the Snickers packet.

He's bitten into a bar. His teeth are sticky with caramel.

Hedy shakes her head. 'I've got to go home.'

'Listen, you should cool it. There's nowhere for him to go . . .'

She doesn't stay to hear the rest. She leaves Scott for the second time with a look of surprise on his face. But this time it's not funny. She's running so fast it hurts her chest. All she wants is to see the pale glint of her brother's hair, his poker back, his aimless trance. To find him around the next corner so that she can let all this worry out in a blast of anger. She's stumbling for the words inside her head, the words to tell him off, to make him sorry. But all she can find is please. Please, please, please.

He's not at home. The bungalow is empty, apart from the boiled wool smell of washing. She calls his name. She's methodical as she goes from room to room, searching corners, behind curtains. She even looks in cupboards in case he's hiding, for fun, or because he's upset. It's possible. Once he fell down and broke his nose and hid in the broom cupboard because he was ashamed that he'd got blood on his shirt. Hedy stares out of each window in turn, searching the street, the garden at the back fringed by trees. She stands in his bedroom among boxes waiting to be unpacked, closes her eyes and wills him to be here, sitting at his desk, engrossed in his scribbling. She opens her eyes, crosses the rug to look at a notepad left on his desk; the pages are filled with his tight, sloping scrawl. She reads some lines . . . *and the huge machine came down, light as a feather. The doors opened. The creatures that came out were green, eyes red as fire.*

Just another of his stories.

Chris never goes anywhere without her. Never. She has a sour taste in her mouth. Mom's told her since she was small, over and over, *look after your brother.* But she didn't need to be told.

The front door bangs, and Hedy flies to the hall.

'Hello,' Ruby says, taking off her hat, patting at her hair. 'Did you have a nice time? Where's Christopher?'

'Christopher?'

Ruby looks at her daughter, and her gaze sharpens. Fear already gathering at the corners of her mouth.

'He's with Scott,' Hedy says, fast as a rattlesnake.

Ruby's shoulders relax. 'He's made a friend? That's nice.' She stands on one leg and then the other to slip off her black patent stilettoes, clattering sharp heels onto the floor, wincing as she wriggles her toes. 'That's better. He won't be long though, will he? I don't want him getting too tired.'

'No,' Hedy says, backing away. 'He'll be back soon. Think I'll go see what they're doing.'

Ruby smiles her unfocused smile. The one she uses when she's going to have a lie-down, an afternoon nap.

He forgot the rule about leaving a trail behind, a scattering of breadcrumbs or bright pebbles to follow home. Instead, when he found the jagged break in the fence, wire torn or wrenched by some creature he couldn't imagine, he pushed his way through, stepping out of the base and into the forest. Then he followed his nose.

Now his nose leads him deeper into the trees under low scratchy branches, the deep moss of dead leaves softening his footfall, allowing him to walk silent as an assassin. The earthy smell is all around, sweet on his tongue, heavy on his senses, so that everything slows and warps like a dream. Airy spider webs catch across his mouth, binding his lips, sticky on his skin. Pine needles come spinning and twirling through dim, green light, catching in his hair, flicking his cheeks and hands. Beneath him, the forest floor seethes and moves. A swarm of ants marching under his shoes. He hopes he's not crushing them. He puts his hand against a sapling, and startles when the

51

bark writhes under his fingers. More ants. He peers at them, the bright tracks they make, running in tributaries. It occurs to him that he's insect like, the way he wears his skeleton on the outside, the way he gets stuck on his back.

He goes on, stumbling out of the thicket onto a narrow track of dark sandy soil. Adult pines stand in rows, creaking, old men with aching joints. It's less dense here, sunlight catches in smoky beams that slip between the canopy above, sparking on coils of bracken, blades of grass. The lack of sky or breeze makes it seem as though he's under water, far from the real world with all its noise and colour, the surface high above glimpsed in snatches of white cloud, marked by tops of waving pines. Birds dive like shoals of brown fish, slipping through the trunks, disappearing into shadows. The endless sameness of the trees disorientates him, shreds his idea of left and right. He's lost. He isn't frightened, just a little guilty, knowing that Hedy will be worried. He feels bad that he didn't tell her where he was going. His fingers twitch with the need to hold hers. He wants to show her everything he sees, to share it with her. But as much as he misses her, it's strangely liberating to be alone. He's never allowed to do anything without Hedy or Mom by his side.

He's certain he passed that same beech tree just a few minutes ago. It's huge girth is different from the tall, straight pines. It was on his right before, and now it's on his left. He's walking back the way he came; except how could that be when he doesn't remember turning around? With the restrictive chin pad, he can't look down to find his own footprints in the sandy soil. There's a rustle to his left and he swings his body towards the sound, peering into the woods, wondering if there's a creature close by. Perhaps animals watch him from behind tangles of twigs, clumps of bracken. He thinks he sees the shine of a yellow eye. Then his gaze snags on something at ground level, something in the grass at the side of the path.

He glimpses the thing from the corners of his eyes. It appears to be a round concrete circle, about as large as a fallen cartwheel, standing proud of the earth by maybe a foot. There's a scattering of brown pine needles covering it. He wonders what it is. It looks too heavy to lift, although it seems to be a covering of some kind, and there's a rusted handle set into it. Like a giant manhole. He thinks it could be the lid to a well. An entrance to somewhere deep underground. He badly wants to examine it further – but how to get down onto its level?

An oak tree nearby has a low hanging branch forked with smaller branches. Christopher chooses a sturdy piece of wood and presses all his weight against it until it snaps. Now he has a crutch. He leans against it, bending his knees until he can just reach his fingertips to the grainy surface of the circle. With a grunt of effort, he lets go and falls onto his knees. He brushes away some of the pine needles and finds a rusted grating set into the concrete. When his breathing's returned to normal, he puts his ear to the grating, expecting to hear the rush or trickle of water. Nothing, just his own blood beating inside his head. Except . . . except . . . if he strains, he thinks there might be a distant shuffle, a faint echo of movement, the scrape of feet against a hard surface, as if far below the ground, someone is walking. He straightens up, confused, and is blinded by a sudden flash of sunlight coming between a chink in the trees. Blinking, he bends to listen again. The noise has gone.

Christopher is hungry. His hips slump to the side. With a grimace, he turns his pelvis further until he's properly sitting. He's not sure if he'll be able to get up again. But he's so tired, he doesn't care. His lids are heavy. He gives in. Closes his eyes.

His wakes with a gasp, pushing damp hair away from his forehead, skin moist with a skim of sweat. His ear tickles. He feels a thing climbing deep inside the whorl of flesh. He sticks a finger in after it and hooks out an ant. It marches over his knuckles, antennae quivering. He tips it onto the ground carefully and then rubs himself down as best he can without being able to see what he's doing. His scalp is itching, crawling. He must be sitting on a nest. He runs his fingers through his hair and tiny bodies tumble out, a battalion of ants. He flaps his clothes to remove the last of them as gently as he can.

It takes a long time to manoeuvre himself onto his knees. He finds the oak branch, and uses it and the concrete circle to push up onto his feet. It's hard. The fibres of his bones tearing apart. Above his own harsh breath, he hears a sound. A child speaking. Then another. The sound of children laughing. Panting, he begins to limp in the direction of the voices.

'Hey!' he shouts. 'Who's there?'

The laughter stops. Abrupt as a tap turned off. Not even an echo washing back. Christopher waits on the path in an agony of listening. The hushed sounds of the forest rush against him: clickings and clutterings, whispers and sighs. No human voices.

'Hello?' he calls again.

A twig cracks to his left, a stealthy snap. He turns towards the sound, staring hard, and plunges off the path, entering the thicket of young trees, pushing his way through a puzzle of branches.

'I'm lost!' he shouts. 'Wait for me. Please.' A sob sticks in his throat.

A laugh, high and loud. And then the sound of feet kicking up the mossy darkness, a chatter of voices, backwards and forwards, like an argument. He sees a flash of movement, a girl, he thinks, younger than him. She's running like a deer. Her outstretched leg shines purple in a stripe of light. Then she's gone. He flounders after her in his jerky half-run, twigs scratching his face. He puts up his hands to try to protect his eyes; his shoulders bump against a tree, jolting his bones, tilting him off his axis.

When his foot catches, he goes down hard, smashing his chin into the ground; the pad jams against his gullet stopping his breath. He's frozen for a second, scared to move. He can see shoes. Pairs of scuffed lace-ups and a pair of sandals. They make a circle around him. Somehow he must get up. With a grunt, he manages to crawl onto all fours; the shoes don't move. He's aware of being the centre of the watchers' attentions, but he can't worry about them, because now comes the difficult part – the stagger onto his feet. He shuffles on his knees to the nearest tree trunk and uses it as a lever, his thigh muscles burning with effort. Holding his breath, his fingers struggle to get a grip on the bark as he inches himself upright.

'What's the matter with him?' a girl's voice asks.

'Dunno. Maybe he's a crip.'

He's back on his feet, spitting out bits of dirt and needle, wiping his mouth with the back of his hand. He pats at his clothes with shaky hands, checking that nothing has broken, no bits of brace or bone sticking out of him.

The shoes belong to three children. Two boys and a girl. He stares at them. They have purple faces. Purple arms and legs. He looks closer and sees that their skin is festering and bubbling with tiny scales that lift and peel. He can't tell if they've painted themselves violet, like warriors, or if their skin really is that colour. They are not entirely purple, he realises; bits of flesh show through, giving them a patchwork look. Their heads are shaved, even the girl.

He thinks back to the strange concrete circle, how it had crushed the grasses around it, as if it had fallen from space. Like the ships in *The War of The Worlds*. He reaches out a hand to touch one of the boys' arms to see if his skin is warm, if blood runs beneath the surface. The boy jerks away.

'Where are you from?' Christopher asks slowly.

'Butley,' the girl says in a strange sing-song voice. 'You a Yank, then?'

Christopher nods. He wonders what kind of place Butt-Lee is, and where it exists.

'Got any gum, chum?' the other boy asks. 'Sweets? Money?'

Christopher shakes his head.

A cunning look creeps onto a purple face. 'Not even a thruppence?'

Christopher doesn't know what a thruppence is. He would like to explain that he would give them one if he had one. He shoves his hands into his pockets looking for offerings and finds nothing but an empty Juicy Fruit wrapper. The children shift and sigh, walking away without glancing back, chattering among themselves in a language Christopher can't understand.

'Wait.'

He blinks and they've disappeared, the forest folding them into itself. He listens carefully; he can't hear their voices any-more. Instead a roar shakes the ground beneath him – branches shudder, birds take flight – the roar becomes so intense he presses his palms over his ears. The noise buries into his skull, and he's smelling burning petrol, the haze of burnt rubber, hot metal, as he stumbles past trunks towards the terrible sound.

56

He can feel the heat now, the whoosh of hot air sucking him in, pulling him closer, as if he's running into a dragon's mouth. With a smack he comes up hard against a chain-link fence. His fingers grasp it. Home.

Pressing his nose between diamond shapes he watches the jet take off. A B-47 he remembers, recalling the respect in Scott's voice as he'd said its name. Christopher clamps his hands over his ears as six engines fire white heat, the silver body thrusting away from the ground.

Ruby lies on the bed, unable to sleep. Her stockinged feet are crossed at the ankles, hands folded, skirt tucked around her knees. She's drawn the newly altered curtains, blocking out the view of the fence at the end of the garden and the pine forest beyond. The trees seem unnatural in their unchanging green. Beneath their canopy, the ground is dry and lifeless, thick with dead needles. The gluey stink of their sap hangs in the air. Thick forest surrounds the base on three sides. All the bluster and roar of the jets, the bombs nestled in bunkers, the ranks of marching men, the commissary and movie theatre, all of it is temporary, she thinks, before the stealthy march of the trees and the things that crawl under the dark branches, between the dark roots.

The weave of red and orange in the curtains lets in tiny pin-pricks of brilliance. The frame of the bed shudders deep beneath her, like the warning signs before an earthquake. Ruby turns her head as ornaments start to tremble on the dresser. She clutches her fingers. The subsonic wail shrinks the walls of the bedroom tighter, shrinks her own skin around her bones. She's used to airfields, but these new machines sear the atmosphere, burn a hole in the sky.

Once she longed for the sound of planes, crouched in a field at dawn, the hem of her dress wet with dew, watching for crosses to appear in a pale sky as she listened for the drone of Fortresses skimming the North Sea. Counting them in, counting them home. Sometimes a crippled plane would make it back, flying low, staggering through the morning mist. She'd strain her neck as they cruised overhead, searching for his plane, Heaven Can Wait painted on the nose. Praying for it to be there, for no red flare to be signalling wounded on board. To know he was alive. Another mission done. The growl of the B-17s was a gladness; it sounded inside her belly, rolling through her blood, a hammering of rebellion, a war cry, a love song.

The night she ran away, he took a truck to get to her, driving through the rain-sodden night without lights, along rutted lanes, past cottages with blacked-out windows, past the huddled shapes of cows in pastures, flanks silver wet in the moonlight. And thank God for the moon, she thinks, otherwise he never would have found his way to her.

An anxiety is growing inside her. It's filling her stomach, climbing into her throat. Where is Christopher? Didn't Hedy say she was going to fetch him?

Ruby swings her legs over the edge of the mattress and sits up too quickly. The room spins and weeps colours. Red. Orange. She pushes herself onto unsteady feet, slips her house shoes on, and goes to the window to pull back the drapes. The forest rustles, wind in the pine needles. Something snags at the periphery of her vision and she turns her head to see a shape moving between the shadowy trunks of trees. Before she has time to work out what kind of animal it is, a face presses against the wire mesh of the fence separating the garden from the forest. Two eyes, a nose and an open mouth. Ruby gasps.

Despite the matted hair around its gaping mouth, and a tangle of greasy fringe hanging over bright, dark eyes, the face is human. A man. With a shock she realises he's staring straight at her. She staggers back and sinks onto the bed, one hand pressed over the thud of her crashing heart. When she dares to creep to the window again, the man has gone.

She edges out of the bedroom into the kitchen, her whole body alight with nerves, and goes to the window, turning her head left and right to see down Roosevelt Road. A car, changing gear, crawls past. The view does not hold the terrible vision of the man, but it doesn't supply the image of her children walking home either. She's looking so hard at the emptiness, she doesn't notice the figure on the pavement outside the wisps of laurel until he's raised an arm to wave at her. She startles, biting her lip. Then she recognises Hank. He's carrying something heavy, a black box. He gestures with his free hand towards the front door.

'Hi. Todd at home yet?' he asks, as she opens the door.

Ruby shakes her head. 'There was a man behind my garden,' she blurts out. 'In the forest.'

'A man?'

'A tramp. I don't know. He looked wild. He scared me.'

'But he didn't do anything?'

'He went back into the forest, I think.'

Hank takes a step closer. 'I expect it was just an itinerant. There are hobo types in the forest, sleeping rough. He can't get over the fence. There's no way into the base. You're quite safe.' He smiles. 'The base is the most secure place you could be. You're surrounded by barbed wire. There're soldiers with guns patrolling the entrances.'

Ruby nods. 'Yes, I suppose so . . . it . . . it just gave me a fright.'

She remembers that she hasn't tidied herself after her nap. She touches her hair. 'Well . . . ' she clears her throat, straightens her shoulders, 'I should get on. I'll tell Todd you called.'

'Wait.' He puts his hand out. 'I have an idea to get your refrigerator going.' He holds up the black box. 'Car battery. See? I think it might work. Where is it?'

She stares at him blankly.

'The refrigerator?'

'In the garage.' She gestures to the left of the bungalow.

Hank's already making his way around the house, dapper in his blues. He's whistling.

'Christopher. Hedy,' she calls after him. 'I don't know where they are.' Her voice falters. 'My children. They're not here.'

Hank swings round. 'Relax – they'll be off having fun somewhere on the base. Everyone watches out for everyone else's kids.' He gives another smile, but it fades when he sees her expression. He comes back, eyes narrowing as he peers into her face. 'Hey now . . . Don't you go worrying, Ruby. Nothing can hurt them here. Nobody can get in and nobody can get out. They'll be home for tea.'

She holds his gaze, and the steadiness she finds there allows her to let go of her fear. It slips away like a creature padding into the shadows. Hank is right. The homeless man can't hurt her or her children. She concentrates on Hank. It's odd, she thinks, how she sees the boy in him, the pimply young man she knew, how he floats just under the surface of this older man like a face under ice, visible but trapped. The sadness of it makes her want to cup his cheek in her hand. He blushes as if he knows her intention, as if she's actually touched him. 'You never married, Hank?' she asks.

'Never found the right woman.' He gives a grimace. 'Guess

I married the military.' He cocks his head towards the garage. 'Todd keep his tools in there?'

While Hank is in the garage, Ruby goes into the bungalow and frowns at her reflection. Her hair has a flattened patch where she lay on it, her face naked-looking without lipstick. She slicks cherry red over her mouth, rearranges her curls. Then she goes into the kitchen to put the kettle on. Those first weeks in the States, she'd missed proper cups of English tea. She remembers an elephant wading through blue and green bushes, while hunched women picked tiny leaves under the Ceylon sun. The picture was on a Lipton tea caddy. Cool in her hands, a rust stain around the lid.

She'd come to love coffee, proper American coffee, not the acorns and chicory she'd boiled on the range at home, the saucepan bubbling its bitter smell, with Norfolk tiles beneath her feet, worn away by generations crossing and re-crossing the kitchen floor. Smoke in the air. A dead rabbit hanging by its feet. A knife in her hand.

Where are her children? She looks out of the window again, the window in her new life, because she's not that girl anymore, the girl on a Norfolk farm. She's a US airman's wife. The kids are playing with other kids inside the perimeter fence. Hank said so. They'll be home soon. She drops three spoons of Folger's into the pot, and even though her fingers are still shaking, she doesn't spill a grain.

When she goes out to the garage to ask if he takes sugar and cream, she finds that he's enlisted the help of a couple of other airmen to help him carry the refrigerator into the house. The three of them ease it along the path. They pant, neck muscles bulging, as they shuffle through the narrow hall manoeuvring the block of white into the kitchen. Hank takes off his hat and wipes his arm across his forehead.

'You mean you've fixed it?' Ruby slips between the men, all of them crammed into the tiny space.

'Yes, Ma'am.' Hank grins at her. 'The battery idea worked. See, I'll show you what I've done . . . '

Ruby claps her hand across her mouth as she watches him explaining how he's made it work. He talks about a voltage inverter, leaning down to prod some wires. He points out a jump lead connecting battery to cable, and a sawn-off plug. She isn't listening to him, just the reassuring hum of electricity. He stops talking. His face opens towards her, proud, shy.

'I can't believe it.' Ruby clasps her hands to stop herself from hugging him. 'I don't know what to say! Thank you.'

Hank colours as he runs a finger around his collar; the other two men are grinning. They salute Hank, ducking out of the house.

'It's nothing. Easy when you know how.' He gives the machine a proprietorial pat. 'Didn't like to see you without it. Seeing as it meant so much to you.'

Ruby feels her eyes hot and blind. They spill. She blinks, cheeks wet. And through the wavering, watery blur a drift of white appears, separating into two blond heads, two pale faces, features clarifying with each new blink.

Hedy and Christopher. Home. Safe. Just as Hank said they would be. Now that she has the flesh and blood reality of them before her, the fear returns from its hiding place, slinking to her like a disobedient dog. She lets out a short sob.

The children regard her warily. She sniffs, frowning. They've brought a smell with them: earthy green branches, liquid sap and peaty soil. A forest in the room.

'Where have you been?' She puts a hand on the cabinet to steady herself. 'You can't just disappear like that.'

'We're fine.' Hedy is sullen.

Christopher offers a sweet smile. 'We're sorry,' he says. 'We didn't mean to make you worry.'

Ruby steps forwards to pick something from the silvery smooth of his hair. A pine needle. 'You haven't been out of the base?' Her voice rises. 'Have you?'

'No,' says Hedy. 'Of course not.'

Ruby looks at her daughter, her unreadable expression. And then at Christopher. She sees the lie in his face.

'You must never, ever leave the base.' She's on her knees gripping his arms. He winces. 'Did you go into the forest? How did you get out? It's not safe, Christopher. Promise me.' A fleck of spit flies from her mouth. It clings to his cheek in tiny bright bubbles. She turns her head and fixes Hedy with a glare. 'You should know better!'

'Mom.' Hedy pulls her shoulder. 'Mom. You're hurting him!'

Ruby stands, the room tipping and spinning.

'Why can't we leave the base?' Hedy is asking. 'It's not fair. Other kids do. They go into town. We can't even explore the forest. It's just a load of dumb trees. What's so bad about it?'

'You don't understand.' Ruby leans down to look into her daughter's face. 'The local people . . . some of them are very poor. Dirt poor. There are . . . men . . . homeless men roaming the forest. There could be poachers. Gypsies. Even wild dogs. If anything happened to you or your brother, there'd be nobody to help. The forest is big. You'd get lost.' She lowers her voice, hissing. 'And you know Christopher can't do the same things you can.'

'He's stronger than you think,' Hedy says, her turned-down mouth stubborn and unrepentant.

Ruby pushes her knuckles into her eyes, making sparks fly, Catherine wheels exploding around her pupils. She needs her Miltown.

'My word is final, Hedy. There's plenty for you and Christopher to do here. There's a playground, isn't there? Other kids? And you can go to the bowling alley tomorrow if you like, for a treat.'

She pats her hair, twitches her lips upwards, chasing a smile that won't stick. Her children have pressed themselves close, as if sewn together with invisible stiches, a thread linking them, pulling them tight. She wants to hug them to her, crush them against her breasts and tell them how much she loves them, but she can see from their faces that they're wary of her. It's her fault. She's made them watchful and worried. She clears her throat and steps back.

'Hank's fixed the refrigerator,' she tells them in a too-loud voice. 'Isn't that wonderful?'

She's a bad mother, a bad hostess. But it's not too late – there's the silver pot sitting on the side, the empty cup and saucer. A jug of cream. 'I made coffee,' she remembers.

But Hank has already gone, a blue figure on the path outside, saluting.

# FIVE

Everything is ready. The table is laid for supper and their hands are washed. Hedy's plaits hang in two straight lines down her back, a bow at each end. Chris's hair is plastered flat over his scalp. They sit in their places, listening for the sound of a key in the front door, the scrape of Dad's feet on the mat. A hot meal is ready to serve from warming plates, delicious smells begging them to eat up. But Ruby says they will wait for their father. 'He'll be here any moment,' she says, folding her hands and staring straight ahead. The clock on the wall ticks on, the minute hand creeping forwards in tiny jerks.

Hedy drums her heels against her chair legs and fiddles with her place mat, pulling strings of raffia apart. Chris sits rigid as a statue. Hedy wonders how much he's hurting. His face is gentle, dreaming with eyes wide open. It's a way he has of escaping his pain, losing himself somewhere in his imagination.

The glistening juices under the meat loaf become cloudy. Tiny drops of fat speckle its sloping sides like fungus. The clouds of steam rising from the dishes of peas and mashed potatoes swirl thinner until they disappear into nothing. Hedy shifts on her chair. Plastic unsticks from her bare legs. Mom made her change out of her slacks. Her empty stomach growls. She picks up her fork. 'I'm hungry.'

Mom stands up, pushing her chair back abruptly, so that it teeters as she leans over the Formica surface, hacking at the crumbling meat loaf, scooping food onto their plates, spilling pools of congealed gravy over the chunks of meat and piles of grey potatoes. She bangs a plate down in front of Hedy. Hedy takes a mouthful and glares at her mother, noticing a red lipstick smudge on her chin.

'Daddy will be home soon,' Chris says quietly. 'I bet he's got lots of important things to do in his new job.'

Mom picks up Chris's hand and kisses it. Her eyes are bright. 'Yes. Of course. I just . . . ' She presses a hand to her forehead. 'I have a bit of a headache.' She looks at Hedy, 'I'm sorry, honey.'

The howl of a jet ripples the water in their glasses. The light bulb above their heads stirs as if a ghost has blown onto it, shadows flickering across the yellow table, the plates of food, the vase of flowers, Mom's red dress and naked arms. Hedy looks out of the window into the night. She thinks about what Chris told her about the forest, the purple children, and the heavy round thing like a doorway into the earth. He said he'd heard footsteps under the ground. Hard to tell if he really believes it, or if it's another of his stories. With Chris, reality and fantasy get mixed up all the time. She wants to explore the forest. They could have an adventure, get away from the boring base. Only Chris says he can't go. He promised Mom. 'Don't be a baby,' she'd said. 'Mom doesn't have to know.' But Chris is stubborn. She'll have to find another way to get him to come with her.

The front door has opened without her realising. Dad's in

the room, handsome in his uniform. He makes the furniture seem small. She feels a surge of joy so physical it hits her in the chest. Now Dad is home, it will be all right. He comes over and kisses Mom, wiping the lipstick off her chin with his thumb. 'Sorry I'm late, honey. Delayed at work.' He puts his hands on his hips and gives an exaggerated sniff. 'Smells good.'

He sits at the table, spreading knees and elbows, and leans across to ruffle Chris's hair, winking at Hedy. She tastes beery, sour fruit breath, sees his unsteady gestures and gets a strange feeling in the pit of her stomach. Mom's eyes are glittering. She doesn't say anything at first, just spoons food onto Dad's plate, smiling and nodding. 'You're here now,' she says in a bright voice. 'That's all that matters. Want me to heat this up? Or are you too hungry to wait?'

Dad forks up some mash and grins, 'Hungry enough to eat a horse.'

Mom arranges herself on her chair with one leg crossed, pats the folds of her skirt, and tips her head on one side to watch Dad eat. With her red lips and red dress, she looks like a movie star posing for a picture.

'You can get down, kids,' Dad says with his mouth full, waving his knife at them. 'Fetch me a Bud from the fridge, son.'

'Hedy, you clear the table. Put the dishes on the side.' Mom doesn't turn her head.

'Baby, this is delicious.'

Hedy piles the greasy plates one on top of the other, clattering knives and forks, a slimy smear of leftovers on her hand, and carries the pile through to the kitchen. She thinks of her father's lie and how nobody pointed it out. Only it was there in the room with them just the same. The thought of it makes her feel as if she's eaten something rotten. She listens carefully to see if an argument is starting, but all she can hear is her parents' quiet conversation, and the clink of a bottle against a glass. She peers into the room. They're sitting at the table. Her father eats, and her mother reaches out to touch his arm. He picks up her hand and presses it across his mouth, her palm sealing his lips.

Here, things are different from America. It's not just the place itself and the funny accents and the weather. It's her parents. Neither of them is acting normal. From the moment they arrived, Mom's been as nervous as a cat in a pack of wolves. And now Dad's behaving like a stranger. Back in the States, when he got home, he'd change into civvies and pour himself a Coke, shoot some hoops with her in the yard, or take Mom by the waist and twirl her around the kitchen table. He never turned up for supper late with alcohol on his breath.

Before they left for New York, Dad got surprise tickets for a baseball match. Just her and him. Walking towards the stadium in the crowd, he'd let her ride on his shoulders, even though her legs dangled down by his waist. She'd hung onto his ears, which made him roar. He'd tipped her off, flipping her over his arm in a somersault, and tickled her until she begged for mercy. Standing in the bleachers, they'd eaten hot dogs smothered in eye-watering mounds of mustard, yelling for the home team until their throats were sore and she was dizzy with happiness.

Naked in the bath, there's no hiding the bruising. Purple smudges run under the metal bars like faithful shadows, decorating his chest and back, encircling his neck.

'My God, Christopher!'

He says nothing.

'Did someone do this to you?' Mommy's voice is tight.

He looks up from the water. 'No. I fell.'

She touches the vivid stripes. 'You fell? I don't understand. Where was Hedy?'

'I . . . I went on my own. It wasn't her fault.'

'It is her fault, Christopher. She knows she has to look after you.'

All his pleasure in the warm water – his one hour of freedom – is ruined because he can feel Mommy staring at the marks, feel her upset and anger changing the atoms in the air, making them dark and hard.

Even after he gets out and lets her dry him, as he's lying face down on the bed, her fingers are angry; her tension pushes into his spine, working into his muscles and sinews, and he wants to tell her to stop. He distracts himself with the memory of Scott's big shoulders, the way he walked with his hands slouched in his pockets as if he owned the world, his narrowed eyes as he followed the path of the Stratojet across the sky.

Hedy comes in, shutting the door with a snap, and plops herself down on the chair in the corner. She hitches up her skirt and sits cross-legged as if she's on the floor. She has a book in her hand, *Between Planets*, ready to read aloud to him when he's in bed. Impossible to read himself when he's lying flat, trapped in the brace.

'Mom,' she says, 'when are we going to see our grandpa and our uncle? When are we going to Norfolk?'

Mommy's hands pause on Christopher's shoulders. He feels the edge of her nails.

'You said we could go.'

'Look at your brother's back,' Mommy says. 'You can't leave him alone. I've told you enough times.'

'It's not my fault.'

'Well, I hold you responsible.'

69

Christopher murmurs, 'Don't be angry at her.'

Mommy sniffs. He tries not to flinch when she presses a bruise.

'What about your family? What about visiting them?' Hedy persists.

'I'm sorry, but I don't believe I actually said we'd visit.' Mommy clears her throat. 'You must have misheard. My parents are dead, Hedy. You know my mother died when I was young, and my father died a couple of years ago.'

'What?' Hedy is breathless with disbelief. 'You didn't tell us our grandpa was dead too!'

'But you never knew him.'

'He was the only grandpa we had.' Hedy's voice is sulky rather than heartbroken.

Christopher twists his head to try to look at Mommy's face. He wonders how she found out about her daddy. A telegram, maybe. Did she cry alone in her room? How would he feel if someone told him Daddy had died? The thought is like tipping headfirst off a cliff.

'Did he die in an accident?' he asks, lifting his head free of the pillow.

'No, sweetheart. He was very old. He had a heart attack.'

'You didn't get to say goodbye?'

Mommy puts the lid on the bottle of oil. 'I said goodbye before I left for America. When I got on the ship, nothing mattered but Daddy. And then you both came along. The three of you – you're my family.'

'But what about your brother? Is he dead, too?' Hedy demands.

Mommy stands. 'Get up now, Christopher.'

'Mom?' his sister's voice persists.

'No, Hedy. He lives at the farm, but he's very busy. Farmers never get any time off.'

'Don't you want to see him? He's your brother.'

Mommy sighs again. 'We were never close. Not like you and your brother.'

'But he's our uncle. Can we go visit him?'

'I don't know.' Mommy sounds impatient. 'Maybe. When he's not so busy.' She hooks a hand under Christopher's arm, helping him sit up. 'Time for bed. Come along.' She rests her warm fingers on Christopher's head and he feels as though she is steadying herself. She strokes his hair. 'Let's get you back into the brace,' she says in a soft voice.

'Is he married? Does he have children?' Hedy stands with her arms crossed.

Mom stares at her. 'No.' She frowns. 'He's not married.'

'What's his name? The name of our uncle?'

'Ernest.'

His name is unfamiliar in her mouth; Ruby can't remember the last time she said it aloud. Ernest. Sometimes she feels his eyes watching her, even though they've been separated for years, an ocean between them. He used to follow her around the house, traipse after her in the yard. He fixed his stare on her as she ran around the school playground. She always knew without seeing him where he was, could feel his gaze following her from whatever corner he'd chosen to hide in at break-time.

She joined in every playground game she could. She remembers a boy being wolf, turning around grinning, 'Lunch time!'

And they were all screaming and running, children scattering like leaves, and the wolf was among them, hands outstretched. She felt the tips of his fingers brush her arm, as her feet went pounding to safety, joy beating in her chest, making her laugh aloud.

'Ruby.'

Ernest's jealous voice claimed her like a rope thrown over her head. He beckoned to her with a nod. She walked over slowly, biting the inside of her cheek to take the grin away. It wasn't fair that she had to be miserable too.

The other kids teased Ernest. They said he was a cripple because his parents were first cousins. 'Inbred,' they called him. 'Crooked.' 'An idiot.' The scoliosis was inherited, but not because their parents were cousins, and there was nothing wrong with Ernest's mind; people just presumed there was because of the way he looked. But Ruby didn't say any of this, instead she sat as far away from him as she could. She didn't want to be an outcast. She was proud of her long, slim legs and her straight back. She couldn't make friends with Ernest always tagging along, glaring at people. Nobody ever came back to their house. Father wouldn't allow it.

In the big classroom, they sang 'My Bonnie Lies Over the Ocean'. She loved the way their voices sounded, so beautiful, like a proper choir, and she wondered what it would be like to travel across a wide sea, to love someone so much you made up a song about them. Mrs Chaffey handed out boards and set some number work. Through a lock of loose hair fallen across her forehead, Ruby watched Mrs Chaffey as she read the newspaper, scratching her chin and yawning. Ruby's hair shimmered like a veil. Ruby wound it around her finger to make a silver ring – a wedding ring. Mrs Chaffey was snoring, the newspaper fallen to the floor.

On the way home, Ruby carried Ernest's bag for him. He limped beside her, dragging his left leg. His spine was hunched into a half hoop. His shoulders lopsided and twisted. The others were playing rounders in the road. Ruby heard the thwack of

72

the ball, the shouts and laughter. She wanted to drop the bag and run back; she wanted to race around the circle of catchers, feet skidding over the gritty road, laughing in the evening sunlight with all the other straight-limbed children.

'You've no more need of school,' Father said. 'You're old enough to take your mother's role at home. Ernest will be leaving too. He belongs here on the farm. Away from prying eyes.'

'But I like school. I like books.'

'You have your bible. Your place is in the kitchen now. It's your Christian duty to mind the house and look after your brother.'

'I won't,' she said. 'Just because Ernest is a cripple. Why should it be me that has to look after him?'

Father took a belt to her. Seven red wheals on her bottom so she couldn't sit down for days. As he raised the leather strap, Father told her, 'God chose the weak things of the world to shame the strong.'

The range was oily with years of soot and spitting fat. Underfoot, flagstones were greasy, carpets ingrained with grit. Her father and brother didn't notice the soft scum of dust on every surface, green and brown stains in downstairs sinks and the lavatory. Ruby scraped grime from the cracks in the pine table, watched it blacken her fingernail. Cups in the cupboard were peaty with tannin. Cobwebs splayed across windows, studded with flies. Spiders knitted in corners. *I know, O Lord, that Your judgements are righteous, and that in faithfulness You have afflicted me.* Their father thought God was punishing him by making Ernest's bones crooked. But why was she being punished? What had she done wrong? Sometimes Ruby thought that there was no God, because what reason could he have for making Ernest a cripple? For making their mother die in childbirth?

Once a week she heated the copper and bent over the washing in the outdoors tub, forcing sopping sheets and clothes through the mangle before battling with armfuls of heavy, damp fabric, pegging it up on the line in the back garden where on windy days, it slapped her face. Her hands were raw, her fingers swollen. Bitterness became a taste at the back of her throat. Sunday evenings, she shut herself into the kitchen with a hip bath of hot water and scrubbed until her skin hurt, washing her hair with baking powder. If she managed to pocket an egg in the morning, she cracked it onto her head, massaged it in before rinsing. A trick she read about in an old magazine. Ruby yearned for a golden tube of red lipstick, like the one she saw in an advert, and a pair of scarlet shoes to match. A pair of magic shoes to carry her away from the farm, from Ernest, and from her father, keeping her like a slave, when everyone said she looked like Dorothy Lamour.

In the kitchen, Ruby takes a Miltown, swallowing it down with a glass of sherry.

She puts the bottle back in the cupboard. 'You want anything from the refrigerator, sweetheart?' she calls through to Todd. She never gets tired of feeling the cold on her face, listening to the hum of the machine.

'Nah, I'm good.' He's in the armchair by the window, staring out at the darkness.

'The kids are in bed.' She draws the curtains. 'Tired? Want a shoulder rub?'

He seems to rouse himself. 'Maybe it's me should be giving you a massage, honey. Come, sit between my legs.'

Ruby kneels down, but she can't settle, can't let the push of his fingers find a hold in the knots of her shoulders. She touches the web of scar tissue tight across her palm. The thought of Ernest is stuck inside her head. The bigger boys used to corner him in the playground, poke him in the chest, tell him he smelt of pigs.

'For Pete's sake, Ruby! Your neck is as hard as a block of wood.'

She slips out from under his hands, and drops into his lap, arms around his neck, nose in the stubble of his jaw. 'I'm fine. Don't worry about me. It's you that's been at work all day, baby.' She kisses his cheek. 'I want to do something for you.'

'Well,' he takes a pull on his bottle of Budweiser and squeezes her waist. 'I can think of one thing.'

She doesn't get up and get washed straight away. Instead, Ruby lies in her husband's arms while he smokes, his other arm holding her close against his chest. But even as he lies right next to her, she has the strange sense that he's getting more and more remote, like a man trudging away across a desert. She nuzzles up closer under his arm, inhaling his salty heat, the beer and nicotine on his breath, wishing she could climb right inside his skin, know all his thoughts. Where was he this evening? Why didn't he say if he'd popped into the bar to get a drink? Stop this, she tells herself. He's entitled to the pleasure of a couple of beers after a hard day. He doesn't have to share every single little thing with her.

She thinks about telling him about the homeless man behind the fence. But something else is already bothering Todd. Coming home with alcohol on his breath and then drinking two more beers over supper isn't like him, and she doesn't want to add to his worries. 'Hedy asked when we'd visit my family,' she says instead.

'What did you tell her?'

'Just that there was only my brother left, and he was too busy for visits.'

'Knowing Hedy, that subject won't lie down just yet.'

She presses her lips into the hair on his chest. 'She'll keep pestering for a while. But she'll get bored eventually.'

'You sure you don't want to pay your brother a visit?' he asks. 'I know you left under a dark cloud, but it's been years . . .'

She shakes her head. 'Ernest isn't the forgiving type.'

'Baby, surely he'd be happy for you, to know you had a loving husband, a family?'

'No.' She wants to change the subject. 'He's a bitter person. Like my father. Bitter people don't know how to be happy for others.' She's struggling to keep her voice from shaking. 'I don't want the children to see that run-down place – to know how I lived. It makes me ashamed to think of it. And I don't want them to meet him. He'll be in a worse state now; it would frighten them.' She picks up his hand and presses her lips against his wrist. 'I was so unhappy,' she says softly. 'My life started when I met you.'

He kisses her hair. 'Okay then. No visits to Norfolk. But there's plenty for them to do here – what with the movie theatre and other kids and school.' He takes a drag and exhales. 'And if they want more, they could go into Woodbridge, visit the shops, play by the river. There's a bus goes in every day.'

'You know they can't do that.' Ruby tries to keep her voice steady. 'It's not safe. Not with his disability.'

'Ruby, he's twelve. You baby him. You have to let him be.'

He doesn't understand, she reminds herself. He's a man. He won't talk about the brace, won't accept Christopher's physical limitations. 'Honey, let me worry about the children. It's my job.' She walks her fingers playfully across his chest, hoping to

76

make him smile. 'And what about yours? You haven't told me a thing yet.'

'It's not exactly what I thought it would be . . . ' he says slowly. 'But it's early days. I'll get the hang of it.'

'So what's it like in those bunkers? Are they big inside? Is it really all underground?'

Todd sits up, dislodging Ruby from his chest. He stabs his cigarette out. 'Goddamn it! This isn't a game, Ruby. Stop asking me questions. Just because you can't see it, don't think there isn't a war going on.'

'I know.' Ruby raises herself onto an elbow, confused. 'I didn't mean—'

Todd's not listening. 'Jesus. Just asking about my job, you're asking me to breach national security. You should know better.'

He lies down, plumping the pillow under his head, settling with his back to her.

Ruby stretches out a hand and places it against his naked shoulder. 'I'm sorry,' she whispers.

Todd doesn't move. She waits for a moment longer, hoping. But his breathing changes, there's a new weight to him, and she knows that he's fallen asleep. She gets up and goes quietly into the bathroom. Todd's outburst has made her throat close up. She struggles to stop herself from crying. She must have touched a nerve. It's this new job. It's a lot of responsibility to have the safety of the world in your hands. She tips a pill into her palm and checks the contents of the bottle. It's nearly empty.

# SIX

When Ruby went into labour with Christopher and Hedy three weeks early, they'd been stationed in Jacksonville, Florida. From her bed in the maternity unit, Ruby could glimpse a row of diamonds glinting on the horizon, the thin line of the ocean. Home was an apartment just outside the base. She was happy cultivating pineapple guava and African lilies in their small garden. Every day she appreciated the exotic otherness of the shocking green grass, honeyed air thick enough to slice, black faces on the streets. The farm in Norfolk seemed a million miles away.

Once, she stood among crowds outside Westminster, raising her voice with other women: pregnant women, women carrying tiny babies in their arms. Her own child curled up inside her, twitching in her belly. Her stomach was already pushing through her clothes, so that she'd had to let out the seams of her dresses. She wanted him or her to be born in America.

'Yankee Doodle Dandy!' the shout went up. 'Give us boats!'

'You'd think they'd be happy to be shot of us,' one woman

said. 'It's not right, is it, keeping us here all this time. Where's your man, then?'

'Back in the States,' Ruby said. 'Waiting for me.'

'Men are all the same – Yanks or Brits. Some of them don't want to take responsibility for what's theirs.' She looked at Ruby's stomach.

Ruby stuck out her hand with the band of gold. 'We love each other. We're married.'

At Tidworth, they made her strip in front of a panel of doctors. Shivering, she spread her legs while a nurse shone a torch inside her, checking for VD. Ruby looked over their heads, pretending she was somewhere else, pretending she was with Todd, dancing under bright streamers. She was one of the chosen ones, the Pilgrim Mothers. From the moment she stepped onto the ship at Southampton, she knew she was sailing off the edge of a map, like those first sailors discovering the Americas. There were eight other women in her berth, and two babies. No room to move, the air rank with the smell of shit and nappy cream. Every night Ruby listened to new-born wails and the chatter of women, while she pressed her hands over her belly and told her own baby about their new life in America. She didn't know yet that she was pregnant with twins. The ship rolled, wallowing across waves big as houses; Ruby lay on her bunk, being sick in a bucket. And then they were there, sailing up the Hudson River, and she stood on deck with the other women, feeling weak with hunger, shivering in her thin coat, looking at the ice floating on the water, the shape of Manhattan rising out of the fog.

Everything she saw and tasted in America was a surprise, taking her further from the familiar, swallowing her up. After Florida came the Iowa posting, a new landscape: drier, dustier, with huge, empty prairies. She loved that, too. She loved everything about the United States.

Ruby gets out the flour and sugar to make a birthday cake. Two cakes. It's tradition to have a joint party for Todd and the twins, their birthdays just days apart. Ruby measures, beats butter and sugar until her shoulder aches and the fat turns pale. She cracks two eggs, mixes in a little of the flour, stirring the gloop, strings of albumen on the back of the spoon. When she became an air-force wife, she'd understood right from the start how it would be. Todd explained about the moving around, the insecurity and loneliness. She'd wanted to laugh at his idea of loneliness – he could never understand how isolated her child-hood had been.

It was after ten B-17s were shot down over Germany, red flares across the Channel, that Ruby let Todd lead her into the belly of the plane and make love to her on the narrow, hard deck. There was hardly any room, and Todd was on his knees, bashing his head on a fuel gauge, cursing, laughing. Her stocking ripped. It didn't matter. He could get her more. *Anything you like, baby*. She looked up at the arch of metal over their heads, the blunt shapes of the machine guns crouched in the darkness. She heard music in the distance, carefree voices bubbling through the night, Todd's breath loud as an explosion in her ear. When she understood that she was pregnant, it was harvest time, and she spent all day in the fields, nails torn, hands scratched by thistles, skin tight with dried perspiration and too much sun. The light blinded her. The sky so blue that any notion of war seemed impossible here, on the ground, where there was nothing but the urgency of getting the sheaves cut and bundled and put away safe before the rains came.

She'd been nervous about telling him, but after a moment of shock, Todd had simply placed his big hand on her nearly flat belly. 'Well now – I'll bet it's a boy,' he smiled. 'I'll teach him how to pitch. How to ride a bike.' She wasn't showing yet, only her breasts different, shot through with blue, heavy and sore.

She puts the spoon to one side and digs her hands into the mix, feeling it under her nails, the slip and slide between her fingers like putty. She squeezes hard, then takes her hands out, unable to stand the feel of it, globs and smears stuck to her skin. She puts her wrists under the hot tap, soaps up bubbles, rinsing with scalding water, watching diluted cake mix sluice down the plug hole.

In the hospital, she was stitched up by a frowning doctor while the babies were taken into another room to be weighed and checked. She'd hardly glimpsed them before they disappeared, swaddled in towels, tiny as kittens. Tired, groggy from drugs, she listened to a mewing noise from behind the closed door, trying to make out if it was the sound of one or two babies crying. The doctor ignored her when she asked if her children were all right, and she thought perhaps he couldn't understand her English accent.

It seemed days later, but it must have been only hours when a nurse told her she'd had a healthy boy and girl. She brought the babies to Ruby's bed in the ward, helped her balance them, one in each arm. Their premature faces were shrunken like little old men, wispy dark hair feathering their bodies. 'Won't be winning any beauty contests,' Todd said, picking up the baby wrapped in blue, whispering into the tiny ear, making plans for baseball games, explaining the joys of jet engines.

Healthy was the word that mattered. Since getting pregnant, she'd been afraid of the illness, afraid it had crossed the ocean with her. But really she couldn't believe her babies would be affected in America, in her new life. The scoliosis belonged to the mud and the wind of Norfolk. It belonged to the family she'd left behind. Her love for Todd was a fire that would burn away any abnormalities. When Christopher was diagnosed years later, Todd never blamed her. Not openly. Before Christopher, as far as Ruby knew, Ernest had been the exception; usually it was the women of the family who were affected. Sometimes she thinks Ernest put a curse on her, that afternoon in the farmhouse kitchen.

The cakes come out of the oven, smelling of vanilla and chocolate. She lets them cool off and calls Hedy to help. Devil's food cake might well be named for the thick, white icing that took minutes of non-stop beating to get right, leaving your arms aching like hell. Hedy comes in from the yard, sweaty from shooting hoops. She slumps at the table, yawning, her apron bunched around her waist. Ruby knows that Hedy likes a challenge. 'Want to make the icing for Dad's cake?'

Hedy beats with the wooden spoon until her elbow's a blur, stirring the egg whites and syrup into a slick consistency. 'Tip it onto the sponge now,' Ruby tells her. 'Smooth it down with the back of a knife.'

Hedy seems to have half the cake around her mouth. The remaining sponge has taken on a lopsided look. Chocolate crumbs mowed into the white, like mud into snow. Ruby looks away. It's only a cake. It doesn't matter. Just because Hedy's a thinner version of herself, her daughter is not her. And that's a good thing, she reminds herself, because Hedy is braver and stronger than she's ever been. A better sister. Loyal and kind.

'Could you lay the table?' Ruby asks Hedy. 'We've got Hank and the Lansenses coming too, don't forget.'

'I don't know why.' Hedy licks her fingers clean. 'Scott's not even our friend.'

'Yes he is,' Ruby says. 'I thought you liked him. You said so. Go and get washed. Put on your pink dress. And for Pete's sake, brush your hair!'

She does her best with the devil's food cake, repairing it with some extra icing and carefully placed sugar flowers. The twins' sponge is perfect, white and pink and blue, with thirteen candles placed around the outside. She's admiring it when she feels her husband's arms snaking around her waist.

'Hey!' She puts her hands over his. 'You're not supposed to see. You're spoiling the surprise.'

'I'm not looking. Got my eyes closed. Promise.' He squeezes, stopping the breath in her lungs. 'Sorry about last night. Guess I'm just tired.'

'It's OK. It was my fault.' She leans into him, her back fitting the curve of his chest. Their fingers entwine. Gladness fills her, warm and gleaming as treacle. She closes her eyes, so that they can be together in darkness.

# SEVEN

At the beginning he will be strange to them. But if he is patient, if he smiles despite their comments, if he laughs with them when they laugh at him, then eventually, they'll accept him. Christopher knows this, because he's been through it all before. So he lets his new classmates call him 'Ironsides', just like the last lot did, and he tries not to get angry or upset when they grab the bars under his clothes and tug on them. *Take it easy. It's only a joke, buddy.*

School on the base is about as bad and as good as school in Iowa. His new classmates' expressions mirror those in Sioux City when they notice his chin pad, his jerky walk, the weird shape of the brace under his jumper. He's become an expert in reading shock, at picking up on pity or disgust.

Brace is a deceitful word, the sly way it slips off the tongue with a hiss, pretending to be subtle and light, whereas really it's hard and cruel, snapping shut like a crocodile in for the kill.

The main difference in this school is numbers. Fewer children, only four or five kids in each grade, means the classes are mixed up, younger and older children sharing the same classroom. Miss Graham soon works out that Christopher is an ace at times tables and gets him helping the younger ones with maths lessons, and he likes that. It feels satisfying to explain things, to see understanding fall through someone like sunlight, and then the way the light ripples on touching new things.

Illuminate, he thinks. A good word.

Outside the classroom, the playground is full of children running and ducking and pushing each other. The spring sunshine is warm on his face; he closes his eyes, letting the heat bake burning spots of red and gold onto them, so that even when he opens his eyelids, the spots are still there, dancing across everything.

He's hoping he'll see Scott in the playground. He's full of new information about the B-47. He's got it by heart now. He can list the revolutionary design of the swept-back wings, the Fowler flaps, the radar-controlled tail gun. He imagines how he'll casually mention the bomb load capacity of 25,000 pounds. Scott will turn, fascinated, looking at him properly, instead of letting his gaze wash over him as if he's uncomfortable with what he sees.

Christopher blinks through the circles of brilliance, and eventually his gaze settles on the silver birch tree at the end of the playground. He loves its fragile leaves, how sunlight has ignited the edges with gold. He watches them shimmer, vibrating against the blue sky. He's so intent on the leaves that he doesn't realise that the bursts of laughter on the edge of his consciousness are getting louder, hitting his face in a fug of candy breath and nervous excitement. He pulls his attention back to his immediate surroundings; several faces stare at him, close-up smirks and big twisted smiles. They are pointing at him. He shrinks inside the brace, confused. What new game is this?

Then Hedy is there, pushing people away, her arms straight as battering rams. She snatches something from his chest and waves it in front of their faces. A white rag.

'Think this is funny? Who did it?'

Christopher sees letters scrawled on the tatty paper in Hedy's angry fist. He pieces it together. *Freak*. He brushes his hands across the front of his jumper, feeling for anything else stuck there. He can't look down, can't see below his nose. They must have pinned it on him while he had his eyes closed. Or even before that. He would like to sit down; he feels suddenly very tired.

'It doesn't matter, Hedy,' he tries to tell her. But his sister hasn't learnt the lesson. She keeps looking for the next fight.

Scott strides over, triumphant in his role as bringer of justice, dragging Jimmy Kisro along by his shirt. The collar has ripped into a long, jagged tear showing Jimmy's skinny black chest. Jimmy's mom will be upset, Christopher thinks; that's a lot of darning. Jimmy's eyes have become rolling whites around dark centres. His mouth is working but nothing's coming out, except strings of saliva.

'You better apologise to Ironsides here,' Scott says.

'Chris,' Hedy corrects him. 'He needs to apologise to Chris.'

'Say sorry to Chris.' Scott gives Jimmy an encouraging shake. The torn shirt is still bunched in Scott's fist, and Christopher hears the grating hiss of the rip getting bigger.

He watches Scott's face, how he looks all the time to Hedy for approval.

Billy and Frank, two of Scott's gang, gather around Jimmy. 'It wasn't me,' Jimmy says, his voice small.

'You saying we're liars?' Billy steps close, his Louisiana tones warm and soft. 'Back home we'd string a boy like you up for something like that.'

He says it with a smile, and it takes a second to understand.

'Hey,' Hedy says. 'That's enough. Leave him alone.'

Scott and his boys shrug, opening their hands as if dropping invisible weapons; and they walk off, giving each other friendly shoves, laughing. Jimmy wipes snot on the back of his hand. 'I didn't do it,' he says, stubbornly. He looks at the ground.

'I know you didn't,' Christopher says. 'Scott made a mistake, is all.'

Hedy purses her lips, lets out an exasperated rush of air.

Christopher gazes after Scott. He's at the centre of an admiring circle. Billy is there too. Christopher hopes that Scott's tearing a strip off Billy for saying that to Jimmy.

'You're not a freak, Christopher. I think you're nice.' Dotty Robbins adjusts the glasses on her snub nose, and reaches out to pat him, as if something is still stuck to his jumper, or he's an old dog. Behind the bi-focals, Dotty's moist eyes have a look he's seen before. He picks up her wrist and gently removes her hand.

'Dotty Robbins is sweet on you,' Hedy tells him as they're walking home.

'No she isn't.'

Christopher knows she's too bored by the subject to pursue it. He can tell by the way she's chewing the inside of her lip that she's got something else on her mind.

'Last night, I got up for a drink of water,' she says, 'and when I looked out the window, I saw something.' She stops and looks towards the horizon. 'Lights in the sky,' she frowns. 'Kind of blinking on and off. And it wasn't a jet. There was one big light, moving slow. Others like stars around it.'

Christopher follows the line of her gaze, seeing the tops of the pines rearing above army buildings and roof tops. He's dreamt about being there again, listening at the stone circle to noises underground. When he's dreaming, he runs and jumps and climbs. But the same nightmare always wakes him: pressed flat as a squashed bug, breathless under a phantom bus or tree. Then his eyes open and his fingers fumble against the metal bars of the brace, and he knows it's real. He's stuck inside his own prison.

'Lights in the sky,' he repeats. 'Are you sure?'

She nods. 'Yeah. Red. Green. Flickering.'

Christopher's heartbeat surges, the rhythm of it reaching his temples in a furious twitch of excitement. 'You mean you think you might have seen a UFO?'

'Maybe. It came down over there. In the forest.'

He's always thought that in another world, more advanced than this one, there might be ways of curing him in a kinder way. He cannot believe that anything as cruel as the Milwaukee Brace would exist among creatures that invented space ships to fly across solar systems.

He stands staring at the dark fringe of the pines, as the howl of a jet starts up, making the ground tremble. 'I promised Mommy,' he says, more to himself than his sister.

'She'll never know,' Hedy murmurs, the noise of jet engines swallowing her words.

Christopher gives a brief nod above his chin pad, as 204,000 pounds of metal screams over their heads.

'OK,' he says.

*

88

Ruby sits beneath a dryer at Glamour Daze, her scalp smarting under a mass of tightly wound curlers. She likes this sense of enforced passivity, and the prick of pain at the roots of her hair is almost pleasant through the fug of her exhaustion. She selects the latest issue of *Ladies' Home Journal* from the pile of magazines on her lap, opening it at an advertisement for PEP vitamins. A man with a square jaw in a suit and trilby is embracing his wife. She's wearing an apron and has a vacuum cleaner in hand. *So the harder a wife works, the cuter she looks!* reads the speech bubble coming out of the man's head.

Maybe that's what she needs, Ruby thinks, turning the pages: vitamins to stop her feeling so tired all the time. She worries that Miltown is doing something to her brain. She can't think clearly anymore. They'd seemed like a miracle when she was first prescribed them, just after Christopher's diagnosis. Taking them helped her cope, helped her be a better wife, a better mother. Now they seem to be doing the opposite, dragging her energy down, making her snap at the kids. But the thought of going without her pills squeezes the air out of her body.

As a distraction, she begins to read an article on How to Have Young Skin at Any Age. Is her complexion looking old, she wonders, rubbing a finger over her cheek. Todd used to pretend to bite the skin there. *Plump as a juicy apple*, he'd say, *hold still while I take a bite*. And she'd scream obligingly while she pulled away, enjoying the sense of his greater strength, waiting for him to tilt her head up and kiss her mouth.

It was a letter from the liaison committee that brought Todd to the farm. Her father read the note with a scowl. 'Request to host a couple of American servicemen for Christmas lunch.' He shook his head. 'Do they expect us to lay on a feast in the middle of a war? Bunch of nosy parker fools.'

'Rendering service with a good will as to the Lord and not to man,' Ruby murmured.

Father cleared his throat and gave a short nod. He folded the letter and put it in his pocket. 'We'll do our Christian duty. The old goose will serve her purpose too.'

Ruby was half inside the open range, face scrunched against the heat to baste the meat, when she heard footsteps. She straightened up, red-faced, feeling half-cooked herself, a dirty apron wrapped around her waist, to find two Americans in the kitchen. The men dazzled her – she'd only seen Americans from a distance. Close up, they were immaculate in elegant, tailored uniforms, like film stars. One was tall and athletic with reddish gold hair, and the other was a short man with a rash of nervous spots and a sweet smile. After the awkward introductions, their guests began to hand out presents, lavish gifts that made Ruby giddy as more and more of them were pressed into their hands: packets of cigarettes, magazines, freshly cooked ham, chocolates and silk stockings. Ruby's father softened a little as he turned the packet of Lucky Strikes over, tapped one out and lit it. She saw how the Americans' eyes flickered over the low, beamed ceiling, stained from years of smoke, tea kettle boiling over the open fire, taking it all in.

Over lunch, she kept quiet, watching and listening, getting up to fetch more potatoes or beer. The talk was men's talk, of the war, how well it was going now that the Ardennes counter-offensive was working, and how the Allies would win in a matter of weeks, no doubt about it. Her brother warmed to the strangers, even laughed with them. Ruby could see that he liked being able to discuss war tactics with real airmen. He told them about the bombing of Norwich and how homeless people made their way into the countryside, sleeping rough in sheds and barns for months afterwards. The Americans talked about General Eisenhower, the D-Day landings, and why their air force hadn't been able to counter-attack from the air on 16 December. 'Fog,' the short one told them. 'Couldn't get off the ground in a white-out. That's what gave Jerry his advantage.'

Suddenly, there was silence, and Ruby realised that the whole table was looking at her.

The tall one was speaking.

'Sorry?' She could feel her face red as a beet.

'Do you like dancing?' he repeated.

She held onto the edge of the table to stop herself falling into the gap he'd carved into the conversation. She sat still, avoiding looking at her father or her brother. She fixed her gaze on Lieutenant Delaney, on the tiny gold airplanes shining on the lapels of his jacket. Then she raised her eyes to his, and managed a nod.

'It's an awful shame about Glenn Miller.' He wrinkled his forehead. 'He was due to play at the base in January. But we're having a dance anyway, in celebration of him. We'll have another swing band playing. I'd be happy to be your escort, if your father would allow it?'

It was as if he'd thrown a bridge across a moat. A chance to escape in full sight of the enemy. Even though village girls were regularly transported on passion wagons, and came back breathy with tales of tables laden with food and live music and handsome Americans, she'd never been allowed to go. But now, her father and brother couldn't do a thing about it. They watched the arrangements being made right in front of them, over the remnants of goose carcass, dirty plates and half-empty glasses.

'We'll take good care of her, sir,' the other airman, Second

Lieutenant Pulaski, assured them. 'Don't you worry about that.'

And her father frowned, 'I suppose it would be all right. Just this once.'

Todd gave her a wink then, as if he knew perfectly well what he'd just accomplished, and Ruby felt something open inside her, like a window thrown wide to let in sunshine.

Her stylist is back, releasing her from the dryer, a heavy metal globe like one of Christopher's cartoon space helmets, beckoning her to a chair before the mirror. She drops the magazine and slumps obediently in the leathery comfort of armrests and swivelling seat, watching herself in the glass with a floaty sensation of detachment as his expert fingers set to work on the rollers.

'Two more hours of my life spent in a beauty salon.' Betty's voice breaks the spell as she slips into the next-door seat.

Ruby blinks at Betty's image. Now she'll be forced to make conversation.

'That's a lovely permanent,' Betty tells her. 'How are your two getting on at their new school?'

'Fine, thanks,' Ruby says to Betty's reflection.

'And what about . . . Christopher?' Betty lowers her voice. 'Is he all right, you know, mixing with the other kids?'

Ruby's jaw tightens. 'Christopher's very clever. He can't run around and play ball. But he comes top in his written work.'

'Oh, I didn't doubt it for a moment.' Betty wrinkles her forehead. 'I just meant, I know how rough some kids can get, with him being a cripple and all.' She waits as the hairdresser combs her hair through. 'Are you visiting family while you're in the UK? Didn't someone tell me you come from East Anglia originally?'

'No family to visit.' Ruby shakes her head. 'My parents are dead.'

'Oh, I'm sorry.'

Ruby gives Betty a steady look. 'Being an air-force wife, it's easier just having my husband and children to care for.'

'Honey, you never spoke a truer word. Ailing parents are a worry. And most relatives we'd never choose for ourselves. Some of us just got to make the best of a bad lot.'

Betty's stylist is flapping his hands, ushering her up as if he's guiding a flock of chickens. 'If madam would like to take a seat at the basins. Michelle will be there directly to give you a wash and massage.'

Betty sighs. She slowly uncrosses her legs and uncoils herself from the leather chair. She manages to appear elegant, even in a pink salon gown with Glamour Daze emblazoned across her chest in gold. She pauses behind Ruby and touches her shoulder.

'Scott never stops talking 'bout Hedy. I wonder if a little romance isn't blossoming right under our noses.'

'Hedy?' Ruby starts. 'I don't think she's interested in boys, not in that way. She'd rather be playing softball. All she talks about is how she misses her league. She played pitcher.'

Betty gives a snort of laughter. 'Well then, I can see the attraction right there. Scott's a sports nut.'

Ruby leaves Glamour Daze. She stands on the pavement, watching her transparent twin in the glass of the salon front. She's not sure what to do, now that the ammonia-scented interior and reassuring simple rituals of the salon are lost to her. Here she is, dressed in her new wool jacket and plaid skirt, with her hair freshly done, as if she's going somewhere – and suddenly she longs to be at a dance, a place filled with music and laughter – one of those war-time dances with Todd sweeping her up in his arms, her face pressed against his uniform.

'Stick close to me,' Lieutenant Delaney had said, that first time. She knew her dress wasn't right. The other girls had pretty crêpe de Chine ones with padded shoulders and tight waists, skirts flipping up, their legs flashing a seam down the back of their stockings as they danced. Oh, but she loved the music, the joy of it, the way it pulled at her limbs and her hips, making her want to jump right into the middle of the sound, as if it were an ocean, or a sky and she was a bird. *Flying.*

Todd didn't care that she hadn't done it before. 'You're the prettiest girl here,' he said, as he took her in his arms and walked her through some steps till she'd got the feel of it, and he could whirl her deep into the centre of the floor, among the jostling bodies. Jitterbugging. Quickstepping. Soldiers in kilts, British sailors, WAAFs, civilian girls in floral dresses, Yanks in their snazzy uniforms, all bumping up against each other. 'What's this music? I love it!' she shouted into Todd's ear.

'"Take the A Train",' he yelled back as he turned her under his arm. 'Look at you! You're a natural.'

The net of balloons above their heads opened, filling the air with globes of colour. Jewel shades floating down, soft touches on her head and shoulders, the sharp snap as they popped under foot, everyone laughing and slapping their hands against the tight skins, punching them back and forth like excited children.

When they stopped dancing, there was food. She'd never seen anything like it. Long trestle tables filled with plates heaped high with chicken, mutton and whole glazed hams. There were pastries, cakes and jellies. Tureens of bright punch and ice-cold beers in buckets. All of it free, just there for the taking. 'Chow time,' the British soldier next to her said. 'How often do we get this kind of grub?'

But she was too nervous to eat anything. Her stomach lurching with anticipation.

94

Ruby realises that she's been standing on her own on the sidewalk, grinning like a fool – she might have even been talking to herself. She glances around to make sure nobody's watching and moves away from the salon window. She doesn't want to go back to the bungalow. The kids are at school and Todd's at work. She's got an hour before she needs to start on supper.

She wanders along, swinging her handbag from her elbow, humming 'Take the A Train', smelling the green of the day. It's spring. She hadn't noticed how the leaves have thickened and how many flowers have bloomed in the last few weeks. She's been cooped up inside. The only place she's visited is the hospital in Ipswich with Christopher for his appointments, and they went straight there and back in a cab. When was the last time she laughed, the last time she and Todd went out together and had fun? She doesn't even like stepping into the garden; she's frightened she'll see the man's face again. She's heard gun shots coming from the forest; hunters moving through the undergrowth. Poachers, probably. It's important the kids stay away from it. She knows there's danger lurking in its shadows.

A familiar roar starts up. Ruby looks towards the airfield. She changes direction, towards the noise, towards the mesh fence, taking delicate, teetering steps in her red heels.

She gets as close as she can to the first fence and stares through the chain-link to the open spaces of the airfield and the signs of activity, the jeeps and the grounded planes, the small blue or khaki figures walking about with such a sense of purpose. Beyond the hangars are those odd grassed-over mounds Hank pointed out on their first tour of the place. After Todd snapped at her, she hasn't asked any more questions, but she knows that his office is burrowed underground under those bunkers, that the work he's organising is conducted away from windows and prying eyes. Secret work that will ensure that America wins the fight against commies.

When he was flying missions into Germany, his work was secret then too. He couldn't tell her when he was going up, or where he was going. Of course she knew the idea was to bomb the hell out of Hitler, but she was never given any details of how they were doing it. It didn't matter, because she watched those great clumsy planes take off and she watched them land. At the beginning, he took her inside Heaven Can Wait, showed her where each of the crew were stationed and explained their jobs; laughed when she asked why it was called the Flying Fortress, pointing out the six machine guns. Then he let her sit where he did, in the pilot's seat, and squeezed in next to her, taking her face in his hands to kiss her. She could imagine what it was like inside that plane on a mission, because he'd told her about the cold, 60 degrees below zero at its worst, how even in their heated, fur-lined boots, they lost all feeling in their feet, and icicles formed in their nostrils and lashes; she knew about the terror and adrenaline, the vibration of the engines, and the drop and lurch as the B-17 rode the bursts of flak.

But she has no idea what it's like in that darkened bunker, or what Todd does all day at a desk, what kind of secrets he has to struggle to keep.

'Looking for someone?' The Englishness of the voice startles Ruby.

A woman is standing near, one hand curled through the mesh fence. She's pretty in a bleached platinum way, with a tight skirt and a blouse cut too low for daytime.

Ruby shakes her head. 'No.'

'I'm Joan, by the way.' The woman smiles. 'Joan Brown.'

'Ruby Delaney.'

'You're English?'

'Not anymore. I married an American.'

'Lucky you.' Joan folds her arms. 'Where do you come from?'

'Iowa.'

Joan laughs. 'I think you know what I meant. Don't tell me if you don't want to. No skin off my nose. I'm from Felixstowe.'

'How did you get in?' Ruby holds her handbag tightly, looking back along the road to where she knows a soldier waits with a gun to check documents and peer into vehicles, looking under car seats if necessary.

Joan shrugs. 'I'm not a spy or anything. I've got a pass. I know one of the brass hats. He works over there.' She nods at the bunkers. 'Comes in useful when I need something pretty to wear.' She points her toe, and turns her slender calf one way and then the other so that Ruby can admire the sheen of her honey-coloured stockings.

'Well.' Ruby touches her hair. 'I have to get home. I have to cook supper for my children. My husband.'

'Ah. Duty calls.' Joan takes out a compact and checks her reflection, holding it up so that her face hovers in a mirrored slice against the sky. 'Good luck to you. Maybe I'll see you again.'

Ruby walks away, red heels catching in the grass, distancing herself as fast as she can from the girl. She's heard about women like her. Ones who thumb rides to the base, with their earrings dangling and skirts nipped in to show the line of their thighs and hips. English girls looking to hook themselves a Yank, aiming to reel him in like a prize fish.

# EIGHT

Hedy's going stir-crazy. Everyone else is allowed to go Wood-bridge or Ipswich, or the local beach, which is by all accounts just a slash of shingle and a mass of brown water, but still, it would be the first time seeing the sea since they left Florida, and then she was a baby, so she doesn't remember properly.

Mom didn't even tell them their grandpa had died. And now she keeps putting off a visit to Norfolk in that sneaky way she has. Hedy's sick of excuses. They could go to the farm this weekend. She wonders what her uncle's like. She imagines a tall man with broad shoulders, skin tanned by the sun because he's a farmer out toiling in the fields. He'll have white-blond hair, like her and Chris and Mom. Ernest. An English name. They studied Ernest Shackleton at school, brave and strong, trudging through the snow of the Antarctic. Maybe Uncle Ernest will be interested in sports, could teach her cricket. All Englishmen play cricket, Dad says.

It's a shame Uncle Ernest isn't married, and that there isn't a tribe of cousins to get to know. But one uncle is better than none. They've crossed a whole ocean to get here; it would only take a couple more hours to get to the farm. Mom always uses Chris as a reason not to go anywhere, but he managed the transatlantic flight, and he goes to the hospital and back in a cab, so Hedy's sure he could sit in a car for a while. She misses her softball team. Dad doesn't even shoot hoops with her anymore, and he's stopped pulling her pigtail and teasing her about when she's going to get a boyfriend. She guesses that working out how to beat the commies must be pretty difficult.

The forest promises purple children, tangled trees, and undergrowth that Hedy imagines as a vast wilderness. Chris thinks there are aliens there too, hiding under a round stone. Sometimes she has to bite her tongue not to say what she really thinks; it's not always easy pretending to believe in science fiction. But sharing his stories with her stops him talking about it to other people who would only tease him and hurt his feelings. Chris has enough suffering already. It's her job to protect him, and if she can make him happy by believing in his fantasies, then it's worth it. The bait worked, her fib about lights in the sky. A little white lie. She knew he couldn't resist the lure of a UFO.

Hedy had no idea that the forest was so big. It seems impossible to navigate – everything looks the same: trees upon trees, tracks that lead nowhere, the filtering light and the rustle of hidden things in undergrowth. Unseen jets scream above the pines, sonic wails echoing between branches like the curses of angry gods.

Chris limps ahead, excited by the thought of finding his concrete circle. 'This is the path,' he says, hobbling faster. Then twenty minutes later, he's stopped, rubbing his cheek. 'No. No.

It must be this way.' They trudge in the opposite direction. He pauses, staring around him.

'I don't understand,' he mutters. Tears clog his throat.

'Tell me what it's like again,' Hedy says, to distract him. 'Tell me what you think it is.'

'I thought at first it could be something that fell from a spaceship.' He blinks at her. 'But the sounds I heard mean it must be a kind of door. There was someone, something, moving under it, far down, as if there's a room or another world underneath. If we could open it ... Scott could help. He's strong.'

Hedy rolls her eyes, thinking of Scott's hunks of muscle pushing up under his smelly boy-skin, his self-regarding smirk and lazy walk, the way he thinks his opinion is the only one that counts. 'We don't want him here,' she says. 'This should be our place. Scott would spoil it. You know what he's like.' She walks his slow swagger, raises an eyebrow in exact mimic.

She waits for Chris to smile. But he's sulking. She sighs. 'Scott won't believe in UFOs. He'll laugh at you.'

'No he wouldn't.' Chris's chest heaves and Hedy hears the asthmatic catch. 'He wouldn't laugh at me.'

She shrugs. 'We don't want him hanging around us all the time. And I don't want to be in his stupid gang.'

'That's mean,' Chris says.

They keep walking, the air between them knotted with unspoken things. Hedy stares into the grass at the side of the path, but there's nothing resembling a large concrete circle. It seems an unlikely object to find, she thinks, so far from any houses. Perhaps Chris dreamt the circle in the first place. He said he fell asleep here. She can see he's getting tired. His legs are dragging, his feet hardly able to clear the ground. Sweat sheens his face.

A deer flits across the path ahead of them, a pale, speckled rump and tiny twitching tail. But when she runs to spot it moving through the trees, it's gone. She thought they would find lots of animals. But the place is eerily deserted, just the flicker of wings as insects and birds flit past. She has the feeling they're being watched. She stops and swings around to stare behind, hoping to catch something out, and hoping at the same time not to. What would she see following them? What creature would loom out of the darkness?

It hurts to see Chris struggling to put one foot in front of the other, the effort it's taking to hold his heavy torso upright, for him not to topple over. He never complains. She wouldn't be able to endure being locked in that thing; she would kick and spit until they let her out. She needs to get Chris home. But she has no idea which direction to take. They could have been going in circles. Every path is identical. Another plane screams overhead. She remembers, with relief, that the noise of jet engines was how Chris found his way back to the base.

She takes Chris's hand. 'Let's look for it another time.' She squeezes his fingers. 'Mom will kill us if we're late for tea. She can't know we've been here.'

He jerks his fingers away. 'Not yet.'

A pine cone hits the ground by her foot. She glances up. Another whizzes past her ear. 'What the ... ?' She's bristling, ready for a fight.

Three children wait under the inky spread of an oak. Two boys and a girl. Her anger evaporates. She nudges Chris. 'Are they your purple children?'

He catches his breath as he spots them. 'I think so.'

'Hey,' she calls over. 'What are your names?'

The children don't move. No more pine cones come flying across the gap between them. She edges forwards as if they're wild animals and might startle; she hears Chris breathing and stumbling behind her. When she's closer and her eyes have adjusted to the shadows, she's disappointed to see that they don't have purple skin, although their heads are shaved, just as Chris said. They're wearing dirty clothes, mended and darned in patches of different colours, like gypsies. One of the kids on the base said to be careful because gypsies in England stole blond children. But these are only small. She could take them on in a fight if she had to.

'I'm Hedy.' She opens her hands, to show she means them no harm.

'Got any gum, chum?' one of the boys says, and all three begin to cackle and snort, laughter tearing from their bellies as if he's said something hilarious.

'You can stop that,' Hedy says, cold and grown-up. She's not sure what the joke is, just that it's at their expense, her and Chris. 'And what's wrong with your heads, anyway?'

It looks as though they've done it themselves with scissors. Not like an army buzz cut. These children have patches where skin gleams through, furry tufts sticking up, and darkened bloody nicks. The girl touches her scalp. 'Nits.'

'Nits?' Hedy asks.

The girl wiggles her fingers and grins. 'Crawling with the buggers, we were.'

Hedy takes a step back. Her own scalp flames with sudden itching. She gives in to the impulse and scratches.

'You were purple,' Chris says. 'Last time.'

'Impetigo. Mum puts gentian violet on us.'

'Do you know a big concrete circle that's around here

102

someplace? Kind of like a cartwheel fallen over. Have you seen it?' Chris swallows. 'It's next to an oak. And some silvery trees.'

The children look at each other. 'Maybe,' one of the boys says. Then leaning closer, 'You got polio then?'

'It's rude to ask stuff like that. If you must know, he's got something wrong with his spine,' Hedy tells them. 'It's not catching.'

Chris isn't wearing his scarf. His chin pad is exposed, jutting under the curve of his throat, forcing his head up. The children are staring at the metal upright that leads under his clothes. 'What's underneath?' the girl asks, peering closer.

Hedy glares, curling her hands into fists. Maybe she'll have to throw a punch after all.

Chris moves his tongue across parched lips. 'If I show you,' he says slowly, 'will you take us to the concrete circle?'

The girl nods.

Hedy inhales sharply as Chris unbuttons his trousers and slips them over his hips, takes hold of the edge of his jumper and peels it up; and then his vest, rolling it out of the way. He stands with blank eyes, half naked, holding his clothes in his fist, bunched across his chest, pulled away from his neck. Hedy can't bear to see. She wants to stand in front of him with her arms held wide to shield him from their curiosity. The stiff prison of the leather girdle is exposed. The sight of his narrow pale ribs rising and falling beneath metal bars elicits an appreciative gasp from his audience. Hedy watches as the children absorb the locked circle around his neck and the pad pushing under his chin.

The girl takes a step forwards, her hand outstretched as if to touch the metal bars, or the goose-pimpled flesh beneath. Chris flinches and the jumper comes tumbling down. Hedy puts herself between them. But the girl just nods. 'I'm Nell,' she says. 'These two's my brothers.'

'My brother,' Hedy tilts her head in Chris's direction. 'Chris.'

He's turned away, doing up his flies, rearranging his clothes. The children are already moving away, single file through the undergrowth.

Chris was right to describe it as like a fallen cartwheel. The circle is about that size and shape, but cast in solid stone. Hedy kicks it with her foot. There's a rusted metal grille and a bar set in the top. She leans over and scrapes some of the dead pine needles away, grabs the handle, and leans back to pull as hard as she can.

One of the boys laughs. 'You're not gonna budge that.'

'Hedy, put your ear against it.' Chris's voice is breathless with excitement. 'Tell me what you hear.'

Feeling a little silly, Hedy kneels in the long grass and does as he says. All she can make out is her own heartbeat and a faint crackle, which could be insects moving in old leaves.

'What're you expecting to hear?' Nell squats beside her.

'Voices. Movement,' Chris says in a tense voice. 'Sounds from under the stone.'

The other boy shrugs. 'Believe in fairies, do you?'

Chris frowns, his bottom lip trembling. 'Anything?' he asks Hedy.

Hedy shakes her head. 'Never mind,' she says quickly, straightening up. 'We need to go home now anyway.'

The lump of concrete is manmade, ordinary. It's a cover for something – perhaps drains or sewage. Chris's imagination has been working overtime. She glances at her brother, puzzled. But he keeps his face twisted away.

They follow the children through a maze of paths. Hedy loses all sense of direction. She sniffs the air, catching an ashy stink of burning. Then one of the boys turns and gestures urgently, his finger pressed to his lips, eyes wide.

Nell tugs at Hedy's sleeve, pointing through the pines towards a spiky structure made of branches. Hedy realises that the smoke is coming from there, rising in a messy trail through the branches. A lumbering figure in a shabby coat stands up, pulling a shawl over his head. There's a low murmur of male voices, a shout of husky laughter. Hedy makes out several other figures squatting and hunched around the smoky fire; they are passing a flask around. A skinned creature impaled on a stick glistens above the flames.

Nell screws up her face and hisses, 'Tell your brother not to make a sound.' She takes a step away and beckons, 'Quick ...'

Hedy reaches behind and grabs Chris's hand. She holds it tightly. 'Stay close,' she whispers. She keeps her eyes on the dark shapes, stooped beside their makeshift structure. If they turn and see them, she'll get between them and Chris. She'll pick up a branch and use it to swing against the men's skulls, hard as she can.

The children walk in silent single file until they can no longer see the men's camp, and the smoke is only a faint tang in the air. The boys begin to laugh and joke, relief making them silly.

They see a blunt tower, like a castle turret. Then they're out of the forest, with the perimeter fence standing high above them. Hedy puts out her hand to touch its cold wire. Between triangles of mesh, jets line up for take-off. There's the usual activity of jeeps and servicemen around the hangars, the grassed-over mounds in the distance. But Hedy realises they're looking at it from a different perspective – they're at the other side of the airfield. The tower belongs to a small church, butted right up against the fence; coils of barbed wire scratching at the ancient wall. The graveyard is overgrown with brambles and creepers; tombstones lean over as if beaten down by the roar of jets skimming overhead. Weeds grow, yellow and blue, cheerful among long grasses.

'Church don't get used anymore – not since the Yanks built the base,' one of the boys says.

Nell points to a cottage with a sagging roof further down the lane. 'Our house.'

Hedy sees washing on a line, brown hens pecking the earth, an old tin bath and a tractor wheel rotting among nettles. A large boxy pram stands next to a pump; a woman with rolled-up sleeves bending over the pram straightens and gestures at the children, glaring, her words swallowed by the shout of B-47 engines.

'The back entrance to the base is along there.' One of the boys waves a hand towards the lane. "Bout five minutes. You'll see it all right.'

'Oh … and if you see Old Joe, don't you mind him.' Nell smiles. 'He won't hurt you. He's not like the others.'

'Who?' Hedy asks.

But the children are running towards the angry-looking mother by the pram, and all Nell does is turn and grin before she disappears into the cottage.

Hedy wants to get Chris home as quickly as possible. But his face is bloodless, hair sticking like damp straw around his forehead. She wishes she was strong enough to carry him down the lane to the gate, but she's not. 'Let's sit down for a minute,' she says.

He doesn't resist when she takes his arm and guides him to a bench, half covered in green, the back eaten by woodworm. She tugs a bramble to one side, cradling under his arms as he lowers himself into a sitting position. He closes his eyes. He looks emptied out. She has the sense they're being watched again, a prickling alertness running down her spine. She turns towards the cottage. The windows are blank, the garden deserted, apart from the pram and hens.

Another jet takes off, flattening the air, wings casting shadows over the land. She winces at the noise, smells the hit of burning petrol and hot rubber; with her hand shielding her eyes from the sun, she follows the spiralling line it makes towards the clouds.

As the plane becomes a distant spark, she drops her gaze to the church, to the holes in the roof, the plain diamond panes of the windows, the cross carved into stone. With a bump in her heart, she sees something move inside the dim porch. A glint of pale, spread like a starfish. A hand, she realises, against the darkness of a long coat, a mane of tangled hair swinging above. The whole thing rises, slow as an animal nosing through smoke. Hedy plants her feet, standing guard over her brother. Chris has his back to the church, unaware.

The thing emerges from the porch, a shambling scarecrow walking in staccato bursts, stopping with a foot raised to stare at them. His chin bobs and jerks like a bird. He seems uncertain. Frightened. Hedy's shoulders relax. She remembers what Nell said. 'Joe?' she tries.

The man stares around him, as if she's casting a trap. He rubs his filthy jaw with a blackened finger hooked like a claw.

Chris opens his eyes, turning a questioning gaze towards her. She puts her fingers to her lips. 'Nell said not to be scared.' Chris is trying to stand, and she bends to heave him up.

When she straightens, the man is there too. She smells the unwashed, fusty stink of him, his feral mushroom breath. Her fingers close protectively around Chris's arm. He looks at the tramp with something like recognition, a shiver passing through him, a fish twisting in his blood.

The man stares at Chris intently under black brows, his eyes glittering.

Chris smiles. 'You live here?'

'Here and there. Under the trees.' His voice is uneven and scratchy as if he doesn't use it often. 'I likes it under the trees best.'

'You've heard the noises in the forest, haven't you? Beneath the stone?'

Hedy has a feeling that the two of them are communicating in a language she can't hear or understand. Words bob to the surface like driftwood, but the real conversation is happening beneath, flickering in currents, brilliant and dark.

'Have you seen lights in the sky?' Chris's voice is tight with hope. 'Not the planes. Something else. Green. Red.'

Hedy wants to tell him she made it up. It was a lie. But she can't, because Joe is nodding. 'Red. Burns. Burns my eyes. Devils,' he whispers. 'Devils in the night. And under the earth. Screaming under the earth.'

'No. Not devils,' Chris is saying with gentle patience. 'They're from another planet. Aliens.'

The man backs away, head bowed, greasy hair falling across his face, his mouth opening and closing, strange sounds coming out.

'Let's go.' She tugs at Chris.

He swivels his head to look at her. 'He knows,' he says, his gaze fever-bright. 'He's heard them, Hedy. The things under the stone circle. I told you. I told you I heard noises.'

Why can't he see that Old Joe is mad? She wants to explain that it's all make-believe and lies. There are no aliens. She opens her mouth; but she can't make his dreams crumble and fall. What would he have left?

Another jet. This time so low, she feels heat on her face. The roar engulfs them, making Hedy shut her eyes, hold her breath. When the plane has gone, Joe has disappeared. There's another sound, a human wailing. She recognises the high-pitched demands of a baby. She glances over towards the cottage; the pram is rocking above big wheels, the children's mother peering under the hood. Hedy pictures Mom waiting at the kitchen window. Mom's eyes are always blinking with nerves, her mouth twitching as if she's about to cry. Hedy knows Mom takes pills to help her keep calm. They don't seem to be working anymore.

'We have to go,' she says, touching his shoulder.

His jaw clenches in acknowledgement, but he doesn't move. She can see thoughts flying through him, snatches of them, like visions, fleeting across his blank gaze. Under her hand his body trembles. Mom was right, she thinks, it's dangerous here for Chris. They won't come to the forest again. Her fingers find his, linking with them, holding tight. He is lost in his thoughts. Cold creeps from his fingers through her own, spreading like frost up her arm, as if scoliosis is travelling through their joined skin into her bones. She wishes that she could mend him. She squeezes his hand tightly, trying to give him her warmth, her strength. They walk towards the entrance to the base, the American soldier waiting with a gun.

# NINE

Ruby worries it'll be too frightening for the children. But it's Saturday night, and this is something Todd and Christopher can do together – they'll never play baseball or shoot hoops – but they can watch aliens on screen, even if Todd thinks it's a joke. So here they are, the whole family, sitting in the front row in red velvety seats while huge pods burst open, spewing out human clones in a mess of bubbles. *Invasion of the Body Snatchers* has already been a hit in the States. Christopher read about it in *Movie Teen* magazine, begged to see it.

She glances across the row, watching Christopher's profile, checking he's comfortable. He's transfixed, his face lit by the screen, his thumb in his mouth.

The screeching music and shouting are making her head ache. Todd shifts his leg against hers, the heat of his thigh pressing through her skirt. Her hand is on the seat rest between them, and he rubs the back of it with his finger in small circles. The pit of her stomach flips, joy tilting through her. Ruby stops watching the film. She looks down at her husband's finger caressing her hand, the contrast of their skins in the flickering half-light.

On the way out, shuffling through the crowded foyer, Ruby recognises nearly everybody: women from the Wives' Club, who smile and wave; the teacher, Lucy, pausing to say hello to the kids. And there's Betty in a yellow coat and matching beret, her arm linked with Ed's, Scott trailing behind, his top lip sneering, reminding Ruby of the singer Elvis Presley. Ed and Todd stop and talk. Betty doesn't let go of her husband, patting his sleeve with her gloved hand.

'Did you like it?' Betty gives Ruby a gracious smile. And Ruby wishes, not for the first time, that Betty wasn't so much taller. 'Not really my sort of movie,' Betty confides. 'Give me a nice musical any day. Bing Crosby. Doris Day.'

Ruby nods. 'The kids loved it, though.'

Scott, Christopher and Hedy are muttering in a huddle; Ruby remembers Betty's words in the beauty salon and looks for a spark between her daughter and that great hulk of a boy. She supposes that one day Hedy will get a crush on someone, but right now her expression is bored rather than flirtatious. It's Christopher who's gazing at Scott, making up for his sister's rudeness. His soft-hearted sweetness can't stand to see another person in any kind of discomfort, even something as minor as embarrassment. He's been locked in the brace all day – their routine disrupted by the evening's outing – but he'd never show that he's in pain. She nudges Todd's arm, 'We should get Christopher home, honey.'

Todd's jaw clenches, but he gives Ed's hand a goodbye shake. 'Time to get the kids back,' he says. 'See you tomorrow.'

As they're walking away, Ruby realises what he's just said.

'Tomorrow? Tomorrow's your day off – we were going to spend it together.'

'Can't be helped, baby. Big-wigs are coming in from the States and Europe on Monday. They'll be inspecting the programme.'

The programme, she thinks. What does that mean? And then she recalls the platinum blonde by the perimeter fence, how she'd displayed her slender legs in their silky stockings, how she'd said she was a particular friend of a brass hat in the secret zone. Ruby closes her eyes and presses her fingers against her temples. She needs to get a grip. The woman wasn't talking about Todd. She clears her throat, composes a smile. 'That's tough, honey. But I know you'll impress them.'

While Christopher wallows in the bath, she opens the cabinet and slips a pill into her mouth. What the hell, she tips out an extra one and swallows that too. Betty was right when she said that air-force wives need all the help they can get. But when she bends down to pick up the towel, the room lurches, blood rushing away from her head. She holds onto the rim of the bath, breathing through the dizziness. Christopher looks up. 'Mommy?'

She sinks to her knees by the side of the tub and takes his damp cheeks in her hands. His skin is plump, heat-soaked and young. She kisses it, wanting to embrace his innocence, kiss away his pain. His wet eyelashes graze her lips. 'I'm fine while I've got you, my darling.' Her voice trembles.

If her own mother had lived, would she have loved Ernest like this? The pain of loving Christopher is a mortal wound, yet Ruby wouldn't know how to exist without it.

When she pulls away, she sees his confusion. She's aware of crossing a line she shouldn't have. Christopher will forgive her. He'll understand.

'Time to get out.' She holds the towel and, out of habit, reaches down to help him stand.

'I can manage,' he says, carefully moving out of her grasp. 'I like to do it on my own when I'm not wearing the brace.'

'Of course.' She straightens, lowering her gaze from his nakedness. 'I forgot.'

She wraps his narrow shoulders in the towel, feeling chastised. 'You loved the film, didn't you? It was fun, wasn't it, going with everyone?' She pats the moisture from his skin, an idea coming to her. 'You know what? We should go to the pictures every Saturday. The whole family.'

'Maybe,' he says, carefully. 'I did like the movie, Mommy.' He looks up at her and smiles. 'The unimaginable becomes real.'

It takes her a second to realise that he's quoting from the film. She grins, and then makes her eyes zombie dead, waggling her head from side to side. 'Who says I'm your mom?' she says in a blank voice. 'Watch out. We're coming to get you.' She hooks her fingers into claws and leans over him, opening her mouth wide.

When she hears his low giggle building into a shout of laughter, she has to touch her chest, because her heart feels as if it's going to burst right through her sternum.


The alarm goes off at six a.m. Todd slaps a fumbling hand on top of the clock. He groans, kissing her shoulder under the frill of her nightie, scratching his head and yawning. Then he's out of bed, the mattress tipping and resettling. His pillow holds the warm indentation of his sleeping head. Ruby places her hand in the hollow.

'Shall I fix you some breakfast?'

He's distracted, looking for his belt. Peering under the bed. He shakes his head. 'I'll have something in the mess hall.' He stops and looks down at her. 'Go back to sleep, hon.'

She hears his stream of piss hitting the back of the toilet. The flush of the chain and groaning pipes. Running water. There's the chink of his shaver tapped against the basin. This house is like paper. She's aware of him in other rooms, scraping a chair back, rustling inside a cupboard, bending to do up his laces, shutting the lid on the shoe box as he gives his toecaps a quick shine. She stays under the covers, hoping he'll come back to drop a final kiss on her forehead. He doesn't. The front door closes with a snap. His heels clip on the sidewalk outside.

Ruby gets up, pulls on her clothes without bothering to wash or look in the mirror. She ties a scarf over her hair, puts on dark glasses, and opens the front door. Todd has already disappeared. She hurries in the direction of the bunkers. But she doesn't catch him up. Is that him, being waved through at the checkpoint? She can't tell from this distance. In uniform, her husband blends in with every other serviceman. She veers off the path across the dew-damp grass and stands with her nose against the fence, fingers clasping the wire, staring at the figures moving far away in their uniforms of blue and brown.

When she turns for home, she half-expects to find herself confronting that woman. Joan Brown. She straightens her shoulders, prepares an impenetrable, polite expression behind the dark glasses. But there are no civilians around at this hour. Not even a woman of easy virtue.

On Sunday night, Ruby presses Todd's shirt to her nose, sniffing the cloth for traces of unfamiliar perfume. She finds only a faint ring of sweat around the collar, a tiny stain on the sleeve that looks like ketchup. He's careless, she thinks, big-hearted, loose-limbed, straight-talking, like a cowboy from the Wild West. One of the good guys. She puts the shirt in the washing basket.

Unfaithfulness would be hard to forgive, but not impossible. A wife should forgive her husband the natural faults of being a man. She sets her mouth in a line, tightening her lips. She reminds herself that she comes from farming stock, born to endure hard work and hunger. But Ruby thinks that she has lost this strength, the enduring strength of her heritage, or that it wasn't scored deeply into her bones in the first place. She remembers her father, his tall, craggy figure striding into a salt wind, words from the Bible falling from his lips. He never touched her or Ernest, except with the sting of his leather strap. The strength in their father had been hard and brittle, unyielding. He talked about punishment and shame, said they were burning in the fire of the Lord. No wonder she and Ernest hadn't been able to love each other; they'd had no one to show them how.

She feels sorrow for those two motherless children growing up on that bleak farm, miles from anywhere, in the cold and muck. There was never any money, nothing extra. Everything had been scraped and saved, patched and mended. She escaped. Ernest didn't. She watches Hedy with Christopher and knows she failed her own brother. But it's no good having regrets. Ernest was impossible to help.

Why does she have the feeling that everything is coming undone? America has made her spoilt, allowed weakness to define her, so that all her fears run free like escaped sows, squealing. She puts her hands over her face. She should see the doctor and ask if this is normal, her dizziness and mood swings, her headaches, the sense that danger looms around every corner. Maybe she needs a different prescription. There must be alternative pills to Miltown. It was just a minor tranquilliser, the doctor said, just a little something to soothe her nerves.

*

On Monday morning, Todd's up early. He stands in the bathroom in his vest, leaning into the mirror, shaving with frowning focus, tapping and rinsing the blade over and over as if trying to remove the top layer of his face, peeling away something that bothers him. He spends half an hour buffing his shoes. Ruby can hardly see the black for the glare of shine. He wouldn't let her do it. Man's work, he said. She hands him a clean, starched shirt, and stands by while he gets dressed in his blues. She darts forwards to do up his tie and adjust his cuffs.

'You're so handsome,' she says, flicking invisible dust from his shoulders. 'You're going to impress them all.'

Todd's left eye twitches. It makes him look suddenly untrustworthy. She reaches up and presses a finger against the flickering nerve. He frowns, pushing her hand away. 'It's going to be a long day.'

'Where are you meeting these important men?'

He pulls up his sleeve to consult his watch. 'At headquarters, then it'll be straight to business in the bunkers.'

'No wives involved?'

He shakes his head. 'Just air-force business, hon. Military only. These guys are real high-ups, they don't have time for a public-relations number.'

Todd has gone. Hedy and Christopher leave for school, swinging their lunch pails. Ruby has one of her bad heads starting, a stab of pain at the base of her skull, as if a crow is crouched on her shoulders, pecking at her with its beak. She ignores it, standing at the kitchen sink to wash the breakfast things. She runs the vacuum cleaner over the floors, makes the beds, dusts ornaments, writes a shopping list through the peck, peck, peck at her head. She watches the early-morning light slide across the laurel leaves, which are fatter and thicker now and more like a hedge, and she wonders what Todd is doing, imagining Joan Brown peeling off his jacket, undoing his top button, kissing the indentation just there at his throat where he has a birthmark blue as a bruise.

She reminds herself that Todd loves her, and anyway he couldn't possibly have made up such a huge lie. One that could easily be checked up on, as the military headquarters is right in the middle of town. The stabbing pain has gone, the bird flown; instead a large man wields a pickaxe, smashing through thin bone into the pulpy interior. Ruby grits her teeth, blinks away the tangles of black and red that interfere with her vision. She must have taken too many pills. She forgot to eat breakfast, took her dose and then two, or maybe three extra ones on an empty stomach. It will pass, she reminds herself. She should eat something. But instead she arranges herself at the dressing table to powder her nose and colour her lips. She takes off her housecoat, fastens her girdle, carefully rolls on her stockings, steps into a tulle petticoat, gingham dress over the top.

She hooks her shopping basket over her arm and sets out with hesitant steps towards the commissary, trying not to move her head or look directly at the sky. She flexes her fingers inside spotless white gloves. Her route takes her past the military headquarters. She's forgotten her list. She squeezes her eyes shut, and begins to recite: *chuck roast, Carnation milk, cream corn, grape jelly, Shredded Wheat.* And there's Todd in a group of others; she recognises Ed and Colonel Anderson. A long inky Packard with an American flag on the bonnet has parked at the kerb, sleek as a beetle; four men in dark suits are getting out of its belly and climbing the steps.

117

Her head hurts. Even her straw hat is too heavy to bear and she wants to rip it off. The pain has become a black box sitting inside her brain, funnelling all her thoughts into its void. Ruby struggles to extract her list: *Carnation milk, cream corn.* There were other items too, but she can't recall them. They've been sucked into the black hole. She doesn't continue to the commissary. She stops, staring up at Todd as he leans forwards to shake a hand. His face swims into focus and she sees his eyelid spasm in a spat of twitches. His eye is all she can see now; it floats towards her big as a football, convulsing and convulsing. Her finger itches to press the nerve, to smooth the skin, to make him better.

She can't reach him from here, standing in the street. He's receded now, standing small and neat, a toy soldier at the top of the steps. She pats her skirt, runs her hands over the tight band of her waist; her petticoat rustles around her knees. These details are life rafts in a dark sea. She wants Todd to notice the way her straw hat tilts across her forehead, how irreproachable she is, how capable, even while her head is exploding.

Ruby edges forwards gingerly as if eggs roll under the soles of her feet. Every jolt is agony, every grain of gravel or crack in the pavement a danger, and she must float instead of walking, carrying the black pain inside her head.

'Honey,' she whispers to Todd. 'I'm here.'

She's managed the steps, and she stands, squinting against the light, next to her husband.

'What are you doing?' Todd's voice is a strangled hiss.

'Mrs Delaney.' The colonel is smooth. A gentleman. 'You must excuse us. We have business to attend to. Military business.'

'But I want to meet your important friends.' Ruby tries to

bring the strangers' bobbing faces into view, finds that they are blurred and inaccurate, features slipping and sliding.

'Chuck Peters and Ted Saunders. Dr Klaus Haugwitz. Henry Sargent.' The names reel past her quickly. Todd has grasped her arm, is squeezing tight, hurting her. 'Time to go home, Ruby. I'll get someone to escort you.'

'Haugwitz?' Ruby is saying, latching onto the one name that stood out. 'Klaus? What kind of name is that?'

She's moving away, a solider guiding her, his gloved hand under her elbow. Ruby swallows, the movement of saliva in her throat dislodging the pain, knives shooting into her brain, making her cry out. There's a flurry of words behind her, a nervous laugh, a door shuts. She slides a look at the stranger beside her. He has a gun. His mouth is a tight line. Something is wrong. She's done something wrong.

When she wakes, she's in her own bed. Hedy is sitting on the edge, looking anxious. Doctor Rowland looms above, his jowls sagging, and puts his large, dry hand on her forehead.

'I've given her a mild sedative,' he's saying.

She wants to ask him about her prescription, the headaches and the feeling of terror, but her mouth is too dry. Sentences don't make it across her parched tongue. The drilling in her head has receded and the room is more lovely than she remembered – buttery soft and fuzzy – and Hedy is an angel bathed in a golden halo. Ruby wants to hold her daughter close, cradle her angular shoulders, rub the frown from her forehead. You are my angel, she wants to say, and I'm sorry I never tell you.

'What?' Hedy tucks her hair behind her ear and leans closer. 'Did you say something, Mom?'

Ruby shuts her eyes, lets exhaustion take her.

# TEN

'Who would have thought this damp old place actually got to have a summer? A real hot one at that?' Betty flaps the air with a Japanese fan, spangles of gold and red falling across her nose. 'Shall I bring a pitcher of my special punch along this evening?'

Ruby nods. 'Thanks. Sandy's bringing potato salad and Joyce is making her Johnny Applesauce Cake. Everyone's being so nice.'

'We're here for you, Ruby.' Betty puts her hand on Ruby's arm. 'We're all concerned for you.'

Ruby swallows. 'Well, there's no need. I'm fine. You can see I'm fine.'

'Maybe Miltown doesn't agree with you ... I've heard a few stories ...'

'Yes, something like that.' Ruby moves away from Betty's touch. 'Just a funny turn. It won't happen again.'

'Don't be embarrassed. It's how it is in this place.' Betty smiles. 'We live in each other's pockets. No guilty secrets! Everyone knows everything. But we watch out for one another, too.'

Three months. Ruby scores the days in the back of her diary as tiny black marks, and then scratches them off one by one, counting the weeks in batches of four, counting the months until they can leave this place and go back to the States. Or anywhere. Just not here.

Doctor Rowland adjusted her prescription after her 'episode'. A nervous collapse, he told her, exacerbated by an overdose of Miltown. Her headaches are less frequent, less severe. She still has dizzy spells and the terror coils like a snake in her guts, but she doesn't tell Todd or Doctor Rowland. She doesn't want them to take away her pills.

When she woke from her sedated sleep, it was night, and Todd had replaced Hedy on the side of the bed.

'God damn it, Ruby,' he said. 'You could have cost me my assignment today.'

The golden light had gone. The room was dim and bleak. Ruby had a sour taste in her mouth. She remembered the afternoon in snatches, the pain in her head, the long flight of steps, four men getting out of a long car.

'Klaus Haugwitz,' Ruby murmured. 'Isn't that a German name?'

'What?'

'I thought the Nazis were our enemies?'

'That was a different war, baby,' Todd said wearily. 'We've got another enemy now – or maybe you forgot – we're fighting the Russians. The Germans are on our side.' He lit a cigarette with shaky fingers. 'Half of them, anyway. Doctor Haugwitz is a respected scientist.' He let out a stream of smoke. 'We're lucky to have him.'

'Sorry,' she whispered.

Todd nodded. Kept smoking, his eyes averted. 'Jesus H

Christ . . . ' He growled, dropping his head into his hands. 'You scared me, Ruby. Scared the hell out of me. I can't manage without you . . . ' He cleared his throat. 'You know that, don't you?'

'I can't manage without you, either.' She reached for him, but he got up abruptly so that her fingers fell into space. 'I love you,' she whispered to his back. Todd had his face turned from her, staring out of the window, smoke drifting around him.

'What time is it?' she asked. 'Christopher . . . ' She struggled onto an elbow. 'I need to get up. It must be his bath time . . . his brace . . . '

Todd shook his head. 'Don't move.' His shoulders were stiff. He stubbed his cigarette out in the ashtray. 'You need to rest. Hedy can help him.'

She'd let her husband down. She heard the disappointment in his voice. She wanted to grab his hand and press it to her lips, beg his forgiveness. But he'd gone.

The kids have been allowed to stay up for the barbecue. Both of them in their best clothes. Christopher smells of Camay soap, his hair damp from the bath. It was Todd's idea to have this party, to present a united front, show everybody that Ruby is perfectly fine. Colonel Anderson said it was important to put any rumours to bed, carry on as normal.

Hedy is opening the door to the first guest. Hank steps into the hall, a bunch of carnations in one hand, a box of beers in his other.

'Oh, I'm glad to see you,' Ruby tells him, as he brushes his cheek with hers. 'Thanks for getting here early. We're out back.' She takes the flowers. 'Todd's been clearing the garden and chopping wood like he's auditioning for *Seven Brides for Seven Brothers*.' She presses her nose into frilled petals. 'Thank you.'

Hank laughs. 'Todd would make a fine mountain man.' He holds up the beer. 'I'll put this in the refrigerator, shall I?'

Todd is standing over a smoking barbecue, tongs in hand. He's into his third Bud. There's a smell of scorched flesh and cut grass. He claps Hank on the shoulder and they light cigarettes, chink bottles together.

'Expecting an army?' Hank asks, looking at the rack covered in chicken legs, ribs and hamburgers.

'Just the usual crowd.'

Betty and Ed arrive next, Betty cradling the jug of her special punch, as promised. She takes Ruby's arm and steers her into the kitchen, where she pours them both long pink drinks from the jug.

'Cheers.' Betty takes a sip. 'Pretty damn good, even though I say so myself.' She puts her head on one side with a concerned frown. 'How're you feeling?'

'Just fine, thank you.'

'You need to get off this base.' Betty takes another sip, leaving orange lipstick on the glass. 'It's too small. Woodbridge is just a short hop by car, and it's really quaint. Genuine Elizabethan houses. In Ipswich there's this darling ladies' dress shop, Lemans. And Footman's department store is nearly as big as the ones back home. I took Scott to the baths in Ipswich for a swim and then got him fish and chips, and boy, was he happy! Your two would love it.' She touches Ruby's hand. 'Why don't you and Todd come with me and Ed this weekend – we're going to pack up a picnic and head for Southwold. It's further up the coast, with a real sandy beach.'

Ruby shakes her head. 'You told me when I first got here I didn't need to set foot outside the base. Remember?' Ruby avoids Betty's eyes. 'You said Uncle Sam would take care of us.'

'Well, honey, I know … but …'

Ruby swallows and meets Betty's eyes. 'We're just fine staying right here. Christopher doesn't travel well. It's uncomfortable for him to sit in cars or buses. People stare.'

'Oh,' Betty takes a long pull on her drink. 'Well, of course. You know best …'

'Yes. I do. Now, I'd better circulate, take these canapés round.'

There's quite a crowd gathered in the tiny back garden. People stand holding plates of burnt meat and potato salad, clutching beers, smoking. Scott, Christopher, and Hedy have taken their food inside, disappearing off into the sitting room. The sound of Sinatra floats through the open window. Ruby worries that her *Songs For Swinging Lovers* LP is getting scratched in Hedy's careless hands. Ed has taken hold of Betty and is dancing her over the grass. 'You make me feel so young,' he sings along to the record, mouth in her hair. Betty is laughing, and Ruby's chest tightens. *For where you have envy and selfish ambition, there you find disorder and every evil practice*, Ruby's father shaking the bible at her. Ruby walks away quickly, collecting dirty plates, smiling and nodding.

'I'm gonna lose my appetite if I have to look at those black faces for one more second,' Sandy is saying in a loud whisper to another woman. 'I mean, really? Niggers at a social event?'

Ruby glances over at Wilson Lester and his wife, Jessie, sipping their drinks alone near the fence. She glares at Sandy and marches over to the Lesters, giving them a wide smile. 'Hello, so glad you could make it. Make sure you help yourself to anything you want.' She sweeps a hand towards the barbecue. 'Got enough to drink?'

Jessie leans forwards and touches Ruby's arm. 'Oh, yes. Thank you. It's a lovely party.'

Ruby feels disapproval like a hard wall at her back, and

knows it's coming from a little knot of guests standing together, Sandy at its centre. When Hank joins her and the Lesters, she gives him a grateful smile. Her hands are full of dirty plates, so after a few more minutes' small talk, she scrunches her shoulders apologetically and makes her exit.

She glances into the smoky garden before she goes into the house. Ed has let Betty go and joined the group of men standing around Todd. She can tell from her husband's big gestures and loud laugh that he's drunk. He's been drinking more since they arrived at the base, but now he's getting drunk with a purpose, cracking open a Bud the minute he gets in from work, getting up countless times to raid the refrigerator.

She stacks glasses in the dishwasher, scrapes gnawed bones into the bin, rinses the plates. She doesn't know how to make amends for what she did. Behaving as if she was out of her mind. They haven't had sex since. And Ruby knows if Todd's not satisfied at home, there are women like Joan Brown prowling the base with their low-cut tops and hungry eyes.

'Need some help?'

She turns to find Hank piling more dirty dishes onto the side.

'Don't you dare.' Ruby picks them up, making a shooing motion towards the door. 'You should be enjoying yourself.'

'I am enjoying myself,' he says. 'I'd rather be here.'

'Are the Lesters OK now?'

'Yeah, they're mixing in all right. Left them chatting to the Jacksons.'

'I thought the war broke up that kind of prejudice. There was a whole black squadron in the States, wasn't there – from Alabama of all places?'

'The Tuskegee Airmen, yeah. Bomber escorts. Brave men and good pilots. They never lost a plane.'

'I thought it would be different here. And anyway, it's been years since Truman issued that order – you know, the one for equality of treatment and opportunity in the military. Todd told me about it.'

'Yup, that caused a ruckus as you can imagine. But things did improve in the war. It's just the Southerners on the base still want to keep to their Jim Crow laws.' He makes a disapproving noise in his throat. 'Dixie-style segregation dies hard.'

There's a whooping noise and some loud laughter. They both turn and look through the open doorway towards the dining-room window, out into the darkness, the shapes of people around the barbecue. Some are dancing. 'Getting kind of rowdy out there,' Hanks says.

'Todd's to blame for that, I'm afraid,' Ruby says. 'I guess he needs to let his hair down.'

'So to speak.' Hank smiles, rubbing a palm over his shorn scalp. 'I'm surprised though,' he goes on. 'To see him hitting the drink so hard. It's not like him. Todd wasn't a big drinker, even between missions. He kept us all sane.' He wrinkles his forehead. 'I've thought about it a lot since. He's the bravest person I know. But it wasn't just bravery, it's who he is. Nothing ruffles him, does it? Not even being shot at by Jerry.'

Ruby dries her hands on a tea towel. 'I know,' she says quietly. 'He's a hero and I'm proud of him.' She lowers her eyes. 'I think it's me. I'm the problem. I let him down.'

'Why would you say that?' Hank takes hold of her arms.

She stares up, shocked by his sudden closeness. He's not much taller than her, so they're nearly eye to eye. She sees the tiny scars pitting his cheeks from long-healed acne.

'I embarrassed him the other day.' She's trembling. 'But ever since we first met, I've known I'm not good enough for him.

126

Never have been.' Tears squeeze her throat shut. Father's voice in her head: *Should have been you God cursed. Not my son.*

'Quit thinking that, Ruby. Todd's lucky to have you. He loves you. Maybe it's taking him a while to adjust to a desk job.' He clears his throat. 'Todd's used to being the hero pilot. Working on top-secret projects means you've got to keep a low profile. Got to stay as anonymous as possible. There's no public glory. He'll get the hang of it.'

She manages a nod and steps away. 'Do you know what they're actually doing out there in those bunkers? All this secret stuff?' she says, pulling out a hanky and blowing her nose. 'Todd doesn't tell me a thing.'

Hank lights a cigarette. 'I'm not part of the programme. And even if I was, I couldn't tell you anything.'

'Yes. Yes. Of course.' Ruby pours herself another one of Betty's special punches. She sips it, tasting cherries and vodka. It's sickly. But she keeps drinking. 'I've heard that the bunkers lead underground. Someone said there are tunnels, lots of them, stretching right under the airfield.'

Hank laughs. 'Someone's been making up stories. True, the bunkers go underground. But I think I'd know about a web of tunnels.'

'I suppose people invent things when their curiosity isn't satisfied.' She slips her hand around Hank's elbow and nods. 'OK.' She takes a deep breath. 'Let's go join them.'

'At your service.' Hank pats her hand.

They step into the garden, the long summer evening faded. Glowing embers simmer red under a smoking grill. Everyone moves with careless, loose-limbed languor, bright cigarette ends fluttering like fireflies. Slurred voices wash against Hank and Ruby as they walk among huddled groups of shadowy figures.

By the dim glow of the barbecue, Todd and Betty are dancing, swaying close, too close. Ruby's stomach tightens. Ed's watching them too, and now he's next to them, cutting in, pulling his wife away.

But Todd keeps hold of Betty. There's a strange tug-of-war between the two men, with Betty being the rope. Then Todd lets go abruptly and Betty staggers, Ed grabbing her arm.

'You've had too much to drink, Delaney ...' Ed's voice is a growl.

Todd is laughing. 'Can't we have some fun, Lansens? Don't you think we deserve it?'

Betty's pawing at her husband. But Ed is shaking her off. Betty's mouth opens in surprise.

Ruby wants to get to Todd, but she can't seem to hurry. Her feet push through treacle. He and Ed are scowling at each other, nose to nose. Betty forgotten. Todd's shoulder folds back, his right hand balls into a fist. Ruby catches her breath.

Then Hank is stepping between them. 'Todd, buddy,' he's saying. 'Come on inside with me. I've hardly seen you since I got here.'

Todd doesn't resist. It's as if Hank's voice has made him forget the argument. He turns away from Ed with a weary stagger. Ruby follows the two men, Todd's lanky frame leaning on Hank's shorter, strong one. She's neglected Christopher because of this stupid party, these foolish people. She wants everyone to leave.

In the kitchen, she finds Hank pouring Todd a drink of water. 'I'll put a pot of coffee on. You go deal with the kids,' he tells her, leaning over Todd, putting the glass to his lips. 'We're fine, aren't we buddy?'

Ruby finds Hedy, Scott and Christopher in the living room,

the TV flickering across their faces. Christopher is sitting apart, dead straight with cushions piled behind him. Hedy and Scott sprawl on the floor, an empty bowl of potato crisps in front of them.

'Switch it off, Hedy.'

She sees a bottle of beer lying on its side, stoops to pick it up. 'Scott,' she says. 'I hope you haven't been drinking?'

'No, ma'am.' He lumbers to his feet.

'I think your parents are just going,' she says briskly. And then she's tidying up the crisp bowl, switching on the side lights. 'Christopher, honey – time for bed. You must be exhausted.'

'I'm fine,' he says. But she hears the effort in his voice. The overhead light reveals his drooping face, the circles under his eyes.

When she stoops to help him up, his body is shaking. 'Darling,' she whispers. 'Let me help you. I'm sorry. Shouldn't have left you here so long.'

Scott hovers by the door. His tall, straight bones are an affront to Ruby. She distrusts his curled lip and sleepy gaze. She doesn't want him to see Christopher limping from the room.

'Off you go, Scott,' she says, her voice sharp. 'It's late.'

He shrugs. 'See you at school, Hedy.' And he slopes away, whistling.

She's coming out of Christopher's room, shutting the door quietly, just as Hank appears from the direction of her own bedroom.

'Todd's out cold,' he says. 'I've undressed him.'

'Thanks,' Ruby whispers. 'You're a life saver.'

'It's nothing.' Hank comes closer. 'I'd get some sleep too if I were you. Everyone's gone now. You must be beat.'

'Yes. I suppose I am.'

Neither of them moves. The silence thickens. Ruby hears the sounds beneath the silence, the breath leaving Hank's body, the wet click of his tongue. She knows she must break the atmosphere before this moment slips over the edge into something undoable. Then she feels his hand on her waist, and he's brushing her cheek with his lips. His mouth lingers. His stubble scrapes her skin.

She jerks back. 'Well.' She touches her hair. 'Goodnight, Hank.' She hears her own voice, how it's too loud, too bright.

'Yeah. It's late.' He rubs his jaw, eyes cast down. 'Goodnight, Ruby.'

She waits in the hall for the front door to close.

Hank's come to her rescue again. Like he did that night on the airfield, years ago. She remembers standing beside the passion wagon, adjusting her neckline, touching her hair. It was a glittering night; a raw wind blowing across the flat, dark space; only she didn't feel it. She was hot with nerves. It was her third date with Todd, and he was supposed to be meeting her off the bus.

'Hey, Ruby,' Hank called.

She spun around, heart skipping.

Before she'd left home, Ernest had twisted her arm with his strong fingers. 'Isn't the Yank bored of you yet?' His voice got lower as he leaned closer. 'Maybe best if he is, Ruby. If it goes any further you'll need to tell him the truth. About our family. About me.'

She'd shaken him off. He was jealous. But he couldn't follow her here to the base. She wasn't going to let him ruin everything between her and Todd.

The other girls were already heading for the hangar, swinging their skirts as they walked, arms linked, towards the party, trails of breath misting the air.

'I'm waiting for Todd,' she told Hank, as she stared into the darkness at the shapes of grounded bombers on the airfield, men gathered in groups, the flare of a match, a glowing cigarette end. 'He said he'd meet me off the bus.'

She recognised the music, 'Chattanooga Choo Choo', coming from the hangar. She longed to be inside the lit-up room, swallowed up by the bright noise of the band as Todd danced her around the floor, his hand on her back. But maybe Ernest was right and he'd got tired of her already. Maybe he wasn't coming. Hank was here to give her the bad news.

'He got held up. Asked me to escort you inside.'

She stopped fiddling with her dress, smiled. 'Sorry. I'm a little nervous.'

'Don't be.' Hank linked her arm through his, patting her hand. 'I'll look after you.'

They strolled together towards the sound of the music, the laughter, the clink of glasses.

'Did Todd tell you that we both fell for you?' Hank asked. 'We left your place at Christmas saying the same thing. We'd fallen for you, hook, line and sinker. Isn't that how you Brits put it?' He laughed.

She turned to him, trying to see his face in the dim light. 'Seriously?' He had to be teasing.

'Sure.' He stopped to get a packet of Camels from his pocket, tapping one out and cupping his hand around it, striking the match with a flick of his wrist. He took a deep drag and exhaled. 'We tossed a coin to see who'd ask you out. Todd got lucky. He always gets lucky.'

Ruby shook her head. 'You're joking?'

Hank blew another stream of smoke. 'I don't joke about love or war. Hey,' he touched her cheek. 'Don't feel bad. I probably shouldn't have said anything; I just wanted you to know there's another guy who loves you.'

'I didn't know you felt like that ...'

'Forget it.' She heard the forced jollity. 'Nobody died. Right?'

He took another drag and dropped the cigarette, grinding it under his heel, and tilting his head back, he said, 'Look at the moon. Kind of beautiful here, isn't it? Nights like this, I can forget about the next mission.'

They waited in the darkness. The music and voices seemed a long way off. It was just the two of them under the huge, blue-black sky, slippery with stars. Her own heart was thudding inside her head. Todd and Hank had been best friends for years, long before they met her. They'd shared terrible experiences up in that icy sky that she'd never know about. She shivered.

'Hey! You're cold, and here's me jabbering on. We need to get you inside.' He stepped close and put both his hands on the tops of her arms and rubbed briskly over the fabric of her coat to warm her.

She felt heat blooming across her skin, felt the kindness of his touch. He wasn't as tall as Todd and she didn't have to get onto her tiptoes to reach his mouth. She closed her eyes. His lips were cool against her own. He tasted of nicotine. The realisation of what she was doing made her feel faint. She tried to break free, but his arms had slipped around her waist. She put her palms on his chest and pushed. He let go and she stumbled; he caught her elbow, blinking at her. 'Been dreaming about that for a while.'

She was breathing hard. She couldn't look at him. She fiddled with the clasp on her purse.

'You know, if I'd flipped that coin differently, it could have been you and me, Ruby.' His voice was low. 'Todd's the good-looking one. But I'm the one with ambition.'

Ruby began to walk over the muddy grass, her heels catching in tussocks. She wiped her hand over her mouth. What had she been thinking? That she could give Hank some sort of consolation prize? The kiss would always be there, a small lie between her and Todd.

Ruby slips in beside her husband with her hands creamed and shiny. He's sprawled on his back, snoring. In the moonlight, seeping through half-drawn curtains, his features are grainy monochrome, like a black and white movie star, handsome as Burt Lancaster. His sleeping face is closed, distant as an actor's up on the big screen, eyelids flickering rapidly.

She puts her sticky palm on his forehead, and he opens his eyes suddenly, making her start. He squints, focusing through the dim light.

'Sorry, Ruby,' he whispers, words slurring. 'I messed up.'

'No . . . ' She leans close.

'I . . . I . . . did something bad.'

'It's all right, baby.'

But Todd is asleep again and he twists away from her, muttering, turning onto his side. He hunches into a foetal position, knees drawn up.

'We shouldn't have come,' she whispers to his sleeping form. 'I knew we shouldn't have come.'

Todd has already gone through the horror of one war. She remembers the day she'd begun to understand what kind of strength he'd needed just to stay sane. She'd watched Heaven Can Wait arrive home safe, and she was counting the rest of the planes off as the last of the B-17s lurched over the horizon, two engines on fire, trailing smoke. She'd been standing in the middle of a ploughed field when the wounded bomber seemed to stall mid-air, hanging inside the blue winter sky before it exploded. The noise blasted her eardrums. She dropped to her knees in the dirt, arms clasped over her head. Jagged pieces of metal and glass, unidentifiable objects raining down. She waited to be skewered through by one of them, until she realised that body parts were crashing into the soil, young men torn up like puppets and hurled from the sky. The casual brutality of it. She couldn't get up from her knees. She kept her face against the damp earth, praying, her hands pressing into the dark clay as if she could bury herself beneath it.

Todd had known each of those men, as he'd known others, shot or blown up over Germany, or the Channel, or like this, in Norfolk on their home run, moments from safety. She'd begun to understand how dealing with danger and death was a skill. And Todd had learnt it. But his war as a bomber pilot had been a battle in the sky. Now he's fighting something invisible underground with weapons he can't talk about. He's working with Germans.

Ruby lies down beside her husband, feeling a precarious lurch of unknowingness. She wants to walk out into a field under a sky empty of planes, and kneel in the soil, squeezing the earthy reality of it between her fingers. She wants to love a man with simple certainty, to understand who her enemies are, and how she will fight them.

# ELEVEN

Christopher sleeps in the bottom half of a bunk bed with a bar above his head to help him manoeuvre. He can't turn onto his side or roll over onto his stomach. Before the brace, he always lay on his belly, spread out like a star fish, snuffling into his pillow. He's had to learn how to sink backwards into unconsciousness, held motionless inside the grip of iron and leather. Hedy told him she'd read that geisha girls in Japan also had to sleep lying on their backs with their heads balanced on wooden blocks, because their dark, glossy hair was twisted and pinned into such complicated and ornate designs that they didn't undo them every day, but kept them lacquered in place for weeks. Christopher spent a long time looking at pictures of geisha girls after that; he loved their pale skin and rouged cheeks, the perfect red bows of their mouths, the folded satin kimonos in lush patterns. They walked like him too, with tiny steps, their heads held unnaturally high.

Mom has left the curtains open and he can see a scattering of stars above the line of the trees. He can't sleep because he's thinking about the evening, about Scott, so instead he watches the inky darkness outside the window. He squints at the moon. One day a human will stand on its surface, and that will just be the beginning. There are so many planets and stars to explore. He's looking for the flash of a UFO. There's other life out there. Just because you can't see something doesn't mean it doesn't exist. And sometimes he feels it so strongly, like someone calling to him, or the ache of homesickness. He wonders if that's what Dad is doing in his bunker, if the US Army has made contact with aliens; perhaps even now, there are visitors from another star communicating with the military. Perhaps the stone in the forest is an entrance into a place the aliens are being kept safe. The thought makes a flutter under his ribs.

But his mind circles back to earlier: the three of them in the lounge with their plates of barbecued chicken, the senseless chatter of adults shut behind glass, Hedy squatting on the floor to look through Mom's records. Christopher wants to relive it again, the moment when Scott stepped forwards to help him into the deep armchair. Scott held his hand and lowered him gently into the seat. They were palm to palm. Christopher felt the shift of Scott's shoulder muscles and the shiver of his bicep as he took Christopher's weight. After that, Christopher had been too flustered to watch TV. Safely behind the other two, he could stare at Scott as hard as he liked, filled with longing to inhabit the bigger boy's loose-limbed frame, to know what it was like to have that uncomplicated grace: a healthy body sprawled carelessly on the floor. There was another feeling inside Christopher too, one he knew he shouldn't have, one that made his face hot. He wanted to press his lips against Scott's mouth.

Christopher concentrates on the glitter of stars, wishing for the distraction of a larger light looming into view. Guilt pours through him, drowning him. He mustn't think things like that. It isn't what boys are supposed to feel for other boys. What would his father say if he knew? What would Scott do? Christopher remembers the note pinned to his stomach. *Freak*.

His body itches to move. But he's pinned down. Trapped. His mind races over to the notebook on his desk, to the story there half-written. His escape. While he's inventing a new plot, he lives on another planet far away. His hero is a boy kidnapped by aliens, taken to their own dying planet because only he can save their race from extinction. He recreates the last sentences in his head, thinking about what needs to happen next. He imagines the lights of the spacecraft, how they flash red and green. And he's the hero. It's him up there, floating above all this, leaving his body to wither inside the brace, while the real Christopher treads stars, talks with creatures of a higher intelligence, saves worlds.

# TWELVE

Hedy wakes early to the sound of her parents arguing. She rolls over sleepily, ears picking up the muffled sentences going back and forth between Dad and Mom in the next room, letting the sounds flutter around her, until she understands what's at stake. Then she's out of the covers, kneeling on the mattress, alert as a wolf.

Mom doesn't want to go, but Dad is insisting. A day in Southwold with Ed and Betty and Scott. 'It's making us all crazy to be cooped up, Ruby,' Dad says. 'Hank said it would be safe to go to town, so a beach will be fine too.'

'With them? You think we should go with them? After last night?'

'It was nothing. I'd drunk too much. Even more important to smooth things over with this trip. Ed and I are on the same team. We need to get along. This project's bigger than us.'

Hedy can't make out the next bit. She presses the side of her head to the wall, and hears what sounds like Mom crying, then a silence.

'Christopher will be safe, because we'll be with him.' Dad's voice is gentle and she has to strain to make out the words. 'A family trip. What do you say? Come on, baby. Don't make me beg.'

Hedy holds her breath, waiting. She's just thinking she should creep out of her room and along the hall to listen at her parents' door, when Dad comes in. 'Help your brother,' he says, opening the curtains. 'We're going to the beach today.'

'Get up, quick,' Hedy tells Chris. 'Guess what? We're having a day out with Mom and Dad. We're going to the seaside! Frank's coming too.'

Chris doesn't look as overjoyed as she'd expected. She waits for him to get a good grip on the bar before she leans over to support him as he heaves his legs over the side. With a grunt of effort, he's upright. She sits on the edge of the bunk while he visits the toilet. When he comes back, she kneels down to guide his feet into clean shorts, carefully averting her eyes as she helps him slide them over the girdle, wondering how many other twelve-year-old girls have to get this close to their naked brother.

'You sure you want to wear long pants? It's going to be a scorcher.'

Chris nods. She knows it's because he's embarrassed by his skinny legs. He puts up his arms obediently for her to slip his T-shirt over his head. For a second, her elation wavers, because Chris won't be able to swim. Grains of sand will get inside the corset and rub against his hot skin. But that's not her fault, and she can't be sorry for wanting to breathe salty air and dive under the swell of the ocean, for being excited.

Mom's in the kitchen packing up a picnic. She's slicing tomatoes, arranging them on pieces of Spam and white bread.

Her fingers move quickly. She's wearing a green sundress with matching earrings.

'You'll have to get your own breakfast this morning,' she says, without looking up.

Mom keeps on slicing, cutting sandwiches, wrapping them in wax paper, her back turned. But Hedy's seen her mother's swollen eyes and blotchy skin. She stares into her cereal bowl, pours too much milk over her Wheaties.

Everyone's trying to ruin this, she thinks. But I won't let them. It's going to be a good day. The best day.

The two families drive in convoy, with Ed taking the lead. Scott turns around to grin at them through the rear windscreen of the Chevy. Hedy and Chris sit in the back of Dad's Buick Roadmaster: shipped from the States, and not a scratch on it.

'Built by the same company that makes P-51 Mustang fighter planes,' Chris whispers to her in Dad's voice, eyebrows raised.

And Hedy, happy that he's getting into the mood at last, whispers back, 'You don't say? Why, I had no idea!'

Leaving the base through the checkpoint, Hedy flattens her nose against the glass as they drive past the soldier on duty. 'Finally,' she nudges Chris. 'We're escaping!'

'About time, huh?' Dad says over his shoulder, turning the wheel with his big hands.

'Yes, sir!' Hedy salutes.

Hedy wonders if Dad sometimes pretends he's at the controls of his Fortress. It makes her feel proud and safe, knowing Dad could defend them from anything. She watches the back of his head, how the light shines through the delicate arches of his ears, showing up a scribble of pink under the surface, secret eddies of blood.

Mom winds down her passenger window and a rush of air

carrying smells of hot tarmac, dry earth, and the pigs in the fields, sweeps into Hedy's eager lungs. Mom ties a scarf over her hair, tucking flyaway strands beneath orange silk.

'Hot enough for you?' Dad shouts into the roar of the wind and road. 'Just the day for the beach.'

'Not as hot as Iowa!' Hedy yells back.

Dad gives a hoot of laughter. 'Nothing's as hot as Iowa!' He leans across and gives Mom a kiss on the cheek, and she laughs too, a lovely bubbling sound that she hasn't made for ages.

Happiness makes Hedy scoot to the edge of her seat and wrap her arms around Dad's neck. He starts and swerves towards the centre of the road; Mom gives a shriek.

'Hey! Watch out, Princess. You'll get us all killed,' Dad says mildly. He takes one hand off the wheel and reaches up to give her fingers a squeeze. She sinks back into her seat holding the guilty thrill of his favouritism close inside her heart. He hasn't called her Princess for the longest time.

Chris has his head turned stiffly to the side, watching the countryside streaking past. Hedy knows he's absorbing everything; he'll remember the details of the pigs, their bald bellies and long snouts, the birds rising up out of the tangle of hedgerow, the people on the tandem who wave at the overtaking car, the woman's red hat and brown legs.

The beach is a long sweep of yellow, with a dozen fishing boats cast up on the shore as if tossed there by a storm. The place is packed with holidaymakers: children licking ice-creams, men in deckchairs with their stomachs straining at white vests, and their faces reddening under the sun. Women kneel on rugs, pouring tea from Thermos flasks, handing out towels to dripping children, shooing away dogs.

Dad strides off with Ed, Scott and Betty, his arms full of picnic rugs, windbreaks, umbrella and picnic box. Hedy wants to dash ahead to get to the sea first – she wants to stare at it all – but she has to hang back to help Mom with Chris. It's difficult for him to push his feet through the rolling grains of sand. People are noticing his Robbie the Robot walk. They turn and whisper, staring at the chin pad sticking up through his T-shirt, the rigid line of his spine. Hedy scowls at each gawking face.

When they reach the picnic spot, Scott is already in his trunks, tall and tanned, light catching the hair on his body, turning it gold. Suddenly, he seems older. Hedy ducks her head, scrambles out of her clothes; her costume's on underneath. 'Race you,' she yells.

Her bare feet push through dry sand and then wet shingle, before she hits the first wave and goes under with her mouth open, swallowing cold. The ocean has her in its strong, green fist. Hedy kicks towards the light, lungs grabbing at oxygen as she breaks the surface. She's come up next to Scott, tossing gleaming droplets out of his hair and snorting like a horse; he lunges for her, stretching a hand towards her head. She swims out of reach, turning her back to the shore and the distant oval of her brother's face, his figure tethered to the upright folding chair under his umbrella, the adults clustered on towels at his feet.

'What's wrong with your mom?' Scott asks, as they float face up, bobbing with the swell. Seagulls hover above, huge wings beating the air. Hedy can see their curled feet, like wheels on a plane.

'Nothing.'

'My mom says your mom's having a breakdown.'

'Don't know what you're talking about.' Hedy flips onto her stomach and swims towards the beach, her feet splashing, hoping she gets salt in his eyes. Her hands carve a way forwards, propelling her through the depths. She doesn't want Scott to know that she's worried about Mom, that recently Hedy's found her standing in the garden, staring through the fence into the forest, her lips working as if she's talking to someone. The feel of this water is different from a pool; it moves against her, sinuous and insistent as a strong animal, a seal maybe. She'll need to explain this to Christopher later with exactly the right words. She can't see the bottom, or even her hands as they slice through the next wave. It's a shock when her knees hit the ground with a bump, scraping across stones. She crawls through the push and pull of the tide, before she manages to stagger out of the sea. Without its weightless magic, her limbs are heavy. She's panting when she reaches the island of picnic rugs and collapses, dripping, next to her brother.

'Your knees are bleeding.' Mom's voice is tight.

Hedy wraps a towel around her shoulders, and shuffles sideways, reaching into a basket to pluck out an apple. 'They don't hurt.'

She flicks open Dad's penknife and peels the fruit, sloughing off ribbons of green. She ignores Scott, arriving back with his big sandy feet and stories about jellyfish. She cuts the apple into quarters, hands the first one to Chris. One for him and one for her. Salt dries in her grazes, sharpening the sting. She spits onto her knees, watching the transparent fizz turn pink before she wipes it away.

'Chris,' she says, 'Do you want to paddle? He can, can't he, Mom? If I go with him?'

*

143

Christopher has been stuck in his chair like an umpire at a tennis match. Forced to turn his head left and right to catch glimpses of a day that belongs to other people, straining his eyes to watch his sister and Scott bobbing in the waves.

Betty is stretched out below in a two-piece costume. Her breasts are jammed together, the skin above freckled and creased like tissue paper that's been crumpled and then smoothed out. He averts his gaze as she sits up to rub oil into her shoulders. The smell reminds him of hamburgers on a grill. He's glad Mommy is decent, covered up in a one-piece with a skirt.

Back from her swim, Hedy brings the smell of salt with her; blood marbles her knees and she's breathless and wet. Her eyes have the wild, angry look he knows well. She peels an apple with furious concentration and asks about paddling.

On the way to the sea, a scum of froth laces the wet sand, netting tiny dead crabs and pebbles. He steps with slow care over it. Freezing water nips at his toes. He stands at the shoreline with his trousers rolled, like an old man or a toddler, Hedy at his elbow. This was not how he imagined his entrance into the ocean. He's surprised by the way the ridged sand moves, hard and then soft, hollowing out and filling up again under the arches of his feet. He didn't expect the strength of the tide, how it tugs at his heels, how the small waves rub against his toes like tongues. He wants to feel it properly, notice the details, but he can't. He's too conscious of Scott, somewhere behind, stretched out on the picnic rug. He can imagine what he must look like to Scott: a cripple teetering in the shallows, with his skinny ankles and deformed spine. 'I want to go back,' he says to Hedy, more roughly than he'd meant.

After lunch, the men and Betty light up Chesterfields, smudging the sky with little plumes of smoke. Mommy fusses around him, rearranging the umbrella to keep him at the centre of his patch of shade. Outside the rim of shadow, the stretch of water and sky are a luminous whole. It makes his heart ache.

To the left, there's the sound of a merry-go-round playing and the rattle of fairground games coming from the blunt nose of the pier. 'What happened to the end of it?' Hedy asks. 'Looks like it's missing a bit.'

Ed scratches his head. 'Well, now. I do believe that part got washed away in a storm last year. I guess they haven't had the funds to fix it yet.'

Scott gets to his feet and stretches. He takes a softball bat from a bag and waves it at the others. 'Who's up for a game?'

Ed, Scott, Hedy and Dad mark out a pitch. Moments later, a couple of other men and three boys join in. Christopher watches the blur of the ball as it flies free, the sudden spring into movement as the players dash from post to post. Dad and Ed are paler than everyone else. From spending so much time in the bunkers, Christopher supposes. And he wonders again what's inside the windowless rooms under the grass. He would like to distract himself with thoughts of aliens, with his latest story, or scribbling in his notebook, but it's too hot and he can't stop looking at Scott in his trunks, shouting as he hits a home run, clenching a victorious fist.

'You see, hon,' Betty says to Mommy, clapping her hands, and breaking off to whoop, *Go, Scott!* 'Look how much fun they're all having.'

'Maybe.' Mommy's voice is low. 'But the beach isn't good for everyone.'

'Oh, Christopher's having fun, too. Aren't you sweetheart?

You don't need to get in the sea or run around to appreciate it!' Betty turns her beetle gaze on him, her sunglasses reflecting his guilty face back at him.

'He's not deaf, Betty.'

The game is over. Dad's got his arm hooked around Scott's neck. 'This one's a mean pitcher. He won the game for us.'

'Just lucky, I guess.' Scott grins, his face wet with perspiration. He takes a bottle of Coke from Betty and swigs from it noisily.

'Kid, there's a time and a place for modesty. And this isn't it.' Dad rumples Scott's hair and Christopher has to look away from them leaning against each together and the dopey look on his father's face. It's not Scott's fault that Dad wishes he had a son exactly like him.

'Here.' Scott leans down, putting a warm, damp hand on Christopher's shoulder. 'Have the rest, buddy.'

Christopher puts the bottle to his lips, the glass chinking against his teeth as he tips the dregs into his mouth.

The sun is low in the sky. The dazzling blue of the afternoon has deserted the water, leaving the sea murky and brown. A breeze gets up, whisking sharp flurries of sand against ankles, scattering grains into leftover sandwiches, granules flying into unblinking eyes. Christopher's neck aches with the strain of sitting for so long. His spine throbs. He looks at Mommy hopefully, and she nods at him and begins to gather their things.

'Anyone want to go take a closer look at the pier?' Ed asks. 'Get some candyfloss maybe?'

Christopher's heart skips a beat. He needs to go home now.

'Nah, I'm beat.' Scott doesn't move from his prone position, a baseball cap tipped over his face.

It's as if Scott has read Christopher's mind.

'Mom,' Hedy asks, as she rolls up a towel. 'How close are we to Norfolk?'

Mommy, packing up the picnic things, stops, hands in mid-air, her eyes full of warning. But Hedy goes on. 'I looked at the map. We've come further up the coast, haven't we? How much further for us to drive to the farm?'

'The farm?' Betty swivels her full attention on them.

'Mom's brother,' Hedy says. 'We've never met him.'

'I thought you didn't have any family left?' Betty takes her sunglasses off. 'You didn't mention a brother.'

'Uncle Ernest,' Hedy says.

Mommy looks away towards the shortened line of the pier, concentration creasing her forehead. Christopher wonders if she's calculating the distance, the time it would take to run there and dive off the end.

Dad clears his throat. 'Ruby doesn't get along with him,' he says. 'You know how it can be in families.'

'Well. Sure.' Betty laughs. 'But hasn't it been years since you've been back from the States? Maybe it's time to let the kids meet their uncle.'

Mommy swings her gaze back to Betty. She struggles to her feet. 'Just. Stop. Interfering.' She drops her hands by her side as if she's very tired. She sways slightly. 'Jesus Christ, Betty. You never let anything go.'

'Hey! There's no need for talk like that.' Ed clambers to his feet too, his face flushed. 'You'd better control your wife, Todd.'

'Let's all calm down.' Dad puts out an arm, as if he's holding back a crowd. 'Ruby's sorry, aren't you? And it's getting late. Time to go.' His eyes fall on Christopher and he frowns as if he's just remembered who he is. 'We need to get Christopher home.'

'No hard feelings.' Betty touches Dad's arm. 'We

understand. You better get on home. We'll finish packing up.' Her eyes are bright. 'Ruby, honey. I'll be in touch tomorrow, see how you're getting along. If you need me before that, you know where I am.'

In the car on the way home, Christopher sings show tunes inside his head to block out the noise of Mommy and Dad arguing. But their voices cut through everything.

'She pretends to care, but she doesn't. I don't trust her. And I told you—'

'I can't do this anymore. You're driving me nuts.'

*I'm singing in the rain. Just singing in the—* It's too hard. He wishes they'd stop fighting. The hurt inside their words is horrible. He can't stand to see them making each other unhappy. Pain is everywhere in his body. He sits very still, but there's no escaping the agony sealed into his bones. He recalls the image of Scott, repeating it in a loop, the gleam of his teeth as his smile sweeps over Christopher again and again. The way he said no to the trip to the pier, the kindness in his voice at that moment, making himself an ally.

Hedy slips her hand into his. She squeezes gently. Christopher can't turn his head to look at her. He concentrates on his sister's fingers, tacky with salt and sand, the texture of her skin as familiar as his own. The thought of Scott can't help him now, nor the thought of aliens – the pain is too bad – there's only Hedy: only his sister standing between him and the void. He grips onto her hand and goes to the place where they become one, flesh against flesh, the line between them fusing and dissolving, her strength seeping into him.

# THIRTEEN

Through swirls of steam, Ruby looks at her son, submerged up to his chin in the bath. She slumps on the closed toilet seat. Her skin is prickly. She hadn't realised she was getting burnt, but a glance in the mirror shows her nose and cheeks red and raw. Christopher, who spent nearly the whole day fully dressed beneath the umbrella, is an intersection of milky shapes under the water. He isn't washing. He looks exhausted, his head tipped back. When she dips a hand into the water to soap the flannel, he opens his eyes. 'Please. I just want to lie here.'

He's worse than usual. Ruby knew it would be unbearable for him on the beach. She hates Todd. Most of all she hates Betty. The hatred is good, like tossing down a glass of neat vodka, setting a flame in her belly. But the thought is there in her head that it's her fault. After all, she's his mother, if she can't keep him safe, then who? With a lurch, she sits back on the seat again, hand to her mouth. She didn't fight hard enough to keep Christopher at home. And it was her refusal to leave the base, her stubbornness, that confused the issue, made Todd certain that he was right in insisting on the trip.

She bends to pick up Christopher's things, and the movement sets the bathroom spinning. She blinks away a rush of stars, the slippery sliding of bath tub, floor, feet. She breathes slowly through her nose until the room settles, and she can fold the T-shirt and trousers and put them in the laundry basket. 'Time to get out, sweetheart,' she says.

Christopher grips the sides of the bath, and hauls himself upright, water sluicing off his spine, twisting down thin legs. Looking at his crooked hips and child's bottom, a familiar silent howl runs through her. He steps over the bath rim, one slow foot at a time. When he's safely upright on the damp mat, she folds him inside a towel and holds him close. He leans against her and she closes her eyes, resting her chin on his unwashed hair.

In his bedroom, they go through the usual routine. He lies on the bunk and she massages his back, hoping that through touch alone, through her fingers against his skin, she can somehow communicate her apology. *God chose the weak things of the world to shame the strong.* She remembers her father raising his belt and the sting on her flesh. In her brief letters home, she'd told her father about the twins, announced their names and weights. It was only later that Christopher's condition became apparent, and by then she'd stopped writing. She never received a single reply. Never really expected to. She'd only written because Todd said she should. Her father probably threw the unopened envelopes into the fire. When she left the farm to marry Todd, she stopped being her father's daughter, her brother's sister.

With Father dead, Ernest will be struggling alone, scraping a living from the muddy land and the herd of cows. She wonders how much he hates her, or if he even thinks of her at all.

The bungalow is quiet. Hedy has put herself to bed, and Ruby doesn't know where Todd is. They'd entered the house without speaking, Todd dumping the picnic remains, folded chair, umbrella and rugs on the floor in the hall, while she'd taken Christopher straight to the bathroom.

She adjusts the girdle, does up the straps, locks the neck ring. Her son lies down inside his prison, and she kisses his cheek, feeling the slight change in his skin, a new rougher texture and musky smell, the beginnings of being a teenager. He smiles at her, but he's not there. He's already dreaming, or thinking of one of his stories. He's gone from himself, gone from her, and she's glad for his sake. Wearing the brace is like a jail sentence. But she knows she's doing the right thing. She won't let him suffer for the rest of his life like Ernest.

Ruby goes back to the bathroom and sluices down the tub, chasing grains of sand down the plug hole with a cloth. She stops at the steamy mirror, rubbing at a patch of glass so that she can apply powder to her shiny skin and a new coat of lipstick. Her eyes stare back, pale blue around pips of darkness, pupils disappearing into themselves like hedgehogs curled up in fright. She's got a whole script of things she wants to say to Todd. She's sorry that they argued. She's sorry she was rude to Betty, not because Betty didn't deserve it, but because she doesn't want to cause trouble for him. She loves Todd. That's the most important part. But she also needs to tell him how lonely she is. It's a different loneliness from the usual one of being an air-force wife. Todd has disappeared, even when he's right beside her. He's lost inside his own head, inside worries that he won't or can't share with her. She misses him. The claustrophobia of the base is suffocating. The other wives are bored and lonely; she can see it in their glazed expressions. And they are afraid: behind their too-bright smiles, they are terrified of what the Cold War will bring – their husbands and children killed, the bomb destroying everything they love. Everyone watches everybody else, because there's nothing else to do, and because any one of them could be a traitor, a commie in disguise. And all the time, there's the dark press of the forest herding them together like sheep. She's afraid for Christopher. She doesn't know why. It's not just the danger outside the base, the constant worry about his health; it's a bad feeling, like the taste in her mouth when a tooth is infected.

She's not sure how well she'll be able to say her lines. She pauses outside the lounge, gripping the door handle. She rearranges her face into a smile, pats the damp edges of her eyes with a tissue. She imagines Todd will be dozing in his armchair, cradling a Bud. But when she turns the handle, the room is empty. There's no sign he's been here at all. In the kitchen, she clicks on the light and glances in the bin. No empties. That's another surprise – a good one. Ruby opens their bedroom door with a lighter heart, hoping to find him getting ready, tooth-paste on his lips, maybe holding out his arms to her. *Come here, baby. You know I love you.*

The emptiness mocks her. Her mouth is dry. She moves through the bungalow searching, even going into the kids' rooms, tiptoeing through their dreaming breath, although she suspects Hedy's only pretending. Todd's not in the bathroom. He's not outside in the back garden either, cigarette sparking in the dusk. The trees lean close to the wire, a black tangle of narrow trunks. She thinks of the man's gaping face. Go away, she hisses into the night, you can't hurt me here. You can't hurt my children.

Standing on the yellow grass under the yellow moon, the heat of the day presses against her bare feet like a cat. A jet tears through early-evening stars. She looks up, half-expecting to see them falling in the wake of its slipstream.

How can she sleep when she doesn't know where Todd is? She wants her husband here beside her where he belongs. When she'd said 'yes' that afternoon on the hill, she knew Father and Ernest would never let her go. They wanted to keep her on the farm, in the kitchen, in her place, clearing out the slops and feeding the pigs, cooking and cleaning, sponging her brother's crooked spine with dark water in the tub in the kitchen. That wasn't a life to give up like a worn-out dress, it was a lock and chain to run from.

It had been a beautiful summer's evening, her heart full of hope, when Ernest came into the kitchen, limping over to the range where she'd been cooking supper. She remembers the sour look he gave her as he sniffed at the bubbling pot.

'Rabbit stew?' He prodded a wooden spoon into the food, his mouth a line of disapproval. 'Again?'

She stared down at the tea towel in her hands. She'd made Todd bring her back to the farm, cut their lovely picnic short to do her domestic duty. Todd's words were still going round and round inside her head, the joy of them making her reckless. *Marry me?* There was a pressure building behind her eyes. She could taste her freedom.

'If you don't like it,' she swallowed, looking at him, 'it doesn't matter, because I won't be doing your cooking much longer, or your housework.'

'What're you talking about?' He stopped prodding the stew,

and looked at her, his narrow gaze noticing details, flushing out differences.

She crossed her arms over her chest. 'I'm going with Todd,' she said.

'Not for long,' Ernest said. 'War's nearly over. The Yanks will go home. It'll be just you and me again.'

'No.' She was standing against the range, its heat against her back. Ernest's crooked shape dark against the bright window. 'I mean, I'm going away with him. I'm going to marry him. He's asked me. Just now. This afternoon.'

'Liar.'

She held out her left hand – she was wearing Todd's signet ring on her engagement finger – and watched Ernest's face, the way his mouth collapsed, the light hardening in his eyes.

'You can't,' he said. 'Father will never let you.'

'I'm not a slave.' She lifted her chin. 'Todd says he can't believe how hard I have to work, how old-fashioned everything is. In America they have washing machines. They have refrigerators.'

Ernest laughed. 'You're dreaming, Ruby. He's not going to choose you. You think your pretty face makes up for all this?' He gestures around the grimy kitchen, and then towards himself. Ernest gave her a cold smile. 'Think he'll take a risk on you?'

'He loves me.'

'He doesn't love you. He wants a whore. He's not going to marry an ignorant farm girl. You've never been further than Norwich.' He came closer. 'You're a slut, Ruby, opening your legs for a Yank. Selling yourself for box of chocolates and a pair of stockings.'

She slapped him. Her hand stinging against the bone of his cheek. His eyes widened in shock. He grabbed at her dress, shaking the fabric in his fist; buttons popped open, flying free, bouncing onto the tiles. He stared at the naked patch of skin above her exposed breast, her dress gaping open. His face sagged, mouth drooping as his fingers reached for the swell of her breasts. Fear made her lash out again, knuckles catching the edge of his chin.

He staggered back with a kind of half sob, half moan, eyes huge in the skull of his face.

'I'm pregnant,' she said, her voice a feather, the words dropping between them like a stone.

His lips opened and closed, making a blurred noise, as if he was drunk.

'I'm having a baby.' She knew she wasn't supposed to be telling him. But the words kept spilling out. 'I'm leaving. I can't waste my life here. It's not my fault. Why should I look after you? Why should I be your only friend?' She put her hand over her belly. 'I'm going to give my baby a future, in America.'

Ernest stared at her stomach. 'Father will kill you. He'll kill Todd too.'

'Father will never know, because I'm leaving with Todd. Tonight. He's coming to fetch me.'

'Your baby might turn out to be like me. And then what? Think he'll stick by you then? The all-American hero?'

Doubt opened a pit in her belly. She clasped a hand around her stomach, feeling the slight swell under her dress, and tilted her chin up. 'My baby will be fine.'

'He doesn't know, does he? I'm going to tell him, Ruby. Somebody should.'

'No!' She shouted the word, clenching her fists. 'You'll never see him again, or me.' Her pulse jumped in her throat. 'I hate you. I hate this place.'

She pulled her torn neckline together. 'You don't understand. How can you? Todd's a real man. When he holds me . . .' she laughs, 'it makes me feel safe. Being with him . . . it's . . . it's like magic . . . as if I'm walking without touching the ground. All I want is to be his wife and make him happy. Being with him makes the world beautiful, when all I've known is ugliness. He wants to look after me. More than that . . .' Her voice drops. 'He loves me. And I feel it. I'm loved. For the first time in my life.' She blinks at him. 'I'm sorry for you, Ernest. You'll never leave here. Nobody will ever love you. You'll never know these feelings . . . these wonderful feelings—'

Before she took another breath, he moved, faster than she thought possible. He had her head between his hands, crushing her skull. She was fighting him using both fists. He was strong, all that farm work, sheer determination making up for his bones. He was forcing her face towards the range. She saw the hot plate beneath her coming closer, the sizzle as a tear dropped. Ruby twisted out of his grip, losing a chunk of hair, but he'd caught one of her wrists, and he was dragging it towards the steaming kettle. A silent struggle. The strain producing grunts, panting, moans, mixed up so she didn't know whether it was him or her making the noises.

Ernest. Her brother. Her flesh. He wasn't letting go. Her left palm was flat down like a griddle cake, slapped straight against the heat. He kept it there next to the kettle. Now she was screaming. White pain leaping up her arm. Her skin raging.

She was scrabbling along the surface with her other hand, finding the knife she used for gutting rabbits. She flailed with the blade, bringing it down hard, the point pinning her brother's finger, a dart going right through skin and bone. He was screaming. Both of them, mouths open, eating each other's pain, swallowing their cries. The smell of her burning flesh. The scent of his blood.

She was backing away, cupping her wounded palm to her chest, watching him hunch over his finger, the knife dripping red onto the stone flags.

Ernest had been right. She'd carried the illness in her blood, and she'd never told Todd. She should have explained it to him, given him a choice. But she'd never meant to get pregnant. She'd been so naive; she didn't even know about birth control – Todd was her first lover, her only lover. She hadn't understood the stakes. Perhaps she should write to Ernest. What could she say? The last time they'd seen each other he'd tried to burn her face in order to take away her future. He'd ended up hurting her hand instead, leaving a scar that will never fade. And yet only one word occurs to her. She writes 'sorry' on an imaginary piece of paper. Then she crumples it up and discards it. He'll never forgive her.

The gleaming numbers on the clock tell her it's three o'clock when the door wrenches open, slamming against the wall. She listens to the lurch and stagger as Todd makes his way to the bed, the rustle of clothes being dropped to the floor, the clunk of his belt buckle as it hits a hard surface. She smells the stink of alcohol even before he falls onto the mattress. She feigns sleep, but there's no need. Todd's breathing has slowed to a rasp. He begins to snore.

It doesn't take detective work to know that he's been with her. Ruby sits up, circling her knees with her arms. Outside the birds have begun to sing. Above them a B-47 roars, shaking the glass in the windows, rattling the ornaments on the dresser, drowning out the chorus.

She keeps watch over him. The grainy dawn touches his

features, distorting them at first, then bringing them into focus, like a net pulling a statue up from the depths. Todd kicks the covers, fingers clenching, muttering a rash of slurred words. She can't make sense of it. He frowns and turns his head from side to side on the pillow, his face puckered. Ruby stares at him, holding her breath. He's panting as if he's in a race. He goes still, rigid, and lets out a choking cry. 'No!' He's shouting that one word, again and again. 'No. No. No.'

She leans over him, gripping his shoulders. He struggles out of her grasp, sitting up abruptly, and his mouth gapes in a high-pitched scream, unlike any sound she's heard him make before. She puts her palms over her ears in shock. He stops, eyes opening wide, giving a sudden gasp as if he doesn't recognise her. Before she understands what's happening, the flat of his hand has whipped across her face. Her head rebounds, a heavy weight on the column of her neck. The blow smacks her sideways, knocking air from her lungs. She crumples, one hand pressed to her cheek.

She scrambles out of the sheets, catching her foot in them and falling onto the carpet on her hands and knees. She stares over her shoulder, thinking he's coming after her. But Todd's sunk back into the pillow. She stumbles to her feet. He looks at her through drooping eyes like a sleepy child. She returns his stare, cheek aching, skin stinging like a burn. Todd's gaze slides across her.

She takes a deep breath. He doesn't know what he's done. He's never raised a hand to her before. She waits for a moment, listening for his snore. In the bathroom, she splashes her face with cold water, holds a wet cloth over the throbbing. She can't stop shaking.

*

158

At breakfast, Christopher is the first to notice her cheek. A gaudy purple bruise decorates the left-hand side of her face. Her eye on that side is bloodshot.

'Mommy?' He sounds scared. 'Are you OK?'

Hedy leans across her cereal bowl, examining her mother's face with interest. 'Wow, Mom! You should put ice on it. Did you fall?'

'Yes. I tripped.' She forces a smile. 'Don't worry. I'm fine.'

Todd comes into the kitchen, heads straight to the counter to pour himself a coffee, and slumps at the table with both hands cupped around the mug.

'Dad, have you seen Mom's face?' Hedy asks.

He raises his head and focuses. 'Jeez, Ruby. What happened? Are you all right?' His voice is hoarse from drink.

She strokes the contusion as if it's a mark that will wipe away. 'I slipped on my way to the bathroom last night. Silly of me. It looks worse than it is.'

'You didn't . . .' Todd frowns, putting his mug down carefully. 'It wasn't another . . . episode?'

She meets his gaze, but she's the first to look away. 'No. Nothing like that.'

# FOURTEEN

They were in his dreams, beckoning him into wakefulness.
The sound of them like bells in his head, clear and bright and
compelling. He knows they're waiting for him in the forest.
Despite his impatience, Christopher stands at the side of the
road, watching the traffic coming in through the entrance to
the base. He's too slow to make it across safely, so he lets the
vehicles go by: a jeep, a Cadillac and a green bus. There are
faces at the bus windows. He's not concentrating, because he's
thinking ahead to how he's going to retrace his steps and find
the stone circle, but the oddness of the faces returns him to
his body, rooted to the sidewalk, and to the children looking
back at him through glass. Details stick and catch in his mind:
the slur of a mouth, a tongue protruding, a small pale hand
pressed against the window, plump fingers like the suckers of an
underwater creature. He blinks and the bus has gone. He turns,
watching it slow and then speed up as it's waved through into
the exclusion zone. He's seen children like that on his visits to
the hospital, once on the street in Sioux City, a drooling girl

with empty eyes, an adult holding her hand, hurrying her along.

The road is clear, and he steps off the pavement, walking over the warm tarmac into the shadow of trees, the sharp scent of pine in his mouth. His girdle pinches his hips and his metal collar presses at his throat as he struggles up the grassy incline towards the fence and the gap in the wire.

As he moves into the interior, across a silt of old, brown leaves, he feels as though he's wandered miles, even though he knows the fence isn't far behind. The trees alter perspective and light, removing the long view, challenging his knowledge of time. He didn't tell Hedy or Scott where he was going. Neither of them likes the forest, and Hedy didn't believe in the footsteps underground. He could see it in her face as she'd bent her head to listen. She thinks the circle is something ordinary. He's afraid Scott won't believe him either, and he doesn't want to endure that betrayal, the shift in Scott's eyes as he looks away, or worse, his sneer as he makes it into a joke.

It's better to do this on his own. He won't be a threat to whatever – whoever – he finds. In movies and comics, aliens are depicted looking a bit like giant insects with bug eyes and armoured bodies, or else they're formless and mucus-dragging like a slug, which, Christopher knows, is really a kind of mollusc and not an insect at all. But he has a different idea; he pictures the creatures under the stone as being gentle and kind, silvery-skinned, long-necked as a heron.

He smiles in relief as he recognises a particular rotting tree, and this patch of rutted earth and squashed grass where heavy pine trunks have been piled up and then removed. He keeps on, limping faster now he knows he's going in the right direction.

The sound stops him. Not sweet, silver voices. Something

odd, something misplaced, like the sound of rain on a tin roof – a sudden, urgent pattering – and the crackle of dead things snapping, far away and then very close, although these noises happen so quickly that they flicker in his consciousness like forgotten memories. He turns, confused, as the herd comes out of the trees towards him, dozens of deer sweeping past. He sees the rough texture of fur, the shine of wild, dark eyes as they brush close, close enough to touch; the deer parting for him, diving around him as if he's a stone in a river.

It takes an age and no time at all for them to pass. Christopher waits, holding his breath. After the small tails have flashed white through the pines, the silence returns, deeper than before, and he feels alone for the first time. He continues on the path, his shuffling feet kicking something. He sees a glint of brass, a flash of scarlet out of the corner of his eye. He uses a twig to touch the ground, sweeping blindly until the twig and the object make contact. It takes a couple of tries to roll it up his ankle and grasp it with his fingertips, but he's learnt that success is about tactics, about not giving up. He holds the thing to his face, turning it in his fingers. A spent cartridge. He sniffs, not liking the sharp, medicinal smell. It leaves a metallic flavour on the roof of his mouth.

He drops the cartridge and walks on, afraid now for the deer, with their soft flanks and dipped faces. He'd wanted to touch his mouth to those gentle muzzles, stroke the long ears. Somewhere in the forest there's a hunter with a stock jammed against his shoulder, sights lined up on a dappled hide.

Christopher listens, but can't hear the sound of hooves on earth, or guns exploding. He doesn't glimpse the herd again. And when he rounds the next corner, he knows he's in the place. He recognises it by the solitary, stunted oak and the cluster of silver birches, pale against the pines. He's found the stone. But his attention is caught by the oak, because it's alive with things dangling and twirling from its branches. Christopher steps closer and understands that the tree is hung with small crosses. They float above his head. Some are made from dark feathers skilfully twisted together with wire. He reaches up and touches the nearest one, formed with plaited grasses and bits of twig. He lets go and watches the tiny crucifix bounce on its tether of string. Christopher thinks of Old Joe, his talk of devils. Perhaps these are his way of warding off evil, chasing away the devils.

Under the oak's branches, the stone lies heavy in the earth. The covering of dirt and pine needles is thick over its surface, coarse grass matted against circular sides. The crosses dangle like tiny hanged men above his head. It is cold here in the heart of the trees. The light is dim, green, like an eternal dusk. For a second, Christopher falters. What if he's wrong? What if this place is bad, like Old Joe said? What if the voices under the stone belong to something dangerous?

To be able to listen at the lip of the circle, he has to get onto the ground. His method is to lean to the side until he's lost his balance and he's dropping through space to catch himself on the palm of one hand, which he does with a grunt and a sickening jolt to his shoulder. Propped on the stone, breathing hard, he uses it as support to lower himself onto his knees. Anything is possible, he tells himself, if he takes his time, free from curious stares to work out the difficulties of his rigid torso and confined limbs. He is triumphant as he kneels on all fours, twisting his neck against the chin pad to get into the right position.

The dankness of underground air, stale and cold, filters

through the grille. He thinks he hears the trickle of ants, a rustle of sheathed beetle wings, the clicking of doodle bugs rolling into armoured balls. His head echoes with the effort of concentration. His heart bangs, blood rushing through him like the sea, and from deep in his belly comes the squeak and rumble of his stomach. The next muffled noise also seems to come directly from the workings of his body, a distant, drawn-out howl like a train through a tunnel. It reminds him of the rip of steel against steel. The bite of iron against his cracked spine. But this noise is something other, something apart from him; it comes from the pit of the earth, pushing up through the thick slab of stone, through the metal grille. It sounds again, closer. A scream. A primal roar. More animal than machine. A coyote in a trap: a creature cornered.

Christopher jerks away in panic, tries to get to his feet and loses his balance, falling heavily onto the grass, twisting onto his back. He's winded, breathless. He stares at distant tree tops moving around patches of blue. The howl is stuck inside his head. A noise from a nightmare. It makes him want to run, run far away from here. His legs scrabble at the earth, hands clawing the air for something to grab onto to help turn himself over. His eyes move to the surface, expecting the stone to open, for something terrible to emerge.

The stone does not open. Nothing moves. Christopher begins to control his breathing, steadying his lungs. *Hedy*, he cries silently, throwing his words across the tops of the trees, willing his voice to speak urgently in her head wherever she might be: *help me*. His eyes flicker into the furthest reaches they can from his prone position, as he tries to think about how to get up from the trap of the brace. He can't be sure that Hedy will come, or anyone. It's a problem to solve alone. He's good at

164

problems; there's no need to panic. But something is there, after all, a presence watching him. It gathers at the periphery of his sight, a twitch of movement, a shadow swooping from the trees to crouch over him, blinding him with darkness. Hands clasp his shoulders. He is too afraid to yell; a scuff of sound grazes his throat. He blinks up at the shape, matted hair hanging, framing an upside-down face that seems familiar. The mouth inside the beard opens, making grunting noises of effort or perhaps words that have lost their meaning. Fingers grip Christopher's arms tight and the world swings and tilts as he's hauled onto his feet. He turns to thank his rescuer, but Old Joe has gone; just his smell remains, musty and dank as a cellar.

Christopher uncurls his fingers and looks down at a small cross made of bracken, new green stalks and tendrils woven together, fixed in place with tiny pieces of wool. He keeps it safe inside his fist. His chest is bruised from the fall. His legs are weak. He wishes now that Hedy or Scott were here. He's not sure how he'll make it back to the base alone.

The sound of the voices has gone. He doesn't understand why they didn't wait. Why they didn't show themselves. The aliens calling in their silvery tones. Disappointment is a sludge in his veins. He tilts his face, wanting the comfort of sunlight. Pine resin catches in his throat, makes him cough, asthma tickling deep in his chest. He longs for the trees to fall away, for the relief of open sky. He nuzzles the air, searching out small ribbons of light that come snaking through branches, beams alive with turning specks of dust and pollen. One of them touches his face. He closes his eyes and lets it seep into him. As he stands in the warmth, it expands, becomes a river, falls over him like a waterfall – a sudden blaze of gold as if he's stepped inside the sun – and he feels strength fizz through his bones.

The metal brace melts away, leaving him unencumbered, full of strength, like a young panther. Behind closed lids he watches himself dance and run and jump.

He opens his eyes into white heat. He's blinded by the glare. He keeps staring into the heart of it, and it pours into him, a rush of crystal: brilliant, healing. He's stunned by the wonder of it.

The light moves across him and disappears, as if a door has slammed, shutting him out. He looks around, dizzy and disorientated. The forest is dark and cold. He tries to move but is caught between iron bars that nip his skin. He puts his hand to his chest, puzzled by the weight of the brace. Inside the light, he had been free. He sobs, rubs his eyes. There is nothing for it but to return to the base, to place one heavy foot in front of the other. The light took away his fear, but now he remembers the howl, and he glances at the stone circle uneasily, checking it's still shut. He limps away, gripping the bracken cross inside his fist.

When he reaches the gap in the wire, he presses his face against the mesh. The base is spread out before him. The road he crossed earlier – the road that leads to the exit – is now empty of traffic; the bungalows and deserted playground lie beyond; army personnel in the distance. A plane blunders along the runway behind the fence. At the junction of the road is the beginning of Main Street with the movie theatre and bowling alley. Further down the street, women in bright summer clothes go in and out of the commissary. It all looks so normal. He pauses, giving himself a moment before the effort of squeezing through the torn wire onto the grassy bank. He's aware of silence, a lull in the roar of the jets, no engine sounds, not even cars moving along Main Street. The birds have stopped singing.

There is only his rasping breath. Inside the quiet he hears Joe's mumbled words. Something he said as he put Christopher back onto his feet. Christopher hears it again as if Joe were close beside him, ticklish mouth at his ear. 'You are the one.'

Christopher is halfway home when it occurs to him that he should tell someone – someone in authority – about the howl under the stone circle. Not the wonderful light, because he couldn't describe that to anyone. He feels a lingering sense of it, like the echo of the distant singing, and wants it to stay inside him. But he should tell someone about the howl. His father would be his usual choice, but Dad has been acting funny recently. His cheeks have a new sandpaper texture, his breath is beery, his eyes unfocused, rheumy, pink. Mom says he's sickening for a cold, or he has a headache, or he's busy and not to bother him.

A jeep pulls up outside the medical centre and Christopher sees that the man who gets out is Colonel Anderson. The most important man on the base. 'Excuse me,' he licks his lips. 'Excuse me, sir.'

Colonel Anderson is tall, square-shouldered, with gunmetal hair clipped short into a silvery carpet. Christopher remembers that the one time he was introduced to him by Dad, the colonel was kind.

For a moment it looks as though the colonel is going to walk right past. 'Please, sir!' Christopher finds new energy and volume.

Colonel Anderson stops. It only takes him a blink to recognise Christopher. 'You're Captain Delaney's son, aren't you?'

He listens to Christopher's story, the spill of words racing each other, and places his hand on Christopher's shoulder, nodding gravely. 'Aliens?' He raises his thick eyebrows. He doesn't laugh. 'Well, well. You did the right thing to report it,' he says. 'You don't have to worry about a thing. We'll send the right people to investigate.' He taps his nose. 'Let's keep it to ourselves, meantime. Don't want to cause a panic.'

Colonel Anderson gets his driver to give Christopher a lift home. The man at the wheel wears mirrored glasses. He hops out to help Christopher into the front seat of the jeep. He takes something from his top pocket, offering the stick of gum with a wink, as if it's something forbidden. He whistles as he drives, salutes Christopher when he drops him off outside the bungalow.

Christopher realises he still has the bracken cross clutched in his left hand. He opens his palm and looks at the smashed crucifix, the snake-green stain on his skin.

# FIFTEEN

Ruby wakes to find the bed empty. She slides over onto Todd's side; the sheet is still warm. She gets up, stepping across the moonlit carpet to open the door and look into the hall. Perhaps he's in the bathroom. She peers inside. The lavatory cistern is quiet, no dripping taps. She walks around the corner and catches her breath. Todd is sitting at the hall table, his head bowed.

She approaches cautiously. 'Todd,' she calls quietly, 'Are you OK, baby?'

Since his nightmare, the blow to her cheek, she's resolved to keep a closer watch on him. And Christopher, too. He disappeared again the other day, coming back with grass stains on his clothes, the smell of pine in his hair. The stink of the forest made her feel sick. She bent down, looked into his eyes and told him in the firmest voice she could find not to go out of the base again. Or else. She doesn't know what the 'or else' could be: taking away his comics? Stopping his pocket money? How do you punish a child already in prison?

Christopher is usually such an obedient boy. She'd lost her temper with Hedy for letting her brother out of her sight for a second time.

She wishes she could talk it through with Todd. But he's so caught up in whatever's bothering him. Since starting his new job he's distracted and distant. He's stopped confiding in her. It makes her feel helpless.

'Todd.' She calls again, a bit louder.

He doesn't seem to hear. Perhaps he's sleep-walking. One of his hands is resting on the telephone receiver, as if he's about to make a call. Ruby feels a lurch of vertigo. Has she caught him just before or after telephoning that woman? Joan Brown. Or maybe it's Betty he wants to speak to. She thinks of them in the dark, smoky garden, Betty's arms twined around Todd's neck. That would be a humiliation too far.

Todd looks up at her slowly. 'Ruby,' he says, as if he's only just become aware of her.

'What are you doing?' She keeps her voice gentle. 'Are you calling someone?'

He looks at the phone. 'No.' He takes his hand off the receiver.

'Then come back to bed.'

He gets up slowly, as if his joints are painful, and shuffles beside her with uncertain steps. This is not the athlete she married, the one who used to do sit-ups and squat thrusts every morning, who prided himself on being a jock.

In bed, he rolls nose to nose with her. She's tight against his chest. They cling together, sharing the fug of their breath, Todd squeezing her ribs until she thinks they'll crack. Ruby is half-suffocating, her bruised eye crushed against his cheek, but she is so relieved she wants to cry. It's like a furious ball inside her, the love and the fear, rolled up together, sitting inside her chest, blocking the air from her lungs. Her lips are squished into his stubble, tasting salt, the comfort of cigarette smoke. She turns her head with difficulty so that she can give voice to her feelings. 'I love you,' she whispers.

'You wouldn't love me if you knew ...' He stops, his voice trembling.

'Knew what?'

'I've done things.' He pushes his face into her hair so she can hardly hear him. 'I'm ashamed, Ruby. Not the man I thought I was.'

'I'd love you whatever you did.' Her fingers grip his arms. 'You can tell me anything.'

She's thinking of her own shame, of how she might still find the strength to apologise to Todd, and then to Ernest.

'I can't tell you this.' His voice is choked back into his throat.

She murmurs to him, her hand making slow circles over his skin. She wishes she had more than these soft words, words that land like snowflakes on the burning, unfathomable landscape of his pain and melt without leaving an impression.

He sniffs and sits up, wipes his nose on a corner of the sheet. 'I hope you can forgive me. I don't deserve it, but I hope so.'

'I have already. I don't care what you've done.' Tears seep sideways across her cheek and into her ear. He's frightening her. Todd doesn't talk like this. Her brave pilot. Her cowboy. The man who doesn't let anyone rattle his cage.

He rubs his eyes with the heels of his hands. 'Damn it. I'm sorry, OK? Just forget what I said. Guess I'm not as tough as I thought.' He gives a dry laugh, which turns into a cough.

She wants to go back into the hug. She's aching for the feel of his arms around her. She must make him understand her love, the depth of it, and how she would forgive him anything, do anything to prove her loyalty. She wants him to give her a test, a challenge: something physical and dangerous where she could excel herself, be brave, be triumphant for him. But he turns over and thumps his pillow, settling with his back to her. She edges close, spooning the rigid curve of his spine.

# SIXTEEN

Ruby tries to cover her bruise with make-up, but it shows through the thickest layer. Her cheek glows purple, black, then greenish yellow, colours creeping through her Coty powder, making her skin look ashen. People notice. They snatch an extra glance, look away, talk about the weather. She begins to open conversations by explaining her night-time fall, the way her face made contact with the bathroom door as she slipped. It is better, she thinks, to mention it than not. But those she tells seem anxious to change the subject.

The only person who doesn't have doubts is Todd.

Hank won't let it drop, keeps asking questions, his expression anxious. 'I've seen a lot of bruised faces in my time, most of them the work of someone else's knuckles.'

'Are you suggesting I've been in a scuffle – a bar-room brawl?' She tries to laugh it off.

'Look. I don't want to interfere. But you can tell me.' His touch on her arm is kind.

'It was an accident,' she says.

There's a small group of women staring at a notice in the window of the medical centre. They're mesmerised, yet a restlessness possesses them, the way they clutch their handbags tighter, adjust hats, while none of them speak or break their study of the sign. Ruby peers over their shoulders.

Ladies – we are sorry
but we are out of Miltown!

Ruby reads and then rereads the sign, mouthing the words as if they might change on her tongue. She looks at the uncomprehending faces around her.

'What do they mean?' she asks. 'For how long?'

Her questions seem to break the spell.

'There goes my sanity!' Sandy Peters winds her finger in circles next to her ear, a bright smile on her lips.

'They'll get another shipment in soon, right?' another woman asks. Dark hair combed high off her forehead.

Ruby goes inside the centre to find more wives jostling at the desk, the receptionist shrugging her shoulders. 'There's a worldwide shortage.' The girl looks over her glasses, impressed with her own importance.

'Can't you do something? You'll have a riot on your hands if you don't.' Betty is there, gesturing towards the door as if to a gang of mutineers, rather than a handful of women. Her white gloves conduct the air like a traffic policeman.

'Doctor Rowland says it's run out in the States, too.' The receptionist is less certain. Her nose twitches. She backs away from the desk, obviously expecting to be overcome by the promised mutiny.

Ruby avoids making eye contact with Betty. She slips away and walks home, heels clicking along at a pace, but preventing herself from breaking into a jog. As soon as she gets in, she goes through the medicine cabinet, systematically tipping out every bottle, rummaging behind cough mixture and jars of cold cream. She empties the contents of all her handbags onto the kitchen table, sorting through the jumble of hankies and combs and dollars. There are two pills left. Only two. *For what we are about to receive may the Lord make us truly thankful.*

Days later, Ruby is hunched over the toilet bowl in a different kind of prayer, retching up acid yellow. Any digested food is long gone, but still her stomach knots and twists. The cramps are worse than childbirth. She slumps on the floor, her cheek resting on the seat, the smell of bleach making her retch again. She's afraid she's dying. It's gone midnight and Todd hasn't come home. She doesn't want him or the children to find her lifeless body in the bathroom. She puts her hands flat on the green and white crocheted mat she made herself, gathers some final residue of strength, and staggers to her feet. Swaying, she presses her damp, cold forehead against her hand, as if she can press back the clattering noises inside her head. She leans on the sink for a moment, avoiding her reflection, and then bends towards the gushing taps, sluicing her mouth with water, splashing her face.

He came when she called him. They sit in the lounge, coffee cups balanced on knees. Ruby takes a sip of burning liquid, her trembling hand clattering the cup in its saucer. A shiver runs through her. Not a bad one. Not like the first ones that turned her bones to ice, but it makes her teeth chatter.

'Excuse me,' she says, clenching her jaw.

'What was it you wanted to ask?' Hank leans forwards, gives his trousers a little tug above his knees. 'Don't want to hurry you, but . . . ' His eyes slide to the clock on the wall.

'Yes, of course.' Ruby waits for a B-47 to pass overhead. She tries to collect the right words and put them in the right order. She practised this before Hank arrived. 'I'm worried about Todd. He's . . . ' She pauses, blinking away the black dots floating in the air between them. 'Remember how we noticed he's drinking a lot? Well, it's got worse. The point is, he's unhappy. It's this place. I know it is.' She knows she's speaking too fast, but she can't stop, the words slipping and sliding on top of each other. 'Everything started to go wrong after we got here. It must be reminding him of the war – all those men he lost, the planes falling out of the sky. Everyone thinks he's so brave. Thinks he can handle anything. But he's just a man . . . Can't you see? It's not good for him, for us. I need to know, is there any way he could get reassigned?'

'Whoa! Slow down.' Hank frowns, blows through pursed lips. 'This is a lot to take in.'

'There's something else.' She leans towards him, lowering her voice. 'I think . . . I think he's seeing another woman.'

'You're kidding me, right?' He shakes his head. 'That's not the Todd I know. He's crazy about you, Ruby. He would never be unfaithful. It's not his style.'

'I've seen her.' The black dots collect in the atmosphere, shaping themselves into the face of Joan Brown. 'I just know.' She closes her eyes. 'The thing is, it doesn't matter. We can save our marriage. But we need to get away from here. We need to leave the base, leave England. You have to help us, Hank.'

She opens her eyes to look at him, aware that her voice is out of control, has entered a different register, high-pitched, sharp, like an alarm. Hank doesn't flinch.

'Ruby,' he says gently. 'I know you like life better in the States. We all do. But asking to leave will hurt Todd's career.' He fixes her with his steady eyes.

She can't trust herself to do more than hold his gaze.

He sighs. 'Any potential reassignment would have to start with his request,' he says slowly. 'But you know how this works, Ruby. There are no grounds for returning to the States. He has no urgent compassionate need. The fact that Todd might be unsettled by memories of the war, that's not going to wash with the military. He signed up for worldwide assignment. It's part of the deal – it's why he gets a pay check. Sorry I can't be of more help.' He sees her face, softens his own expression. 'I can talk to him though, if you like, sound him out, see if there's anything we can do to make him happier.'

'Don't tell him it was me. Don't mention the affair.'

'I won't. And don't give this other woman another thought. Todd's a family man.'

She nods again. She'd hoped for more. But it's something. Perhaps it's something. She can taste metal in her mouth. Blood. She must have bitten her tongue.

'What else is worrying you?' he asks, his voice gentle.

It's her chance to keep talking about Todd's strange state of mind; and although pain hammers at her temples, she tries hard to give him the right information, to say the one thing that will make Hank understand how serious it is. He listens, his hand on her arm. Then he rubs his chin, gets up and hands her his empty cup. Their fingers brush. She pulls away. How easy it would be to lay her head on his shoulder.

'There was one other thing . . . ' Ruby enunciates slowly. 'I

take Miltown. For my nerves. They've run out. I ... um ...'
She pats her hair, crisp with spray. 'I'm finding it hard to cope
without. Doctor Rowland says there's not a single pill anywhere.
I don't suppose you know of a way of getting hold of some?'

She is proud of herself – how calmly she offers this possibility
to him, as if it were a casual request.

Hank frowns. 'Hmm. I don't have much to do with doctors.
But I can see how much pressure you're under. I'll ask around,
see what I can do. Maybe I'll be able to pull some strings.'

She stands in the hall to say goodbye and he takes her cold
hands in both of his, rubbing them, warming her. 'I'm worried
about you. About all of you. I'm sorry this didn't work out.' He
moves her wedding band around her thin finger. 'I feel responsible. It was me that recommended Todd. Thought it would be
good to have some of the old team together again.' His mouth
twists in a sorrowful grimace. 'Guess I was wrong.'

'None of this is your fault.' Ruby leans forwards, kisses his
cheek with dry lips. Like a bird pecking at grain, she thinks, not
a woman with the gift of love inside her. She sees it in Hank's
face – his loyal face – a brief whisper of distaste, or fear, or pity.

Three days later a brown package addressed to her drops
through the letter box. She opens it in the bathroom behind a
locked door. There's no note. Three bottles of pills fall into her
lap. They're not labelled, but she knows what they are.

# SEVENTEEN

Christopher writes the sentence down in his notebook. *You are the one*. He chews his pen. 'I am the one,' he tells the empty bedroom. He sits at his desk and puts it all down, writing like it's a made-up story, because this way he's not breaking his promise to the colonel. He tells it from the perspective of someone else, a healthy boy without a bent spine. But he writes it in the order it happened: the oak hung with crosses, the stone circle, and how he got down on his knees and listened at the metal grille. He describes the howl, the way it came from the pit of the earth, the fury and agony of it. He tells how he warned the colonel. Then he tries to describe the way the light felt on his face. How it was something alien and beautiful. From another world. Words fail him. He can only think of how wonderful it was. He writes *The Wonderful*, and underlines it.

The howl under the stone had been full of terror. But the light had been good, like a blessing. He can't put the two together, doesn't understand what it all means. He wonders when Colonel Anderson will send men to investigate and what they will find.

He can't tell Hedy or Scott anything about it. He promised. He writes that down too, how he was sworn to secrecy by the colonel.

Days pass and nobody mentions the forest, or the stone, or the noises he heard, and Christopher understands that whatever they found is to be kept a military secret, like the work his father does.

Hedy pulls her baseball cap low, stamps and kicks at the ground, a bull in a ring. The girl with the bat looks nervous, practises a few half-hearted hits, the wood stroking the air rather than slicing it. Christopher feels sorry for her. The female softball team Hedy's managed to scrape together is not in his sister's league, nowhere near, and she's a tough coach, wanting to get them into shape for a competition with another US team. Hedy slaps her leg and makes a funny little bow before her pitching arm swings in two fast underarm circles and the ball flies at its target. The girl in bat lets out a cry as the ball makes contact with her left thigh. She hops away, sobbing, the bat trailing behind. Hedy stands shaking her head.

'Strike two,' Scott says, snapping gum between his teeth.

Christopher watches them play for a little longer, to show support. But the game drags, and anyway it's only a practice. He's tired and there's no shade to stand in, so he gives Hedy a quick thumbs-up to tell her he's going home.

Scott rolls off his heels after him.

They walk together in companionable silence, Scott slowing to Christopher's pace. 'She's not bad, your sister. For a girl,' he says after a while. He spits efficiently, leaving a neat blob on the pavement. 'Smart pitching. Spins the ball well.'

'Yeah.' Christopher wishes he had something interesting to add, wishes now that he'd listened to all those baseball conversations between Hedy and Dad.

'Want to get a soda?' Scott nods towards the com.

Late summer sun blasts the grass to stubble, makes dusty leaves droop. Parked cars shine like mirrors, the baked metal too hot to touch. Christopher sweats under the tight girdle. His wet skin rubs against the leather, opening his sores. He's afraid he smells of rot.

They stop outside the com and Scott buys two bottles, the frost on the sides dissolving under the warmth of their fingers. They clink. 'Cheers,' Scott says in an English accent.

Christopher waits, his drink untouched, watching Scott, the tilt of his chin, his undulating throat. A trickle of spilt liquid crawls over his skin, gathering in one shining droplet at the base of his neck.

Scott stops gulping, and wipes his mouth with a sigh. 'Boy, I needed that,' he grins at Christopher.

His big teeth blaze from his mouth, which is wide with the simple happiness of being alive, drinking soda on a hot day. Christopher stands inside the sweet warmth of Scott's pleasure, and it's almost as perfect as standing inside the wonderful light. I am the one, he reminds himself. And anything seems possible in that single moment.

His hand is on Scott's cheek. The shape of his fingers fitting the curve of bone with an exactness that breaks his heart. Scott's skin burns hotter than Christopher imagined. Gently, he brushes away the last of the soda dribble, his touch moving across Scott's parted lips.

# EIGHTEEN

Hedy walks along Main Street, dangling the catching mitt by its laces, the weight of it bumping her knees. She pushes her cap off her hot forehead. Strands of ticklish hair cling to her neck; her plait unravels down her back. She'd like to cut it off, but Mom will never let her. She knows she played well today. She's gotten the knack of the wrist snap now; her elbow is up; she can get real backspin on the ball. The black line is visible every time. Coach in Iowa told her, look out for the black line as the ball leaves your hand, then you've got heat in your throw. But if she can't get these candy asses into shape, they'll lose the match next week.

She'll talk to Dad about it. He could come and coach them. Except he may not be at home, even on a Saturday. Mom said he was working extra time. Mom pretends he's just getting in late and leaving early, but his toothbrush in the cup in the bathroom is dry as straw, his shaving soap untouched.

Scott appears at the end of the street, walking with that disturbing pull and push energy, as if his feet are shackled while his top half ploughs forwards, shouldering the air, splitting its seams. The best thing about Scott is his ability at baseball, his knowledge of sport. She wants to ask him what he thought about the match; his opinions of the team would be useful. He stops on the sidewalk, noticing her, and it looks for a second as if he might cross the street to avoid her, which is weird, but he changes his mind and keeps on coming.

When he gets up close, she can see that he's in a mean mood.

'What's up?' She takes her baseball cap off, pushes her fingers through her damp hair.

'Tell your brother that if he comes near me again, he's dead.'

Hedy tries to see the smirk lurking under Scott's scowl, because this has to be a joke. She screws up her face, shrugs her shoulders. 'I'm slow to catch on, so you'd better get to the punch line quick.'

'You know he's a pervert, right?'

Something snags in her throat. She swallows. 'What are you talking about?'

'Your brother's a fucking pervert. A fag. He needs to be locked up.' Scott's skin mottles, his eyes are slits.

'Don't talk about my brother like that.'

He shoves past, his elbow catching her ribs. 'Get out of my way.'

'There's something wrong with you!' She yells after him. 'It's you that's nuts!'

He turns and opens his arms. 'I'm gonna tell everyone what your brother did – tell him that from me, too. Shit. He might even get lynched. Serve him right. Maybe I'll get the cops. They'll put the spaz behind bars. He's a fucking criminal.' He stops, as if searching for a word, and then spits it out. 'A deviant.'

She feels winded, as if Scott has landed a blow in her stomach. She glances around to see if anyone's heard and walks on fast, breaking into a run. Her baseball cap falls from her fingers and she doesn't stop to retrieve it, the red and white writing on the front announcing, *Diamonds Flash, Softball Team 1955*. They'd smashed that season, won every game.

Chris is sitting at his desk with his back to her. He's not writing anything – just staring into space.

'What happened?' She closes the door behind her. 'I saw Scott.'

Chris doesn't move.

'Chris? Answer me. What's going on?'

She stands beside him, touching his shoulder. He glances up in a kind of dull surprise, hardly acknowledging her presence. He's pale, his skin bleached of freckles.

'Are you ill?' she asks.

He moves his head irritably, as if her words are a swarm of mosquitoes.

'What did you do?' Her voice is louder.

'Leave me alone,' he whispers.

There's a shout from the hall. Their mother's voice. Hedy is alert, listening. Another voice interrupts, deep and male.

'Dad's home,' she says, a sob breaking inside her, her heart rising like a balloon, both at once.

'I wish it would fall,' Chris says in a toneless voice.

'What?'

'The atomic bomb. I wish it would fall right now.'

'Jesus, Chris!' She shouts. 'Just shut up!'

Dad will make all of this go away, she thinks, crossing the room in three strides.

Dad's in the kitchen. But there's something wrong. He's in uniform, but his clothes are rumpled and creased, his tie undone. He's standing utterly still, his feet fixed under him, body rigid as if he's balancing on a tightrope, braced against a strong wind. The expression on his face is one of terror.

'Todd?' Mom asks. 'Todd? What's the matter?'

'Don't move,' Dad hisses. 'Don't move or you'll fall in. The floor. It's gone.'

Hedy's confused. Is it one of his jokes?

'Todd?' Mom sidles towards him and touches his arm. 'Stop this. You're scaring me. Look, the floor is right where it always was.'

Dad shakes Mom off and stares into the corner of the room. His eyes are red blind, but behind the glaze of unseeingness is another deeper vision, as if he's looking inside himself at a different world, a terrible one, and this ordinary life is the vision that passes him by. 'The thing,' he breathes. 'The creature. Spying on me.'

'Dad,' Hedy says quietly. 'What creature?'

'Please,' Mom is begging. 'I don't understand. What do you mean?'

Dad staggers forwards, lumbering onto his knees, hands out-spread to touch the floor with cautious fingers as if he's uncertain of its existence. He looks up with a wild gaze and flinches at something only he can see. 'They're coming for me . . .'

He makes an odd, urgent scuttle sideways, scrambling under the table, where he curls up, whimpering, 'Stop them. Please, please stop them.'

Mom has got down onto the floor and is tugging at his sleeve, trying to make him get up. It's an impossible task. Dad is immovable. He cowers, wrapping his arms across his head in the 'duck and cover' position they practise at school. 'Make them go away!' he cries.

'Todd!' Mom shouts. 'Stop this!'

The doorbell rings. It keeps ringing and ringing. Someone outside has their finger pressed down hard.

Mom and Dad don't seem to hear, they are caught in their

awkward half-dance, their tangled embrace, faces close, almost close enough to kiss. She's trying to pull him out from under the table, and he's refusing to move. 'I know they're here,' his voice breaks, becoming a hysterical whisper. 'They follow me. Watch me.'

'Todd. Sweetheart. There's nobody here but us.' Mom is talking in a gentle voice now, crouching next to him, her arms around him. 'Let me get Hank. He'll know what to do . . .'

Her father stands up fast, banging his head on the table. He runs his fingers through his hair, as he backs away from Mom, the whites of his eyes huge around the dark centres, a sheen of sweat on his brow. 'Monsters. They're monsters.'

She's walking towards him with her hands up.

'Get away from me!' Dad shouts. 'Get off me! You're one of them!' And then he stops, shaking his head, rubbing at his eyes. 'Am I mad?' His voice breaks like a child's, taking on a pleading helplessness. 'Am I going mad?'

The bell keeps ringing. Hedy opens the door. Four men in dark blue uniform crowd the entrance. USAF Security Police. She tries to slam the door shut. But the men flash a badge at her and tumble inside. They're taking hold of Dad, attempting to separate him from Mom, who's clinging to him like a drowning woman.

Dad is being marched to the car waiting at the kerb outside, his arms cuffed behind his back, two police either side of him jostling close, guns at their hips. Dad is thrashing between the men. 'Help me,' he's shouting. 'Help me!' Every window opposite is full of a staring face. Hedy can't understand. His behaviour is mortifying. Terrible. He's more drunk than she's ever seen him, or anyone. He needs to tell them they've got the wrong man, he needs to clear up the misunderstanding, but nobody will believe him when he's like this.

Mom is curled on the floor. She moans, one long animal noise, pulling at her hair with both hands. She's staring through the open door to the space where the car was. The car that took Dad away.

Chris hasn't even come out of his room, even though he must have heard the shouting and commotion. Hedy goes to him. 'Dad's been arrested,' she tells her brother's back, the metal bars of the brace. 'Maybe you don't care.'

Chris turns his face slowly, his chin rotating above the pad like a robot. He looks at her dumbly, blindly; no concern or surprise flickers across his features. Her hands are shaking. Seeing Dad like that has broken something inside her. She feels a painful, terrible release coming from the broken place, anguish and anger spewing out.

'It's your fault.' Her finger jabs at him. 'You. You're the one. The problem. This is all your fault. Scott hates you. I hate you. You're disgusting.'

How could she not have seen his unnatural sickness, the girlish way he cries over sentimental things? Even without the excuse of his bent spine, even without the brace, he would always have been a disappointment to Dad, an embarrassment to his family. He's got something wrong with him – something in his head. A deviant.

I hate him, she tells herself. This is all his fault.

She has to get away. She slips out of the room and leans, trembling, against the closed door, holding the handle as if to stop him from coming after her. Rage and grief beat at her ribcage. Mom is still on the floor, slumped over. Hedy knows she should go to her, but she can't. Her body is locked. Her legs won't move. She watches her mother swing her head against the edge of the oven, the sickening thud, the way she does it again and again.

187

# NINETEEN

Hank scoops Mom off the floor, carrying her as easily as if she's a doll. Hedy didn't think he was so strong. Hank puts Mom on the bed gently and slips off her shoes, talking all the time in a soothing voice. 'You'll be all right, Ruby. You lie quiet now. A good sleep and you'll feel better.'

Tears slide across her cheeks. Her breasts shudder under her dress, straining against thin fabric. Without shoes, her feet are exposed in nude stockings, the shape of them, toes bent under nylon. Hedy glances away. It's a relief when Doctor Rowland arrives with his black bag and Hank and Hedy leave the bedroom.

They stand in the kitchen, and Hank pours himself a glass of water, drinks it fast. 'I'm sorry you had to see your dad like that,' he says.

'Where is he?'

'At the military jail.'

'Why?'

Hank rinses the glass and puts it upside-down on the

draining board. 'I'm afraid he broke his promise to the US government and air force.'

'Dad would never do that.'

'He's been under strain recently. He's been drinking.'

'Under strain? Like . . . Mom, you mean?'

Hank nods. He looks serious and sad.

Mom's always had her turns, needed her afternoon lie-downs, needed to take her special pills, but not Dad, not her funny, baseball-loving father who liked to look at the facts, who was brave and strong, and sometimes silly, but never crazy.

Doctor Rowland comes out of Mom's bedroom. He treads over the carpet, shoes rolling under his weight, his steps marking a trail through the plush. 'I've given Ruby something to help her sleep. A sedative.'

'Will you be OK, Hedy?' Hank asks. 'I can get one of the other wives to come over to cook supper and watch you. Betty's a friend of your mom, isn't she?'

'We don't need watching,' Hedy says. 'I can look after Chris. And Mom.' She bites her thumbnail. 'What about Dad? When will he come home?'

Hank takes a moment to answer. He clears his throat and glances at Doctor Rowland. 'The charges are serious, Hedy. I won't lie to you. He was working on something important, something our enemies have been trying to find out about. Any breach in security has to be dealt with thoroughly.' He puts his hand on her shoulder. 'Try not to worry. Be a good girl and look after your mom.'

Hedy goes back into the kitchen to stand at the window, watching Hank and Doc Rowland leave together. Their low voices reach her as an indistinct muttering. They shake hands and part on the pavement, walking in opposite directions. The doctor's stomach weighs him down, makes him waddle, the black bag clutched in his fist. Hank marches off, moving as if he has important places to get to, his uniform without a crease, hat on straight. She wishes he'd stayed.

Hedy remains at the window, staring at the street. She remembers one of the bubblegum cards saying how in Russia people can get taken away at any time, hauled off to prison for no reason, without fair trial or appeal. There's no justice in the USSR. 'That is life under communism!' the card read. But here they are in England, under American military law, where things are fair and good and people are not punished for no reason. Dad would never do anything bad. He'll have a trial, and they'll realise there's been a big mistake.

Somehow hours have passed and the burning sun is low over the pines. Dusk reshapes things, blurring edges, dimming colours, turning a passing black cat into a small panther as it disappears under a parked car. Hedy startles when she hears boys' voices. Three of them have come into view, strolling down the centre of the empty road with lazy, scuffing feet, tossing a ball back and forth, shouting to one another. She knows them – Billy, Frank and George – boys in Scott's gang. Frank once tried to kiss her and she punched his face. Her hand hurt like hell, but it was worth it. They glance over at the bungalow, three faces turning in unison, eager eyes searching something out. Billy slaps Frank on the shoulder, making him stagger. She hears laughter. Hedy shrinks back, crouching under the level of the window, listening for their receding footsteps, their fading voices.

A bluebottle rises heavily, buzzing around her. It bangs against her forehead before veering off towards the window.

Why did Dad think there was something hiding in their kitchen? She's never seen him like that before, as if he'd been having a nightmare, except he'd been awake. He'd been like a crazy person, or maybe a wild drunk – only she hadn't smelt beer on his breath.

After the boys have gone and she feels safer, she realises she's hungry. She opens the refrigerator and takes out some milk, drinks it straight from the bottle, her teeth knocking against glass, liquid spilling over her chin. She finds a cold chicken leg and rips into it, swallowing without chewing. She puts the bone back in the fridge on the shelf. She thinks about taking Chris something. But if he's hungry he can get food for himself. He's not helpless. He's not a baby. Dad told Mom that all the time.

Hedy hopes that Mom is awake. But she's on her side, knees drawn up, hand flat on the pillow beside her cheek. She hasn't put on her nightie or brushed her teeth or rubbed cream into her face.

'Mom?' Hedy crouches beside her, shakes her shoulder. 'Mom?'

She's so quiet that Hedy thinks she's dead. Panic turns her insides to water. She grabs Mom's arm and yanks on it. Mom mutters, moving chapped lips and swollen tongue, sour breath hitting Hedy.

Hedy opens the window. Sluggish air hangs like a cloud outside. Nothing moves, just the planes overhead. She goes into the bathroom, her guts releasing in a rush, then gets onto the bed beside her mother, fully dressed in her softball uniform, and lies down on Dad's pillow. Her face is itchy with dried sweat. She smells curdled milk on her shirt. She watches the remains of the evening light spangling the ceiling, how the dull gold fades into nothing, and suddenly the bedroom is full of night. Above the trees the moon surfaces like a drowned face.

\*

Birds sing. Hedy listens to their warbling as she stares up at the same ceiling as the night before, except now it's lit with lemon yellow. She woke with the sunrise, hearing the first lone song-bird before the rest joined in. A jet roars over the roof, hurtling into the far blue, a glittering speck. In the outside world, the day begins as if nothing is wrong. Beside her, Mom sighs and turns on the pillow, licking her lips, clearing her throat. She opens bloodshot eyes, stares at Hedy, uncomprehending. Then she takes a short, shallow breath. 'No,' she says. 'No.'

'What about something to eat?' Hedy scrambles out of bed. 'Or coffee? I know how to make it.'

Mom puts her fingers over her eyes. 'Pills,' she murmurs. 'Give me my pills.'

'But you've been asleep a long time.'

Mom sticks out her hand silently like a beggar. Hedy finds a small brown bottle beside the bed. She squints at it, looking for a label. There isn't one, but she remembers that Mom usually takes two tablets. 'Here.' She tips the yellow capsules into Mom's palm, passing her the water from the table.

Mom throws her medicine down, gulps the liquid. Then she pushes her feet out of the sheets and stumbles from the room. Hedy can hear her peeing, the flush of a chain. She comes back, winding her way to the bed, uncertain feet hardly clearing the ground. Her crumpled, slept-in dress is twisted to the side. Hanks of hair hang around her sallow cheeks. She falls onto the pillow. 'Christopher?'

'He's OK,' Hedy says. 'I'll get him dressed. Give him breakfast.'

Mom nods and her eyelids flutter and droop. She's gone again. Hedy wants to drag her mother out of bed, shake her into behaving right. Mom needs to act as if everything's going to be fine, because it will be as soon as Dad is released. Mom should

192

be up and dressed, her mouth bright with lipstick; she should be cross with Hedy for sleeping in her clothes; she should be making breakfast with an apron tied around her waist.

Hedy waits for a moment outside Chris's door, touching the handle. She feels bad that she said those terrible things. She didn't mean any of it. She feels guilty that she didn't help him into bed last night. He must have struggled alone. He missed his bath. He was stupid to mess with Scott, but it doesn't matter now. He's her brother, whatever he did. Only Dad matters, getting him back, making them a family again.

She turns the handle. She'll apologise. She'll whizz up Chris's favourite milkshake, and then read the rest of *The Day of the Triffids* out loud. They'll laugh about Scott, if not today, then sometime soon, when Dad is home and Mom is better.

But the bottom bunk is empty, the sheets pulled up neatly. She drops onto the cover, resting her hand on the smooth white pillow. The bed hasn't been slept in. She won't let herself panic. Think, she tells herself. Think. Her chest is tight, her heart squeezed flat. Hedy looks out of the window towards the forest, where sunshine tips the pines, the sky above sketched with vapour trails.

She bangs on the door of number five with a clenched fist. Betty answers, her face surprised, and then at once interested, listening. Hedy can see she knows about Dad, but hopes Scott hasn't mentioned Chris and what happened yesterday.

A radio is on somewhere in the house, Elvis Presley's shaky voice singing 'Don't Be Cruel'. There's a smell of fried eggs. Coffee. Scott's voice shouting over the song, 'Hey, where's my green shirt?'

Hedy takes a step back, her gaze fixed on the shadowy interior. 'Please would you go to our house and watch Mom,' she says quickly. 'She's sick.'

'One of her turns again? Oh, Lord! I can imagine. Want me to come right away?'

Hedy nods.

'It's in your drawer, honey,' Betty shouts over her shoulder. 'Why is it men can't find anything?' She tut-tuts, batting blackened lashes. 'I'm sorry to hear about your dad.' Her voice is hushed, as if he's dead. 'Let me get my things.' She reaches behind her for a red handbag, opens it, takes out a pair of dark glasses and slips them on. 'I'm popping over to Ruby's,' she yells into the house. Then to Hedy, 'Are you hungry, sweetie? Have you and your brother had breakfast? Want me to fix you some pancakes?' Over the top of the sunglasses, Hedy can see her noticing the dirty softball shirt, milk-stained, the ratty tangle of her plait.

'No thank you. I have an errand to run.'

'But Hedy . . .'

Hedy turns and walks away. She can feel the snag of Betty's unspoken words trailing behind her, knows that Betty's standing on the doorstep staring. Rolling her shoulders, Hedy breaks free of Betty, Scott and all the rest of them; she strides out, jogging and then sprinting along the sidewalk towards the perimeter fence.

Before she plunges into the trees, Hedy takes one last glance behind her. Behind barbed wire, a shimmering wave hangs over the airfield, a gasoline mist, grounded jets mirrored in the runway.

The forest closes around her, cool and dappled. Hedy thought she'd remember the way to the stone, but the trees all look the same. She listens to the green hush of their exhalations, feeling them bending towards her, watching her with wooden eyes. The lack of view makes her disorientated, and she's tramping round in circles like last time, shouting Chris's name into the silence, hearing it echo back. There are spent cartridges on the ground. She prods them with her toe and wonders who's been here with a rifle, what they killed. Rabbits? She's hoping she'll see the kids so they can help her. Maybe Chris is with them. She looks at her watch. She's been in the forest for over an hour. Panic fills her throat. Mom might be awake. Hank might have come with news of Dad.

'Chris!' she yells. 'This isn't funny. Come home. I'm sorry, OK? I didn't mean those things. Chris!'

She finds herself among beech trees, the air different here, a gleaming yellow, bright moss under her feet. She doesn't recognise this bit of the forest. She finds herself back at the perimeter fence. 'Damn.' She touches the mesh and remembers that the kids' house is next to the fence on the other side of the runway. She just has to follow the wire. Keep it on her left.

The path winding alongside the base is knobbled with tree roots that catch her feet, making her stumble. She jumps when a rabbit springs in front of her, skidding away under the fence. She looks at her watch again, glances up and sees the church tower poking above the mesh. The kids' house is right around the next corner. Her legs flash under her, red and white, dust-streaked.

The way the roof sags in the middle makes the cottage look broken-backed. She unhooks a loop of twine, goes through a low side gate into a garden. A collection of outbuildings cluster next to a ragged hedge. Dismantled machines, including a small tractor, squat in the dirt, leaking oily shadows. There's an air of neglect, a lot of bird shit, but when Hedy turns to look at the wide vegetable garden, she sees that it's busy with nets, neat trellises strung with beans, raspberries glinting under green leaves.

Hedy can't see anyone. 'Hello?' she tries. The air is thick with heat, threaded through with the sound of bees. She stands in the sunlight, squinting at the darkened windows, at the hens scratching in the shade. She feels oddly invisible, and very thirsty. She looks over at the pump; she has an urgent need to splash her face, drink from her cupped hands. She goes over and grasps the long, curved handle.

A door in one of the tarred sheds opens and a bald man comes out. She moves back from the pump. He's holding up both hands, shining red. Drips from his fingers roll down his wrists, twists of scarlet, like ribbons. He has an apron wrapped around him, dark and slick with the colour.

Hedy is transfixed, unable to move. She's not invisible after all, because he's watching her, his gaze a line, hooking her in with his narrowed eyes. He brings the stink of a butcher's counter with him. He stops at the pump and pushes the handle with his elbow, sticks his hands under the water, and all the time he's staring at her as if he can read something written on her forehead.

The water gurgles, spouting out, becoming pale pink in the sunlight, falling into the trough, into dark water littered with sodden feathers. He looks back to the shed, the open door. Inside the dim interior she can make out a shape, a fleshy heaviness. Flies have followed him in a hungry cloud; their senseless buzzing batters around them; one of them bounces off his shiny scalp. A streak of blood there like paint.

'What do you want?' He dries his hands on his trousers.

Hedy can't remember the names of the children. Is this their father? Her throat closes. 'I'm looking for my brother.'

'Not here.' He blocks the sun. She's trapped inside his shadow. She looks down, sees the knife at his belt.

She clears the gate in one stride, and she's running past the derelict church, stumbling towards the fence. Beyond the mesh, the distant base is an impossible mirage. She can't reach it. There's no way over. All those soldiers, and not one to help her. There's a shout behind. And Hedy falters, slows, glances over her shoulder, because it isn't the man.

The girl – Nell – is following her. She covers the ground without seeming to touch it. She's hardly panting as she catches up, grinning, 'Scared of blood?'

Hedy looks past her at the cottage and the shed.

'My dad. He's gutting deer. Went out last night. Poaching. That's why he didn't want you around. Didn't know if you'd snitch on us.'

Hedy remembers her real purpose with a sick jolt. 'Have you seen Chris?'

'The crip?' Nell's hair's grown out a bit; it wisps close to her head like a halo. She pulls at a strand, winding it around her finger, and shrugs. 'No.'

Hedy's lungs falter. Panic rising. 'I need to find him.' She spins around to face the forest, colours blurring. 'Take me to the stone circle. Please.'

Nell folds her arms. 'Which one?'

Hedy stares at Nell. There's nothing inside the other girl's expression to say that this is a trick. Nell's small face tilts to the side. 'You mean the one we showed you before? By the oak?'

Hedy drops her head, her arms hanging. 'I didn't know there was more than one.'

'Come on then.' Nell walks. Her bare feet etched with scars, straight toes pointing the way. 'There's a few scattered about,' she's saying. 'Old Joe likes the one near the oak best. Sleeps there all night sometimes, like he's guarding it.'

'What about those homeless men we saw? Would they hurt Chris?'

Nell doesn't reply, just sets off at a jog. Hedy follows. Nell veers away from the path, between the trees. She parts bracken, steps over rotten stumps, her body slipping around obstacles, touching them as if she loves each one. Her naked feet are silent, spread like paws. Hedy envies Nell's certainty, her belonging. A squirrel balances head down, gripping the bark of a pine trunk, tail twitching over its shoulder. It watches them, turns and scurries up the tree.

They keep going. The pines fall away and become gleaming beeches. Pines again. Scratchy low branches, the ground crusty and dead in the deep shade. They get back onto a path.

'Over there,' Nell says. And Hedy recognises the silver birch trunks, their scattering of leaves, shining coins under the dark pines.

At each footstep, her heart thuds, drum beats softened inside earth, a pulse echoing through her bones. The air pools around them like stagnant water closing over their heads. Hedy's throat is thick; she can hardly breathe. Nell feels it too – the wrongness – because she stops, lets Hedy go on without her.

At the foot of the oak tree, there is a twist of shadows, and with a shock she realises that Old Joe is there, hunkering down between the roots. He moans when he see her, puts his hands over his face, rocking back and forth on his haunches.

Above her something creaks and turns. A shadow slides across her, darkening the space, dark on dark, making her shiver. She looks up. A boy stares down. His eyes ripped buttons. His mouth a slash of flesh. His head is bent at an odd angle, rope choking under his chin, his face mottled purple, bloated into a cruel cartoon of his real one. Chris. How can that be him? Dangling among leaves. There are little crosses hanging from the branches all around him. One of his shoes has fallen to the ground. The rope above him creaks and turns.

She opens her mouth to scream. A white sound slicing the air. Her twin's name rips from her throat, over and over, his name repeating, stuttering wildly through the branches, making the birds fly up.

She's on her knees, the trees tilting and whirring around her. The ground sinks and shifts. She's crawling through the dry crackle of needles and leaves, ants under her fingers. She crouches below his body, and then she is reaching up to claw at his foot in a red sock, clutching the bones of his toes, stiff through slippery fabric. She has to get him down. The sock comes off in her hands, red sliding between her fingers, revealing milk-pale skin, a thin naked foot dancing alone in the space above.

'Help me,' she cries. She looks behind her. Nell has disappeared. Old Joe takes his fingers away from his eyes and stares through the bristle of hair, but he doesn't move. His mouth gapes.

'Help me get him down!'

At last, Joe limps forwards, the palms of his hands turned outwards, so that she sees fresh sore marks there. He opens his mouth and strange, ugly mutterings and squawkings come out, more animal than human.

She glances at the inflamed wheals on his palms, the raw flesh. Nausea rises into her throat. Rope burns.

She sobs as the full realisation swoops through her, and she edges backwards, away from the old man, slipping on fallen leaves and roots. Fear is a pulse under her grief, a drum beat inside her skull.

Then there is the crackle of static, the snap and rustle of feet through undergrowth. Joe blinks, tortoise-slow, and turns to watch a line of men approaching. They come through the trees, leaves stuck into their helmets, moving in formation, quick hand movements directing each other. Military authority, loud as the shouted instructions that stutter over the walkie-talkie, fills the space, makes the moment real but impossibly distant.

A man in uniform, his face blackened, takes her arms and leads her to the side. She watches another man untie the rope lashed around the tree, while two of them lower Chris gently, working hand over hand to take him down through the branches and leaves, taking him into their waiting arms, gathering him to them tenderly.

There are questions, kind, practical. She can't answer, can't speak. Steel glints as handcuffs snap around Old Joe's wrists. He doesn't resist, just keeps looking at her with pale eyes, his mouth making those broken sounds inside the tangle of hair.

Four men carry Chris between them, and she's confused by the unfamiliar softness of her brother's body, the limpness of his cradled spine. The group in combat clothing winds through the pines, a solemn ritual procession, towards two jeeps parked near the fence. She keeps her gaze on Chris, watching as he's handed onto a stretcher, lying on the narrow canvas as if he's sleeping, the lines of his body fluid as they never were when he was alive. His chin is folded onto his chest, one arm dangling before it's placed beside him. Someone has unlocked his neck ring, undone the girdle and iron bars. Someone has taken him out of the brace. Old Joe.

Old Joe has killed her brother.

# TWENTY

Betty comes and goes, as do several of the other wives. They've set up a rota, taking it in turns to arrive on the doorstep with casseroles, fried chicken and Miracle Whip. They make cups of coffee or tea. They run the vacuum over the carpets, unload bags of shopping onto the kitchen table. Mom does not get up. She lies in her darkened bedroom. Doctor Rowland visits. He brings more bottles of pills. Through the open door, Hedy watches as he slides a fine needle into Mom's arm. The skin on her arm around the tributaries of veins is brown like a bruised peach. The narcotics tilt her back over the edge, make her sleep and sleep.

Hank is there sometimes, too. He sits with Mom, talks to her quietly when she opens her eyes. She whimpers, her fingers working against the sheet, trying to tug it over her head. Hedy knows that she wants to disappear, to follow the part of her already lost.

Behind closed doors, Hedy hears the to and fro of whispered conversations that stop as soon as she enters the room. The adults look at her as if she's a problem they have to solve. Betty combs out Hedy's ruined plait, and puts her into a hot bath. She kneels beside it and makes Hedy soap herself all over with rose-scented bubbles and then hands her clean clothes to put on. 'There. Much better. Nice to see you in a dress.' She aims a drier at Hedy's wet hair and brushes it out. 'Such a pretty colour,' she murmurs, as she weaves it tight and sleek.

'What about my dad?' Hedy asks Hank. 'Can I see him yet?'

Hank holds her wrists with both his hands. 'I'm sorry. He's facing a court martial. He can't see anyone right now.'

'Does he know? Does he know about Chris?'

Hanks nods.

'I want to see Dad,' she whispers.

'Of course you do.' Hank places his hand on her shoulder. 'I'll try to arrange a visit for you.'

'How did the soldiers know?' she asks.

'Know what?'

'How did they know Chris was dead? How did they know to find us by the oak?'

'They were practising manoeuvres. A routine exercise. Lucky for you they were. It was too late for your brother. But if those soldiers hadn't arrived when they did,' Hank shakes his head, 'that man would have hurt you, too.'

It should have been her with the rope round her neck. Not her brother. He never did or said anything bad in his whole life. He can't be gone. She keeps thinking he'll limp through the door. She gets out all the exercise books filled with his neat writing and reads his stories. Spaceships and aliens. His words pull her inside them, make her forget for whole moments at a time where she is and what has happened. In his room, she flips through his collection of ten-cent comics, *Weird Science* and *Strange Worlds*, *Astounding Super-Science Fantasies*, running her fingers over the colourful images, over paper his fingers have touched. She lies on the bottom bunk with their copy of *The Day of the Triffids* clutched to her belly. They only had one chapter left to go. She stares up at the grab bar above her head.

His clothes are folded in drawers, and she pulls them out in armfuls, scattering them on the carpet in a tumbled pile. He will never wear them again. The image of Chris hanging in the tree comes back, his blue protruding tongue. She gasps and drops to her knees as if someone's struck the back of her legs with a baseball bat. Why did she say those things? The last things she ever said to him. Shame withers her insides, bones and organs deflating like old balloons, disintegrating, collapsing. She scoops up a T-shirt, pushing it against her eyes. The pressure of her grief forces her down, and she slumps on her side, curling into a ball among the jumble of clothes, burying her face in them, sniffing for his smell. She can drowse for a while like this, wrapped in his shirts, one of his stories clutched in her hand. She wakes with dribble on her chin, stiff from the floor, her shoulder aching.

She takes off the dress and stuffs it into the waste-paper bin under his desk. She picks up a jumper from the mess on the floor, the indigo one with darned elbows, and then she drags out his favourite blue jeans. She zips them up over jockey briefs. The jeans fit, the jumper's baggy from being stretched by the brace. His Keds are too big, so she wears her own. She chooses the polka-dot scarf to wear around her neck, wrapping it close against her, inhaling the metal of the brace, worn-in sweat, his freckled skin.

Hedy pads silently into the bathroom and locks the door. She finds Dad's razor and grabs her plait, slippery and clean, pulls it over her shoulder and hacks at it with the blade, sawing through it strand by strand, until she holds it in her hand like a small pelt.

She drops the plait in the bin, uses Mom's nail scissors to neaten up the ragged ends, cropping close to her ears. She leans across the basin, nose to nose with the mirror so that Chris will come closer. He's just inches away, looking serious and tired and almost like himself. Her breath mists the glass, smudging his face. Her lips find his cold, hard mouth. 'I'm sorry,' she says. 'I'm sorry. I'm sorry. I'm sorry.'

Sandy is in the kitchen with the radio on, making supper. Hedy can smell frying onions and something greasy. She goes into Mom's bedroom, approaching the bed softly. She sits next to the shape swathed in the pink coverlet.

'Mommy.' She prods her thigh. 'Mommy. Wake up.' She leans over her, raising her voice. 'Wake up.'

Mom's face twists on the pillow, frowning, eyes closed.

Hedy takes her mother's hot hand from under the sheet and squeezes, nails nipping feverish flesh. Mom stirs, rising to the surface of herself reluctantly, a half-drowned swimmer coming up from the depths. Her dull eyes open slowly. She gazes at Hedy, her expression changing as it clarifies with recognition, brightens with joy. She opens her mouth, a sound coming out, half gasp, half sob. Their fingers tangle. Mom struggles to sit up, reaching to scoop Hedy into her arms.

Hedy leans her cheek on her mother's shoulder. She buries further in, pressing her nose through folds of nightdress. Mom's skin smells medicinal and sharp. Hedy nudges into the hands stroking her shorn hair, her naked neck. She knows that Mom believes she's holding Chris in her arms, and Hedy wishes she could really become her brother – then he would be in the world instead of her as he deserves to be, and Mom would be happy because she always loved Chris best. Mom's chest convulses with sobs. The dry rattle of her inflamed throat is at Hedy's ear as she whispers his name.

*Christopher*, she croons. My *baby*.

Tapping her mother's back with quick pats. *Yes. It's okay, Mommy. It's me. I'm here.*

They are twins, and that means more than anyone else understands or knows. They used to have the same dreams – exactly the same. She felt his pain in the aching of her own spine. When they touched he took strength from her, energy flowing like milk through their joined hands. Hedy finished his sentences, understood his fears. She was his protector. Death can't separate them. She will wear him on her skin, carry him with her. She can change the way things are. She can make him stay.

# TWENTY-ONE

Hank squats on his haunches beside her. 'It's best you live with the Lansenses for a while, until your mom's well again.'

'I don't want to.'

'I know it's hard. But you can't stay in the house alone. Betty's offered to take you.'

She's too tired to fight. It won't be for long, she thinks.

Betty arrives with a bright smile and bustles around, opening drawers and cupboards, packing a case for her. When she leaves the room, Hedy opens it up again, throws her skirts and knickers in the garbage and repacks it with the rest of Chris's things.

Betty's mouth tightens when she finds the clothes in the trash. 'Come on now, sweetie. Let's at least take some of these pretty things, too. You don't really want to look like a boy, do you?'

'Let her, if she wants to wear her brother's clothes. What harm can it do?' Hank says when he comes to drive them to Lincoln Avenue. 'She's been through enough already.'

At number five, Betty shows Hedy where she can put her

stuff, opening up the white chest of drawers and wardrobe in her new room. But Hedy's not going to unpack anything. She doesn't want to settle in the Lansenses' spare room with the apricot bedcover and matching lampshades. Dad will have his trial and be acquitted and Mom will come home.

Along with Chris's clothes, she's taken Dad's transistor radio, Chris's favourite sci-fi novels, and all Chris's notebooks with his stories written out in his neat writing. On the first night, she tells Betty she has a tummy ache so she can miss supper, and she lies on top of the apricot bedcover and reads the last chapter of *The Day of the Triffids* aloud. And then she turns over onto her side and sobs. She sobs until she can't breathe, sitting up to gasp for air, her eyes so puffy that she's blind.

'They're packing up your house,' Scott says as he shovels waffles into his mouth. 'I saw when I cycled to the com this morning.'

Hedy runs all the way to Roosevelt Road, and it's true, there's military personnel all over the bungalow and a removal van parked outside. She tries to stop them, beats her fists against the man who is going through the rooms with a clipboard, and the two men in overalls carrying Dad's armchair and Mon's vanity table out onto the sidewalk.

The man with the clipboard takes her arms, holding her away from him when she tries to kick his shins. The others laugh until they understand who she is. 'Sorry, kid. Another family's moving in,' the man in charge tells her. 'All your possessions are going into storage. They'll be safe.'

Betty arrives, breathless, her dark glasses on, handbag swinging, and takes Hedy's hands, gripping tight. She apologises to the men in her grown-up voice and pulls Hedy away. 'Let them do their job, hon. It's just procedure. There's a wait list for families needing housing. Let's go to the com, shall we? What candy do you like best?'

'I'm not five.' Hedy tugs her fingers from Betty's.

Back at Lincoln Avenue, Hedy goes straight to the spare room and shuts the door. She has to do something. She tears a blank page from one of Chris's exercise books, sits on the bed, and writes to President Eisenhower at the White House. She tells him about the unfair arrest of her dad, and how he's a war hero who would never do anything to hurt his country. She asks Betty for an envelope and overseas stamp and Betty, busy fixing her face in front of the vanity mirror, gives it to her without asking questions. Hedy goes to the end of the road and posts the letter. She doesn't know how long it will take to get to America, but knowing she's sent it makes her feel better. They won't let her see Dad, but she'll write him a note too explaining what she's done and that he'll be home soon. She'll give it to Hank to deliver.

That evening they have meatballs, with apple pie for dessert. Hedy sits opposite Scott. He keeps his head down, ignoring her. There's a knock on the door, and Ed goes to answer it. She hears Hank's voice. Ed calls Betty away from the table and they go into the living room together and shut the door.

Scott shakes his head. 'What now? Bet it's something to do with your dad or your mom.'

Hedy sits still. She has the same feeling, only she wouldn't admit it to Scott. A falling-down feeling inside her bones.

'Why are you being mean?' she asks.

He picks his teeth, forehead wrinkling as if he's considering the question. 'Look, I'm sorry your brother died. But he was a freak,' he raises an eyebrow. 'It's the truth. You're all right. But your family is nuts.'

'Did you do something to him? If you did I'll kill you.'

'Cool it.' He smirks.

Blood rushes to her face.

'Course I didn't do anything to him,' Scott drawls. 'Just told him a few home truths.'

Hedy half-stands, hands curling into fists. She is shaking with rage. But the adults are back, standing in a little huddle, and Betty says to Scott, 'Sweetie, could you just go to your room for a few minutes? We need to talk to Hedy.'

Scott sighs. They listen to him thumping down the corridor and the slam of his door. Hank pulls up a chair and sits with their knees touching. She can see from the look on his face that whatever it is, it's bad. She closes her eyes and puts her hands over her ears. Hank peels them away gently.

They got Doctor Rowland to come afterwards. He gave her a shot in her arm. She went to sleep under the apricot spread, diving backwards inside herself, down and down, and as she fell her last thoughts were about the atomic bomb, because it came, exactly like they said in school, smashing into the earth out of the blue. Bang. Her world burning up, and her crouched on the floor among the broken, fried leftovers, somehow the last one left alive.

Dad's funeral is days later. Betty makes her wear a navy dress and Hedy doesn't argue because she feels groggy and her tongue is furry and difficult to move. The fabric scratches her legs and makes her feel like someone else. She stands between Betty and Ed watching the coffin slide through the curtains. Betty reaches down and puts her hand on her shoulder. Her big diamond ring presses into Hedy's skin. The Stars and Stripes pleats as it gets caught in the mechanism until someone pulls the flag away from the bare wood, folds it up in their arms. The flag isn't for burning. Just Dad.

'Your father didn't deserve a military funeral. He was a traitor,' Scott hisses afterwards.

'Why did Scott say that?' she asks Hank back at the house, where the grown-ups are drinking whisky and talking in hushed voices. 'About Dad being a traitor?'

'A traitor?' Hank leans down and sighs. 'Nothing was proved. What we do know is that he was a war hero. That's what you need to remember.'

A war hero who hung himself in his cell.

In the evenings, Hedy switches on Dad's transistor radio, the one he listened to games on, the one he played music on in the evenings when he and Mom danced in the kitchen, laughing. She runs scenes behind her lids, choosing the happiest memories. She rereads Chris's favourite books, turning dog-eared pages. She listens to baseball games on the radio. She wears her brother's clothes, sees his reflection in the mirror. Nothing brings them back.

September comes and Mom isn't better. Hedy hasn't been able to see her yet. She's still resting at the asylum. They make Hedy go back to school. An invisible barrier stands around her, keeping people away, her own high fence with rolls of wire, prickly spikes of misery and shame. She sits in Chris's clothes and stares at her desk.

# TWENTY-TWO

A door opens. Ruby raises her head with difficulty. Her skull is heavy. A young woman with a freckled face stands over her. 'Time for your treatment,' the young woman says and holds out her hand to help Ruby up from the bed. They walk down a corridor painted eau de nil. Ruby is tired and it's hard to pick up her feet properly and sometimes she stumbles and the young woman tightens her hold on her elbow. They go through a doorway into a small room and the door shuts behind. There is a gurney and a crowd of men in white coats, smiling. They are all smiling. They pat the bed as if it's a treat for her, an afternoon lie-down. Ruby is glad to stretch out on the bed. She would like to sleep. The freckled face comes closer. 'Open your mouth.' She puts a rubber block tenderly between Ruby's lips. 'No need to be afraid.'

But the block in her mouth feels like a stone, and she can't breathe. They are putting straps and shackles across her. Pulling tight. Panic thrashes. No. No. No. She's caught. Hands press on her shoulders, arms, legs, pinning her down. Something sticky and cold on her temples and a voice telling her to count backwards. Bam. Every nerve in her body alight. She's on a plane powering through the sky, but it's all gone to hell. It's hit, metal ripping into scraps, searing her limbs, tearing her muscles, setting fire to her hair as she falls down, down, down through the screaming blue. *Todd*, she's trying to yell, but there's a stone in her mouth and blood on her tongue.

Vicious, crippling headaches. Her body bruised and sore as if she's been hurled to the bottom of a steep flight of stairs. Thoughts in her brain bob up like balloons. What has Hedy done? Where is Chris? Why doesn't Todd fetch her home? If she asks the questions out loud, they give her pills, cold baths. Whatever she says or does, they take her back to the room, to complete her course, to make her well.

She falls from the sky over and over until she's good. She swallows her medicine and keeps her arm steady for the needle. She doesn't turn her head to look at the door as she passes through the eau de nil corridor, her slippers slapping beneath her on her way to the dayroom. She doesn't want to go back there. She can smell the burning rubber, singed flesh. Ruby puzzles through her memory, trying to find paths to follow, but all that comes back is the noise of jets and dark pines behind a bungalow, a ring of them around the base, like a higher fence, impenetrable, seeming to encroach a little more every day. She lost people in that place, her children, her husband. She doesn't know how it happened, where they are now, why they don't come.

# TWENTY-THREE

The pines behind the fence bristle with dark green, but the leaves on the tree outside the bungalow in Lincoln Avenue are turning orange. After school, Hedy changes direction from her route back to the Lansenses', and walks down Main Street, keeping on across the outer road towards the gap in the fence and the forest. It's taken her this long to pluck up courage. She's going to visit the stone circle, even though she's scared. Something felt wrong about her memories from that day, not just the horror of it, something else catching at the edges of her thoughts.

She walks up the bank, standing just where the gap should be. But it's not there. Puzzled, she touches shiny new wire, a whole section that's replaced the torn fencing between the stone uprights. She stands and stares at the trees, her fingers curled through mesh. She's about to turn away when she hears a shout.

Someone's coming through the pines. A thin girl in an old coat and bare legs appears through the branches. 'Bloody hell,' the girl says. 'I thought you were a ghost. You look just like him.'

Nell's hair is longer and her face is sharper than Hedy

213

remembers. Hedy wasn't expecting to see her; it makes her feel confused.

Nell stares. 'Why are you dressed like him?'

Hedy's mouth is dry. She swallows, the words not coming.

'I've been here after school nearly every day,' Nell goes on. 'Thought you'd show up some time or I'd see you and shout. I was going to break into the base, but they mended the fence the day after.'

'Break into the base?'

'I wanted to tell you something.' Nell curls her fingers through the mesh next to Hedy's, and leans her face close to the wire. 'About your brother.'

'I hate Old Joe.' Hedy's words come out in a rush and a sob thickens and sticks in her throat. 'Why did he do it? I hate him. I hate him.'

'Old Joe didn't do it.'

'Yes. He did.' Hedy's heart starts thumping at her chest. 'He's in prison.'

'No.' Nell shakes her head. 'I told you. He's harmless.'

Hedy's frown deepens. 'You're wrong.' She backs away from the fence. 'He was mad. He killed Chris.' Mad people. Drunk people. Bad things happening everywhere. Mom always said so. Hedy didn't understand before. 'I was there . . . I saw what he did to my brother . . . ' She slams her fists against the wire. 'You don't know. You've got no right to talk about Chris. You've got no right to say those things . . . '

'All right,' Nell says quickly. 'I just . . . I can't believe it was Joe.'

Hedy folds her arms. 'Well, it was.'

'That's a rum 'un.' Nell bites her lip and frowns. 'Maybe I was wrong about him. I heard about your dad, too,' she says in a hushed voice.

Hedy starts. 'How?'

'My nan. Works as a cleaner at the bowling alley.'

'What did she say?'

'She said ... she said he killed himself.' Nell lowers her voice to a whisper and edges closer, her mouth at the wire. 'She said he must have done it 'cos he didn't want to face the electric chair.'

'Electric chair?'

'Yes. Because he was a spy, your dad, wasn't he? For the Russians.'

Hedy steps back. The ground tilts under her feet. 'No. That's wrong. Dad would never do that.' Her head is full of thunder crashing between her temples. Her mouth is dry. She growls, 'Take it back.'

Nell looks at her steadily. 'I only said what I heard.'

'Take it back.'

Nell shrugs. 'He wasn't a spy then. He's your dad, so I suppose you know.'

'Tell your nan she heard wrong. Tell her to stop spreading lies.' Hedy has a sickness in her throat. She spits onto the ground and hunches her shoulders. Her stomach hurts. 'I've got to go. I'll be late for dinner.'

She walks away, slipping on the grassy bank. Nell's calling after her, but the scream of a jet erases her words. The engine's roar gets into Hedy's bones, shaking them loose. She can't listen to Nell. Hedy saw Old Joe with her own eyes, saw the rope burns on his hands. Dad was a good man, a hero. She'll fight anyone who says different.

Scott has his gang round. They've shut themselves in Scott's bedroom. Hedy lies on her bed and switches on the radio. The news is on, and she's only half-listening, just wanting to block out the sound of the boys in the next room. *Antonio Vilas Boas, a Brazilian farmer, claims he's been abducted by extra-terrestrials,* the news reader is saying. *Boas claims to have seen a red star while he was ploughing a field at night to avoid high temperatures. He's reported being taken on board a spaceship and having encounters with beings from another planet.*

Hedy sits up, turning the dial. She presses a hand to her mouth. Hedy imagines Chris's reaction, hears his voice. *I told you there were aliens!* She knew Chris better than anyone. Nell doesn't know anything about him. She wasn't by the oak tree that day. If Old Joe didn't murder Chris, then the only other explanation could be that he killed himself. And then it would be her fault, because she didn't help him, because she left him on his own the night they took Dad away. Because she said those terrible things.

She wants to roll time up like a carpet, roll it back to the moment she failed him, and do it all differently, be the sister she should have been, the one he deserved.

Hedy hears Scott and the others coming out of his bedroom, then the front door slamming and Betty yelling at them. She goes to her window and lifts the curtain, watching them strolling down the street. Frank, Billy and Scott, easy in each other's company, with their big shoulders nudging one another and their hands thrust into pockets.

Betty and Ed are in the living room watching TV. Hedy doesn't want to join them, noticing them shift position on the sofa, suddenly more formal, watching her out of the corners of their eyes, with Betty saying silly, cheerful things, as if Hedy's life hasn't been blasted into a million pieces. If she could just go back to Mom and Dad sitting together after supper, Chris, clean-smelling from his bath, his hair damp, lying on his bed listening to her reading from a novel, she would promise anything, give up anything.

She opens her door into the hall, hearing the roar of a TV audience's laughter. She waits for a moment before she goes quietly to Scott's room and turns the handle, slipping inside. He never lets her past the threshold. There are empty Coke cans and candy wrappers all over the floor. The place smells of feet and old sweat. His baseball mitts dangle from the back of a chair. She'd like to take out some of her fury on something he cares about, rip up a comic or chuck one of his stupid trophies in the trash.

There's some kind of folder on the floor, half pushed under the bed. Hedy gets onto her knees and slides it out. It's a scrap book. She didn't think Scott and his lot were the type to collect stamps, or even baseball cards. She opens it. The pages are covered with articles torn out of newspapers and old pamphlets stuck down with globs of glue. She starts reading, and her breath quickens, her skin suddenly cold. Reports of beatings and burnings and lynchings. Blurry pictures of black people hanging from lampposts and trees. Men in white hoods. She's heard grown-ups making racial comments and jokes, seen the way Jimmy and the other black kids get bullied. There's no segregation on the base and not everyone likes it, especially not Southerners, she knows that. This book though, this book is disgusting. Evil. She kicks it back under the bed and sits down hard on the covers. She wishes she could punish Scott for being cruel to Chris, for saying mean things about him after he's dead, for telling lies about Dad. But he wasn't guilty of murder. It wasn't Scott who killed her brother or her father. They've been stolen from her, and there's nothing she can do about it. There's nobody to rage at. She slips off the bed onto the floor, sitting with her arms over her head, brow against her bent knees, sobbing into the dark cave of her own body.

# PART TWO

## The Farm

# TWENTY-FOUR

## 1958

Hedy stares out of the train window. The countryside is wet and tumbled, cows in fields, thickets of trees. Rooks rise from tall oaks, a swarm of black wings tugging at the sky like rain. Her reflection floats in between. The ghost of Chris hovering over leaves and wings. She blinks and looks down at her hands holding onto each other in her lap, reaches up to touch the shorn line at her neck, the collar of the plaid shirt.

'We were hoping your mom would be better by now,' Hank told her at Christmas. 'But she needs a little more time, so I think it's best you stay with a relative for a while. Your uncle in Norfolk has agreed to take you. We haven't managed to track down any Irish relatives yet. But if you'd rather ...'

'No.' Ireland was too far away from Mom. And she already knew her uncle. Ernest. Inside her head, she knew him.

Hank took her to the station and waited with her. When the train came, he found her a seat and put her case on the luggage rack. The whistle blew. Before he got off, he pressed a bag of lemon sherbets into her hand, stooped to kiss her short hair. 'Be brave, kid,' he said. She wanted to cling to his waist, ask if she couldn't live with him. She'd be no trouble. Instead, she got into the compartment, put her bag on the rack. As the train jerked and started to move, she yanked the strap to lower the window, leaning out so that she could keep him in her sights for as long as possible.

When she gets out, there's hardly anyone else on the platform. The guard signals with his flag, the train already disappearing on its way to somewhere called King's Lynn. A tall man with white-blond hair should be easy to spot, she thinks, the farmer in his big boots, carrying her mother's likeness on his face, an explorer who can pull a sledge over ice fields. Hedy stands, alert, watching the entrance. A station porter disappears through a doorway carrying a brown paper package. A boy, a bit older than her by the looks of him, leans against the wall, smoking, watching her before he flicks his cigarette onto the tracks and wanders away. She sits on a bench with her case beside her. She holds onto the handle. It's cold, and she shivers, pulling her coat closer. The minutes slip past, the afternoon fading into dusk. Her eyes close.

'I was expecting a girl.'

She sees his boots first, mud-splattered. Her uncle's big wellingtons. The man who's wearing them leans heavily on a stick, his body twisted to the side, one shoulder higher than the other. His torso, wrapped in a battered jacket, seems strangely foreshortened. His hips tilt like a listing boat so that his left leg is longer than his right. His hair is the colour of hay. Inside his pale eyes she glimpses Mom. He grunts, taps her leg with his stick. 'What's your name, boy?'

'I'm not Chris,' she says quietly. 'I'm Hedy.'

'What?' He scowls at her.

'My brother died. I'm his sister. I'm the girl.'

'You look like a boy.'

'I'm wearing his clothes.'

'A boy would have been more useful.' He turns away from her. 'Well, I haven't got all day.' He's limping away, and she picks up the bag and hurries after him, stumbling over her numb feet. He's opening the door of a small, box-like car parked outside. She goes to the boot to put her case in, but the man – her uncle – is holding out a metal stick, bent like a piece of old pipe.

She takes the stick from him, stares down at it without really seeing it, puzzling something out in her head: how could he mistake her for Chris? The only explanation is he doesn't know her brother had scoliosis and wore a brace. That means Mom hasn't had any communication with her brother since leaving England. Not a word between them all that time.

'Never seen a starting handle before? Slot it into the front and give it a good thwack.'

Hedy finds the right place after fumbling along the bottom of the bonnet, under the bumper. She bends her knees for balance, sticks in the handle, grips it tight.

'Mind you keep your thumb up,' comes his voice.

The starting handle is cold in her hands. When she pushes, it's stiff and hard to turn.

'Pull it towards you,' he's shouting. 'Then let go.'

She manages after the third try, and the engine stutters into life. She climbs into the narrow front seat, cramming her bag into the footwell. The case forces her to sit with knees raised high. She doesn't know what to do with the handle, so she holds it across her lap, leaving oily smudges on Chris's best Levis. Her uncle releases the throttle and the car rolls away. Hedy can't see where they are, or where they're going, because the windows are made of a crackling brownish plastic. Her uncle peers through a hole he's cut in the windscreen, squinting into the wind.

Hedy strains to glimpse his hunched shape crammed behind the wheel in sideways glances. The not-knowing of it makes her dizzy. He is the reason Mom locked Chris into his neck ring and girdle, why she set her mouth whenever Chris cried to be let out. Why didn't she tell them?

The car jolts, and jolts again, and she guesses they've left the road and are lurching over a rutted track. The air coming through the hole in the windscreen brings new smells: sea salt and the deep, sweet stink of manure.

She has to open a gate. She watches the car drive through, and then hauls the gate closed after it, securing a metal hook through a ring. She glances around at a watery landscape, flat as Suffolk. Flatter, maybe. Channels of brown water dissect fields. There's more sky than land, and hardly a tree to break the monotony, reminding her, unexpectedly, of Iowa. In the distance, a couple of horses stand with their tails to the wind. Some red cows dip their faces at her through a wire fence.

The next time they stop, her uncle gestures that she get out.

She stands in a yard slick with mud. The light has almost gone, but she can make out a brick house, broken-backed like Nell's cottage, standing among a jumble of barns. Nothing is straight. The roof of the house drops and rears up. Each of the windows is a different size and shape. All the outbuildings are crooked too, lopsided walls patched together with wire fencing and rusted panels of corrugated iron. Several large pink pigs are asleep in a sty. She can hear the cawing of rooks, the wind in the trees.

With a fierce, hard bark, a dog comes barrelling out of the shadows at her. She sees teeth, a red throat. She raises her hands.

'Down!' her uncle shouts.

She thinks he means her, but the brindled dog has dropped

to its belly, and lies prone, a half-whine, half-growl gurgling from its broad chest.

'Don't touch him. He doesn't like strangers.'

The kitchen is so dark that Hedy can hardly see, and her uncle doesn't put the light on. She can taste smoke. The embers of a fire glow inside a wide fireplace, the silhouette of a kettle hanging over them. She follows him towards a door, banging her shin on an edge of something. The floor under her feet is slippery and uneven.

'There's soup on the range. Help yourself if you're hungry. I'm going to bed. I'll show you your room.'

She trails behind him up one flight of stairs, along a landing and then they mount a narrow, winding staircase. He hauls himself up, one step at a time, his hand on the rail, dragging air into his lungs as if he's been fished out of the sea. She worries that he might collapse in front of her. How would she move him?

It's an attic bedroom: black beams and little windows set into a sloping ceiling. There's a bed with an iron headboard, made up with white sheets and a blue blanket. A chipped chest of drawers slopes at an angle on the listing floor, and there's a stand with a china bowl and metal pitcher. It's cold. Hedy shivers. 'This was your mother's room,' he says, the words caught up in his wheezing.

Mom's room. She puts her case on the low-sprung mattress, then sits next to it. Her legs are too weak to stand; she's not sure she'll be able to take her clothes off.

'I'll expect you at five tomorrow. Sharp if you want breakfast.'

She didn't imagine the farm to be like this; she thought there'd be neat white fences, piles of fresh-smelling hay: a homely place like in *Anne of Green Gables*.

Shivering, she gets out the transistor radio and places it on a stool next to the bed. She switches it on to hear something comforting. But it only hisses with static, strange disjointed voices snapping in and out, sliding into a roar of nonsense. Slipping between icy covers, she tucks her feet up under her, hugging her arms around her knees. The sheets smell stale and unfamiliar, rough against her skin. The spongy mattress sucks her in, rolling her into the middle where her hip bone presses against something hard. A broken spring. She stuffs her fingers into her mouth to stop herself from howling. She wants to go to sleep, and wake up at home on the base with Mom cooking pancakes, Dad whistling in the bathroom, and Chris waiting for her to help get him dressed. But the picture of Dad in his cell slots behind her eyes, his feet kicking above the cold floor; and she tenses against a sudden swinging vertigo, knowing her father will never lie in a bed again, never stumble out of it in his striped pyjamas, yawning, flinging open the window to let in the morning.

Dad was decorated for bravery, but grief isn't a thing you can fight with weapons. He must have killed himself when he heard about Chris. Hank said her father was a hero at the funeral. But he also told her that Dad was going to talk to someone about his secret work. At least, she thinks Hank said that – now she can hardly remember. It's all muddled up. When she thinks of a spy, she sees a man with a shifting gaze under a trilby hat, a communist with a Russian accent. She rolls her cheek into the scratchy weave of the pillow. Sobs come from the pit of her belly, hard and tight. Tears flow, making her pillow wet and her eyes raw.

When she wakes, the room is still dark. There are no streetlights here, no cars crawling past or the noise of heels on sidewalks. But she can hear movement downstairs. Outside a cockerel crows. It must be morning, although it doesn't feel as if she's been asleep for more than moments.

# TWENTY-FIVE

It's warmer down here. There's a pan bubbling on the range, a wooden spoon sticking up. There's no sign of her uncle. Hedy sniffs warm oats; her stomach gurgles. She never did have any soup for supper. But as she moves around the table towards the pan, she hears a snarl. The dog is beneath her, sprawled on the floor next to the heat. He lifts his head, ears back, and his trembling lips show long teeth and mottled gums.

Hunger makes her brave. 'Good dog.' Hedy puts out a hand, letting him reach up and sniff. He gets up and moves away on stiff legs, the growl in his throat a low, discontented rumble. She scoops out a bowl of lumpy porridge and eats it standing up, without milk or sugar, keeping her eye on the dog.

Uncle Ernest comes in from the yard, stamping on the mat. The dog slinks to his side. He nods at her. 'Ever used a shovel?' He waves towards the door. 'Some lads are out there digging ditches. You can help. First you feed the cattle.'

'What about school?' she asks.

'You start Monday. There's a bus that will take you, goes from

227

the end of the lane. But you'll be doing chores before and after. Got to earn your keep. I've had no money from the air force.'

'It's only till Mom gets better. I won't be here long.'

'Maybe you won't.' He scowls. 'Maybe you will.'

Hedy shivers in Chris's checked jacket. She wishes she had gloves and a hat. A heavy, dank mist hangs in the distance, wrapping the fields in white, a gathering of ghosts watching and waiting. The dog follows them, lifting its leg against the wheel of the car, trotting around the yard, nose to the ground. Ernest limps over to a pile of muck and straw, pointing. 'Dig out enough mangels and swedes to fill that wheelbarrow and then I'll show you where to take it. Quick sharp.'

Ernest doesn't wear gloves on his reddened hands. The first finger of his right hand is missing from the middle joint, the flesh splayed and blunt. She glances away before he notices her looking, and picks up a pitchfork to root through the straw. The wood is rough, the pitchfork heavier than she'd imagined. Beneath the surface, she finds wizened vegetables. She forks them out, tossing them into the barrow, some of them disintegrating into pulp as they land, the stink of rot in her nostrils. When the barrow is full, she grasps the handles and pushes it after Ernest to the big barn. Cattle move towards the door, their eyes soft and yearning. The air around them is smoky with their breath. These ones are black and white, not the red ones she saw before. Ernest nods towards the manger and she tips the tumbling vegetables in, watching the cows push each other to get their noses into the trough.

'You do this every morning. Mangels and swedes, then over there, silage and grain. Hurry and pour it in. These animals rely on you now. You'll learn to milk them, too.'

Close up, the cows are much bigger than she'd thought. Powerful and broad-boned. One of them reaches a huge, dipped head towards her, blowing through a wet nose. She swallows and takes a step back.

'Friesians. Good milkers.' Ernest's voice softens. 'This is Betsy.'

Hesitantly, she puts a hand on its thick neck, feeling heat and soft fur against her chilled fingers. She glances up at her uncle, smiling. But he's already limping across the yard.

Hedy spends the rest of the morning digging with three boys. They are older than her, their chests and shoulders broad under their jumpers. It's hot work and they've taken off their coats and rolled up their sleeves. They don't say much at first, watching her struggle with the spade. The one with red hair laughs. 'Fancy Cole sending a girl to do man's work. Reckon you're new to this?'

The black-haired one joins in. 'Not much meat on you.' He pinches her arm, nearly encircling her bicep with the span of his hand. 'Why do you dress like a boy?'

She glares at him. 'I want to.'

'How old are you?'

'Thirteen.'

'You might be a tiddler, but least you have a straight spine,' the redhead says.

'My dad says there were other Coles with crooked spines too,' the black-haired boy says. 'A witch put a curse on their family.'

'My granddad says that Cole's father and mother were first cousins. Says that's why he's the way he is,' the smallest boy says.

'That's all just talk,' the red-haired boy says. He seems to be in charge. The others call him Peter. 'It's a disease, got some long name I can't remember. It goes down the generations. That's why she's lucky.' He nods at Hedy.

Hedy says nothing, keeps shoving the blade of her shovel against the hard earth. Peter leans on his spade. 'But I feel sorry for you anyway.' He jerks his head in the direction of the house. 'He's got the devil's temper.'

Hedy is weak from hunger. Blisters have appeared on her hands, some of them weeping, the skin peeled pink. Gripping the shovel is agony. The ground is cold and unyielding, like striking concrete with steel. The jolt goes through her whole body. 'Isn't it lunchtime yet?' she asks.

They laugh. 'Cole keeps to the old ways. We wait till Fourses. Mrs Rose will call us in. You better get your back into it or there'll be trouble.'

Two ditches are dug: deep pits carved out of the dirt, like graves. But there's more to be done, cutting switches to line the base of the ditches, covering those up with straw.

'Why are we doing this?' Hedy asks Peter, as she throws an armful of straw onto the network of branches.

'Drainage. Land would be a bog otherwise,' he says. 'Place got flooded out last year. Reckon the sea wants it back.'

When the day has gone from dusk to dark, a bell rings from the house and the boys gather their coats, following the sound and the glow of the lighted windows across the ground. In the kitchen, a tall bony woman in a floral apron takes a steaming cauldron off the range. This must be Mrs Rose, Hedy supposes. It's impossible to tell her age. Her face is the opposite of a rose. She seems carved out of rock, something pulled from a mountain, hardened by time, but then she smiles and her flint face changes, becomes petal-pinked. 'So you're Hedy,' she says, dishing out bowls of gravy with dumplings and hunks of bread. 'Wasn't there a film star with that name?'

The boys eat. There are no words, just slurping sounds, and the chink of spoons scraping the bottoms of bowls. Hedy swallows without tasting, scalding her tongue.

After the boys leave to cycle back to the village. Mrs Rose sets a cup of tea on the table and turns back to the sink, elbow deep in a washing-up bowl. Hedy watches her sinewy arms working, the twist of grey hair at the back of her head held up with kirby pins. She misses Mom. The missing is an ache closing her throat, different from the new ache in her bones and muscles. She has never felt so tired. She turns her hands over, looking at the raw mess.

'The state of you,' Mrs Rose says. 'I'll find some iodine for those blisters. What you want, young lady, is a bath.'

Hedy nods, thinking of the bliss of soaking in bubbles, remembering Mom's lavender salts. 'I'll go up now.'

But Mrs Rose is laughing. 'There's no bathroom in this house. There's a hip bath in the washhouse and hot water in the taps, thanks to the range. I can fill you a tub here before the fire, seeing as you're new to the place. I don't mind.'

Hedy doesn't want to be naked in the kitchen. What if her uncle came in? She shakes her head.

Mrs Rose makes a sound in her throat. 'I've had three children of my own. A grandchild, too. You don't need to be shy.' She smiles. 'I'm finished for the evening anyway. I come in every afternoon to cook supper and do a bit of tidying for the old man. I'll be off home and the old man is in bed – goes to sleep early. He won't be down again till morning. You can have a proper soak without worrying about interruptions.'

The tub is small and squat with a high metal back. Mrs Rose

drags it in and positions it next to the range. After she's filled it with buckets of hot water, she hands Hedy a sliver of green soap and a towel and leaves. Hedy undresses quickly, kicking herself out of her clothes, and steps into the tub. She lowers herself into the heat, and sits with her knees drawn up to her chest. The water's steaming, the bottom of the tub gritty against her buttocks. Mrs Rose left the door of the range open, and the smouldering coals give the only light in the room, smoky and dim and red. She sits without washing, letting the water grow cool, tensed for the sound of her uncle's uneven footsteps. She's rammed a chair under the door knob, just in case. But all she hears is the small tumble and spark of burning coals in the fire, and the snoring of the dog. She hugs her knees and leans her forehead against their bony shelf. Exhaustion dulls the ache of homesickness.

She gets out of the tub when the water is cold and dries herself on the scratchy towel. The dog raises his head to watch her, but he doesn't move from his basket by the fire.

In her room, there's one small looking-glass high on the wall. The night has turned the window into another mirror, her reflection coming back at her out of the darkness. She stares at her blurred face, seeing Chris there too, both of them stuck together, one the drawing and the other the tracing. Looking closer, their faces dissolve, disappearing into the landscape outside.

If she'd got to the oak tree earlier, could she have saved Chris from Old Joe? Stopped him from putting the rope around her brother's neck? And if Chris hadn't been murdered, would Dad still be alive? She doesn't know the answers to these questions; she only knows that if she'd been kind, if she'd been a proper sister, then everything would be different.

Curled in between cold sheets, wearing socks and a jumper, she holds her cupped hands to her face, blowing softly onto the sores. Tears come as soon as she puts her head on the pillow, a slow seeping of salt water. She presses the sheet over her face, blows her nose on its edges. She doesn't know how she's going to get through the days here – but perhaps it's her punishment, she thinks: what she deserves.

She wakes from a deep sleep into a room milky with moonlight, her heart beating fast. There's a damp patch under her as if she's wet herself. She did that once in a dream, thought she'd gone to the toilet and woke up in a soggy bed. She switches on the light and pulls back the sheet; a smear of red glistens in the middle of the bed. Hedy reaches between her legs, feeling the crotch of Chris's pyjama trousers; her fingers coming away sticky.

# TWENTY-SIX

The hip bath is still in the kitchen, the metal tub half-full of cold, scummy water. The dog is sleeping on his side before the range. He must be getting used to her, Hedy thinks, because he can't be bothered to move, observing her out of one half-closed eye. She snatches a few mouthfuls of the simmering porridge, eating it straight from the pan with the wooden spoon, keeping a watch out of the window for her uncle, ears pricked for the drag and thump of his step on the stair.

Outside, a hard rain is falling through early-morning darkness. It doesn't look as though it's going to let up. She finds an oilskin hanging from a hook in the boot room and puts it on, the material crackling around her. She pulls the hood up over her face, and pats the back pocket of her trousers; all the money that Hank gave her is there, more than enough for train tickets. She has the address of the place where Mom is being looked after, where Hedy imagines that she's having a lot of afternoon naps with her shoes off and the blinds closed.

Hedy looks left and right cautiously as she leaves the house.

The water is seeping into her Keds before she's made it half-way across the yard. A ripe animal smell reminds her of her neglected duty. She feels bad about the cows. But she can't stop. With every step, she expects to hear her uncle's angry shout, her shoulders hunched against the thought of it.

He said there was a bus that went into the village. He said it went from the end of the lane. The silver frost has gone, sucked away in mud and filthy puddles, but the air and ground are spiked with its icy chill. Hedy walks along the rutted track, head bowed against sharp fingers of water. She has cramps in her stomach. Dribbles of rain slip off the edge of the oilskin hood, finding their way under her clothes.

She's ripped up a T-shirt and folded wads to line her jockey shorts. She's heard other girls call their time of the month the curse. She can see why now. It hurts with a dragging ache deep inside. She wants Mom. She needs her. Hedy can't stay on the farm with Uncle Ernest. The thought is unbearable, like another kind of curse. He doesn't even like her. She has to make Mom better.

It's the first bit of good luck, when a lorry stops at the bus stop and the driver asks if she wants a lift. She's been waiting ten minutes on the deserted country lane, uncertain even if she's in the right place, and with every minute the likelihood of her uncle coming to find her increases. The man at the wheel has a cigarette stuck to his bottom lip, a cap pulled over his eyes. He calls her lad and tells her to hop in, jerking his head towards the rear.

By the time the train pulls into Ipswich station, Hedy is almost asleep, the heating under the seats sedating her, making her clothes steam. She stands on the platform, shivering, and counts the money left over in her pocket, deciding that she has enough to get a taxi to St Peter's. She has her first glimpse of the asylum through yellow leaves, a sprawling redbrick building. The taxi leaves her. She stares up at blank walls, bars on the windows, a stony sky above the roof, and feels a moment of doubt. She runs her hands over the damp wool of her jacket and trousers, and touches the short back and sides of her hair, reminding herself that she has to be her brother, because if Mom thinks she's Chris, like she did last time, then it might be enough to jolt her out of her madness. They only have each other now.

There's a bell to ring. When the door opens, a surprised-looking nurse stands on the threshold in a blue uniform with white apron, a fob watch pinned to it.

'I'm here to see my mother,' Hedy says. 'Mrs Delaney.'

The nurse jangles the bunch of keys hanging from her waist. 'I'm afraid Mrs Delaney is not receiving visitors.'

'I'm her son, she'll want to see me.' Hedy scrabbles around trying to find a convincing argument. 'I've come a long, long way. I don't have the money to get back. Please.'

On the last sentence, her voice wobbles and she stops, chewing the inside of her lip. The nurse shows her to a wooden bench at the side of the entrance hall. 'Don't move.'

She unlocks a door and disappears. Hedy stares around. The floor is chequered in black and white, the walls panelled in dark wood, with two paintings of landscapes facing each other from opposite sides of the room. She notices buzzers beside each of the three locked doors. There's a small window set into the wall, with a mesh screen across it. After a few minutes, Hedy gets up and looks through the mesh, seeing a long corridor, and the stern nurse approaching with efficient speed in her shiny shoes.

'You're to be allowed a short, supervised visit.' The nurse's mouth turns down. 'Doctor Ashby is letting you use his own office for the purpose. But you mustn't come unannounced again. It's unsettling for patients. When Mrs Delaney is ready for visitors, you will be told the official times.' She beckons. 'Come along. Follow me.'

The white corridor is long and straight with doors and side corridors leading off it. It's a place to get lost in, an Alice in Wonderland world. Hedy glimpses a ward with lots of beds, like a real hospital. An elderly lady is coming towards them, shuffling slowly. She's in her dressing gown, even though it's mid-afternoon. A plump nurse holds the woman's arm. When they are close, the woman looks up. Hedy sees that she is very old, her face fallen in on itself like a rotten apple. 'I am the queen of the United States of America,' the woman says in a surprisingly loud, authoritative voice. 'You will not address me, child. Be careful what you say.'

'Now, now, Joyce.' The plump nurse raises her eyebrows and tugs at the woman's arm, moving her on.

Hedy has to step smartly to keep up with her nurse. Behind them, there's a series of child-like, breathless shrieks. Hedy's skin prickles. The stern nurse stops at one of the polished oak doors, knocks, and they enter. Hedy is aware of flowers, two large bouquets bursting with pinks and purples, a stained-glass window speckling the room in triangles and circles of luminous yellows and blues, and a man with a moustache rising from a seat behind a large desk holding out his hand.

It's only as she steps forwards that she sees another figure in the room. A woman hunched in a chair in the corner, hands moving continuously in her lap. She's wearing a dressing gown too. Her lovely hair is dull, hanging against the slope of her cheeks. She doesn't look at Hedy. She's staring at the flowers with an empty expression.

'Mrs Delaney,' the doctor says gently. 'Your son, Christopher, is here to see you.'

Mom doesn't appear to have heard him, except her dry lips move, whispering to herself. Her eyes stay fixed to the same spot.

'You may approach her. Try talking. But her medication will be making her sleepy.'

'Mommy.' Hedy pulls another chair up and sits on the edge, so their knees are touching. 'It's me. Christopher.'

She remembers how his name pulled her mother up from the void before, how Mom clung to her when she thought she was cradling her son, vividly present, hands full of love. Hedy is aware of the doctor watching. She squares her shoulders, blocking him out. Mom won't look at her. Close up, Hedy sees the frazzle of split ends in Mom's hair, the sleep grit at the corners of her eyes. Her breath is foul, as if all her teeth are bad.

'Mommy, I need you to get better, so we can go back to Iowa. We have each other, don't we?' In desperation, Hedy takes hold of her mother's left hand, separating it from the other, breaking off the actions of washing or warming that Mom's been enacting since Hedy came in. Hedy squeezes. 'I can't manage without you. I need you. Look at me,' she says. 'Please.'

Mom's eyes widen and she snatches her hand away. She swivels her head, levelling a direct gaze at Hedy, a look so cold that it makes Hedy's heart falter. 'What have you done?' she asks quietly.

Hedy leans back, blinking.

'What have you done with him?' Mom repeats, louder, her voice hoarse. She's reaching for Hedy, grabbing her arms with sudden force. 'Where is he? Where's my son?' Clumps of hair fall into her eyes. Inside her open mouth, Hedy sees a grey, furred tongue. Mom's fingers are strong as iron.

Two men are in the room. They are pinning Mom's arms by her sides. But she's gone limp as a dead creature, her mouth slack and her eyes unseeing.

'I'm sorry. It's best if you leave now,' the doctor is saying. 'I'm afraid your mother wasn't quite ready for the excitement.'

The men are taking Mom away, her legs dragging like broken things, her head thrown back, a tumble of dirty hair pale against the dressing gown.

As Hedy follows the nurse back along the corridors, she's afraid she might fall; her knees lack the ability to bend, ankles flimsy as paper. In the hall, a man in uniform rises from one of the benches. 'Hello, Hedy,' he says.

She begins to cry then. The surprise of him being there. The relief of Hank still being Hank. His calm, familiar face. The American accent sounding like home.

His arms are around her. 'Let's get you into the car.'

It's stopped raining. They are driving through wet, autumnal countryside, cutting through puddles, sending dirty spray into the hedges. The Cadillac so wide it takes up most of the road.

'How did you know?' Her voice is small.

'They called me when you arrived. It gave me a shock, I can tell you, when they said a young man called Christopher Delaney had come to visit his mother.'

'I thought if I dressed like Chris ... if I looked like him ... I thought she might think I was him. And it would make her better.'

'Why would you think that?'

239

'Because she loved Chris best.'

'I'm sure that's not true.'

Hedy shrugs. 'She loved him because he needed her most. I was supposed to look after him. But I wasn't there when . . .'

'Hedy.' Hank's voice is gentle. 'You couldn't keep fooling her for long, could you? She's your mom. She can tell which is which when it comes to her own kids.'

'She knew it was me this time . . .' Hedy says. 'And she was angry.' She swallows. 'She blames me.'

'You mustn't say things like that.' Hank shakes his head. 'She's confused at the moment. She doesn't know what she's saying.'

Hedy stares out of the window at the brown and grey hedges going past in a blur. She hopes that Hank is right – she wants to believe him. 'Where are we going?'

'I'm taking you back to the farm, back to your uncle. He'll be worried. I haven't been able to reach him on the phone, so I haven't been able to tell him that you're safe.' He glances at her. 'I'm presuming you made this trip without his permission?'

'Don't take me back there. Please.' She puts a hand on his arm and feels it tense against the steering wheel. 'I hate it there.'

'It's all just a bit strange right now.' He's trying to sound cheerful, but there's a quaver in his voice. 'That's natural. But you'll get used to it.'

'No.' A sob breaks in her throat. 'No, I won't.' She looks at his frowning profile. 'My uncle doesn't like me.'

Hank doesn't take his eyes off the road, but his eye twitches. 'There's nowhere else I can take you.'

'Can't I come back to the base with you?' She sits up straight, hands folded in her lap. 'I could live with you. I'd be good.'

He makes a noise in the back of his throat. 'Sorry, kid. No

can do. Your uncle's said he'll have you. Look, he's not used to kids. It'll probably take him a while to adjust. Give it some time, OK?' He glances at her. 'For me?'

She slumps lower in her seat. 'I'm not staying long.' Her voice is dull. 'I . . . I can't live there for ever.'

'Not for ever. I promise,' he says. He glances at her again, one eyebrow raised. 'He knows you're not Christopher, doesn't he?'

She nods.

'OK, then.' He reaches across and pats her knee. 'That's good. You can't go around lying about who you are. Got to start off with a clean slate.' He taps the wheel with his thumbs.

Hedy stares at the scratchy trees, the muddy, flat horizon.

'Is Mom going to get better?'

There's just the noise of tyres against the road. 'She's very ill,' he says eventually. 'But they're doing everything they can to make her well.'

She sinks further into her seat, biting her nails, stripping them back to the quick.

'It's been nearly fifteen years,' Hank says, blowing out cigarette smoke. 'But heck, thought I'd find my way back.' He shakes his head. 'All this mud makes everything look the same.'

'You and Dad were stationed here in the war, weren't you?'

'Just a few miles away. Got around on bicycles. Used to know these lanes, even in the dark. No lights allowed. And the farm, of course. Your dad and I first visited the Coles' place when we were invited to Christmas dinner. We arrived all spruced up, loaded down with gifts, excited to see inside a genuine English home, and bingo, we walked in to find Ruby, face flushed and looking real pretty.' He scratches his nose. 'Guess you know that story, huh?'

Hedy turns her face to the window. She's heard the story lots

241

of times. Dad loved to explain how he'd first seen Mom with her head in the oven, cooking a goose. Hank and Dad were best friends. Best friends know everything about each other. 'Why did Dad kill himself?' she asks.

Hank scrunches up his face. 'I . . . I just don't know.'

'Why was he in prison?'

'I wish I could tell you – but it's classified. There's an investigation going on right now. Sorry, kid.'

'But . . . you don't really think . . .' Her voice is small. 'He couldn't have spied for the Russians, could he. Not my dad?'

Hank grimaces and throws his cigarette out of the window. 'Hell, the whole thing's out of character. But,' he sighs, 'war does strange things to people.'

'He was a hero. You said so. He'd never do anything bad.'

'No. Of course he wouldn't.' Hank leans across and squeezes her hand. 'Remember what a great dad he was. He loved you very much.'

They don't talk after that. Hank recognises the village pub, The Hare and Hounds, and finds his way at last. They drive across a bridge, the canal smooth and deep below, and then they're bumping along the farm track. Hedy gets out to open the gate, whistling softly at the red cows. Peter told her that they're Red Polls, beef cattle that came over to Norfolk with the Romans. When they pull into the yard, Hank switches off the engine and twists around in his seat, says straight off that he can't stay.

'Please,' Hedy tries. 'Come in with me.' She thinks her uncle won't be angry if Hank is there, cloaked in all his military authority.

'I'm on duty,' he says. 'Got to get back to the base. You can take it from here.' He gives the end of her nose an affectionate press.

242

Getting out of the car is another kind of leaving home. She can smell Dad in the American leather seats and the fug of Camel smoke. She stands and watches Hank reverse past the muck pile, turning the wheel with the flat of one hand; she wants to run after the Cadillac, bang on the window, make him take her with him. Then he's gone, saluting her in the wing mirror. The black and silver car looks like a spaceship cruising through a foreign landscape of dirt and dank water.

# TWENTY-SEVEN

The dog lets out a warning bark as she goes into the kitchen, before sinking onto his belly with a sigh. Mrs Rose puts soapy hands on her hips. 'Wondered who it was in that fancy car. Where have you been?' She raises her eyebrows. 'Mr Cole wasn't too pleased to find you'd gone off without even a say so.'

'Hank . . . Major Pulaski telephoned to tell you where I was.'

'Oh, he's been at it again.' Mrs Rose looks towards the hall. 'The old man hates the noise. He will keep taking it off the hook.'

'I went to see Mom,' Hedy says in a quiet voice.

'Well.' Mrs Rose goes to the fire and lifts the kettle off the hook. 'No harm done. I expect you could do with some tea. Something to eat.'

She puts a plate on the table, smelling of the sea. 'Mussel pudding with suet. Eat up. Things are always better on a full stomach.'

Ernest hobbles into the room. He stands at the other side of the table in concentrated silence, observing her as if she's a rabbit destined for the pot. She stops chewing. He pulls out a chair, scraping the legs over the stone, and sits down hard with a grunt. 'Thought I'd got rid of you.'

'Hedy went to visit her mother,' Mrs Rose explains, handing Ernest a plate of food.

'Told you before, girl. If you want to get fed, you need to work for your supper.'

'I saw Mom,' she says. 'She isn't any better.' She drops her head, throat tight. 'She was like a sleepwalker ... her eyes all red and her hair dirty. She didn't look like her.'

He pushes the chair back with a screech of wood against stone. 'The girl's whining's taken away my appetite.' He gets to his feet, shrugging off Mrs Rose's hand. 'You still need to do your chores.' He gives Hedy a cold look. 'And you can help Mrs Rose in the kitchen, too.'

'Don't mind him. Pain makes a person sharp, makes them snap when they don't mean to,' Mrs Rose says when he's gone. She gets up to clear the table, and pauses by Hedy's chair, puts a hand on her shoulder. 'Your poor mum. You must miss her.'

Hedy can only manage a nod. Mrs Rose sits down next to her and takes one of Hedy's hands inside her papery fingers. She sighs. 'Your uncle isn't a bad man. He's not used to children. We never have any company on the farm. He doesn't like to see strangers. And, well, I might be speaking out of turn, but I think he argued with his sister, your mum, before she left for America. That's what everyone says – that him and your granddad didn't want Ruby to leave – but she did anyway, and that caused a lot of bad feeling. Bad blood.'

'Is that why he doesn't like me?'

'Oh, child. He doesn't dislike you. Give him some time. He'll come round.'

That's exactly what Hank said, too. Hedy can't imagine Ernest coming round, she's not sure how that would happen, but she has no choice but to stay here for now. The dog heaves himself to his feet and stretches, pads over to touch his cold nose to Hedy's hand before he goes to the door, wanting to be let out. She leans against the frame, watching him stroll away, sniffing at the muck. The hens lift bobbing heads, watching him with wary eyes. He ignores them, cocking his leg against the barn wall.

She looks at the puddled yard, chickens scratching in the sludge, the pigsty next to tarred sheds, crooked roofs against an oatmeal sky, and takes a deep breath, tasting bitter silage, salt from the sea. This place will never feel like home. The brindled dog comes panting towards her, his muscled flank pressing against her as he goes into the house, but she stays where she is, fingers against the doorframe. There's a ghost moon in the sky. A pale circle pinned to the clouds. She squints up, imagining that she can see the bungalow up there, a tiny building with the laurel hedge at the front and pines at the back, Dad's barbecue in the garden, glued like an upside-down toy to the belly of the moon.

Hedy and Mrs Rose are preparing supper. Hedy fetches potatoes from a big sack in the cellar, her fingers black with greasy earth. 'This is last year's crop.' Mrs Rose explains as they stand at the kitchen sink together, scrubbing the soil off under the tap, 'They last a good few months if you keep them somewhere cold. Time to plant potatoes is on a Good Friday. Less chance of a frost. It's a tradition when starting up a vegetable patch to bury the body of an animal first. Makes the earth rich, you see. Keeps it fed for years to come.'

'What did you bury?' Hedy glances down at the potato in her hand.

'One of the carthorses. Star, his name was.'

'A whole horse, under the garden?'

'It's a big garden,' Mrs Rose says.

Mrs Rose brings some of her niece's cast-offs with her the next morning, getting them out of her bag like a magician conjuring coloured ribbons out of a pocket: darned cotton frocks in faded flower prints. The washed-out fabrics are soft in her hands, but Hedy can't abandon Chris's clothes, not while his smell lingers. She likes wearing trousers; it feels more natural to be able to stride out in them, to be able to sit down without worrying that she's showing her knickers.

Before she goes to sleep, she reads another of Chris's stories written in his exercise books. *The Wonderful*, he's called it. It's about a boy who hears a scream coming from under a circular slab in the ground, the sound of an unearthly creature trapped far beneath the surface. Afterwards, he sees a wonderful bright light from a spaceship. He tells a colonel about the aliens that he's sure are landing on earth; but then the story just stops, as if he was halfway through writing it.

As she lies in bed, she thinks that the story isn't like the ones he usually made up; Chris's other tales are about faraway planets and invented creatures. This one has a real setting: the stone by the oak, the place the kids led them to, where he asked her to listen for noises underground. She closes the exercise book; it makes her dizzy to think that he wrote about the place where he was later murdered.

# TWENTY-EIGHT

Hedy has started at the village school. She keeps her head down, minds her own business. She'll always be a Yank to the other kids, an outsider, the girl who dresses like a boy, the one with the funny accent. She doesn't care. It's dangerous to have friends. People can disappear at any moment. Her only friends here are Peter and Mrs Rose.

Ernest is no friend to her. He doesn't behave like an uncle, either. He grunts if she asks a question, and leaves the room when she comes in. Then one morning, after breakfast, he asks Peter to teach Hedy how to drive the Fordson Major. 'She's tall enough to reach the pedals,' he says, looking at Peter and not at Hedy. 'She can start to pull her weight on the farm.'

Peter and Hedy go out into the yard, to the shed where the green tractor is kept. Hens cluck around the wheels, and perch on the seat. Peter shoos the chickens away and shows her how to drain the TVO and check the fuel line, how to use the pull-out choke and set the mix of petrol and TVO. She watches carefully. She used to help Dad when he was tinkering with the Buick Roadmaster. She remembers Dad, happy under the bonnet, showing her how the engine worked. 'Did I tell you that she's built by the company that makes P-51 Mustang fighters?' he'd ask every time.

'It's tricky to start in the cold,' Peter tells her. 'You need to be firm with the old girl. Show her who's boss.'

Hedy bends over, grabs the crank at the front and gives a skilful yank, using the technique she learnt starting Ernest's car, hoping to impress Peter. But the tractor crank turns grudgingly, and the engine clicks, but refuses to catch. She grits her teeth and leans into it. On the third go, the machine roars, deafening her.

'Couldn't have done it better myself.' Peter nods approvingly. 'Farmers need to be mechanics now. Up you get.' He gestures to the seat, covered in sacking. Hedy swings herself up, looking down at his red hair and broad smile. He leans an elbow against the big mud-encrusted wheel. 'This thing belongs in a museum,' he says. 'Try and persuade the old man to invest in one of the new tractors. Make all our lives easier.'

'He doesn't listen to me,' she says, doubtfully. 'And even if he did, I don't think there's any money.'

'I know.' Peter pats the vibrating bonnet, wipes oil on his overall pockets, adding to the smears already there, ingrained into the worn blue. 'No money in farming. Can't stop wishing, though,' he says. 'Put both hands on the wheel. Foot on the clutch. Give it some revs.'

She pushes her foot flat. She feels the engine respond, the life of the machine flaring below.

'Not too many!' he yells. 'Put her in first gear and move forwards. Slowly.'

The tractor rolls forwards and Hedy panics. 'Watch out! You'll lose your toes!'

Peter steps out of the way. 'I said, slowly!'

Hedy inhales the heady scent of oil and diesel. From her elevated perch, she can just make out the glimmer of sea in the distance, across the flat, brown fields. The tractor judders and moans, and she glances at the gauge between her knees to check it's not overheating. Peter's behind her, walking up the track, shouting instructions she can't hear. She doesn't need to be told what to do – it's an instinct. Her shoulders have relaxed, hands firm on the steering wheel; and for the first time since Dad and Chris died, something opens inside the closed fist of her chest.

Early darkness falls through smoke-stained air, and the ghostly shape of a white owl swoops past the window, turning its round face towards the ground. The complaining clatter of the rooks stops abruptly as the last of the light disappears from the sky. Mrs Rose has gone for the day, and Ernest limps in from the yard, bringing the cold with him, the dog at his heels. He pulls off his muddy wellingtons at the threshold. Hedy looks away from his struggles. She waits until she hears the thump of both boots hitting the flagstones.

She stoops to pick them up and set them straight by the others next to the door. 'Did Peter tell you?' Hedy can't prevent herself from grinning. 'I had my first lesson. He said it was as if I'd been driving her all my life. He said I was a natural.'

Ernest grunts. 'We'll see about that,' he says, his breath catching in his throat. He pours himself a glass of water from the tap, keeping his back to her.

'I thought you'd be pleased,' Hedy says, scowling down at her dirty hands. She goes to the door. 'I'm going to bed.'

He doesn't reply. Fine, she thinks. You're nothing but a mean old man, and I won't try to get you to like me anymore. The sharp noise of coughing makes her turn. His hands are fluttering helplessly at the front of his shirt; his watery eyes stare through her. She hears the rasp of his breath and her heart quickens, remembering Chris's asthma attacks. Ernest's eyes squeeze shut as he wheezes and hacks, and suddenly he slumps forwards, fingers flailing to find the table edge. He leans there, misshapen ribs shuddering.

Hedy puts a hand towards his shoulder and snatches it back. It seems wrong to touch him. 'What shall I do?'

He gestures towards his throat. His mouth works, no words coming, and then, 'Can't ... breathe ...'

She steps close and her fingers fumble at the buttons of his shirt, undoing them, pulling the fabric away from his neck. With her hand under his elbow, she guides him to a chair. 'Sit down. Try to breathe slowly.' She remembers Chris struggling to catch his breath. Keep him calm, Mom used to say. Talk to him. Get him to breathe in through the nose and out through the mouth. She couldn't have a cat because Chris had an allergy to fur. She can't believe that it ever mattered to her, that she ever begrudged him anything.

White spit is caught at the edges of Ernest's cracked lips. His chest whistles like a boiling kettle. His frightened eyes move towards the dresser. 'Potter's ...' he manages.

She searches through the dresser shelves, fingers sweeping past tins of tea, bundles of opened mail and candle stubs, until she finds a green tin with the words Potter's Asthma Cure in black lettering. She forces herself to read the instructions on the back, and with shaking fingers spoons out some of the aromatic powder. There's a box of matches kept on the shelf next to the range; she strikes one, but it hisses and dies. She bites her lip, tries again. She holds the small gold and blue flame under the bowl of the spoon. Ernest staggers close and leans over the fumes, eyes closed. He takes a jagged breath, then wheezes out and in again, his lungs filling.

The worst has passed and he slumps at the table, breath still laboured, but getting air into his lungs. She puts the kettle on.

'Mom always made Chris a cup of something hot afterwards,' she says as she places the mug on the table beside him. 'For comfort.'

'Ruby?' He raises his head. There's a skim of sweat on his forehead. 'Your brother ... he had asthma too?'

She nods.

He takes a wincing sip of the liquid. The dog comes over and places his muzzle on Ernest's knee, his tail wagging slowly. Ernest places his hand on the dog's head. The kitchen clock ticks. Hedy is startled to notice that it's been an hour since the attack began. She glances back at her uncle.

'Don't look at me, girl,' he says in a low voice. 'You're always staring.'

She sits back in her chair with a jolt as if he's slapped her.

'I don't want your pity.' His face twists as he looks down, stroking the dog's ears.

'But I don't ... ' She leans forwards. 'It's not that. Chris had scoliosis, too. Very badly. He had to wear a brace.'

Ernest's head snaps up and he looks at her for the first time, properly. 'Ruby's son?'

She nods. 'Mom didn't tell you?'

He scrunches his face into a frown. 'I haven't spoken to her since the day she left the farm. She was pregnant with you then. You and your brother.' He stares down at the table, rubbing his thumb in the whorls of wood. 'Well ... so she had a child like me, after all . . . ' He looks up. 'And your father . . . he stayed?'

'Dad? Of course.'

'Not every man can cope with having a son that's . . . that's not like other boys.'

'Didn't your father cope?'

Ernest rubs his cheek with the stump of his finger. 'He wanted to keep me out of sight. Locked away. His curse. I wasn't supposed to leave the farm.'

'That's terrible. I'm sorry . . . ' Hedy leans her elbows on the table.

He makes a grumble of sound. 'It's a long time ago. No point talking about it.'

'Why don't you come with me next time I visit Mom, in the asylum?' Hedy clasps her hands tightly. 'Maybe it would help, if you came.'

He shakes his head. 'I don't leave the farm. It's too difficult.'

'Oh, but—'

'I said no.' He hauls himself to his feet. 'I'm going to bed.' He pauses at the door, clears his throat and looks at the floor. 'Thank you.'

She waits, listening to the drag and thump of his feet in the hall. The dog sits in his bed by the range. He looks towards the door, ears cocked, listening too. When the sounds of Ernest's uneven gait stop, the dog sighs and curls up, tucking his nose under his tail.

# TWENTY-NINE

## 1959

On her way back from the turnip field, perched on the hard metal seat of the Fordson, Hedy sees the swallows. She can't hear them above the roar of the engine, but there they are, just as Peter said: first ones of the year swooping through the cool evening, dipping low to the grass and then up into the blue, tucking under the eaves of the house. She never noticed different kinds of birds before coming to Norfolk. The world changes with knowledge, details that were always there emerging into view, like a photograph in developing fluid. Peter's taught her so much: the names of birds and how to recognise their songs: thrush, robin, blackbird, hedge sparrow and chaffinch. Last year, out in the orchard, he lifted the spiky leaves of a nettle to show her pin-pricks of white. 'Eggs of a peacock butterfly,' he said. 'This patch of nettles will be thick with butterflies soon.'

Hedy's body has changed. She's broader across the shoulders, her biceps tight; she's got an all-weather tan, freckles running rampant from the hours spent outdoors, hands rough and scratched. When she climbs into the tin bath in the kitchen on wash evenings, she discovers the budding of her breasts, the curve between her waist and hips. She doesn't like the changes; her new body feels awkward. She can't bring herself to ask for a brassiere. She can still fit into Chris's shirts, but she's had to acquire longer trousers, hand-me-downs from Mrs Rose's sons. She belts them in tightly, rolls up the hems. Mrs Rose begs her to let her hair grow, but Hedy prefers it clipped into her neck, soft under her fingers like animal fur.

Hedy's chores mean she never has much time to herself; there's always something to do: collecting the eggs, throwing tail-corn to the chickens, milking the cows. Skimming the cream and churning it for butter. She's doing proper farm work, too – every weekend, and after school, she helps with whatever needs doing – hoeing and drilling, driving the tractor down straight furrows, making perfect rigs, and then a turn around the headland like a professional.

Ernest's ribs are compressing his lungs. It's a slow suffocation. He's terse and tight-lipped, uncomplaining. His mouth whitens, waxy with strain. Mrs Rose whispers the details of his ailing health to Hedy. 'It's not just his lungs. His heart's being crushed like a walnut,' she says. 'He's already lived years longer than they thought. Weakness, he calls it. But there's many a strong man couldn't have endured the pain he's had to.'

In the kitchen, Mrs Rose is chopping potatoes, stirring a stock on the range, steam filling the room with smells of rosemary and onions. The three farm hands eat with elbows propped on the scrubbed table, cups of tea and a plate of bread and cockles in front of them. Mrs Rose has made Nelson Slices, and Hedy's mouth waters for the taste of crusts soaked in marmalade and rum. Peter looks up. 'Noticed the swallows, Hedy?' he asks.

'Feels like the beginning of spring when they arrive,' Mrs Rose says. 'But my old dad always said the later they come, the better the summer.'

Hedy takes the kettle from the hook in the fireplace, pours more strong brown liquid into their mugs. As she leans over, Peter coughs. 'They're playing *The 39 Steps* at the picture house in town this weekend.' He studies his hands, a deep colour rising from his collar, spreading over his neck. 'Would you like to come?'

Hedy thinks of the chores she has to do, her homework for school. She opens her mouth to say no.

'Course she'll go with you, you lummox,' Mrs Rose says. 'The girl needs to get out. It'll do you good, Hedy.'

'I'll pick you up.' Peter manages to raise his eyes, face a startling scarlet. 'Seven o'clock. Saturday.'

The other farm hands are laughing, elbowing each other in the ribs, but they stop when Ernest comes into the kitchen.

'Still in my kitchen?' he says. 'I don't pay you to loaf around my table.'

The men rise at once, wiping their mouths with the backs of their hands, shuffling awkwardly to the door, darned toes against the flagstones, tripping each other in their hurry to shove their feet into their boots left just outside.

Hedy picks up their dirty crockery and plunges it into the bowl in the sink. Washing off the crumbs, she thinks of the swallows, coming back each year, returning to reuse the mud and saliva nests that take them so long to make, such tiny creatures going back and forth from Africa to Norfolk, finding their way home to the exact same farm house. They must believe their nests will still be there: a kind of unquestioning faith in the rightness of the world.

They're sitting in the front row in itchy red seats; the screen is loud and close up, the actor's faces looming over them like giants. Hedy hasn't seen the black and white version of the film; she didn't know it's about a spy ring. When she understands, she shifts uncomfortably, thinking of Dad. She can't connect him to the shady crooks who are stealing military information from the government. She's immersed in the story, and jumps when she feels Peter fumbling to hold her hand. It's awkward, their fingers squashed together, hot and sticky, and she makes the excuse of blowing her nose to break free. After that, she keeps both hands in her pockets. She senses Peter's puzzled expression from the corner of her eye. She's glad she hasn't told Peter about her father. She wouldn't want his embarrassment at the subject matter of the film. After it ends, they trudge out together. A couple in the back row sit with their faces stuck together even though the lights have come on. They are oblivious to the disapproving stares of the people filing past. Hedy looks away quickly, still thinking about the film, about Dad. When Peter reaches for her fingers, she snatches them away. 'Don't,' she says.

He looks startled and then hurt, hanging his head.

'I ... I only want to be your friend,' she says. 'I can't be your ... girlfriend.'

'Sorry.' Peter coughs and turns red. 'I thought ...'

'No,' she says, trying to soften her voice, to let him down gently. 'It's not you. I don't want to be anyone's girlfriend.'

When he calls her from the kitchen the next day, she's worried he wants to try to be her boyfriend again. She follows reluctantly, traipsing out towards the low field. Peter stops by the patch of green nettles and points. 'Look. They've come out of hibernation.'

The field is alive with brilliant reds and purples shining in the light. Peacock butterflies rising into the sky. Peter tells her that the wings are brown as dead leaves underneath for protection from birds. One lands on her hand, light as breath, blinking at her. 'See how the pattern on the front looks like an upside-down owl's face,' he whispers.

They lie back in the long grass, and he plucks a stem and tickles her nose with the feathered end; she bats it away, laughing. She's relieved that he's not being odd with her. She doesn't want to lose his friendship.

'Would you tell me about your family?' he says hesitantly.

She stops laughing. 'What about them?'

'Well ... you know how people talk. I heard that your brother was ... was ...' He lowers his voice. 'Murdered. Is that really true?'

She sits up, hunching her shoulders, and draws away from him.

'I shouldn't have said.' Peter folds inwards, dropping his chin to his broad chest. 'Don't tell me anything if you don't want to,' he says quickly.

She sits for a moment without speaking, the horror of that afternoon pushing behind her eyes, feelings she's suppressed for months leaking out. She takes a deep breath and presses the heels of her hands against her eyes, letting the swell of emotion rise and settle, storm water lapping, threatening to drown her.

'Forget I said anything.' She hears Peter's worried voice.

The sun is warm on the back of her neck. She takes another breath and opens her eyes. 'No,' she says, blinking into the brightness. 'I want to tell you.'

Words come quickly. She speaks Old Joe's name aloud for the first time since leaving the base. She explains how they first met him in the abandoned church yard: his ancient face, wrinkled and burnt by the wind, the wild thatch of his hair, and how he lived rough in the forest. She repeats the things he said to Chris about lights in the sky, about devils. She tells Peter about the rope around her brother's neck and how it was slung over the highest branch of the tree. She tells him that one of his shoes had fallen into the grass. She describes the military arriving and how it took three men to untie the rope and lower her brother through leaves and branches into their arms.

When she finishes speaking, she's exhausted, but glad she's shared it with someone. Peter is staring at his bent knees. He's been picking grass and shredding it with his nails and his fingers are green-tipped. He looks puzzled. 'So, this old man, Joe,' he says hesitantly. 'Where did he get the rope from?'

Hedy turns to stare. It wasn't what she was expecting him to say. 'I don't know. Why does it matter?'

Peter blows into his cheeks, like he does when he's thinking. 'It's only that, well, a good length of rope's expensive. And heavy. I was wondering how he managed to buy it and then drag it through the forest and then ... do what he did ... if he was old and poor, you know, like you said?'

Hedy's mouth is dry. Her pulse jumps at her throat. She's never thought about the practical difficulties of hanging Chris. She never thought of how Old Joe would have got hold of a rope. 'But he must have managed it somehow,' she says. 'Maybe he stole it. How would I know? He had rope burns on his hands.'

'So you think he planned it all out before?' Peter rubs his chin. 'Was he waiting for your brother? Did he know he was coming?'

Hedy's chest is tight as a wrung-out cloth. Peter's questions are like physical blows. She cowers under them.

'Did you see him ...' he lowers his voice, 'did you catch him ... in the act?'

She shakes her head. 'Stop. I don't know.' She moves away from him, folding her arms across her chest. 'I don't want to talk about it.'

Ideas are rustling inside her mind, dry wings battering at her, confusing her, so that like a bird, she cannot tell what she's looking at anymore, a leaf or a butterfly. *He's harmless,* Nell's voice says. But Hedy hadn't wanted to believe her, because otherwise she'd have to face the fact he'd killed himself. But now Peter's pointed out the financial and physical impossibility of Old Joe hanging her brother, she can see it was never going to be possible for Chris to commit suicide that way either. Only who else, she thinks, would have wanted her brother dead? Who would kill a crippled boy, except a madman? In her head, she remembers characters from the film last night: the upright professor with a smoking gun in his hand; the pretend policemen pushing the hero into the car.

She stands up, brushing grass seeds from her jeans. 'We should go in. I've got the milking to do.'

'I'm sorry.' He stumbles after her. 'I didn't mean to upset you ...'

She walks quicker, wanting to be alone with all the rustling thoughts, trying to make sense of them, to see them for what they really are.

# THIRTY

Hedy's become used to the long, flat horizon, unbroken by anything taller than a tree. Despite its bleakness, there's a strange relief in that hard, clean beauty. She's not nervous of the cows anymore. She loves the steady, ruminating nature of them, big-boned and broad, belonging to the earth, the way they touch her hands with their grey noses, nostrils flaring, the calves' rasping tongues insisting on her fingers, their long-lashed gaze.

She's caught Ernest's habit of singing to the herd as they come into the milking parlour. She's humming, an old dance tune that Mom used to sing, as she leans her shoulder into Betsy's warm side, fingers working at the teats; the warm, sweet smell of fresh milk and the silage scent of the parlour is comforting.

She senses another person behind her, glimpses a pair of legs in wellingtons under the crook of her arm. Betsy stops eating to turn a quizzical gaze over her shoulder.

'Are you avoiding me?' Peter asks.

Hedy doesn't stop milking. She still has six cows to do after

Betsy. She shakes her head, turning her cheek into the soft give of white and black hide. 'It's just ... you've given me a lot to think about. Old Joe's in prison. But now I'm wondering if they got it wrong.' She sits up on the stool and slaps her hand on the cow's wide cradle of rump before she pushes herself to her feet and takes the stool into the next stall. 'But if Old Joe didn't do it, and Chris didn't kill himself, then I don't know who else it could have been.'

'I'm sorry,' Peter says. 'I tell it how I see it. Plain speaking.'

Hedy frowns. 'There were other homeless men in the forest. We were warned to stay away from them. But they had no reason to do anything so terrible.'

Peter has taken down the other milking stool and has settled himself with the next cow. Hedy hears the sound of the stream hitting the bottom of the bucket. Ernest has talked about updating the parlour, getting some of the new machinery that plugs straight onto the udders.

'There doesn't always have to be a reason,' Peter says in a low voice. 'Not for evil.'

'I've been thinking about Old Joe and those marks on his hands. Do you think,' she says, 'that he could have got those because he'd been trying to get Chris down?' She coughs, clearing the lump in her throat. 'Trying to save him?'

There's silence from the other stall, apart from the rhythmical sound of liquid hitting bucket. Then Peter's voice comes, 'It's possible, I suppose ... just from what you've told me ... well, it could be that he found your brother hanging and tried to help.'

'But how I am ever going to find out?' She presses her forehead into the mud-slivered belly of the cow in despair.

'Maybe you just have to accept that ... that it's a mystery,' Peter says. 'You can't know everything in the world. It's full of things beyond our understanding. That's what God is for – so we can trust that He knows best for us.'

'I don't think I believe in God.'

'Doesn't matter. He loves you anyway.'

She coughs, not knowing how to answer. 'My brother loved science-fiction stories,' she says instead. 'He wrote them himself, too. He was good. I think he would have become a real author, if he'd lived. He thought there were aliens in the forest. Said he heard them just where he was murdered. He wrote a story about it. It's odd, isn't it? A strange coincidence.'

'Could I read it?'

'It's not finished,' she says, surprised. 'It's only a couple of pages long. But if you want to ... only don't lose it ... or spill anything on it.'

'Of course not,' Peter says gravely.

Hedy stands in the kitchen making Ernest's favourite soused mackerel. She chops off fish heads and tails, then uses a sharp knife to slit open their skin, taking out the prickly spines before carefully rolling them up. She drops the silvered coils of fish into boiling vinegar and water.

Mrs Rose sniffs the air. 'You've become a dab hand at that.'

'I'll never like them, though,' Hedy says, poking the coils of fish with a fork.

'The old man is happier these days,' Mrs Rose says. 'Have you noticed? Something's softened inside him. It's having you here that's done it.'

Hedy swallows a smile and blinks. 'He's still a grumpy bugger.'

'True,' Mrs Rose laughs. 'You can't change all the spots on a leopard at once. Little by little, that's what I always say.'

'He won't come with me to visit Mom. I wish he would.

Seeing him might help her, and then maybe they could sort out their differences.'

'Don't expect too much from him,' Mrs Rose says. 'He's afraid of leaving the farm. He's locked himself away for years. He hates people staring. You can't force people to do what you want, especially not a stubborn old goat like your uncle.'

Peter is waiting for her at the kitchen door. He hands over the exercise book. 'I see what you mean about it being unfinished,' he says. 'It's good, though.'

Hedy takes the book back, holding it to her chest.

He scratches his head. 'You could finish it for him, couldn't you? Make up an ending?'

Hedy stares up at him. 'Me? But I'm not a writer ... it's not my story.'

'You were twins. I thought maybe you'd have the same talents – be good at the same things.'

'He was the writer. Anyway, I couldn't finish what he started,' Hedy murmurs. 'It wouldn't be right.'

'Maybe he'd want you to.'

'You don't know anything about him.' She squares her shoulders. 'Sorry. I know you're trying to help – but you keep saying all these things, and it just makes me more confused.'

In her room, Hedy looks at the story again. She knows the words off by heart. Chris's words. She couldn't try and guess what he would have wanted to come next. She puts the exercise book in her drawer, pushing it under a layer of folded clothes.

# THIRTY-ONE

## 1961

A woman with hair like raven's feathers walks into the classroom. She doesn't look much older than Hedy. There's an intense prickle of interest as the class observes their new English teacher. She is not what they expected. Miss Ward had been a giantess, her shapeless body constrained in the same floral frock and dun-coloured stockings every day, impossible to tell her age, just that she was old. This girl, with her smooth, pale complexion, is wearing a slouchy shift dress in an odd bronzy green, and most extraordinary of all, the short hem line reveals legs in matching green tights. Hedy feels a rush of pity. She's going to get torn to pieces by the boys.

The teacher stands at the front regarding each one of her pupils with a steady gaze. She says nothing. The clock on the wall ticks. There's throat clearing and feet shuffling, the room full of nervous expectation under the weight of silence. The boys at the back, lolling on their tilted chairs, break first.

'Cat got your tongue?' one of them calls.

There is relieved laughter, the tension pricked, the atmosphere returning to normal. The teacher strolls between the desks to the back, pauses, and walks to the front with an expression of concentration as if she's measuring how long the room is with each stride. Her brown heels tapping the floor. And as easily as that, she regains their attention.

'Silence is powerful, isn't it?' she says, as if she's in mid-conversation with each one of them. 'This term I want us to consider how an author can use it. After all, he or she is dealing in words, a constant flow of words. So where is the space for silence in a book? Where can it be hidden? That's what I want you to think about. Think about it on your way home, or when you're eating your supper or cleaning your teeth.'

There is a ripple of unease. People glance at each other. What is she talking about? Is this homework? Nobody speaks. She appears not to mind; with a little hop she sits up on the desk, her green legs swinging into space, and gives them a radiant smile, showing a glimpse of tongue. 'I'm Miss Banville. Welcome to your first year in sixth form. I want to help you make the most of it.' Her eyebrows draw together as she leans forwards. 'I expect hard work. I expect dedication. So anyone who thinks this is a class that doesn't matter, who wants to mess around, I suggest you leave now.'

She slips off the desk, agile as a dancer, and goes to the door, opens it. 'I won't be offended.' She gives them a pleasant smile. A muted version of the first. 'If you stay, then you accept my rules. I want your passion. Your promise to work. And I'll be here for you. I won't let you down.'

Hedy can hardly breathe. Her heart is thudding in her chest. She's never heard anyone speak like this.

One of the boys stands up, but slumps back down when his friends pluck at his arm. There's a murmur that falls into a hush at the signal of Miss Banville's raised hand.

'All right,' she says, closing the door.

She picks up a piece of chalk and writes her name on the board in large, rounded letters. She turns. 'You know who I am. Now, I want all of you to tell me your names. Starting with the front row.'

Hedy realises it's her turn to speak. She clears her throat. To her horror, her voice is an uncertain squeak. Someone at the back laughs, but stops when Miss Banville glances in their direction.

'Hedy,' she repeats. 'What an interesting name.'

'How was it?' Mrs Rose asks. She's peeling apples. A ripe, sweet scent fills the kitchen. She finishes one long, skilful uncoiling of skin.

'All right,' Hedy says, the apple smell making her think of a day at the beach, her knees stinging with salt, Chris limping to the shoreline, his pale feet. Was that the moment things began to go wrong for all of them? No. It began almost as soon as they arrived on the base, a change in the atmosphere like a storm brewing, headachy, all the air squeezed shut.

'At least I'm another year closer to leaving school,' she tells Mrs Rose's back.

'I left school at fourteen,' Mrs Rose says. 'Girls don't need an education, not when you're going to get married and have children. Going all the way to the grammar school in town seems a waste of time to me.' She puts a bucket of apples on the floor. 'There – you can sort through the windfalls.'

Hedy picks up a bruised apple and puts it into another pail for animal feed. The old dog is asleep in his basket by the range.

His paws twitch with dream-running. His arthritic limbs only take him into the yard and back now.

'I know I keep on about it. But you could be pretty if you dressed like a girl and let your lovely hair grow out.'

'I don't want to get married. I don't care about looking pretty.'

'I know somebody who'll be disappointed to hear that.' Mrs Rose raises an eyebrow.

'Peter?' Hedy looks down at the fruit. She frowns. 'He's my friend. Nothing more.'

'When you inherit this place, you'll need a man to help you run it. And let me tell you, a friend is a good place to start, especially when you're thinking of spending a lifetime together.'

Hedy concentrates on the apples, dropping maggoty fruit into the feed pail for the pigs. She doesn't intend to get married to Peter, or anyone. Girls in her class are always going on about film stars like Clark Gable and Gregory Peck or giggling about some boy at school. They stand in the toilets at break, pinching their cheeks to bring pink to their skin, talking about clothes and laughing like idiots. She can't join in – she doesn't want to, and wouldn't know how if she did. She'd rather play rounders with the boys.

She thinks about the surprise of Miss Banville, suddenly there in the chalky classroom. She'd looked at Hedy as if it was Hedy herself that was interesting, not just her name. Hedy hadn't been able to return more than a half twist of a smile before she'd dropped her gaze to the scratched wood of her desk.

# THIRTY-TWO

*Hedy, Hedy, Hedy . . . can you hear me? I need to tell you some-*
*thing about the light. It was wonderful. Every evil thing extinguished*
*and only good remaining, a bright well of goodness falling over me.*
*I felt no pain. My spine was straight. I could run and jump. I could*
*fly. They took my hand in theirs. And that's when I understood –*
*they were the light – and I didn't need to be afraid.*

Hedy wakes with a rushing heart. She pushes her legs out of the
covers, and stumbles across the listing floor to find the switch.
The bare bulb glows, shadows flickering across the wash stand
and iron bedstead. She pours a glass of water and drinks it too
fast, catching sight of herself in the mirror, a blond boy-girl with
hair sticking up, eyes puffy with sleep.

Chris was here. She couldn't see him. But his voice . . . he
could have been standing beside her – cinnamon breath, his
apple-scented hair, the smell of him all around her.

Ever since Peter put doubts in her head about Old Joe mur-
dering her brother, she's thought long and hard about who else

might have wanted to kill him and there's only one name that slides into her head: Scott. He had a motive: he hated Chris. He thought he was a pervert. A deviant, he called him. He'd even said that he deserved to be lynched. She thinks of the newspaper clippings she found in the album in his room. It makes her chest tight to think that he could have done it, and that he's alive and happy somewhere, believing that he's got away with it.

The sky is silver, apricot light seeping across the horizon, the morning full of chattering, chirping birdsong. Hedy swallows a yawn, and leans over the pen to scratch one of the pig's ears. She used to think pigs were dirty creatures, wallowing in muck. Peter appears out of the barn, pitch fork in hand.

'You're up early,' he says. 'Even in my book.'

'Been awake for hours,' she says. 'I've been thinking about my brother again – about what happened to him. '

'Your brother?' Peter coughs, rubs his neck. 'So many years have gone past since it happened, Hedy. Maybe it's time... maybe you have to let it go.' Peter drops his gaze, staring at the ground. 'Do you want to come to the dance on Saturday?' He shuffles his toe in the dust. 'At the village hall. Might cheer you up.'

Hedy shakes her head. 'I'm not much of a dancer anyway.'

But she's not concentrating on Peter; she's wondering how she'll ever find proof that Scott killed her brother. She doesn't even know where he is, or any of the other boys. They were kids from military families – they could have been posted anywhere in the world – and they'll be young men now, maybe in the army themselves.

'How was your mother? You saw her at the weekend?'

Hedy shrugs. 'The same. She doesn't know who I am.'

'Why do you keep going, then?' Peter lowers his voice. 'It just makes you sad.'

'I have to try. One day she'll recognise me. She did once, when I first went.'

Peter puts his hand on her arm. 'Don't like to see you disappointed.'

She moves away. 'The cows will be waiting.'

'I'll help. Easier with two.'

'No.' She swings round, gives a quick smile. 'I can manage.'

She heads for the lane leading to the small pasture, knowing he's watching her. He'll be leaning against the side of the pen, perhaps lighting a cigarette, his eyes following her with a hurt expression. She can't change the way things are, can't force feelings into blooming where there's nothing in the soil, no bulb or roots. There must be something wrong with her. She thinks of Scott again, remembers him hot and angry on the sidewalk shouting about Chris. He called him a fag. A fucking pervert.

She needs to tell someone. Hank. He'll know what to do.

# THIRTY-THREE

Hank is waiting outside St Peter's in his car. A new Cadillac with fins at the back like a mermaid's tail. He waves to her through the windscreen as she comes down the steps.

'Usual place?'

Sliding into the passenger seat, she nods. Depending on his work commitments, Hank sometimes ferries her from the train to the asylum, or he picks her up and they have tea or lunch together at a café near the station. He's stopped asking how Ruby is. The answer is always the same. But if she needs to talk about her mother, he listens. 'Your mom was so damn pretty,' he says. 'Could have been in the movies. And such a good dancer, people stopped to watch.'

In the café, he orders a pot of tea and some cakes.

'Don't take this the wrong way, but when are you going to start dressing like a girl?' He takes a bite out of a scone, cream squeezing onto his fingers. 'You won't get a boyfriend if you don't act like a lady.'

She shakes her head, smiling. 'It's 1961, Hank. Girls wear trousers all the time, cut their hair short.'

'You know what I mean.' He drops his voice. 'You started all this after Christopher . . . Maybe it's time to move on, is all I'm saying.'

She plays with the crumbs on her plate. 'At first, when I dressed like my brother, I was in shock. I suppose I did it to try to bring him back in some way – to see his face in the mirror instead of my own.' She bows her head. 'I felt guilty. I should have been able to protect him. But,' she touches his arm lightly, 'this is who I am. I'm not pretending to be my brother, or anyone else. I like wearing boys' clothes. More practical for farm work, for a start.' She folds her hands together and leans forwards. 'Hank. There's something I need to tell you . . . something important.'

He looks at her, head on one side, chewing.

'I don't think Old Joe killed my brother.' It comes out in a rush.

Hank stops chewing. He wipes jam from his top lip. His eyes narrow.

'Scott did,' she says.

'Scott?' Hank's face relaxes. He raises his eyebrows. 'Now, why would you think a thing like that?'

'Something my brother did made Scott really angry. And then, later, I found a scrapbook in his bedroom and it had clippings in it – photos and reports torn out of newspapers from the States. It was horrible . . . stuff about the Ku Klux Clan and lynchings.'

'That's not enough to accuse him of murder, Hedy. Scott was just a kid.'

'He was a bully.'

Hank smiles. 'I remember he liked to act the big man. But lots of boys do. It's just show. He might have been angry with your brother, but killing him?' He shakes his head. 'You say Scott was collecting clippings about racial things. That's got nothing to do with Christopher, has it? Besides, we caught Old Joe with your brother and the rope. He confessed.'

'But what if it wasn't him, and he's in prison?'

'He's guilty, Hedy. He had a fair trial. He's in a secure unit for the insane, not a regular prison. He's being looked after. You don't have to worry.' He wipes his fingers on a napkin, pulls his seat closer to hers. 'Listen, it's my turn to tell you something.' He gives her a steady look. 'I'm being posted back to the States.'

She picks up a teaspoon and grips it. 'When?'

'Soon. A month.'

She can't speak. Finally, she nods, 'I'll miss you.'

The last link with Dad, with Mom. She has to stop herself from begging him not to go – it reminds her of that day on the base, when he put her on the train to Norfolk.

'I'll miss you, too. But at least I know you're fine. You're building yourself a new life, and I'm proud of you, kid. Your mom and pop – they'd be proud, too.' He stops, swallows. 'I'll give you my address. If you need anything, let me know.'

'We can stay in touch?'

He leans over and taps the end of her nose. 'You bet we will. We'll write each other. It'll be fun.'

'I can't stop thinking about what happened to Chris.' She turns the teaspoon between her fingers. 'There's something else that bothers me.'

She catches a frown creasing Hank's forehead. A quick flash of impatience.

'You know Chris wanted to be an author,' she says quickly. 'Well, I have his notebooks.'

'Notebooks?' Hank looks puzzled.

'His science-fiction stories.'

Hank stares at her.

'There's one story, *The Wonderful*. It's set in the forest by the base. In the story he hears a scream from under a stone circle.' She swallows.

Hank sits back and lights a cigarette. 'Go on.' His voice is tight.

'The thing is, the place he talks about, it was where I ... where I found him. Where he was murdered.'

'A scream?' Hank blows out a stream of smoke. 'From underground? What did Chris believe was down there?'

'I don't know. He describes the scream as being like a wild animal in pain. Then he saw a brilliant light above the trees. A spaceship or something.' She rubs her nose. 'His character in the story tells the colonel everything, and the colonel says he'll investigate, in case aliens have landed.'

'Spaceships?' Hank knocks ash into a saucer. 'Those manhole covers are Forestry Commission property. They don't cover anything more interesting than a drainage system. If he heard a scream, I imagine he heard a rabbit in a trap nearby.'

'So you don't think that there's a connection between what Chris heard and saw and the fact that he was found there?'

Hank shakes his head again and smiles. 'Are you asking me if I think there are aliens in the forest?'

'Well ... no ... I don't know ...'

Hank waves his hand. 'Chris was in the wrong place at the wrong time. That's all there is to it. I'm sorry. It's just a story, Hedy. He had a vivid imagination. If he'd written more I expect he would have gotten to the part where aliens crawl out of the hole and take over the world. Look.' He softens his voice, puts his hand over hers. 'I don't think you should keep going over this. It won't bring him back.'

She nods. Takes a sip of her cold tea. 'You're right.' She sits up straighter.

Hank looks at his watch and snaps his fingers, calling for the waiter She gets the feeling that she's annoyed him, bringing it all up again. She's sorry to have spoilt their time together. 'And what about you?' she asks. 'Are you pleased to be going home?'

He crosses his legs and smiles, stubbing out his cigarette. 'Aside from leaving you? It'll be good to be back in the States.' He taps the table with one finger. 'It's time to go home. The work I've been doing here has had some excellent results. Things that will help keep the whole world safe.'

Hank drops her at the station. She watches the red fins of the Cadillac disappear. He wrote his new address down for her, and she folded the piece of paper and slipped it between the pages of the novel she's reading. She turns and makes her way to the platform, a kind of homesickness swilling around her stomach. Seeing Hank does that, brings back the loss. But knowing that he's leaving makes it worse.


Hedy visits the library every week. She loses herself inside pages, eats up the stories of other people's lives. She reads passages aloud, imagining Chris there on the bed, listening. *Don't stop*, he says. *Just another chapter. Please.*

English lessons are exciting. Miss Banville paces the room quoting lines from a poem, or she sits on the desk with her feet swinging. Her enthusiasm even touches the boys at the back, stops their muttering and sly grins. Her clothes are brightly coloured. Her wrists clatter with wooden bangles.

Hedy spends each lesson yearning for Miss Banville's approval, wanting her to look at her, and equally badly wanting to hide under her desk. When she found the courage, Hedy put up her hand and answered a question. Miss Banville nodded as she listened. 'Good,' she said quietly. 'You're thinking for yourself.'

Once she told her, 'Go away and read some poetry. Try Owen, Sassoon, Rosenberg. The First World War poets. Come back when you've found the common themes in them. Not the war – something else.'

Confused, Hedy started to rise from her desk. Miss Banville leant over and placed her hand over Hedy's. 'After the lesson,' she whispered, smiling.

Hedy dropped back into her seat before anyone noticed her mistake. She spent the rest of the lesson touching the hand that Miss Banville had covered with her own. The skin tingled.

Hedy notices a pile of papers on Miss Banville's desk, and knows they're the creative writing assignment. Her toes curl inside her shoes. She's written a story about a lost spaceship marooned on Mars, the surviving crew having to make decisions about who will live and who will die as their oxygen supply runs out. Stupid. She regrets it now; it's silly, just a lot of made-up nonsense. She wrote it for Chris. She heard his voice in her head while she wrote, helping her find the words. She sits with her arms folded across her chest, staring at her lap.

Miss Banville's heels click on the floor as she gives the papers out. She murmurs words of encouragement as she passes desks. When Hedy's story is put in front of her, she keeps her gaze lowered. Miss Banville says nothing. She moves on. Slowly, Hedy raises her eyes.

'I haven't given marks,' Miss Banville is saying. 'This was an exercise to get your imaginations going.'

Disappointment and relief make Hedy pick up her paper.

There are a couple of red lines through spelling mistakes. At the bottom, Miss Banville has written. *Come and see me after class.*

Hedy chews her nails. She hated it, she thinks. I'm not a real writer, not like Chris. She's let him down. When the bells goes, the other children pick up their books and file out of the classroom, chatting. Hedy waits for them to leave, before she approaches the front desk. Miss Banville looks up at Hedy. 'This is your last lesson, isn't it?'

Hedy nods.

'Then I'll walk with you, if you don't mind. I could do with some fresh air.' She slips her pen and a small pile of books into her bag and slings it over her shoulder. They leave the school building and cross the playground. It feels odd to be walking with a teacher. Hedy wonders if anyone has noticed. Miss Banville is smaller than her and takes quick, determined strides, her red skirt swishing around her knees. Hedy has to hurry to keep up.

She wonders when Miss Banville is going to tell her what she thought of the story. Maybe she's disappointed, perhaps she'll suggest that Hedy drop English as a subject.

'Your story . . .' Miss Banville says, as if she can read Hedy's mind. 'It was startling.'

'Startling?' Hedy's not certain if that's a good thing.

She stops and looks at Hedy. 'You're a natural writer.' She emphasises the word *writer*. 'But you have to hone your skill. There are things to learn. You're telling too much, for example. You need to show more.'

'Show more?' She sounds like a parrot.

Miss Banville nods. 'With scenes, with action and dialogue. Be braver. I can tell you're holding back. You need to practise, keep on writing.' She nods again, silky hair slipping across her eyes. She tosses her head. 'And read. It's essential to keep reading.'

'I do,' Hedy says. 'I read all the time.'

'Good.' Miss Banville smiles.

'What shall I write about?'

'Anything. But whatever your subject, you must write every day. It's your work. Can you do that?'

Hedy manages to move her head up and down. She doesn't want to jolt herself out of this moment. She wonders if she's dreaming.

'I can read your stories, if you like.' Miss Banville touches Hedy's wrist. 'I'd be happy to help.' She raises her head, squinting into the light. 'I think that young man over there knows you.'

'What?' Hedy turns, dazed.

Peter is parked across the lane, waving out of the window of the farm truck. Miss Banville grins. 'See you tomorrow. I'm looking forward to reading the next one.'

'What was that about?' Peter says as she climbs into the passenger seat. 'Who's the woman?'

'My English teacher.'

'She looked about twelve. Funny clothes, too.' He starts the engine and turns the wheel. The truck rattles.

Hedy has to shout over the noise. 'I think she's stylish.'

'Stylish?' He gives her a sideways glance. 'What was she saying? Were you getting a telling-off?'

'No,' Hedy says. 'Not exactly.'

That's the second time Miss Banville has touched her. She looks at her wrist, the point of bone. Her chest feels huge inside her ribs. As if her heart has been pumped up like a balloon. She's so excited that she wants to scream out of the open window into the rush of air. She wishes she'd written the whole conversation down so she could relive it, hear Miss Banville's words again and again. She doesn't want to forget a single thing.

There's no desk in her room, and Hedy feels reluctant to write at the kitchen table, where Mrs Rose, Peter, or even her uncle, might read over her shoulder. She's embarrassed to admit what she's doing. Whatever Miss Banville says, her efforts will never compare with Chris's. So she waits until all her chores are done, her homework finished in the kitchen, before she goes to her room and sits cross-legged on her bed, balancing the exercise book on her knees, chewing her pencil, writing and crossing out, and writing again. She writes the kind of stories that Chris wrote, the kind he'd want her to read to him. She's imagining new planets and strange creatures, believing in the impossible for as long as it takes to finish a story.

# THIRTY-FOUR

Hedy comes in from her chores with fresh milk on her fingers. Mrs Rose is outside, hanging sheets in the sunshine. As Hedy scrapes out the remnants in her bowl and puts it into the sink, Ernest limps into the kitchen. He nods in her direction, sitting heavily at the table, waiting for her to fetch him his breakfast. He looks tired, she thinks, as she pours him his tea and sets his porridge in front of him. She hears the rasp of his breath as he picks up the spoon.

Standing at the sink she's shocked by the sudden sound of a metallic clatter and spins round to see the spoon lying on the floor, Ernest pushing himself back from the table. His chair sticks on the stone flags as he attempts to get up. Air rattles in his throat; his eyes bulge.

'Don't move. I'll get the Potter's.' She turns towards the sideboard.

But he's still struggling to get up. Hedy's fingers close around his arm. 'Stop,' she says. 'Sit still.'

His skin is sheened with grey. Panic blinds him. He's choking.

His leg catches under the table. Hedy grabs him, but he twists out of her grasp and tips off the chair, landing on his hip. He cries out, curled in a half-circle, his breath coming in jagged gulps. The old dog snuffles to his side, licking his face and whining.

'Mrs Rose!' Hedy yells as she crouches.

Ernest stares up with unfocused eyes. Her reflection is shrunk inside his pupils, a stick creature trapped behind the black of his gaze.

Mrs Rose is there, the door banging behind; she bends down, bringing the scent of washing powder, the clean cotton of the sheets. She shoos the dog away, and places a hand on his forehead, slips her fingers to his wrist to feel his pulse. 'Call Peter,' she says.

Peter takes one shoulder and Hedy takes the other; together they hoist Ernest up the stairs. They try to lie him down on the bed, get him comfortable, but his hands claw at his throat; his mouth gapes wide and the shrill whistle of his breath makes Hedy want to cover her ears. 'You two go on now,' says Mrs Rose. 'Call the doctor, Hedy, then boil the kettle. I'll do the rest.'

Hedy glances over her shoulder as she leaves the room. Mrs Rose is sitting on the bed, undoing Ernest's shirt, smoothing the hair from his forehead, their faces close. Hedy has a sudden memory of Mom lying in her darkened room, Hank comforting her.

Last bell has rung. Pupils push past, careless with the relief of the day's ending, storming towards freedom. Among the voices and clattering feet, Hedy hears her name being called. She slows and turns.

Miss Banville shines out of the crowd of uniformed pupils, bright in a yellow dress. 'Is everything all right? I was worried. It's not like you to be late. You slipped away so quickly afterwards.'

Hedy hangs onto the strap of her bag. 'My uncle. He's not well.'

'Oh, my dear,' Miss Banville steps closer, her voice gentle. 'I'm so sorry.'

Hedy's throat closes. She struggles to speak, but there's something hard lodged in her throat.

Miss Banville takes a deep breath. 'Hedy,' she says.

There is so much inside that one word, the weight of it, her name spoken aloud, the simplicity of being known by another, that it releases something. Hedy begins to cry. She finds she can't stop. Snot and tears are sticky on her face; through a blur, she rifles inside her bag for a hanky, unsuccessfully. She can feel the interest of pupils and teachers as they pass by, the curious stares and whispers.

Miss Banville takes her arm. 'Come.'

She lets herself be led away, across the playground to the car park, where her teacher unlocks a blue Morris Mini and opens the passenger door for her. Hedy slumps in the seat, eyes blurry, her sleeves sodden from being dragged across her cheeks and eyes and nose. She doesn't ask where they're going. A part of her doesn't care; she supposes that Miss Banville is driving her to the farm.

They stop outside a terraced house that Hedy doesn't recognise. Miss Banville puts on the handbrake. Turns to her. 'We're going to have a cup of tea. Give you some time. Then I'll take you home.'

When Hedy doesn't move, she laughs. 'I won't bite. My landlady, Mrs Durant, might, but if we're quick we can get up to the second floor before she emerges from her kitchen.'

Hedy manages a small smile. She follows Miss Banville up the path, into a gloomy, overcrowded hall, smelling of furniture polish and boiled vegetables. They hurry up the stairs and her teacher unlocks a door. Inside, there's a different smell, peppery and musky. The sitting room is covered in rugs and cushions in shades of purple, orange and red. There are no chairs, no sofa. A wooden chest seems to serve as a table. Wild flowers spill out of vases, a lampshade is covered with beaded fabric. The brown wallpaper is almost invisible under dozens of drawings and paintings. Hedy stares around. She's never been anywhere like it.

'Make yourself comfortable. I'm going to put the kettle on.'

Hedy goes to have a closer look at the pencil drawings tacked to the wall. She recognises the Norfolk landscape, big watery fields, canals, horses grazing, and some long, windswept expanses of sand with dunes, the dark waves of the North Sea rolling under huge skies.

Miss Banville comes back, two steaming mugs in her hands. 'Here. It'll make you feel better.'

'Did you do the drawings, miss?'

She nods. 'Keeps me busy in my spare time. I paint, too.' She lowers herself onto one of the cushions, 'Sit. Relax. And while we're out of school, please call me Claire.'

'Claire.' Hedy tries the sound of it on her tongue, soft as a sigh. She folds her legs under her, sinking onto a cushion. It's funny to be sitting on the floor with her teacher. It feels informal, almost like a game.

Claire smiles. 'To tell the truth, when someone calls me "miss", for a second I think they mean someone else.'

Hedy takes the hot cup in her hands. Boiling water with a clump of green leaves floating inside like weeds in a pond.

Claire laughs at her expression. 'Mint tea. Drink.'

Hedy sips cautiously. It's sweet, and the leaves make the water taste fresh. She nods. 'Where did you get all your stuff? All these fabrics and cushions?'

'Morocco, mostly. I spent a year travelling with friends. They serve mint tea there with lots of sugar. It's a real ceremony to make it properly.' She watches Hedy over the rim of her mug. 'Tell me about this uncle of yours. I hope he's not very ill?'

Hedy thinks of Ernest's broken body, his mouth thin with pain. 'I'm afraid he is.' She swallows. 'He's the only family I have left.'

'Oh, I'm sorry.' Claire looks concerned.

Her listening face encourages Hedy to keep talking. 'I've only lived with him for three years. I'd never met him before. I used to have a ... a proper family. But then my brother died.' She takes a deep breath. 'My dad died, too. My mom couldn't cope. She's ill, in an asylum. I used to think she'd get better.' Hedy rubs her cheek. 'But it's been years. She doesn't know who I am.'

Claire has gone pale. 'My God.' She clasps her hands. 'I had no idea.' She shakes her head, dark hair falling into her eyes as she shifts position to sit cross-legged. She puts her mug on the floor. 'All this grief and loss, all your feelings ... I think you should try to put them into your writing. Your work will be more powerful, and it will help you, I think, to write it down.'

'I don't know that I'm good enough.' Hedy looks into her mug. 'I don't feel like a proper writer. Not like my brother – Chris.'

When she glances up, Claire is nodding. 'You have the talent,' she says. 'It will take hard work, though. You'll be frustrated, full of self-doubt. You'll know rejection. But if you're a real writer, you'll keep doing it anyway.'

'When I'm making up a story, it's as if Chris is with me, somehow inside the words, inside the story.' Hedy bites her thumbnail. 'It's him I'm writing for.'

Claire nods as if she understands. 'Writing is healing. It's your connection to him.' She pauses. 'Was he younger?'

'Yes, but only by minutes. He was my twin. He was different from other people. Not just because he had a deformed spine. He was better, kinder.'

Claire widens her eyes. She leans forwards, head on one side. 'How ... do you mind me asking? How did he die?'

Hedy picks at one of the damp mint leaves, tearing it apart. 'He was murdered.' She can feel the older woman's shock, a tightening of the air between them. 'He was hung from a tree. I don't tell people. Nobody knows what to say.'

'From a tree?' Claire's voice is low and hesitant. 'Like ... like a lynching?'

Hedy jerks up her head. The word jolting her suspicion of Scott back into life. The teacher stares at her lap as if she's thinking, and then she lets out a long sigh and touches Hedy's arm. 'We don't have the right words,' she says quietly, 'for something so terrible. That's why people don't say anything.'

Hedy closes her eyes and opens them again. The relief of talking has made her dizzy. She has the urge to keep on until she's told Claire everything. 'After Chris died, my dad killed himself in a cell on an American airbase.' Hedy clenches her fingers. 'He'd been arrested. They said he'd betrayed his country. I still can't believe he would have done it. It seems crazy to think he might have been a spy.' She rubs her eyes, sparks bursting behind her lids. 'But I don't know. There's so much I don't know. And there's nobody to ask. The only person I can ask can't tell me, because he's not allowed to.'

Claire stands up, tucking a strand of hair behind her ear. She walks across the room and stops by the window, staring out into the street. 'You really think your father could have been a spy? A double agent, you mean, for the Russians? Like the Ring of Five.'

Hedy blinks up at her. 'Who were they?'

'A group of Cambridge students who were turned after meeting at university. I followed the story in the papers. They were idealists. Communists. From what I've read, most spies become double agents for their ideals, although I think it can be lucrative, too.'

'I don't know what would have motivated Dad to do something like that.' Hedy is crushed by a sense of helplessness. 'He seemed so patriotic. It's hard to believe he was capable of betraying anyone, let alone his country. He was a bomber pilot in the war. A hero. But I was so young. I didn't really know him. Not like that. I only knew him as my dad.'

Claire paces the floor, rubbing her chin. 'This is all incredible.' She swings round to face Hedy. 'Are there any clues, I wonder ... anything about your father ... his life ... his choices ... that might help you understand?'

'Like what?' Hedy scrambles onto her knees, hope flickering. 'I've gone over and over everything I can remember.'

'Well,' Claire frowns, 'for example, did you ever get stationed in an Eastern Bloc country? Um ... could he have come into contact with any communists, East Germans?' She presses her fingers together. 'Russians or North Koreans?'

Hedy shakes her head, slumping onto her hip. 'But I suppose he could have met a communist anywhere. I guess they don't walk around with a sign round their necks.'

'No. Of course not.' Claire's voice is disappointed. She sits on the floor next to Hedy. 'What about that person – the one you said knows something?'

'Hank.' Hedy chews her lips. 'He's in the military. A family friend. But my dad's case is classified. So he can't tell me anything – not yet.' Hedy runs her fingers through her hair, sweeping it off her forehead. 'One day though, one day it will stop being classified. And then ... then I'll know the truth.'

Claire puts her arm around Hedy's shoulder. Hedy sits very still, aware of the length of the limb lying against her, the scented roundness of her flesh. 'I hope you find out soon.' She moves away, standing up. Hedy feels the lack of her like a small grief, a folding inwards.

'Do you like music?' Claire is bending down, sorting through some LPs. 'I think you'll like this.'

There's a record player in the corner of the room. She slips a black disc out of its paper and sets it down carefully. The needle crackles and there's a rushing sound. The room is filled with music. It's like nothing Hedy has ever heard before. It is rich and delicate at the same time, a flood of melody held against a steady rhythm. A man's voice, sweet and fine, rising and falling. Claire sits down and closes her eyes. She opens them when the record comes to the end. 'Bach Cantata number fifty-four,' she says. 'The piano was being played by Glenn Gould. A genius.'

Hedy says nothing, because she can't think how to describe the record or how it made her feel. Soothed and excited, happy and sad. It's too complicated to talk about, like the thoughts that Claire's words have released into her head, chasing each other round and round. Claire seems to understand. She stands up. 'I should drive you home now.' She picks up the mugs and disappears with them. Comes back with the car keys in her hand. Hedy glances around again, storing up a memory of the room for later. She would like to hear the music again. She thinks about the way Claire Banville said the word *genius*, and feels a lurch of envy.

# THIRTY-FIVE

Hedy knows all the staff by name, can find her way about the building without any help. But there are rules, and visitors must always be escorted. 'She's not having a good day today, I'm afraid,' Nurse Grey says, her plump face crumpling in sympathy. She's Hedy's favourite nurse because she seems to genuinely care about Mom.

Hedy's got used to the smell of stale urine, bleach, and overcooked food that sharpens the air of the building. She recognises faces in the day room: the elderly woman with the blue girlish bow in her wispy hair who cries as she knits baby blankets, and the younger woman who stares at everyone with malicious, shining eyes. Hedy finds her mother in her favourite rocking chair by the window in the day room.

Mom sits and rocks back and forth, her hands continually moving in her lap, pressing her fingers into the scar on her palm. She never told them how she got the scar. 'Oh, I don't remember,' she used to say, even though nobody could forget an accident that left a mark like that.

Mom closes her eyes and moans. Hedy draws up another chair and sits down quietly. When her mother is like this, she must be careful not to trigger an outbreak of hysteria. She must not frighten her.

Hedy's discovered that talking in a calm voice, telling Mom about her day, about the farm, can act like a lullaby to a fractious child. So she begins as if she's telling a story. 'I've just come from the train. I know each bit of the journey now – could almost draw the countryside and villages from memory. I like it when the train passes the same houses, and I see the lights come on in the evening, see mothers calling their children in for their tea.'

Mom's face relaxes. She stops moaning, sitting with her lips parted and her eyes glazed as if she's seeing comforting visions in her head.

'How are you, Mom? It's me. Hedy.'

There's no response. Not even a flicker behind the eyes. She knows her mother spends most of her days sedated. She thinks of the pills Mom used to take for her nerves, and how her fingers trembled when she tipped them out of the bottle.

'I have a new teacher at school. Miss Banville,' Hedy tells her. 'Claire. She's not like anyone I've met before. There's something about her, as if she has a fire in her belly, a passion. She seems to feel the world with a greater sensitivity than other people– a bit like Chris used to . . .' She glances at her mother to see if she'll react to the name. But she's rocking quietly and staring into the garden.

'She's encouraging me to write stories. I know I'll never be as good as Chris.' Another quick glance to check for a response. Her mother's face is calm and blank. 'But I really like doing it. It's hard. It's more exhausting than playing a baseball match or digging a ditch because it's pulling a story out of nothing, creating whole characters from nothing . . .'

She sits quietly and looks at her mother. She'd like to explain how it feels to sit near Claire Banville, how her heart jumps and her skin feels raw and naked, how she longs for their hands to touch. She looks around at the inmates and nurses. She can't admit it – this feeling – it's the way she's supposed to feel about a man, not a woman.

Mom's placid smile has gone. She's frowning, her hands clamped over her ears, moaning, a low, anguished groan.

Hedy shifts her chair closer and touches her mother's leg. 'What is it, Mom?'

Her mother stares at her, her palms still stuck to the sides of her head. 'He keeps telling me the same thing,' she hisses. 'He keeps saying that Christopher is dead.'

Hedy swallows. 'Who?' she asks quietly. 'Who's telling you?'

'Where is Hedy? She should be with him. Where is she?'

Hedy feels sick. The room tilts and sways as if it's her in the rocking chair. 'I'm so sorry,' she whispers. 'I let him down. I let you down.'

Her mother looks at her sharply. 'Who are you?'

'It's OK, Mom. Don't upset yourself. I'll get someone.' Hedy crosses the room and finds Nurse Grey, tugging on her sleeve. Hedy leaves the ward, not letting herself look back. She's learnt to protect herself from the disappointment of Mom not being Mom, but it still unbalances her, takes the strength out of her bones. She remembers how she felt after that first visit, walking down this same corridor with shaking legs, and how Hank was there to meet her in the reception hall. The gladness and relief in her heart when she saw him there, waiting.

# THIRTY-SIX

## 1962

Summer. Rain and more rain. The cows wading up to their hocks in mud, and dark water lapping at the brink of the canals, the sea creeping up the defences.

Hank is keeping his promise; she's received several airmail letters since he left for America.

> *Our new president is handsome as a film star, according to the ladies. But he's serious about the Apollo mission, and getting a man on the moon. I believe it will happen this decade. On the subject of handsome men, I met up with Scott Lansens. He's at the Colorado Military Academy, training to be a pilot. Good to see the kid in cadet uniform. He'll make colonel someday. He sends you his best. Says it's a damn shame what happened to your brother.*

Scott. The name is a shock. Panic scrabbles at her insides. Then anger, making her shake. How dare he talk of her brother, send messages to her? She scrunches the paper, screwing the sentences into nonsense, and flings it into the bin. Whatever Hank said, she can't stop thinking about Scott; she can see it playing out behind her lids, how Scott and those boys pulled Chris out of the brace, slipping the noose around his neck, and laughing. Laughing.

Hank sends a package with candy bars and a pair of hooped earrings. Hedy holds the fine circles in her hands. She positions them by her ears and looks at her reflection in the mirror. She doesn't have pierced lobes. She keeps them on her mantelpiece. She likes the silvery shine and moon-like curve of them. At night, she stares up at the real moon, at the faint shadows across its surface, marking out possible meadows, mountains, rivers. She imagines the long-necked, gentle beings her brother wrote about up there somewhere, watching over her.

'Was it Scott?' she whispers into the night. 'Chris? Tell me what to do. Tell me how to find out.'

She's reading all the time – *The L-Shaped Room* by Lynne Reid Banks, *The Country Girls* by Edna O'Brien, *To Kill A Mockingbird* by Harper Lee – Hedy is dazzled by the possibilities of life, comforted by the characters she finds inside the pages, people who are outsiders, conflicted, struggling, alone. Atticus Finch sometimes wears the face of her father, and night after night she stands with him in the town square turning back the mob from the jail, facing down the men who surely have rope looped in their hands.

Upstairs, Ernest is propped on pillows. He wheezes into starched hankies that Mrs Rose boils and irons every day, the bloodstains fading to pale rust. When Hedy enters his room to bring him a drink or a meal on a tray, he doesn't open his eyes. His intractable silences are the condition of his life. She understands now that loneliness has calcified around him; a lifetime of living as a solitary creature has scratched away at his humanity.

The rest of the house is different. Peter and the farmhands linger over their tea; there's humour and running jokes in the kitchen. None of them are tensed for the sound of Ernest's footsteps limping down the hall, his stick hitting the flagstones.

Hedy stands in Ernest's room with a bowl of tomato soup in her hands, steam curling in an aromatic cloud. She gives a small cough. 'I have your supper here. Best to have it while it's hot.' She sits beside him and hands him the bowl, the spoon. 'Do you want me to help?'

He shakes his head.

'There's more salt if you want. Chris liked tomato soup too,' she says. 'He was always asking Mom if we could have it for tea.'

'Chris,' he repeats the name as if it's a foreign word. 'You said he had scoliosis too? Was it ... was it very bad?'

'Yes,' she says, trying not to sound too eager, wanting to talk about Chris. 'But he wore a brace to straighten his bones.'

'A brace?'

'The Milwaukee Brace. Like a torture contraption. He hated it. But Mom said it would cure him.'

'Ah. Nothing like that when I was a boy.' Ernest blinks at her. 'It must have been hard ... hard for her to see him suffer. I worried that her child would be afflicted. It was always a risk.' Ernest looks worn out from speaking, his voice getting weaker and weaker. He lifts a spoon to his mouth. His shaking fingers mean that half of the liquid spills, and Hedy has to prevent herself from dabbing with a napkin. She remembers how Chris wanted to do things for himself whenever possible. Although there was one thing he was always happy to let her do.

'I have an idea.' She stands up. 'Won't be a minute.'

She comes back with a book in her hand, and Ernest doesn't object when she settles in the chair in the corner and begins

294

to read. He appears to be listening, she thinks, glancing up in between paragraphs. When she finishes the second chapter, she sees that he's fallen asleep.

It's a habit now to read to Ernest every evening after his supper. He lies looking up at the ceiling, concentration creasing his brow. He enjoys crime novels best: Agatha Christie, Dick Francis.

'Which do you prefer?' he asks one evening. 'Miss Marple or Poirot?'

'The funny thing is, I get Mrs Rose and Miss Marple mixed up in my head,' she smiles. 'I think it's the practical mind and stout shoes. So I'm very fond of Miss Marple. But in the end . . .' she raises one eyebrow, 'it has to be the man with the little grey cells. What about you?'

Ernest makes a noise which is half wheeze and half croaky laugh. 'Oh, I think Miss Marple. I admire a capable woman. Mrs Rose has been a friend to me. A good woman.'

She gets through three or four chapters before he's snoring. His face looks relieved in sleep, pain drawing back from the surface. Hedy straightens the covers, switches off the light, looking down at his skull, which seems every day to shrink further into itself. She touches his forehead, smoothing her fingers over the hard-etched frown lines. Then she picks up dirty cups and goes to her own room, where she stays up late, puzzling over plots, editing her work.

There is a new clarity to her days. She didn't think even this small connection with Ernest was possible. Visiting Mom has become more bearable, too. She doesn't expect recognition now, and that helps to make the visits easier. Mrs Rose packs up gifts of shortbread or flapjacks to take to Mom, jars of apple jelly, bunches of flowers picked from the garden. Sometimes Mom buries her nose in the blooms and smiles, eats a biscuit and says it tastes good. Little things are all that matter, small comforts and pleasures that might make Mom's life in the asylum easier.

# THIRTY-SEVEN

Hedy hasn't been invited to Claire Banville's flat again. She can see that it might be difficult for a teacher to become too friendly with a pupil. But she keeps re-imagining going up the cabbage-smelling stairs and in through a door that leads into another world – one of travel and adventure, art and music – and she knows that that is how she would like to live one day.

As Hedy goes past her uncle's bedroom, she stops, aware that the struggle of his breathing is louder than usual. The summer's day is blocked by half-drawn curtains, the air thick with the fusty, stale smell of sickness, the stench of the chamber pot. She steps over the threshold. The dog, usually banished to the kitchen, is lying on the floor next to his master's bed, and he raises his head, giving her a sorrowful stare.

Ernest has to sleep propped on a mound of pillows to get any oxygen into his crushed lungs. He waves a skeletal hand, beckoning her closer. She treads over the carpet, leaning to pat the dog. 'Shall I open the window? Do you want me to read to you?'

'I need to tell you . . .' He's turning his sunken face towards her. 'I need to talk about your mother . . .'

Hedy sinks onto her knees by his side, closing her lips, giving him space to tell her more.

'She ran away. Did you know that?' He looks at Hedy. 'We argued. Said things. Terrible things. There was a fight.' His arms stir on the sheet, the stump of his finger twitching. 'I was angry for a long time.' He coughs, a strangled sound that becomes a struggle for breath.

She picks up the glass of water on the side table and holds his head, putting the glass to his lips. Water dribbles over her hand onto the sheets. His skull is heavy, strands of hair clinging.

'Mom would never talk about her family,' she says. 'About the farm.'

'Our father was a cruel man. He hid behind God. Used the Lord's name as an excuse when he took the rod to us. He was ashamed of me. It made me angry and I took my anger out on Ruby.' He blinks, his mouth open to gasp air. 'I was jealous because she had everything that I didn't . . .' He closes his eyes. His breathing is harsh. His chest struggles in its rise and fall under the sheet. His eyes open. 'And in the end, she could run away, and I couldn't. I hated her for that most of all. But I don't hate her anymore. I want you to give her a message . . . tell her . . . tell her . . . I'm sorry.' He coughs and scrabbles for Hedy's hand. 'You will tell her . . . won't you?'

'Yes.' Hedy holds his fingers firmly in her own. 'Of course I'll tell her.'

'I didn't want her to leave . . .' His head rocks on the pillow. 'I was frightened. I didn't have anyone else. We didn't have the words to explain feelings. But now . . . I know . . . I know why she left. I don't blame her . . .'

Hedy keeps holding his hand. She thinks he's fallen asleep. His eyes have closed.

'I'm glad you came.' His voice is a thread of sound.

In the attic, she closes the door and leans against it, putting all of her weight against the wood as if someone is in pursuit, crashing up the narrow stairs behind her. Loneliness crushes her, a hard, cold, breathless thing, with dark wings smothering her. She closes her eyes, pushing it away. It belongs to Ernest – his stubborn, solitary life – his unhappiness. She doesn't really understand what happened between him and Mom, but she knows there's been a waste – a waste of love, of years, of opportunities – and it's too late to recover any of it. She wonders what terrible things sister and brother told each other, and then thinks of her own terrible words, the ones she spoke to Chris. She wishes someone could take a message to him. She recites it every day, the sentences silent in her head, or roared into the wind: *I'm sorry, Chris, my twin, my love, my other half. I never meant to hurt you. I never for one moment wished that you were not you. I only ever wanted to heal you and make the pain go away – but not like that. Never like that.*

At least Ernest's message for Mom is safe in her head. One true thing. But she doesn't know if Mom will be able to recognise the words.

She has to tell someone. There's only one person – only one person she wants to talk to. But it's the school holidays. Hedy catches the bus into town. It's a long trip through dusty lanes. The tangled loveliness of summer is spread across the flat, Norfolk landscape. At the horizon, the sea moves, shedding salt into the air. Most of the crops have been cut. Stubble fields are alive with rabbits and hares, larks hovering on brown wings above the gleaming earth. White eglantine weaves through leafy hedges, flowers full of bees; the blood-red, papery-skinned poppies are overripe, petals falling open, dark hearts burning in the sun.

Hedy gets off the bus when they reach the centre of town. She's surrounded by buildings. Light slices between shadows. The town is crushed under the blazing sky. Walls trap hot air. Tarmac melts, giving off a burnt, chemical tang. She stands on the gritty pavement and glances up and down terraces of narrow houses. They all look the same. With a jolt of dismay, she realises she can't remember the name of the street where Miss Banville lives. Hedy puts her hands on her hips, hoping for inspiration. There's a particular energy that emanates from her, even in stillness, a crackle inside the spaces she occupies. Perhaps she will feel the pull of it. Hedy walks away from the shops and cinema to back streets, where the only noises are muted by distance: the stutter and roar of engines, children's voices, a busy lawnmower.

Hedy envisions herself sitting on the floor in the shade of the purple drape, a red cushion under her elbow. She'll sip her mint tea and tell Claire what her uncle said. Hearing about Mom and Ernest's falling-out has made her own confession rise up; an urgent need to talk about Chris presses into her throat, a need to explain exactly what happened the night Dad was taken away, to repeat the things she said to Chris. Hedy imagines her teacher listening in that concentrated way she has, nodding her head, before she says something wise. Or perhaps she will be disgusted, horrified by Hedy's callous behaviour, and she'll turn away. Hedy has to take the risk.

Her feet are tired. Sometimes she finds that she's walked the same length of sidewalk as she did ten minutes ago. She has a blister on her heel and a terrible thirst. She looks up and notices a parked car covered with a red tarp; the shape and colour trigger a memory. This is the right street. At last. Pacing past each house, Hedy gazes up at second-floor windows, her heart lifting when she recognises the swag of purple patterned fabric hanging at the third house – 'from Morocco,' she breathes.

She rings the doorbell, keeping her finger on the buzzer for longer than necessary in her relief. The door opens, and a sallow woman in a housecoat and slippers glares from under a headscarf. 'I'm not buying anything.'

Hedy attempts a smile. 'I'm looking for Miss Banville.'

'She's not here.'

Hedy steps closer, trying to peer past the woman into the dark hall. She can't believe she isn't there, waiting for her, somehow knowing how much she's needed. 'Are you sure?'

'Calling me a liar?' The landlady pulls her chin into her neck, and shoves the door. Before she's aware of what she's doing, Hedy's stuck her foot between the edge and the frame. 'When will she be back?'

'I'm not her keeper,' the woman scowls. 'If you don't take your foot out of my door, I'll call the police.'

Hedy retreats back onto the street, standing in the middle of the road, shading her eyes to stare up at the window. The purple fabric seems to mock her now. Nothing moves. No shadow flits across the glass. Hedy doesn't know where to go or what to do. She keeps staring up at the window as if by looking hard enough she will reverse reality and conjure Claire's face smiling down. A car comes along, sounding its horn with irritated beeps, and Hedy moves reluctantly out of the way. She sits on the edge of the kerb and slips off her shoes to massage aching toes, inspect the bubble of blister. She holds her disappointment close, a heaviness in her belly. She will wait.

There's shade under a large shrub climbing over a wall on the opposite side of the road, and Hedy folds herself up in the dust beneath it, fitting herself inside the shape. She can hear the sound of a vacuum cleaner coming through the open windows of number three. The slam of a door. A woman towing a little girl by the hand crosses the street, notices her with a start, and walks on at a faster pace. The child hangs back to stare; she clutches a lolly, orange dribbles making patterns across her wrist, dripping onto the pavement in sticky drops. 'Come along,' the woman tugs at the child.

A blue Mini pulls up, and the passenger door opens. Hedy struggles to her feet. A stranger emerges from the car: a slim, brown-haired woman unfolding herself gracefully. She's wearing a pink blouse, gingham shorts cut to show long, tanned legs, and she carries a picnic basket. In the other hand, she swings an opened wine bottle. Claire appears from the driver's side, jangling her keys and laughing. The two link arms and walk towards number three. The way they lean into each other, keeping pace, their bobbed hair touching, makes a fierce surge of wanting and despair flood Hedy's chest. The brunette looks about the same age as Miss Banville. She holds herself like a dancer, her shoulders back and her spine long. She'll be the one sitting on a red cushion sipping mint tea, not Hedy. She'll suggest putting on a record, and they'll reminisce about their picnic and open another bottle of wine.

Hedy hovers in the shadows. Why did she come? Coming to her teacher's home uninvited – she's been deluded, a dreamer, to think that Miss Banville would welcome her, would even want her here.

Hedy trudges up the cinder track to the farmhouse, dragging her disappointment with her, her unspoken confession sitting in her chest like a rock. She's sweaty and hot; her shirt sticks to her back, damp under her breasts. She passes silent outbuildings and animals sleeping in the shade. It's a relief to get into the dim cool of the farmhouse kitchen. The dog whimpers from under the table and comes to sit at her feet. 'What are you doing down here?' She strokes his ears.

Peter appears in his shirt sleeves, dirt streaking his flushed face. He pushes the hair from his forehead and clears his throat. 'Hedy . . .' He looks at his feet. 'I'm sorry.' His voice is nervous, oddly formal.

She doesn't speak, turns and runs to the stairs, scrambling up the steps two at a time. At the threshold of Ernest's room, she looks at the bed, the shape of her uncle there, unmoving.

Mrs Rose is tidying the clutter of an invalid's possessions, collecting bottles of pills, a tub of Vaseline and discarded hankies. She glances at Hedy and shakes her head. 'He's gone, child.'

The doctor is there. He snaps his black bag shut, and nods at Hedy with eyes averted as he leaves.

Hedy falls onto her knees and clutches Ernest's hand inside her own. She presses her lips to his rough fingers; warmth lingers in his skin, and she feels it seeping away. 'We still had so much to say,' she whispers.

Mrs Rose sits on the bed, and pats his knee under the covers. 'He's at peace now.'

Ernest's eyes are closed, his skin seems more fabric than flesh, the colour of ash. Despite the warmth of his body, he looks as though he's been dead for centuries, a hollow cadaver, an unearthly creature. Hedy buries her face in the sheet. Ernest's message repeats in her head, impossible to forget: such a short, important sentence. She's not sure if Mom will ever understand.

# THIRTY-EIGHT

'She's having a good day,' the nurse says. 'She's been doing some sewing with the other ladies. And she's been given the job of mopping the floor this week.'

Mom is leaning back in her favourite rocking chair, pushing with her feet to make it tilt and swing. Her cheeks have a pink glow. Her hair is neater, tidied into a bun.

'I hear you've been sewing?'

Ruby nods eagerly. 'I hemmed some hankies. I embroidered Todd's initials onto the corners.'

Hedy falters. It hurts to hear her mother talking about Dad as if he's still alive. She takes a breath, making her voice bright. 'And you're on mopping duty, too?'

'Francesca is jealous . . .' Her mother lowers her voice. 'She tries to take the mop from me. She wants it. But I won't let her.'

'Good for you, Mom.'

'Francesca eats coins and buttons. Puts them in her mouth and swallows. Everyone knows they aren't good to eat.'

'I'm here to tell you something.' Hedy drags a chair close and sits down. She doesn't know how to deliver Ernest's message; she's scared that it will trigger a bad reaction. 'Do you remember your brother?' She looks into Mom's face. 'Ernest?'

Mom begins to hum. She stares past Hedy's shoulder, unblinking.

'I'm afraid that he died. Just a couple of weeks ago.'

'I like to watch TV,' Mom says. 'Can I watch it now?'

'He wanted to tell you he was sorry.' Hedy knows it's no good. She touches Mom's hand, finds the scar on her palm. 'This is important, Mom. He said he was sorry. He said he understood why you left.'

Mom yanks her hand from Hedy's grip. She turns her head, twisting it from side to side, her eyes anxious, but blank. 'Why can't I watch my programme?'

Mom pushes herself to her feet and moves slowly in her odd, stilted gait towards the huddled figures that sit in a half-circle in front of the muted televisions. She drops into an empty chair, her expectant face reflecting the images that flicker and leap from silent screens.

Once Hedy thought she could make her mother better. Once she thought she could take her away from this place. She's not sure if that will ever be possible now – with every passing year, it seems more and more unlikely. At least her mother is being cared for, she thinks. Hedy misses her mom, her real mom. But maybe wanting her back is selfish. If Ruby remains here, inside the walls of her own delusions, inside the routines of the asylum, she is protected from the unbearable truth. She is safe.

# THIRTY-NINE

## 1965

Peter got engaged and then married in a matter of months; his bride is a local girl from Stiffkey saltmarshes.

'She's a good woman,' he'd said, when he first told Hedy about the engagement. 'She's keen on me.'

'I don't blame her. She's a lucky girl,' she told him. 'I'm happy for you.' And she was. It was a relief to see Peter happy and settled, to know that they were free to be friends without her worrying that she was accidentally leading him on.

'You were my first love,' he'd said then, staring hard at his shoes. 'But I'll be a good husband to Lily. The past is the past.'

Hedy's finished with school. She's running the farm now; she couldn't manage without Peter. She thinks about what happened at the base all the time. But however much she tries to recall events, she's no nearer to understanding how her family came to be destroyed, as if a bomb had fallen out of the blue, blowing them apart. She's certain she's missing vital details; there's a part of the picture she can't see yet. She can't let the past go – not like Peter; the weight of her history is an anchor tethering her. She's stuck with her feet buried deep in mud.

The only time for writing is at night, when her shoulders ache from driving a fork into the earth, her fingers blistered and ingrained with dirt. She's invested in a second-hand typewriter and mastered a basic form of typing, and even though her self-taught technique only uses the first fingers on each hand, it's quicker than using a pen. She's working on another novel.

'A useful learning curve,' Claire had said of the first. 'Now write another. You have plenty more books in you.' Her gaze had darkened, her eyes steady and intense. 'You need to find your own voice. You can't do that if you're relying on me.' She'd cleared her throat. 'You've left school. It's time, Hedy. You need to do this on your own.'

There were no more meetings where they sat together in the library, knees brushing under the table as they bent over Hedy's latest chapter or story. There had been occasions when Hedy stopped hearing her teacher's words, so preoccupied was she with the uncomfortable prickling desire to press her leg against the older woman's, and to feel her press back. She had a crush, she told herself. A silly crush, like the ones the girls at school had joked about in the changing rooms. But she knew what she felt was more than schoolgirl infatuation. She didn't have a name for her feelings. She couldn't use the word 'love' without experiencing a furious twitch of embarrassment, humiliation coursing through her, making her blush even when she was alone, berating herself for making a fool of herself; but what other word was there for the anguished aching that inhabited every part of her body: her eyeballs, her kidneys, her scalp, the pores of her skin?

Hank's blue airmail envelopes flutter onto the doormat. She props each envelope in the kitchen, while she moves around the table brewing tea and cutting bread. She makes a ceremony of slicing open the rectangle of fragile paper with her uncle's brass letter blade and reads Hank's words over breakfast, not allowing herself to rush sentences that are full of facts and opinions about politics and the times. Hedy is gratified that he thinks she's old enough to be given such information.

After Ernest died, Hedy had a bathroom fitted in one of the upstairs rooms, a blue plastic bath and matching basin and WC: no more lugging hot water from the sink to fill a hip bath. And she bought a TV set and put it in the parlour; there it sits, a blank-faced ugly box, but at the turn of a switch it becomes a portal. Drama and science and astronomy fill the room. She loves *The Avengers*, never misses *The Sky At Night*. She switches on the news every evening.

Hank's latest letter is mostly about Vietnam. He says President Johnson has at last sent US combat forces into battle. *It's essential to stop the communist threat. Once one Asian country falls, another will follow suit. Of course, China and the Soviets are right behind the North Vietnamese, but our troops are better trained and better equipped.*

He finishes with his usual wish. *I hope you've taken to wearing dresses at last and have found yourself a nice young man. You're not far off the age your mother was when she met me and your father.*

The thought makes her panic. It means life is passing her by.

Chris's unfinished story – *The Wonderful* – is still in her drawer. She knows it off by heart, going over it in her mind, sifting through the handful of sentences as if they might contain a clue to his death, because she's beginning to seriously consider that perhaps it's fact, not fiction, however unlikely it seems, and that Hank is mistaken. She can't stop wondering why it's so different from his usual stories in style and content. She suspects that it's linked into his disappearances into the forest, telling what happened on the occasions he slipped away from her. But she has no idea where the light would have come from, or what creature could have made such a noise, and if these things have anything to do with his death. It can't be a coincidence that he was murdered in the same place that he experienced them, can it? She knows Chris believed there were aliens in the forest. She also knows that sometimes just wanting to see things is enough to conjure them. She's run up to complete strangers before, believing that a certain tall man seen at a distance was her father – the crushing disappointment as he turns and she looks into the face of a stranger. But for a few moments she'd made Dad appear; she'd seen him alive, walking the earth. Perhaps all of it was in Chris's imagination – but he believed it had happened.

It's time for the cows to come in from pasture to winter in the barn. The grass is crisp in the mornings, the last of the leaves nothing but withered scraps. Last spring, Hedy removed urine-soaked straw in wheelbarrow loads; today she's scrubbing the stone floor and sluicing out the mangers. Her favourite job comes next, laying down fresh straw; she loves the musty smell of it, the crumbled remains of summer meadows, disintegrating nettles, scraps of poppies. She's in an old pair of overalls, filthy sleeves rolled up, feet in men's boots. She's let her hair grow a few inches, and it tickles the back of her neck, falling into her eyes when she's working, so she's pulled it back with a headscarf.

Hearing the bump and scrape of wheels turning into the yard, she presumes at first that it's one of the farm hands, or perhaps the postman. But the engine sounds aren't familiar. She stops with her arms full of straw and peers through a chink between the planks. A blue Mini is parked outside. She lets the scratchy heap fall at her feet. Claire gets out, elegant in a pair of green slacks and a matching smock.

Hedy doesn't move, standing behind the slatted wall of the barn, her eye to the gap. She's noticed a passenger in the car, recognises brown bobbed hair. Claire goes up to the kitchen door and lifts the brass knocker, rapping a couple of times. The sound echoes in the yard. Everyone is out. Mrs Rose only comes up during the week, and it's a Saturday. There's no barking, because the old dog died soon after his owner. The farmhouse is implacable, keeping its silence. Claire bends forwards and shades her eyes to peer through the kitchen window, her nose against the glass. Then she turns and surveys the yard with a puzzled expression. Hedy drops to her haunches, pulse jumping. A part of her wants to run out and greet her, but not when the brown-haired woman sits in the car watching.

She can hear her teacher walking across the yard, hear her making clucking noises at one of the farm cats, and then a car door slams and there's muffled conversation between the two women. Hedy strains to make out what they're saying, thinking she catches the word 'shame'.

The doors slam again and the engine starts. Hedy straightens up and watches the Mini reverse and drive away down the cinder track.

Hedy finds an envelope pinned to the door.

She opens it with shaky fingers.

*Dear Hedy,*

*I was hoping to see you, to tell you in person that I'm moving away. I'd already given in my notice, but a new opportunity happened very suddenly. I have a part-time teaching position in the south of England, in Cornwall. It suits me better, as it will allow me more time to concentrate on my drawing. A gallery there has offered to show some of my work. I'm enclosing my address; please keep in touch. We are renting a cottage by the sea and you will always be welcome to stay.*

*Keep writing. Hard work and perseverance are the keys. It was a pleasure to be your teacher.*

*With fond love*

*Claire Banville*

Hedy sits at the table. She pours herself a sherry from a dusty bottle left over from a long-ago Christmas. She knocks back a sticky tumbler of the pale brown liquid. It's sweet and strong and makes her cough. She refills the glass, looks at the word 'we'. Miss Banville – Claire – uses it with brutal carelessness. She will be sharing her cottage with the brown-haired woman.

'They.' 'We.' 'Us.' Hedy pushes the heels of her hands into her eyes. Why should she mind? It makes no difference to her. She knew there was no future for her and Miss Banville. But there's a pain in her chest, and she lifts the empty glass and hurls it at the wall. She thinks of Ernest's loneliness, and feels it like the wings of a great, dark creature, the rustle of its feathers coming to claim her.

# FORTY

## 1970

A package arrives and then six postcards, one after another. The package contains a leather-bound notebook. Miss Banville has written on the flysheet, *For your next novel*. The cards show scenes of Cornwall. The messages on the back mention her show at the gallery, her new pupils, the landscape and how it differs from Norfolk. At the bottom of each card, she signs her name with a flourish, *Claire*. But Hedy doesn't want to think of her as Claire anymore. In each, she asks about Hedy's writing.

Hedy doesn't reply, doesn't explain that she'd sent the second book to a publisher and got the manuscript back with a rejection letter weeks later, or that she'd tried another publisher and got an almost identical rejection, the pages of the manuscript more ragged and dog-eared. The postcards stop. The farm consumes Hedy's energy. She's got permanent smudges under her eyes from late nights at her desk and early mornings in the milking parlour, from staring at the pages in her typewriter under poor electric light, words blurring.

Hank's small, forward-slanting scribble reminds her of her father's writing. In his last letter he described meeting Buzz Aldrin, actually shaking his hand. He said Aldrin had told him the dust from the moon smelt like seared steak. Chris would have loved to know that. In Hank's opinion, *Nixon is the right man to keep America – the whole world – safe from nuclear threat.* It's the kind of thing that Hedy imagines Dad would write.

She wishes Chris had lived to see men land on the moon.

Early evening, darkness lapping at the kitchen window panes. Peter and two farm hands are finishing their cups of tea. Mrs Rose buttons up her coat, tut-tutting at the bruised sky. They leave together, calling goodbyes. The beating of Hedy's single heart isn't enough to hold back the loneliness. A tapping noise comes through the wall, the sound of Ernest's stick as he limps over the flagstones. She tells herself it's nothing, just the wind in the eaves, the knocking of a piece of loose metal, but her mind is skittish and dark as the weather. She walks through the shadowy passageway and shuts herself into the parlour, switching on the television, turning up the sound of a living voice.

A depressed-looking newsreader is halfway through a piece about the power cuts. *Nationwide power cuts averaged at 31 per cent yesterday and hospitals faced their most critical twenty-four hours of the strike so far with staff struggling to keep going by candle and battery power.*

After that there's a clip of demonstrations against the Vietnam War: young Americans waving placards. A reporter talks to a girl in bell-bottom jeans with flowers in her hair. The girl looks straight at the camera. 'We've had enough of carnage and hypocrisy.' She makes a sign with her fingers. 'Peace and love,' she shouts. 'Peace and love.' The crowd behind her take up the chant. Wilted flowers slip across her forehead. Hedy shifts closer to the set. When Hank last mentioned the war, he said it was tough going on the ground, that they'd encountered more losses than expected, but they were winning. Hedy wants to reach through the glass to tell the girl to keep faith with the president.

The weather man stands before a map of England, pointing to the east with his stick. Snow is on its way. Hedy gets up and turns the switch. The screen shrinks to a white dot and turns black.

She finds the candle and box of matches; the electricity is due to shut off in a few minutes and she just has time to get into bed. Hedy sees pale flakes falling outside the window before she lies down. The sheets are icy and she hugs a hot-water bottle. Even dressed in pyjamas, two jumpers and socks, she's shivering. The noises of the night dampen to a hush, a deep quiet that only comes with snow. The girl with flowers in her hair, the young protesters waving words at the camera, are creatures walking a separate planet, strange and wondrous and unreachable.

She knows that she's dreaming, but she can't wake up, can't even blink. The light is intense. She is staring straight into brilliance. She anticipates the searing of her retinas. Instead, her sight goes beyond the heat towards a shape moving towards her; she's sure it's the silhouette of her brother – her chest releases. The light is a pathway, a beckoning. She takes a joyful step, then remembers that this is a dream.

The light shuts off, and she's left standing on the forest floor under a leaf-speckled canopy of trees. She's here again. There's the stone, shifted to one side. And here's the oak tree. She puts a hand on the wrinkled bark and looks up into its branches, fearful of seeing Chris, his body hanging. But there's only leaves and acorns. Hedy approaches the edge of the hole cautiously, peering over the lip of earth into the void. She picks up a handful of earth and pine needles and drops it into the darkness, hearing it scatter, scratching the air as it falls.

She shivers, certain that Chris was standing in this exact spot only minutes ago. Why didn't he wait?

She wakes, her eyes wet, her pillow damp. She pushes herself upright and sits with her arms wrapped around her knees. She smells boy sweat, cinnamon breath. She says his name again, calls it loud into the room and hears a tide of emptiness rushing around the hole it makes in the air. She pushes her feet out of the covers, and goes to the window. Her arms hug her ribs. Under a rash of stars, the dark farm buildings are dense with the slumber of animals. She leans her forehead against cold glass. A movement outside the window makes her start. A snowflake sweeps past, and another. More snow. She watches as the sky is filled with them, and they settle, a thicker layer of white covering fences and trees, softening the landscape, brightening the air.

She switches on the light, pulls on an extra cardigan and wraps a blanket from the bed around her, then sits at her desk at the typewriter, winding a sheet of paper inside it with purpose. She hauled the desk from the spare room up here ages ago. There is a story that needs to be finished, even though she has no idea yet of its form, or how it will end.

She starts with the only thing she's certain of: the title. She writes, *The Wonderful*, and stops, her hands falling into her lap, thinking about the light in her dream, so real and compelling, and how it had been impossible to look away until it disappeared, as if a switch had been thrown or a curtain dropped.

She sets her shoulders, touches the keys and begins to type.

# FORTY-ONE

## 1972

There's a blue car bumping up the track through the fields, dust rising behind. As it gets closer, Hedy sees that it's a low-slung Ford Mustang. There's nobody she can think of who'd have a vehicle like that, except Hank. She puts down the spade and stands with her hands on her hips, gladness building inside her, pulling the edges of her mouth into a smile.

The car stops in the yard. She glimpses uniform and a square jaw through the windscreen. She goes forwards to scold him for not warning her of his arrival, to welcome him back. But when the driver emerges from the other side of the car, she sees he's too tall. Too young.

He takes off his hat and scratches his scalp. 'Hedy,' he smiles. 'You dressing like a boy still? God damn it, didn't think I'd set eyes on you again. And here you are. I'm glad to see you. Even though you look a mess.'

'Scott?' She folds her arms, body fizzing with shock. 'What are you doing here?'

316

He rubs his jaw. 'I've been posted to Lakenwoods. Flying F-4 Phantoms. Can I get a drink? Don't suppose you've got cold beer? Coffee maybe?'

'I don't have any beer or coffee. Water, if you like.' She walks into the house, hearing his steps following behind. Her cheeks are burning and her heart hammers at her ears. She wants to turn and tell him to go to hell. She wants to turn and batter her fists into his face.

He stands next to the sink, easy as a cat, handsome in his uniform, and drinks from the glass she gives him, throwing back his head, wiping his mouth with the back of his hand. He looks exactly as she would have predicted: huge shoulders, big-boned face, a sense of entitlement about him. He takes a seat at the table, legs spread.

'Got a lot to catch up on.' He pats the chair next to him.

'I was in the middle of something.' Her lips tighten. They stare at each other, but she can't read his face. She's searching for the murderer inside it. 'All right,' she says, sliding into the seat reluctantly. Now that the shock is ebbing, she understands that with Scott here in front of her, there's the possibility of discovery. The truth, perhaps. She taps the table with her fingers, an urgent, erratic drumming. 'Just for a few minutes.'

'Well, well. Never thought you would have ended up a farmer.' He looks around the kitchen, making wet clicking noises behind his teeth.

'How did you know where I was?'

'Hank gave me your address years ago, because I said I wanted to write you, but when it came to it, I couldn't get my words in order.' He smiles and scratches behind his ear. He looks puzzled for a moment. If she didn't know better, she'd think he was embarrassed.

'Why are you here, Scott?' she asks. 'It's been years. We're not friends. What do you want?'

He coughs and looks at his fingers spread on his knees. 'I guess I owe you an apology.'

'What for?' Her chest is tight.

'I wasn't too nice to you after your brother died. And then your dad and everything. It must have been pretty rough.'

She clenches her fists. 'You could say that.'

'I've been in Vietnam. Flying out of Thailand. Bombing raids.' He glances away, his voice low. 'We had it easy compared to the troops on the ground. I saw a lot of crazy shit. Being there. Seeing it all. Doing things. I don't know – it changed me.'

'And now, Suffolk?'

'Yeah. Soft option. But I've done my time in hell.' He blinks. 'Glad to be out of it in one piece, but I'm glad to leave the States, too. Lot of hatred towards war vets there, and all those hippies kicking up a fuss, burning draft papers and having sit-ins. Off their faces on drugs. Then there's the civil rights nonsense. Blacks taking our jobs and housing. The country's in a mess, frankly. I'm not sure if Nixon's the man to sort it out.'

Hedy remembers the pages torn out of newspaper, stuck in a folder. 'You don't agree with civil rights?'

'Blacks and whites shouldn't mix. It's not natural.'

'I disagree. And so does the government.'

He stretches, arms hooked behind his head. 'Makes no difference around here, does it? Looks like you're pretty isolated.'

'Mud and cows mainly,' she snaps, getting to her feet and grasping the back of a chair. 'But that's nothing for you to worry about.'

'Aren't you lonely?'

She looks at her knuckles flaring white against the chair, and then shrugs. 'Sometimes.'

'You're not getting any younger. Don't you want to get married?'

She shakes her head and stares him down.

Scott seems undaunted. He smiles. 'I got myself a sweet girl. We're getting married next year.'

'What about your dad and mom? How are they?' She slips back into the chair beside him. She has to get to the point. Ask him for the truth about Chris. She needs to get him off-guard before she springs the question.

His mouth twists. 'Not so good. They're divorced. Dad left the air force. He's working in his brother's garage in Texas. Drinks too much.'

'I'm sorry.'

'Mom had an affair.'

'Betty?'

'I didn't know at the time. It happened on the base in Suffolk. They kept it from me for years. Then Dad said something to me about it before I went off to Vietnam. He wouldn't tell me who the man was, said go ask your mom. So I did. And, Hedy . . .' He looks at her, eyes wide. 'You won't believe who it is.'

Hedy pushes her chair back, suddenly dizzy. 'Actually, I think I do have some coffee.' A cloud of bees is inside her head, buzzing. 'I'll make some.' She goes to the cupboard, opens up the coffee can, rattling the lid. She starts to spoon it out, spilling grains over the surface. Her fingers are shaking.

'Hank.'

The name sounds behind her. She spins round, stares at Scott. 'What?'

The buzzing stops. The kitchen is silent. She'd been

319

scared that Scott was going to say her father's name. But, Hank? She swallows; the pulse of moisture loud in her head. Sounds rush in: birdsong, a car in the distance, the clock on the wall edging its second hand to the next number. Scott scratches his chin.

'Yeah. Sly old dog. Never gave me any indication all these years that he was banging my mom. He was the reason my folks split up, but he slapped me on the back and looked me in the face like he had nothing to be ashamed of.'

'Hank and Betty?' Hedy sits down. She turns her head. Her neck clicks. 'I had no idea.'

'Nobody did. Mom said it didn't last long. He was seeing someone else, too. Some English tart that came up to the base.'

Hedy realises she's been holding her breath. She breathes out.

'It was like being in a pressure cooker, wasn't it?' Scott says. 'Living in that place. Everyone on edge.'

'It's what I remember: people's fear– of the bomb falling, of each other even. That whole paranoia about . . . ' she swallows, 'spies. And my mom, scared all the time. Convinced Chris was in danger.' She frowns. 'But she was right.'

'I guess she was.' He rubs the back of his neck. 'I'm sorry about your dad. Shit. First Christopher, then him.'

'He was drinking heavily, and then he kind of went off the rails before they took him away. I thought later, well, something must have really been scaring him to make him behave like that. Maybe,' she bites her lip, 'maybe he knew they were onto him. Maybe he was being blackmailed.'

'He was working on the same programme as my dad. I could see it took a toll on him, too.'

'I think . . . I think maybe Dad could have been spying for the

Russians. I don't want to believe it. But I can't think of another reason why he behaved so strangely and then was arrested.'

'There was a lot of rumour about it afterwards.' Scott raises an eyebrow. 'Fed into all that craziness. Reds under the bed. And it's true the commies would have been trying real hard to find out what they were doing inside those bunkers.' He shakes his head. 'But there was something my dad said once. He said Todd Delaney was a good man. Said it was a crying shame what happened to him.'

Hedy gasps. Her head is ringing with confusion. 'Did you hurt my brother, Scott? I need to know.'

He gives her a puzzled look. 'Hurt him? No. I said some hurtful things, I'll admit that. Might have pushed him away even. I can't remember. He tried to kiss me. Turned my stomach. But I didn't fight him. He was a cripple.'

Hedy gets up and stands with her back to him. She looks out across the fields, the light shimmering in the distance. The view is cleansing, spare and lean. Scott has brought the darkness of the past with him. She pushes her face into her hands. She doesn't want to think about what Scott's told her about Hank; he'd been her saviour – the only adult who helped her after everything went wrong.

'I know I behaved badly when I was a kid. It's been weighing on me. I'm sorry you lost your dad and your brother. I really am.' He coughs. 'I'm glad to see you again, Hedy. I could come and pick you up, take you out for a drink or something sometime?'

She shakes her head. 'I don't think so.'

'Call me if you change your mind.' He puts on his hat. 'I'll leave you my number. You need company. Need to get out of this place.'

She watches him drive away, edging the sports car across the

321

bumps, taking it slowly. The cows at the fence stare at the shiny blue vehicle, backing away, snorting. Hank had been right all along. Scott didn't murder her brother.

The package is solid and heavy, wrapped in string, with a London postmark. She knows exactly what it is. She's been expecting it. Hedy opens it on the kitchen table, nerves and impatience making her fingers fumble, ripping the paper. She pulls out three books, three copies of the same novel, hardbacks with a design of a dark fir tree on the cover, dwarfed by a vast white circle behind it. At the centre of the light, a small, black figure with a domed head hovers. Hedy runs her finger over the title picked out in scarlet letters: *The Wonderful*.

Her science-fiction novel. Hers and Chris's. She wrote it for him, finished it for him in his name. Hedy doesn't know whether to tell Hank her news. She doesn't see how she can express her disappointment in him and celebrate the novel in the same letter. In the end, she doesn't mention what she knows. The sense of betrayal stays with her – but really, his affair with Betty didn't affect her or her family – good men do stupid things, she knows that.

*Remember I told you about Chris's unfinished story? Well, I finished it for him. A science fiction about two different kinds of aliens arriving on earth at the same time: good ones through a wonderful light, and evil ones through tunnels under the earth. And now it's been published. I didn't tell you before, because I couldn't believe it would really happen, even when I'd signed a contract with a publisher. But now the finished copies have been sent to me and I can hold it in my hand. I'll mail you one soon.*

She writes to Miss Banville as well. She spends ages composing sentences, only to scribble them out and rewrite them. It takes her a long time to get the words right. But after she signs her name, she sits with the paper in her hands. It's been years since they've had any communication. Hedy thinks of the brown-haired woman and imagines her with Miss Banville inside a cottage overlooking the Cornish sea. They pour each other glasses of wine and smile across the glassy rims. Hedy rips the letter up and drops the fragments in the bin.

Through the gloom, a shape unfolds, a red spark moving. Peter is out in the yard, having a smoke. She comes close.

She likes the smell of cigarettes. It makes her think of Dad and Hank.

They stand in silence for a while. From inside the walls of the barn, there's the sound of a cat yowling, the noise they make when they've caught a rat.

'Outbuildings all need a new coat of tar,' Peter says. 'Won't do another winter without.'

She nods.

'So, you're a full-time author now?'

Hedy sighs. 'I can't manage the farm and write too.'

Peter puts his hands in his pockets. 'Then give up the farm. Henderson will jump at the chance to buy it. You've worked hard for this. I used to hear the typewriter when I was off home late some nights. See your light on.'

'It won't earn money.' She bites her thumbnail.

'Sell the herd. You'll get a good price for them.'

'Without the cows we won't have a farm. We're not making a profit on grain.'

He sighs, impatient. 'That's what I'm saying. Time to get out. Every small farm is struggling. You're not a farmer, Hedy.'

She turns away from him. He's right. She should be glad to get rid of the farm, to leave this place that her mother hated. It was Ernest's prison. Just as it's been hers for the last fifteen years. But it was also the only home her uncle ever knew, and in his own way, she knows he loved this land, belonged to it. When she sells, it will be the last of him. A pale shadow cuts low above their heads. The barn owl. She tilts her face to watch it pass, a heaviness belonging to the air.

# FORTY-TWO

Hedy is on the train to St Peter's on her way to see Mom. She opens the *Telegraph* she bought at the station. The front-page story is about an air crash in England. No survivors. Wreckage and the dead flung across the Surrey hills. She hasn't been on a plane since that flight from New York. She'd been a child then, fearless and full of unquestioning trust. She wonders how her father stayed safe when he piloted his Fortress through flak and bullets from Messerschmitts. He'd beaten the odds and survived. A lifetime of luck used up in a couple of years. Another headline catches her attention. Five men have been arrested while attempting to bug the Watergate building in Washington DC, something to do with Nixon's re-election campaign. She guesses that Hank's next letter will be full of the story, his indignation at the crime. Hank is behind Nixon's campaign, approving of his fight against communism. *He's not afraid to make the hard decisions, Hedy. He'll break eggs to make an omelette.*

Nurse Grey meets her in reception. 'You can go through to

the dayroom. Tea trolley's there if you want anything. Ruby loves her tea and biscuits.'

For a long time, it was as if Mom's removal from life had stopped the ageing process, kept her looking like a dishevelled, absent version of herself. Now there's a snarl of grey in the blonde; her jawline is softened and drooping. She's thin, her shoulders brittle.

They sit opposite each other across one of the card tables scattered around the dayroom, her mother unwilling at first to leave the rocking chair by the French window, until the offer of biscuits did the trick. Hedy is always taken aback by her mother's awkward crab-like steps, the way her arms dangle against her sides like a sleepwalker. Ruby sips her tea and looks at Hedy, her eyebrows in wary wrinkles. They talk of inconsequential things. Then Hedy slides the book out of her bag and places it next to her mother on the table. 'It's a novel.' She's not sure how much to explain.

Her mother is staring at the cover, her lips moving silently as she reads the title and author name; a slow smile spreads across her face. 'Christopher Delaney.' She speaks the words hesitantly, fumbling over the shapes they make in her mouth. She picks up the book and examines it, turning it in her hands, bringing it to her nose to smell. 'Christopher wrote this,' she says; and this time she sounds certain, excited even.

Hedy tips forwards on her seat, afraid to breathe.

'My son.' Ruby lifts the cover to her face and caresses it with her cheek. 'My son. He was such a clever child. Good with words. People thought he was stupid, because of the brace. Even Todd didn't understand, couldn't see beyond the outside. But I knew that one day he would be cured, and then the world would see his brilliance.'

326

It's the first time Mom's talked coherently. Hope takes a hammer to Hedy's defences; she's hungry for her mother to say something else. Ernest's last words gave her glimpses of a different Ruby, scraps of history, and Hedy yearns for more, to sew the story together. She mustn't do anything startling, mustn't frighten her. She wants the real Ruby back, not just her Mom, but the woman she never knew. 'I wrote the book under his name, because it was his,' she explains quietly. 'It was all his idea.'

Mom nods, eager, distracted. 'Where is he now?' She strains her neck, looking around the room.

Hedy clenches her hands. 'He's . . .' She tilts her chin up. 'He can't come today.'

Her mother smiles, relaxing. She says in a confidential tone, 'He visits me. He brings me presents.'

The disappointment hurts. But if Mom has come close to the surface of herself once, she can do it again, each time stepping nearer, like a wild horse. Mom's heart thumps with blood, her bones have flesh – there's still a chance, even after all these years, that she could return to her body from whatever place she's lost herself.

Hedy thinks of Ernest's words, her promise to him. 'Mom, do you remember your brother, Ernest? He wanted me to tell you something.'

Mom sits up straighter, looking expectant. Hedy takes a deep breath. 'He says he's sorry. He said he understands why you had to leave.'

Mom doesn't move, except for a twitch in her jaw. Hedy reaches out and takes her hand. 'You remember him, don't you?'

'Ernest?' Mom's eyes are very wide. 'He said that?' She begins to stroke the scar on her palm. 'Will he come and see me?'

Hedy lowers her voice. 'Those were his exact words. But he's . . . ' She swallows. 'I'm sorry . . . He's dead.'

Mom balls her hands into fists and raps at her skull. 'Dead, dead, dead,' she mutters, hammering at her head with her knuckles.

Hedy tries to take her mother's wrists, to stop her from hurting herself. 'Don't.' She grabs one bony wrist. Her mother is surprisingly strong. 'Stop. Mom.'

Her mother twists her arm, yanking free. 'Get away from me! Who are you?'

Hedy sits back, holding her hands up in a gesture of peace. 'It's just me. Hedy. Your daughter. It's all right, Mom. I'm not going to hurt you.' She takes a deep breath. 'I went to live with Ernest. I still live at the farm. Your old home. I sleep in the attic, in your room.'

Ruby looks scared. She frowns and clasps the book tighter, leaning away from the table, angling her body half out of the chair. 'What do you want? I didn't talk. I didn't tell anyone. It wasn't my fault.'

'What wasn't your fault?'

'I didn't tell anyone about Todd,' Ruby says with careful emphasis, as if she must get every word right. She puts her finger to her lips. 'I didn't say anything about it.'

'What do you mean, Mom?'

'I don't have to tell you. You can't make me.'

Hedy takes a deep breath. Questions crowd her throat, but Mom's face is slack with confusion. 'Would you like some more tea?' she says instead.

Mom's shoulders are hunched by her ears; she sticks her jaw out. 'I told Hank. That's all. I only told Hank.'

'Hank?' Hedy can't keep the shock out of her voice. Mom's never mentioned Hank before. 'What did you tell him?'

Her mother's hand shoots out and knocks her cup from the table; it clatters onto the floor, spilling liquid everywhere. She's pushing away from her chair, the book clutched to her chest. 'Leave me alone!' she shouts, stumbling to her feet, waving as if she's drowning. 'Dream words. They were only dream words. They didn't mean anything.'

Hedy knows to do nothing. Any movement, any attempt to reassure her will only make it worse. Two nurses are at her mother's side, soothing her, taking her away. Hedy sits alone at the table, cold tea slopping around her own cup, darkening the biscuits. A girl comes with a cloth to clear up the mess. The brief moment of confusion is over. Staff and patients have returned to their own concerns. The atmosphere reseals itself after the disturbance, as it does each time confusion or rage rips it open. A somnambulant, drugged peace prevails. It always prevails. Hedy can't catch her breath, wants to leap to her feet and run down the white corridors, past the wards, past the nurses with their fob watches and jangling keys.

She gets up and walks quickly towards the door. What did her mother tell Hank? What did she mean? Or was that memory as false as her imaginary visits from Chris? Outside, on the gravel driveway, she takes gulps of summer air to steady herself. Her usual cab is waiting, the driver smoking and reading the newspaper at the wheel; he crumples it onto the passenger seat and starts the engine when she signals to him.

# PART THREE

## The Forest

# FORTY-THREE

The base is only half an hour from the asylum. Hedy leans into her driver's window. 'Change of plan.' She knows it's still occupied by the United States Air Force. She's thought about coming back lots of times, but she didn't want to see the wire and the bungalows, would always have been afraid of running into Scott or Betty. She watches yellow and green fields roll past. She thinks of her mother and how she'd understood Ernest's message, her face clearing and brightening with that understanding, becoming herself again, even if only briefly.

The cab stops on the verge near the entrance to the base. Hedy's looking at the tall mesh fence. Through it she sees familiar streets, American cars, the brick bungalows. It's as if nothing has changed. A fierce mechanical wail makes her jump. She'd forgotten the noise of the jets. The driver turns in his seat. 'We're here, love. But I can't take you any further, not unless you have a pass?'

She spots the soldier at the entrance, his face impassive under his helmet, rifle on his shoulder. Of course. She shakes her head. 'Drop me a bit further along then, by the first entrance into the forest.'

She winds the window down, smelling pine, hot sap, the tinder of dry wood. The car pulls off the road at the entrance to a path leading through the trees. 'You sure about this?' her driver asks. 'I can wait for you.'

She shakes her head. 'I don't know how long I'll be.'

She pays him and sets off, feeling his curious gaze on her back, and then hears the engine turning over, the grate of tyres on tarmac. Solitude claims her. As she walks, the path narrows and trees block the light, shielding the sky. She's disorientated. Smells and sounds press against her. She's never come into the forest by this entrance before, but she guesses that new trees must have grown and old ones been cut down, the topography of the place shifting and changing. The stone circle and the oak tree will still be there, though, she's sure of that. She listens to the roar of grounded jets and walks towards the noise, hoping to recognise a landmark, to find her way to the right path.

She passes through a waste ground of severed trunks, upturned stubs of roots clinging to the burnt earth. Then she's back among living trees, and the sound of birdsong returns, the rush of the wind in branches like distant waves. An instinct makes her turn off along a narrow track. The ground here is vivid moss under bracken, tall fronds curling as high as her elbows. The path shrinks to a tiny deer track. She wades through thick, ticklish plants, stopping to look at the canopy above her head; three butterflies dart through a sunbeam, red wings flashing. The brilliance of the light makes her blink, sun spots spinning behind her lids, and when her vision clears, she has the sense that she's nearly there.

She's moving forwards with new purpose, holding her breath,

her feet moving softly. She feels a sudden need to be silent, to stay hidden. Blood rushes in her ears. The birds have stopped singing. All she can hear is the roar of her own heart. The trees around her have become familiar in the queasy sense of having seen them before in a dream; the path opens and widens, becoming sandy, curving around a corner. She knows she'll find the stone and the oak just around the bend, and she is gripped with a terror that Chris will be there, neck broken, blind button eyes accusing.

She approaches the spot slowly, staring at the oak. It's an ordinary tree, thick with summer green, its growth stunted under the taller pines. There are no crucifixes dangling from its sturdy branches. It's hard to believe that she saw her brother's lifeless feet dangling inside the rustle of its leaves. She clenches her hands, remembering the feel of his toes under the slippery fabric of the red sock. The stone circle is half hidden by long grass. She looks down at the concrete surface. Pine needles lie in a thick blanket, partly obscuring the grating and a red sign. Hedy squats and brushes them away, touching the white lettering: *Keep Out. Danger. Property of US Military.*

Hedy stands in the spot where Chris was murdered, closes her eyes and waits. She thought she'd experience something: a new insight, a buried memory rushing into consciousness, a ghostly visitation or voice revealing the truth. But the forest hums and turns around her, implacable, uncaring. She opens her eyes, and the tree and the stone remain just that: a tree and a stone. She walks until she finds the perimeter fence. She peers at grassy bunkers, sleek jets on the runway. Sunlight sparks on metal. The tarmac shimmers in a heat haze. She follows the edge of the fence, her fingers trailing the wire, knowing it will lead her to the sandy path where tufts of heather grow.

She arrives at the abandoned church. Bricks have crumbled from the tower, missing slates leave dark gaps, brambles swamp the tombstones. The children's cottage is transformed. The roof is straight, the garden neat. The tumbledown sheds are no longer there; instead there's a smart garage. A woman comes out of the house and lights a cigarette, stands with her face tilted to the sun. Hedy doesn't recognise her. She's disappointed. She'd imagined the children, heads shaved, faces violet.

She's tired. Her sandals have rubbed her heels, and the grit from the forest floor has got between her toes. She doesn't know what she's looking for – just that she hasn't found it. She wonders how she'll get to the station without any transport. As she walks along the road past the back entrance to the base she notices five new-build houses standing in a terrace. Fresh paint on doors and windows. Washing hangs from a line in one of the small front gardens. A young woman comes out and begins to unpeg the clothes, dropping them into a basket. A small boy clings to her legs, his thumb in his mouth. The woman's slim, muscular legs, angular face and set of her mouth are familiar. 'Nell,' she says, approaching the garden. 'Hi. You're Nell, aren't you?'

The woman turns, the basket hitched on her hip. 'Who's asking?'

'Hedy. From the base. My brother and I . . . a long time ago, we met you and your brothers in the forest.'

Nell's expression changes. She softens and nods. 'Hedy. Well, I never. I recognise you now.' She rubs her chin. 'You'd better come in. I'll put the kettle on, shall I?' She's already walking into the house, her child stumbling behind, one small fist clutching the hem of her skirt.

They sit in the small front room. The bellow of a jet makes the windows rattle. The child plays on the floor with wooden bricks; he's breathing loudly through his mouth, a bubble of snot at one nostril. Hedy balances her cup of tea on her knee. 'He's yours?'

Nell nods. 'Poor kid's got a summer cold.'

'I walked past your old cottage.'

'Owned by different people now. We got this place off the council. I prefer it. Easy to look after and everything works. My dad's dead and my mum's gone to live with her sister in Eastbourne.'

'And your brothers?'

'All married. With kids. They live locally. Ned's a policeman, would you believe?'

Hedy smiles and sips her drink.

Nell leans across her child's head and says, 'I'm sorry about what happened to your brother.' She keeps eye contact, unblinking. 'That day in the forest. Like a horror film.'

Hedy clears her throat. 'I know you think Old Joe didn't do it. But there's no other explanation.' She flexes her fingers, places them on her knees. 'I've thought about it for years. I worried that Chris had committed suicide. But he couldn't have managed it on his own, even if he tried. Then I suspected Scott, an American boy. But Joe was convicted. He confessed.'

Nell snorts. 'Old Joe would have confessed to anything. He wouldn't have understood.'

'You're wrong.'

'He's dead, by the way. Died in that place. I don't even think he knew why he was there.'

Hedy looks down at her hands. She doesn't know what to say.

The child's tower of bricks collapses into a pile, and he begins to wail, holding up his arms to his mother. Nell heaves him onto her lap. 'It all happened very quickly, didn't it? Never a mention in the papers. I remember my parents talking about it, saying it was fishy. Then your dad was in jail and you were all gone.'

Hedy's heart thuds against her breastbone. 'Fishy?'

'Look, I'm just saying what I heard. But the whole thing seemed to be hushed up.' Nell takes a tissue out of her pocket and gives her child's nose an efficient wiping. He wails louder, protesting. She puts the tissue back in her pocket. 'I saw those men coming through the trees with their faces blacked out and their guns that day, and it was as if they already knew your brother was dead.'

Hedy sets her empty mug on the floor. She is cold. 'What are you saying?'

Nell gives her a sharp look. 'Just wondering aloud, that's all.' She kisses her boy's tear-stained cheek, and his cries quieten into hiccupping sobs.

'No. You've got it all wrong. I asked about that. They were in the forest for routine manoeuvres.' Hedy grips the side of her chair. 'It was luck, Nell. Old Joe would have tried to hurt me too if they hadn't come.'

Nell looks uncomfortable. She shifts, hugging her child tighter. 'Maybe they were on an exercise. Or maybe they were there for some other reason. Like I said, it happened a long time ago.' She gives a quick, determined smile. 'Looks like you're doing okay now? Someone said you live in Norfolk, with your uncle?'

'He died.' Hedy can't concentrate. In her head, she sees the soldiers coming through the shadows, hears the crackle of the walkie-talkie. 'I'm running the farm,' she manages.

'Sorry for your loss, but inheriting a farm, that's good, isn't it?' She nods. 'Got a young man?'

Hedy gets up. 'No. Too busy for that.' She brushes her hands over her trousers. The small, hot room, crammed with toys and furniture, is making her claustrophobic. 'I should go. I've taken up enough of your time. You've got your hands full.'

'Where's your car?'

'I came by cab.'

'I'll get Phil to drive you to the station; he's due home any minute.' She holds up her hand when Hedy protests. 'He'll be happy to do it.'

Phil turns up in oily overalls, his empty lunch box in his hand. He simply nods when Nell tells him that he needs to turn around and take Hedy to the station. He doesn't say a word for the whole journey, and blushes when she thanks him as they pull into the car park.

She's grateful for his silence. She keeps seeing the red sign on the stone. Those letters. Property of the US Military. She'd thought that the manhole covers belonged to the Forestry Commission. Now she remembers an old rumour about a web of underground tunnels. The stones could easily be air vents. In which case, the scream that Chris heard might have come from a military person working inside a tunnel. But even if that was true, it doesn't help Hedy understand what happened to her brother. Nell is stubbornly hanging on to her conviction that Old Joe was innocent, yet can't offer any other name. Hedy can't think of another suspect, either. Hedy rubs her eyes, frustrated by running into the same blank wall again. It's been years since it happened, years since her father was arrested. If she knew what his crime was, it might help her understand what happened to him; there might even be a connection between his crime and why Chris was murdered. Perhaps her brother's killer was Russian. A communist spy. She'll write to Hank and ask him when her father's case will stop being classified. Then she remembers, he hasn't replied to her last letter yet.

# FORTY-FOUR

## 1974

Hank never writes Hedy another letter. She sends several more, thinking his has gone astray, but doesn't receive a word. She keeps writing anyway, keeps looking on the doormat for a blue envelope. Eventually, it occurs to her to ask Scott. She finds the number he left and puts in a call. 'You certainly took your time,' his voice says down the line. 'Thought I'd be posted abroad before I heard from you again. Changed your mind about that drink?'

'Scott,' she says. 'Have you heard from Hank? He's ... he's just disappeared. He used to write to me regularly. But I've had no communication for ages.'

'Haven't heard from him, either. Not that I was expecting to. But I'll ask some questions, see if I can track him down. I'll let you know.'

It's an August evening, bats flitting through the twilight, mosquitoes hovering above the water butt. Mrs Rose and Hedy sit crammed together on the sofa in the airless parlour, the TV on loud. It turns out that Nixon was in the wrong after all, and now he's resigning. The whole of the news is dedicated to the story they're calling Watergate. Mrs Rose and Hedy listen to his speech in silence. Hedy imagines Hank is watching too; he might even be there in Washington. He'll be devastated by this. He's been betrayed. The whole of America has been betrayed. Nixon reads from sheets of paper, staring through the screen.

'He's talking,' Hedy says. 'But he's not saying anything.'

'He's a slippery character, that one.' Mrs Rose puts down her knitting. 'You only have to look in his eyes. Shocking to think the President of the United States is a criminal.'

'Mrs Rose.' Hedy turns to her and takes her hand. 'I'm selling the farm.'

The old lady squeezes Hedy's fingers. 'A wise decision. You don't want to spend the rest of your days cooped up here.'

'I wish I could feel settled in Norfolk, but I can't.'

'I've never been further than Norwich. Never wanted to. I've found everything I wanted in this place. I'll die here and be content. But everyone's different.' She looks into Hedy's face with a steady gaze. 'There's something inside you that's restless. You're looking for something. So I say, best get on with it.'

Hedy opens her mouth to protest, and then closes it. She sits on the edge of the sofa. 'But what about you?'

'Oh, bless you. I'm past retirement age. I only keep coming up here to see you and Peter. I don't need the work anymore. My knees have all but given out. You're like a daughter to me, Hedy. And that's why I'm telling you to get rid of the place. It's holding you back.'

Hedy's eyes blur with sudden tears. The room wavers. She

doesn't know if it's Mrs Rose claiming her as a daughter, or the relief of being set free. She blinks and brushes away the wet on her cheeks. Gratitude fills her chest, making it tight. 'I ... I don't know what I would have done without you. All these years.' Hedy takes the old hand and squeezes it again. 'You've been so kind to me.'

Mrs Rose laughs. 'Now you're being soft. I'm not one for fancy words. Come on. Let's switch this nonsense off. I need to get home.' She rolls up her wool. Puts it into a bag. 'You've told Peter?'

Hedy nods. 'He's already been offered a job by the new owner.'

'That'll be John Henderson? He's been after this place for years. I hope you got a good price.'

Hedy grins. 'I should probably have got you to make the deal.' She puts her arms around Mrs Rose's bony shoulders and holds her in a tight embrace. 'Thank you,' she says into the older woman's grey hair. 'Whether you want me to say it or not, I do love you, Mrs Rose.'

Mrs Rose returns the hug for a brief moment before she wriggles away, brushing imaginary dust from her clothes. 'Now, that's enough of that,' she says. But the smile doesn't leave her face.


Scott wants to meet in the village. He wouldn't tell her much, just that he'd found something out, and he wanted to tell her in person. 'I'll be at that pub I drove past last time on my way to you. The Hare and Hounds.'

It's lunchtime. The sun is high and she wishes she'd put a hat on; heat sears her scalp. She's on an ancient bike she found at the back of one of the barns. She and Peter fixed it up. She pedals past the cows, over the bridge, and onto the lane into the village. Thick summer hedges tower above her, a welcome shadowy breeze on her face. The freedom of cycling fills her with excitement, but she can't stop a feeling of foreboding, a sense that she's pedalling towards something unpleasant, something bad.

He's sitting at a wooden table outside, and rises to his feet as she leans the bike against the wall. 'Warm beer?' he asks. 'Or something else?'

'Cider,' she says. 'Thanks.'

They settle across from each other, and he takes a sip from his glass. She does the same. Her top lip is wet and she wipes it with her hand. 'So?'

He leans towards her. 'There's something big going on. Some kind of investigation.'

'Where?'

'Back home. In the States. I couldn't find out exactly what it was about. But there are some important people involved. Military high-ups. CIA.'

'What's it got to do with Hank?'

Scott takes a breath and lets it out slowly. 'He's been arrested.'

Hedy stares at him. 'Arrested?'

Scott rolls his shoulders. 'Nobody will say why.'

'My God.' Hedy scratches her head and frowns. 'I don't understand. Maybe it's a mistake . . .'

Scott grabs one of her hands. 'Or maybe there's a link between this and what happened on the base. Your dad being arrested and you never finding out why.'

Hank, with all his authority. His calm air. She thinks suddenly of his capable and sturdy hands. It's too incredible. Hedy pulls her fingers free of Scott's hot grip. 'I can't take it in.'

Scott sits back and his face hardens. 'Serves him right,

arrogant bastard. Never could forgive him for what he did to my parents.'

'He was kind to me.' Hedy fiddles with her glass, twisting it round, cold seeping into her skin. 'I don't know what I would have done without him. My world blew up. He helped me survive.'

Scott takes out a packet of cigarettes and offers her one. She shakes her head. He lights up, taking a deep drag and exhaling into the blue. The smell catches at the back of her throat. Hedy coughs.

'Why would Hank be arrested?' She licks dry lips. 'And why all the secrecy?'

Scott blows out smoke and shrugs. 'Like I said. I have no idea. But don't you think there are parallels here?'

'I don't know . . .' She scrubs at her eyes with her fists. 'God, I'm so sick of it,' she scowls. 'Of not ever knowing anything. All of this stuff about Nixon, too. It makes me wonder if anything is true or real. How can I ever get straight answers?'

'When it comes to the military or government,' Scott looks at her, squinting through smoke, 'all you can do is wait. Truth comes out slowly, like rats out of holes.'

'It's been years, and I still don't know about Dad.'

'Someone will know something,' Scott says. 'We'll stay in touch.'

They finish their drinks. He asks if she wants another and she shakes her head. 'Do you still have that scrapbook?'

He looks confused.

'I found it in your room. It was full of horrible pictures. The Ku Klux Clan.'

His cheeks colour. 'That was a long time ago. I was a kid.'

'But you don't believe in civil rights?'

'I just think we're different, black and white. Different needs.'

'That's bullshit, and you know it.' She stands up. 'You went to war, Scott. You said it changed you. Where's your humanity?'

'War doesn't teach you about humanity.' He blinks up at her. 'It just sucks away any faith you had in the world. Tramples it to death. War just makes you tired of life, is all.'

Hedy shakes her head. 'Thanks for the information about Hank. And the drink.' She tastes sweat on her lips. 'But we can never be friends. Not when you say things like that, think things like that.'

'That's a shame, Hedy.'

She nods. 'It is.'

She cycles home through the brilliance of the day. Dragonflies stitch the air, needles of electric green and blue. The wheat fields ripple, burnished gold. How can this be the same world, she thinks, as the other one? It feels as though she could stretch out her hand and rip the fabric of the day apart, expose the ugly darkness behind, letting the ragged edges trail through. Hank told her once that war changes a man. She wants to believe in this clarity of light, this earthly beauty, the possibility of believing in another person, to know their goodness to be unchanging. She thinks of her brother, his true and shining heart.

Hedy is packing up the house. Mrs Rose is upstairs. She's insisted on washing down the woodwork, even though Hedy told her that there was no need. Hedy has cleared out the cellar. She's hauling the last bits of old broken furniture, half a stove, and rotten sacks dirty with coal dust up the stairs and out into the yard. It's a relief to get rid of it all. Rubbish is going onto the back of the truck, ready for a trip to the dump. She's in a pair of shorts, and a man's shirt covered in cobwebs and dirt. She stops when she hears a vehicle bumping along the track, shielding her eyes from the sun to see who it is. She doesn't recognise the car. Light bounces off the windscreen. Hedy stands with her hands on her hips as the car rolls to a halt in the yard and the driver's door swings open.

Black hair layered around her face like Jane Fonda in *Klute*. She's wearing a pair of purple bell-bottoms and waistcoat, and she takes off her dark glasses and smiles. 'Hello, Hedy.'

Hedy takes a step towards her and falters. 'Miss Banville.'

She comes forwards. 'For goodness' sake! Call me Claire.' She takes Hedy's filthy hands in hers. 'I've come to congratulate you.'

Hedy is blank.

'I noticed *The Wonderful* in a book shop. It took me a minute to realise. You've written under your brother's name.'

Hedy nods. 'You've come all the way from Cornwall?'

Claire squeezes Hedy's hands. 'From London.' She looks around her. 'Looks like you're having a clear-out?'

'I've sold the farm. I'm moving.'

'Why didn't you write? Why didn't you answer my cards? At least tell me that you'd got published?'

Hedy remembers the note she tore up. She feels ashamed. 'I was going to but . . . I didn't think you'd be interested.'

Claire lets go of her hands and gives her a puzzled look. 'I have a present for you.' She leans into the car and brings out a bottle of champagne. 'We need to celebrate. I'm so proud of you.'

In the kitchen, Hedy finds that the glasses are all packed and unearths two teacups from the cupboard instead. Claire uncorks the bottle and pours out the champagne. They clink the rims of the cups together and drink.

Hedy sneezes, the bubbles going up her nose. Her first

champagne. Claire leans forwards and touches the ends of Hedy's hair where it curls onto her shoulders. 'It's longer. Suits you.'

'Yours is different, too.'

'How many years has it been?'

Hedy takes a step back; she's finding it hard to believe that this conversation is happening. She looks out of the window towards the parked car, as if she might see the silhouette of someone there. 'Where's your friend?'

Claire takes a sip of her drink. 'My friend?'

'The woman with bobbed brown hair.'

Claire frowns. 'Lucy? I didn't know you'd met each other. She went off to live in Cambridge. She got offered a post there. She lectures on medieval history. I think she's happy.'

Hedy turns away on the pretence of finding something to eat. 'There's not much in the larder. I could make us some soup?' She can feel heat in her cheeks and waits for it to subside before she turns back.

'Soup and champagne?' Claire sits down and crosses her legs. 'What could be nicer?'

Mrs Rose comes into the kitchen with the bucket and empties it into the sink. 'All finished upstairs.' She wipes her forehead with her apron. 'Who's this?'

'Claire Banville. My ex-English teacher. This is Mrs Rose.'

'Would you like some champagne, Mrs Rose? We're celebrating Hedy's success as an author.'

Mrs Rose gives Claire a lingering look and then glances at Hedy. 'No thanks, dear. I'll leave you girls to it. I'm off home.'

The evening lies ahead, long and sultry; the sun across the fields burns red and amber. One of the farm cats stretches out in the dust, eyes half-closed, glinting at the low-flying swallows.

They eat the soup and finish the bottle of champagne. Hedy,

a little drunk, tells Claire about the afternoon that she came to find her, how she sat outside the flat. She explained seeing Claire return with her friend. It's a relief to confess it, even though she sounds like a mad stalker. Claire looks stricken; she leans across the table and touches the back of her hand. 'I'm sorry. I wish I'd known you were there.'

Claire's touch burns. Hedy looks at their joined hands, wanting to pick up Claire's pale fingers and kiss them. Did she want to do that at school? She thinks so. She nods and pulls her hand away into her lap.

'You were easy to talk to, kind . . . ' She stops and glances up at Claire. 'That day that I came to find you, I wanted to tell you something about my brother.' She swallows. 'Something I've never told anyone else. You see, the very last words I ever said to him were cruel. I was angry and upset. I took it out on him. And now he's dead and I can never unsay the words, never tell him I'm sorry.'

Claire takes a deep breath. 'That's why you have that look in your eyes . . . you've been blaming yourself all this time. Hedy.' She grips Hedy's hands. 'Listen to me. He knew how much you loved him. The words you spoke that day wouldn't have changed that.' She gives Hedy's hands a squeeze. 'It's hard . . . hard to love. We make mistakes all the time. We hurt those we love the most. But you can't give up on it – you can't protect yourself, because it's all that matters.'

Hedy can feel her throat closing. She doesn't trust herself to speak.

Claire nods as if Hedy has spoken. As if there has been an agreement. 'I've got a new job,' she says, standing up to clear the table. 'In London, teaching. But I'm painting, too. There's a gallery in London that's interested in my work.'

'Will you stay the night?' Hedy asks. Heat floods her cheeks. 'I mean, it's too late to drive all the way back to London now, isn't it?'

'I'd like that. Thank you.'

They climb the stairs, each creak and wheeze of the joists louder than Hedy remembers. She hesitates at the bottom of the climb to the attic, and turns left along the landing, showing Claire into Ernest's old room. It's neat, cleared and cleaned by Mrs Rose. 'I'll fetch some bedding,' she says. 'Do you have anything in the car? Otherwise I can lend you a toothbrush and something to sleep in.'

They make up the bed together, tucking sheets in, putting slips on pillows, working in silence like a team, as if they've always shared domestic tasks. Hedy pushes open the window to let in some air. The night is dark at last. She switches on the side light and moths come blundering into the gold circle on bewitched wings. Hedy has fetched a spare toothbrush and one of her clean night shirts. She is awkward now, hovering at the threshold.

Claire comes close. 'I'm glad to be here.' She leans forwards and brushes her lips lightly against Hedy's cheek. 'It's good to see you again. You've grown up, Hedy.'

Hedy swallows. 'Can you stay? For a few days?'

'I can make myself useful. I'm good at cleaning. And packing.'

Hedy can't sleep. She sprawls across her mattress, the crumpled sheets pushed to the bottom of the bed. A mosquito bite on her ankle itches and she scratches, making the skin flame. The window is thrown open, but there's no breeze and she's sweltering. Her limbs are tingling with the knowledge that Claire is sleeping just a floor away.

Claire and Scott both made their way up the cinder track back into her life. What if they'd never come? She's been stuck here waiting all these years, like the girl in the tower from the fairy-tale, like someone under a spell, or a last surviving astronaut on a lonely planet.

The next day, they have breakfast together. Eggs fresh from the hens, and some stale loaf toasted over the range. Straight after they've finished their cups of tea, Claire is as good as her word. She gets on her hands and knees to clear the cupboards, packing the rest of the china in newspaper and putting them carefully into boxes. Mrs Rose arrives with a black treacle tart she made at home. It's Hedy's favourite: sticky, and flavoured with lemon. Mid-morning, Peter comes in, red-faced and yawning.

'Someone didn't get much sleep,' Hedy grins. 'Peter and his wife have just had a baby,' she explains to Claire. 'A beautiful little girl.'

They all sit around the table eating slices of treacle tart for elevenses. Peter is laughing at something that Claire's said, and Mrs Rose gets up to put boiling water in the pot.

Treacle melts on Hedy's tongue, and sweetness seeps through her, dripping into her bones, filling every part of her. It's the sweetness of sitting around a table like a proper family, she realises; not the food itself, but being with people she knows and trusts. She watches the three of them, how easy they are with each other – Mrs Rose refilling cups, Peter offering Claire the jug of cream – and it makes her want to weep with happiness. She can't stop sneaking glances at Claire. The heart-spinning joy of having her here. And under that, a recognition of a rightness she hasn't known since before the base.

The phone rings. The sound is a rarity, and for a moment, Hedy thinks of ignoring it. Sighing, she pushes open the door into the back hall, stumbling over the uneven flagstones, blinded by the dim, cool space, and picks up the receiver. She can't think of anyone she wants to speak to. Everyone she loves is in the kitchen.

'Yes?'

'Is this Hedy Delaney?'

The voice is American. Male. For a second she thinks it's Hank and her heart jumps. Hank and Mom are the two people missing from the table.

'This is Leonard Tenet from the Joint Intelligence Objectives Agency. We would like to invite you to our London office to discuss a classified matter involving a settlement from the US government on behalf of Captain Todd Delaney.'

The words run into each other like nonsense. She clings to the only thing she understood. Her father's name. 'I'm sorry . . . I'm not sure I . . .'

'I'm afraid I can't say any more at this time, ma'am. You will need to bring proof of identity. If you could take some details down, I'll give you further instructions.'

Hedy can hear the others laughing in the kitchen. Outside the sky is blue and the sun is shining, but she's blinking through shadows, writing down instructions that a voice on the phone dictates.

# FORTY-FIVE

## 1957

Major Hank Pulaski goes through the security check at the entrance to the tunnel. He keeps his expression blank, his eyes empty. He doesn't indicate to the soldier that he's seen him. Even on home territory, he can't let his guard down. His job requires complete discipline at all times. It reminds him of the war, when he manned the controls of the Fortress. Every nerve in his body set to maximum, every sense on full alert. Danger could come out of the clouds at any moment, from any direction. He couldn't afford to relax. Hell, he couldn't afford to blink.

The door clangs shut behind him. The narrow, windowless tunnel is lit by flickering fluorescent tubes. It smells dank. He paces it out under his breath, knowing exactly when the tunnel will take him under the perimeter fence so that he's walking under the forest floor. He passes observation rooms, each one fitted with one-way glass, some with the blinds drawn. Other people are using the narrow tunnel: military personnel on their way back to the bunker, or exiting an observation room. All speak in murmurs. They salute as he passes. Scientists in white coats scurry past, peering through their glasses at him. The end room is fitted out for the new experiment.

Delaney is there with his clipboard, waiting. He salutes. Hank gives him a fleeting wink. An acknowledgement of their history, their friendship. 'Is the subject responding?'

Delaney licks his lips. 'Not yet, sir.'

Hank steps up to the window. Inside the room, a man wearing an American football helmet, the visor blacked out, is strapped to a chair. 'How many times are you playing the loop?'

'Twenty a day, sir.' He coughs. 'As instructed.'

'Let's make it thirty.'

They stand and watch the seated figure. He doesn't move. The subject's fingers on the chair rest are the only thing that betray inner life as they scrabble and tremble, bitten nails raking the plastic. The blacked-out helmet gives him the appearance of a giant insect. Hank finds he can't remember what the face under the visor looks like.

'The subject was in a state of distress before we started the tape.' Delaney's voice breaks. His left eyelid twitches. A nervous tic.

'Maybe he needed more preliminary shocks,' Hank says. 'Get the psychiatrist's reports on my desk this afternoon. Haugwitz is due in a couple of weeks.'

As Hank moves away, Delaney hurries after him. 'Hank?'

Hank turns, his eyes cold and reprimanding.

'Sir,' Delaney corrects himself, clears his throat. 'The children. Is it really necessary?'

'This is critical work, devised by experts for the protection of our country. It's not up to you to question the method, Delaney.' He waits for a beat. 'Is that clear?'

It's interesting, he thinks, how a man like Todd cracks under pressure, a different kind of pressure from the stress of flying a bomber at 45,000 feet over enemy territory. Cold War work requires a gritty internal strength, an unwavering dedication to the cause, a talent for secrecy and making difficult decisions. There's no outer glory, no room for individual action. Hank knows that Todd thrives on adrenaline. He needs the admiration of other men. He lets his emotions interfere with his work. Hank's always understood that those weaknesses will betray Todd in the end. Now it's happened. The great hero, vulnerable at last. Hank smiles.

Ruby's bruised eye has faded to a sickly green. She's tried to hide it with some sort of pale powder, but that makes it look worse. Despite his probing, she's sticking to her story that she fell in the night, bashed herself against a door frame. Such admirable loyalty and so misplaced. He wonders why she's asked him to come. She's as much of a mess as her husband. Her fingers pluck at her clothes, touch her hair. Her mouth twitches.

They sit across a low coffee table. Hank balances his cup on his knee, waiting. A jet roars across the sky. Ruby sips her drink, her eyes cast down, avoiding him while the thunder from the B-47 shakes the ornaments on the dresser.

'Remember how we noticed Todd's drinking?' she says haltingly. 'Well. It's got worse.'

She's choosing her words carefully. From the tension around her mouth, the tick of a vein in her neck, he can see what this is costing her. She's weighing it up: the conflict between keeping her husband's secrets and her need to protect him from whatever is driving him to drink. But she trusts Hank.

'It's this place,' she bursts out. 'I know it is.'

He keeps his expression neutral. It's best to leave the space open for her to talk.

'Is there any way he could be reassigned?' She has real hope in her eyes as she says the words.

She must know that it's an impossibility. Yet still she asks. He understands that she is desperate. What else has happened, he thinks, beyond the drinking, besides her husband hitting her?

'I think he's seeing another woman,' she's saying.

He has to stop himself from laughing. She's on the wrong track, after all. 'That's not the Todd I know,' he says gently. 'He's crazy about you.'

He almost feels sorry for her. She made the wrong choice years ago. And now she's paying for it. He glances at the clock and stands up. She's trembling. He could probably take her in his arms now and she would submit, would be grateful for the comfort. She's run out of Miltown of course, and that's adding to her jitters. But there's more to this meeting than she's revealed so far. She's hiding something else. He takes her hand, strokes the back of it in soothing circles. 'What is it? What else is worrying you?'

'He talks ... in his sleep,' she says.

'We all talk in our sleep sometimes.'

'But it's what he says.' She blinks and swallows. 'Lately I've heard him say ...'

'Go on,' he murmurs.

She glances at the door and leans towards him. 'I heard him say, "not the children".' Her mouth crumples. 'I thought he meant our children. But last night he said it again and yelled ... I don't know, but it sounded like, "release the straps". Then he said a name. Haugwitz. Very clear. And I remembered it's the name of the German that came to the base. I don't understand what it means. But I think . . . I think it's something to do with his work.' She lowers her voice. 'It must be connected to what's going on under the bunkers.'

Hank squeezes her hand. 'You're under a lot of stress. Try not to worry.'

She follows him into the hall.

'It was me that recommended Todd,' he says. 'Thought it would be good to have some of the old team together again.' He sighs. 'Guess I was wrong.'

'None of this is your fault.' She leans forwards and presses dry lips to his cheek.

He leaves the bungalow, shutting the door behind him. Tilting his hat straight, he walks quickly towards the airfield.

Captain Delaney has become a security risk. But now he has the opportunity, unbeknown to him, to play a different part in the programme. A valuable part. This was what Hank had hoped for, why he'd invited Delaney to work on the programme. Todd will continue in his duties, watched by an agent who will observe and monitor the effects of the drug. LSD has been given to various guinea pigs obtained through prisons and mental hospitals. Regular operatives have also volunteered for the programme. But what the firm wants are military guinea pigs: trained men with discipline and moral scruples. And these subjects must not have awareness. They are to be tested blind.

Hank has never been guilty of sentiment. Of course, he has fond memories; he wouldn't be human otherwise. Culling rats with .45 automatics, peppering the walls of the Nissen hut with bullet holes, blasting away their restless boredom. Cycling through God-forsaken Norfolk lanes in search of a pub, falling off into hedges on the way back, vision fuzzy with warm ale.

He smiles. He and Todd went through twenty-four missions together. Todd was a great pilot. But these are different times, and they call for different heroes. Those last months, on the final missions, Todd was loose-tongued, criticising orders, bleating about the wholesale obliteration of the German people. But Hank understood the bigger picture, the necessity of human misery to force the turn against the leaders. A justified means to an end.

Delaney, a military hero, is the perfect candidate for LSD. Hank writes 'the full dose', and signs the document on his desk, stamps it with a red *Classified*, and passes it to his secretary.

Details of Colonel Anderson's conversation with Christopher Delaney are reported back to the head of the covert research operation. Although a breach of security, of course, it would not normally necessarily be one to take offensive action on, but this particular manhole is directly over the crucial psychic riding experiment. The Haugwitz experiment. Noises were heard by civilians. The man known as Old Joe has been interrogated. He and the crippled boy heard human sounds of distress. It is enough to cause a serious risk. Hank lights a Camel and leans back in his seat; he taps his pen on the blotting pad. The phrase, to kill two birds with one stone, comes to mind.

# FORTY-SIX

## 1974

Hedy steps out of the London train onto the platform where Claire waits, a small figure in a red coat. But Hedy stumbles past her, unable to speak, and wrenches the door of the Mini open. She collapses into the seat, hunched up, her arms around her knees. Claire slips into the driver's side behind the wheel. She doesn't turn the ignition. 'What happened?' she asks. 'What did they say?'

Hedy stares through the windscreen. 'He wasn't a spy.' She swallows hard, blows air through her mouth. 'Dad wasn't working for the Russians.'

Claire puts her hand on Hedy's knee. 'What happened to him?'

Hedy can't draw oxygen into her lungs. A weight presses down on her, bands pulling tight around her ribs, hard as iron, like Chris's brace. Inside the tightness, she flails, trying to catch her breath, drowning inside the small, compressed spaces of her body. Panic squirms free. Her mouth is open, gasping.

Her fingers grab at her chest, yanking at her coat, wrenching off a button.

Claire opens her window, leans across to open the passenger side. 'Try to breathe in through your nose, out through your mouth.' She starts the engine. 'Breathe. It's going to be OK.'

'I didn't believe in him,' Hedy gasps. 'I thought he was a traitor. I thought he'd done what they said. I let him down.'

'You didn't let him down. Hold on. I'm going to get you home.'

'Oh, God, oh, God, oh, God.' Hedy squeezes her eyes shut. Opens them again. 'Help me.'

The landscape outside streams past, the colours of early autumn, amber and brown, blood-reds. The bands around her chest are shattering her bones, squeezing her lungs like dishrags, squeezing and squeezing.

At the farm, Claire helps Hedy into bed, brings her a hot-water bottle, because even though it's not cold, she is shivering, her lips blue, teeth chattering. She curls into a ball in the centre of the mattress and closes her eyes. When she opens them, it is night. Claire is there, sitting on the edge of the bed. She has a cup of steaming tea in her hands.

'Here,' she says. 'I've put sugar in.'

Hedy sits up and takes a sip, wincing at the heat and the sweetness.

'Do you want to talk about it?'

'I want to kill Hank.' Hedy puts the cup down. 'If I ever see him, I will kill him.'

'What did he do?' Claire asks quietly.

'He fed my father drugs. Gave him LSD without telling him. As an experiment, to see what it would do to him. The last time I saw Dad ... I couldn't understand what was wrong, why he was behaving so strangely. I thought he was drunk. But he was having a bad trip. He didn't even know it himself. It must have been terrifying. Then they arrested him, put him in a cell and gave him some more. That's why he killed himself. They drove him mad. He didn't know what he was doing.'

'My God.'

'Hank lied about everything. He was an undercover CIA operative. He was in charge of the programme, the same one Dad was working on.' She bites her thumbnail. 'They were looking for the perfect truth drug. They were inventing new methods of mind control by experimenting on human subjects – prisoners, mental patients – then they began to give LSD to unsuspecting citizens, military personnel. It was completely illegal.'

'Didn't the army know? The government?'

'Apparently not. They knew what the programme had been set up for, but not the methods being used. It was psychological torture. Worse. And, Claire . . . ' Hedy sobs. 'They even experimented on children.'

'Children?' Claire's face contorts in horror. 'And now? What's happening now?'

'It's been shut down. The case went to the Supreme Court. They had former Nazi scientists working for them. War criminals. It made me sick to hear some of the details. And my dad mixed up in it. He must have been desperate. He must have been out of his depth.' Hedy drops her face into her hands. 'I thought it would be a relief to know the truth.' She shakes her head. 'But it's like a nightmare. I didn't think that anything this rotten could happen, in the name of what? Fear? Fear of each other, of a war that wasn't even happening, not really.' She gasps, her dry throat aching. Strange sounds are coming out of her: hard, knotted sounds, retching and coughing.

Claire puts her thin, surprisingly strong arms around Hedy's shoulders and holds her, holds her tight to stop the shaking. She strokes Hedy's hair back from her face. 'But your father was innocent. He was a good man. You can rebuild him in your memory. Resolve to do something for him, in his name.'

Hedy hears Claire's words, but all she can do is concentrate on Hank, his face, his voice, the things he said. The lies he told. If he went to the electric chair, she would throw the switch, she would watch his body frying. There is nothing that she could do to punish him enough for his betrayal, for what he did to them all.

# FORTY-SEVEN

## 1977

Hedy sways into a seat on the top deck of the double-decker, and takes her ticket from the conductor. She sits with the stub of paper in her hand, staring down onto a muggy evening in early June; people gathered outside pubs in the last of the sunshine drinking beer. Union flags flutter from windows, strings of them fastened from one lamp post to the next, lining the roads with red, white and blue. Only two more days till the Jubilee celebrations. Street parties have been planned all over the city. As the bus makes its slow journey past narrow South London streets and across the river, rows of identical brick houses give way to green garden squares and stucco dwellings six storeys high. Hedy glimpses the grand facades of department stores down the King's Road, watches unknown faces in crowds of commuters, girls in short dresses.

The bus groans around Hyde Park Corner. Glancing down, Hedy sees two horses cantering through the park, hooves throwing up dark sand. The riders' black hats bobbing. They pass the Royal Academy and Fortnum & Mason. She catches a glimpse of bright dresses on mannequins and a towering display of perfume bottles through gleaming plate glass. The conductor rings the bell, and Hedy braces herself against seats as she makes her way along the swinging bus, then clings onto the rail as she goes down the winding stairs, jumping off the running board as the bus pulls up at her stop.

The exhibition is in one of the galleries in Burlington Arcade. Hedy hurries inside. The small room is already busy with guests. A waiter hands her a glass of sparkling wine. The paintings are nearly obscured by banks of people, gossip and chatter thick as fog, thick as the smoke coming from dozens of cigarettes. She looks around and finds Claire at the centre of a small group. Perhaps she's talking to eminent art critics. Hedy waits, not wanting to interrupt. She likes to watch Claire as if she's a stranger, seeing her as if for the first time. A small woman with long dark hair framing an eager, quizzical face defined by a strong nose and olive skin, so that Hedy imagines that there's the possibility she might be of American Indian descent, although Claire says more likely Spanish by way of Ireland. But Hedy only has a moment before Claire glances up and raises a hand, beckoning.

'How's it going?'

'OK. I think. You know what these things are like.'

'Any buyers yet?'

Claire nods. A man in a purple suit interrupts, kissing Claire on both cheeks flamboyantly, fragrantly, his black felt hat tilted to the side to show grey curling hair. 'Wonderful show, darling.'

Hedy slips away, taking gulps of wine as she negotiates groups of people in the tight space. She wishes for the end of the evening, when it will be just the two of them, and all this noise and small talk, the clutter and confusion of the opening will be over.

The house in Battersea is not far from the park and the river. It has a small garden that Hedy tends, space for the kitten they brought from the farm with them, a feral creature, now a plump purring moggy that sleeps under the roses on dusty summer days or curls up on the end of their bed on winter evenings.

The deeds are in both their names, making them legal partners, joint owners. The compensation money from the US government, added to the small amount left over from the sale of the farm after the debts were paid, meant that they could buy it outright. When Hedy planned the walled garden, she dug in plants for her father and Chris, wanting to have living things to remember them by. For her father, acanthus: strong, heroic plants with bold flowers, cultivated by the Romans and then lost to cultivation before being reintroduced. For Chris she chose gypsophila: white flowers spreading in dreamy clouds, their petals reaching for the light on a branching of slender, straight stems.

Hedy gave the notebook containing Chris's story to Leonard Tenet. She'd requested another meeting and shoved Chris's original story of *The Wonderful* into his hands, explaining that those pages in her brother's handwriting were not fiction, but the clue to his death. Reading it as fact, not fiction, makes sense now that she knows what was going on in the tunnels under the forest floor. Chris reported hearing the scream to the colonel, who would have informed Hank. The colonel made Chris swear not to tell anyone. Nobody knew about the tunnels stretching out from under the base; nobody knew about the illegal and cruel experiments being conducted down there.

But Old Joe and her brother heard things that would have been enough to threaten the secrecy of the project. If Hank could give his old friend large doses of LSD without his permission or knowledge, then have him arrested and locked in a cell, Hedy knows he would have been able to arrange Chris's death, too. She can picture how it went as clearly as if she's watching it unfold on TV: Hank took advantage of Mom's breakdown and Dad's absence to get Chris out of the house and into the forest, where Old Joe was being held by his men: Old Joe, who heard devils underground. A mad man and a boy in a brace. It wouldn't have been hard for them to set the scene, to haul on the rope. When she got there, Old Joe had been trying to save her brother.

But the exercise book came back in the post with a note: not admissible as evidence. She has nothing conclusive to confirm her theory. Hank will not be prosecuted for Chris's murder. When she got the note, she threw her head back and howled. Claire came running.

'He'll be court-martialled for causing the death of your father,' she said, reading the note. 'At least you know that. And, it says here, for his fundamental disregard for human life in the course of his work.'

'But he did it, Claire. I'm sure of it. He killed Chris.'

'I know.' Claire held Hedy in a tight embrace.

Mom had been so frightened of the forest, so afraid for Chris. But it wasn't a monster lurking in the pines, a madman dressed in rags, a creature from another planet that had fulfilled her fears. It had been an old friend, a man in uniform smiling among them.

Hedy crushed his present of the silver hoops, bent them into crumpled angles between her fingers, then she burnt his letters.

She took the ashes and threw them off Albert Bridge, letting the wind and the brown water carry the remains of his words away. It was Claire's idea. A way of dealing with all that anger. A rage that made her sick for months. Casting the ashes away was her method of killing him, killing the memories of him. He is dead to her. She doesn't want to hear his name or allow the thought of him to enter her mind. But she can't forget the things she knows, can't stop reliving her time on the base with her new knowledge filling in the gaps.

It's obvious to her now that as soon as Dad started his job in the bunkers, he was under terrible stress. He'd been working on the psychic riding experiment, a programme invented by Haugwitz – a convicted Nazi war criminal, fresh from his experiments conducted in the concentration camps. The programme involved putting a 'subject' into a drug-induced coma. Then they were woken with electro-convulsive therapy: the voltage and frequency of the shocks much higher than any used in asylums and hospitals. They continued until the 'subject' could no longer produce a seizure. It was only then that they were confined in a blacked-out helmet and made to listen to a message played on a constant loop. The aim was to strip away the individual's personality and 're-pattern' them. This is what her brave, decent father was expected to arrange and oversee. No wonder he started to drink, to behave strangely.

In a time of paranoia – when the government were convinced the Russians and Chinese were ahead in the Cold War – Hank was just one of many who were given absolute power to succeed in their mission to overtake the Soviets. Hank was accountable to nobody and unconcerned with any constitutional limitations. It was only after Watergate and in the wake of a growing public distrust of the government that President Ford began to investigate illegal CIA activities around the world, including those at the base in Suffolk.

Hedy remembers her mother's slow unravelling, her fears for their safety, especially Chris's. Mom had been taking tranquillisers. Hedy remembers the pills in the brown bottle, the one with no label. Knowing Hank's access to drugs, she wonders what that bottle had really contained and how the contents had affected Mom. Whatever drugs she was on, it must have been terrible for her to watch her husband's distress and not to know the cause or be able to help him. And Mom would have been thinking of her long-lost brother, too – so close, in the next county. The fact that she never told her children about him, never disclosed the fact that Chris had the same condition as his uncle, makes Hedy wonder how much guilt her mother suffered for abandoning Ernest.

Hedy and Claire get off the bus early so that they can walk home across Chelsea Bridge and through Battersea Park. The evening is still warm and there are people in the park, walking dogs, having picnics on the grass with bottles of wine and punnets of early strawberries.

As they leave the park and walk up the street towards their flat, they hear the Sex Pistols' version of 'God Save the Queen' playing out of a window. Claire does a good impression of Sid Vicious in her red pant suit, snarling the words, and shouldering towards an invisible microphone. Children playing on the pavement, chalking out hopscotch squares, look up, laughing, and take up this new game, following along behind for as long as the song can be heard.

The ginger cat is waiting for them on the front wall. He

arches his back, purring, asking for food. They unlock the door and go through into the sitting room, the walls covered in Claire's framed drawings and paintings, bookshelves full of novels and poetry, with Hedy's books stacked together on their own shelf, spines turned outwards, Christopher Delaney picked out in red, silver or black.

'Hungry, my love?' Claire asks.

Hedy shakes her head; they've nibbled on dips and crisps all evening.

She drops her bag onto the Moroccan carved table, steps around the red and purple cushions on the floor and holds out her arms. Claire walks into them, smiling.

'You—' Hedy begins to say. But her words are cut off as Claire kisses her.

Because of Claire, Hedy has learnt to love her body. The first time they went to bed together had been revelatory: after the ripping away of clothes had come the sheer relief of feeling the full and naked expanse of each other's skin, and then the slow and sometimes fumbling discovery of being unexpectedly twinned with another – the mirroring and the sameness and the sense of belonging – the knowledge that she would not be alone again.

# FORTY-EIGHT

## 1980

Hedy is sitting in a crowded café in Soho, several bags of sale shopping slumped on the floor at her feet. Misted-up windows give the street beyond a pale romance, muting the traffic and neon signs. Customers sit with their hands around hot drinks, grateful to be out of the cold. Their discarded outdoor garments steam with condensation. Hedy stirs her coffee and thinks of ordering a croissant. The man at the next table blows his nose with such an extravagant explosion, she can't help glancing up. That's when she sees the headline of the newspaper he's reading: *Unexplained Lights, UFO in Suffolk say US servicemen.* She screws up her eyes and tilts her head, trying to read the small print. The man gives her an irritated glance.

'Watch my things for me, please,' she says, bundling herself into her coat.

In the shop next door she buys three different papers and takes them back to the café, orders a refill of coffee, and sifts through the reports one by one.

A security patrol reported seeing bright lights descending into Rendlesham Forest, Suffolk, on the evening of the 26th December. Thinking it was a downed plane, the servicemen entered the forest, where all four of them witnessed a metallic object with coloured lights hovering through the trees. Getting closer, they were blinded by a brilliant light. After daybreak the servicemen returned and found burn marks in the earth, broken branches, and a high level of radiation when they tested the area. Local police were called but reported no unusual findings; they believed the flashing lights came from a local lighthouse.

A hoax, one paper called it. Another said it was possible that this was a genuine UFO sighting. No danger to the public, the report concluded, no need for panic.

She stuffs the papers into her shopping bags and gets the bus home. She needs to be alone, to think. The traffic is slow, and each new passenger crowding on lugs straining plastic bags. There is barely room to move. Hedy stands with a plump woman's elbow sticking into her ribs and someone's wet umbrella dripping onto her foot. Hanging above the top of the bus are Christmas lights, all of them still bright with electricity. Elaborate giant snowflakes, fleets of reindeer and different kinds of Santa Clauses bob up and down in the wind.

There's a message on her answerphone from her agent. A reporter is asking for her opinion on the UFO story. 'And didn't you live in that area once? Call me back when you can.' The message clicks off. Hedy erases the tape.

She sits on a cushion in the sitting room, the bags discarded in the hall. The Christmas tree in the corner is losing its needles, the floor underneath prickly with faded green. The faint smell of pine. The cat jumps on her lap. It's cold in the room. Hedy keeps her coat on. She imagines the servicemen moving through dark branches, their fearful, hopeful faces fixed on the sky. Flashing lights can be caused by any number of things, she reminds herself, lighthouses or falling stars.

It's human to want to believe we're not alone, that God or aliens must be out there, maybe both. She knows that Chris believed his wonderful light was something from another solar system. It's shaken her to think there might be a connection between what the servicemen saw and her brother's experience, that it's more than a coincidence. It's hard to admit that she'll never know the truth, and that there won't be a last reckoning for her brother's death, a final answer to the mystery. She makes up stories for her job, shaping tales out of nothing, creating beginnings, middles and ends. People need help to make sense of things, need a narrative, a purpose, an ending. Chris was just the same – it was why he wrote in the first place, to help him make sense of his own pain, or at least to cope with it.

She misses him. She misses him. She kept hoping she'd have the dream again with his wonderful light shining on her. It was the last time she dreamt of the forest. The closest she's come to being with him. She felt such joy, knowing he was there, inside the brilliance, waiting.

The phone rings. Hedy presses her face into the cat's vibrating body, wiping tears on ginger fur. He doesn't seem to mind the dampness. There's a shift inside her, a flicker of energy passing through, like a star falling light years away. When it's gone, she's left with a kind of acceptance of what is known and what will never be known. The phone stops and there's a new silence in the room. Outside the window she notices that snow has begun to fall.

# FORTY-NINE

## 1981

'My bonnie lies over the ocean, My bonnie lies over the sea, My bonnie lies over the ocean, Oh, bring back my bonnie to me.' Once they lived in Iowa, in a bungalow with the Stars and Stripes flying in the yard. Before that it was Florida. The sea shining on the horizon.

Ruby holds the novel in her hands. *The Wonderful*, it says on the cover. And then his name, his beloved name. Her son. Christopher. She runs her fingers over red letters, raised like Braille. Her tears fall, splat, patches of wet dampening the paper. He was a beautiful child. She hated locking him inside the brace, but she had to put him in prison to set him free. And then they took him from her.

This is the novel that Hedy wrote. But inside the covers is Christopher's story. Ruby remembers Hedy reading to him, all of those science-fiction books they went crazy for. 'Look after your brother,' she'd told her. But she didn't need to. Since they were born, Hedy always watched out for Christopher. If she half-closes her eyes, she sees them both, her children, blond heads together under the blazing sun.

She is so much better now. She knows a lot of things, although the electric currents have taken some things away for ever. Ruby sits on her bed on the pink cover. It's not the right time for outdoor exercise, but she is dressed in a coat and hat. 'You'll need to wrap up warm,' the nurse said as she helped her with the buttons. Outside the windows, outside the bars, the January sky is filled with falling snowflakes. There is a reason she's sitting here, waiting. She is going home at last. Not to Iowa, or to Norfolk. She knows that those places aren't home anymore, just as she knows that Todd and Christopher are dead. And Ernest, too. Getting better has been hard.

She also knows that Hank was not a friend, not ever; her memory of that time is fragmented, broken like a smashed mirror, but in the jagged, shining pieces she sees reflections of truth. The drugs from that little brown unlabelled bottle had made her hallucinate, had put her into a dark, uncertain world where she lost control of everything – including her children. And then, leaning over her as she lay in bed, Hank whispered things to her, terrible things, blaming Hedy for Christopher's death. Telling her that Todd was a spy. His words followed her here, came back to her every night, emerging to haunt her in the marshy wasteland of her days.

'Ruby,' the voice would begin softly, 'I know you can hear me.'

And she'd recall a room full of a dull gold light. Orange curtains rustling at an open window. The shadows of pines behind a mesh fence.

She'd push her head under her pillow, or press her palms to her ears. But it was no good. The voice would not be silenced.

*You're going to a place where you'll be looked after. You know you're not strong. You can't trust yourself. You let Todd down – it was you who gave him away, who signed his death sentence. Your mind plays tricks on you. Christopher is dead. Remember how I told you that there'd been an accident? It was Hedy's fault. Don't cry for Todd, he was a spy – he betrayed his country. You don't have a family anymore, Ruby. All of that's gone. You're on your own now.* On and on, the whispers rising and breaking inside her like waves.

Then one night they didn't give her any meds, and she remembered him leaning over her as she lay in her bed in the bungalow behind the pines. She recognised his words.

'Hank.' She spoke his name aloud into the darkness. His face materialised above her, wide with surprise. 'I trusted you.' She kept her eyes steady, watching him. 'You lied to me. You lied about everything. Todd. Hedy.'

His mouth twitched, in anger or amusement, she couldn't tell.

'Liar,' she said again. But he was a figure in blue, moving away towards the voices beyond the door, towards a time that was gone and could never be retrieved.

Ruby woke in her cot, half-suffocated by the smell of other women's bodies and breath, her mind oddly bright, as if it had been emptied of stones.

'Hedy,' she whispered with wonder in her voice. 'My daughter. My angel.'

And then the real horror came, the memory of loss. Her husband. Her son. Gone. The knowledge cutting chunks out of her heart – but pushing her up out of a slip-sliding bog of uncertainty into a hard, clean light.

She plucks at the sleeve of her coat. A dull navy wool. It's not her coat, really; she's been given it by the home. It's thick and heavy. It still smells of the last owner. She keeps her feet pressed together, lined up in sensible shoes.

'Well, you've certainly been here a long time,' the nurse says. 'It says 1957 on your notes.'

Ruby tries to remember what it's like out there in the world. Sludge-coloured fields under a ragged flight of rooks. The burning dust-driven plains of Iowa. Heaps of spires and rooftops in some great city. There will be choices to make. To forgive, or not to forgive. What to eat for breakfast. What time to go to bed. The freedom waiting for her seems very fine, almost noble, but frightening, too. How will she walk without a nurse to watch over her? How will she sleep in a room that is dark? Her fingers move to her palm, to the scar. She won't be alone. And her fear is only fear of the unknown, and that is the beating blood of life itself.

The door opens and her daughter comes in, walking with the athletic swing she's always had, as if she's about to break into a sprint. Her cheeks are flushed with cold. She's wearing jeans and a jacket, and she brings the smell of the frozen outside with her.

'Hello, Mom. Are you ready?'

Ruby stands up and touches Hedy's face. 'Ready as I'll ever be,' she says.

Hedy picks up the holdall with Ruby's possessions. The way she stands, with her feet spread and her knees soft, looking ahead for the next obstacle, the next battle, reminds her of Todd. Because he's been there all along, in the bones and spirit of their daughter, in the words that she's saying now, 'It's all right, Mom. I'm going to take care of you.'

No amount of electric shock can erase love. Even when she couldn't remember her own name, there was the memory of it inside her, like a separate creature moving under her ribs, pulsing under slabs of bleak, dark nothingness. Very small. The feeling of her children's breath, the heavy warmth of them in her arms, Todd's mouth on her own. And long before that, the distant memory of Ernest – perhaps two or three years old – holding her hand, and her the stronger one leading him across the farmyard, picking up feathers to thread into his hair, making him laugh. Her brother, her flesh: before his bones betrayed him, before she betrayed him. All of that, packed up into a tiny pulse.

Hedy takes her hand, the one with the scar, and folds it inside her own. 'There'll be three of us. My friend, Claire, lives with me. I think you'll like her. And I hope you'll like the house. We've converted it. But none of that matters.' She smiles. 'There's a garden to sit in when it's warm. You'll have your own room.'

'Can I sleep with a light on?'

'Of course. We can get you a night light. Maybe one of those ones with a moon and stars.'

A small group of doctors and nurses gather to say goodbye; they look proud and concerned, like parents seeing a child off to school on the first day. Ruby looks resolutely forwards and keeps hold of Hedy's hand, in case they change their minds, say it's all a mistake and call her back. Together they walk slowly down the long corridor. The door opens. 'You first,' Hedy says.

Ruby steps outside, and the white world rushes to meet her, sunlight catching on freshly fallen snow setting a blaze of brilliance that blinds her; she thinks she sees the silhouette of Christopher inside the light, his shape imprinted on her eyes. She blinks and he's gone. She puts out a hand to steady herself, hears Hedy murmuring words of encouragement, and such joy enters her that she's giddy, giddy as if she's spinning under Todd's arm, the dance urging her on.

# AUTHOR'S NOTE

The experiments going on under the bunkers in the novel are taken from the Project MK Ultra programme. This was a programme of experiments conducted on human subjects: mental patients, prisoners, military personnel. Even children. The programme was designed and undertaken by the CIA and organised through the US Army. It began in the 1950s with the aim of discovering methods of exerting mind control over individuals through torture and interrogation. Drugs like LSD were also administered to civilians and military personnel, like Todd, without their knowledge or consent. At the time, the US believed that Russia already had a 'truth drug', and were desperate to find their own. Former Nazi scientists were recruited to work on the programme. Experiments were conducted using drugs, chemicals, sensory deprivation, isolation, induced comas, and other forms of psychological torture. The MK Ultra programme was officially ended in 1975 after a commission was called to investigate its often illegal methods.

MK Ultra experiments were performed in different locations throughout the United States, but to my knowledge they never happened on an American airbase outside the USA. That part of the story is pure fiction. The airbase in the novel is based on Bentwaters in Suffolk, used by the USAF during the Cold War. It is surrounded on three sides by a pine forest.

This same location in Suffolk, Rendlesham Forest, is also the place that the alleged December 1980 UFO incident was reported by US airmen.

# ACKNOWLEDGEMENTS

Thank you, Emma Beswetherick. How very lucky I am to have you as my editor; I'm also privileged to have the talented team at Piatkus working on my behalf. Dom Wakeford, Kate Hibbert and Andy Hine, I appreciate what you do.

I am, as ever, hugely grateful to my agent, Eve White. You made everything possible. And thanks to Ludo Cinelli for all your help.

I am indebted to my early readers, who are patient enough to wade through uncorrected and not-yet-working manuscripts: Sara Sarre, who brings love and dedication to her role as BF and first reader; Alex Marengo, who is not just willing, but happy, to discuss plot points in the middle of the night; Ana Sarginson, my very earliest reader, aged five; Anil Malhotra, who read nearly every draft and gave me considered and useful feedback. Many thanks as well to my writing group: Mary Chamberlain, Viv Graveson, Laura McClelland, Cecilia Ekback and Lauren Trimble. It's wonderful to belong to such a loyal and talented group of writers. Sophie Hutton-Squire, I am always thankful for your thoughtful and thorough copy-editing.

Right at the beginning of my research, I was fortunate to make contact with Joyce Berch and Ruth Cunha, who were both kind enough to talk to me about their lives on Bentwaters airbase in the 1950s; everything you told me was fascinating and valuable. Thank you so much. If I've made any factual blunders in this novel, they are completely my own.

Lastly, I couldn't do what I do without my family – their love and support is central to everything I am and everything I do: my siblings, Alex Sarginson and Ana Sarginson, my partner, Alex Marengo, and my children: Hannah, Olivia, Sam and Gabriel.

# how it ends

# ends

Reading Guide

# READING GROUP
# DISCUSSION POINTS

- What are the main themes explored in the story?

- Do you have a favourite character, and why?

- Does setting play an important role?

- Can you think about family, parenthood and childhood in relation to all the main characters? How do they inform decisions in the story?

- The story is set in the 1950s, but many themes still resonate today. Can you discuss?

- How important are sexuality and identity in the story?

- Can you discuss the sibling ties between Hedy and her twin brother?

- Did you get a feel for the US airbase and its surroundings?

- The story moves between points of view. Who, in your mind, has the strongest voice?

- Did you see the end coming and how did it make you feel?

- All the characters in the novel are lonely to one extent or another: who, in your opinion, is the loneliest, and why?

- Christopher is trapped in a brace – who else is trapped in the novel, and in what way?

- Can you discuss why Hedy dresses in her brother's clothes?

- Can you comment on Christopher's experience of the wonderful light in the forest?

# BEHIND THE BOOK: A CONVERSATION WITH SASKIA SARGINSON

***How It Ends* is the fifth book you've written. Does the writing process get easier with every book?**

I hope that the experience of writing multiple books has helped me hone my craft and learn more about my 'voice'. But each new story needs a different structure and approach – and the problems arising from this always feel different. When I begin a novel, I'm filled with excitement; when I finish, I'm filled with nervous anticipation of how it will be received. That never changes. Neither does my joy and frustration and obsession with the process of writing.

**What has been the most enjoyable part of the writing process?**

For me, the most enjoyable process is always in the re-making: the editing and re-writing of drafts. It's liberating when I've got the research behind me and the bones of the plot down, because that means I can play around with the way I'm telling the story. Best of all, I love tweaking, editing, and polishing the text.

**What has been the most difficult part?**

The hardest part is definitely getting that first draft down – facing blank page after blank page. Working out how to tell the story inside my head can actually feel quite exhausting. I tend to eat a lot of toast and honey and drink a lot of coffee during this stage!

**The setting of this book really makes it stand out. Is there a reason why you decided to write a novel based on an American airbase in the 1950s?**

I grew up in a pine forest in Suffolk with an American airbase on our doorstep. In the 70s and 80s, there seemed to be a glamour to the lives of the American military personnel and their families, living separately from us behind a tall, wire fence. I was also aware of the reported UFO sighting in the forest by American airmen in the 1980s. I always wondered if there was any truth in it, or if there was another explanation, and if that explanation would be mundane or sinister. It occurred to me that I might be able to write a story that used the base as a setting, and weave in the UFO sighting. Going back to the 1950s, and the decades that followed, appealed to me for lots of reasons: the intense interest in outer space and the excitement about putting a man on the moon; the lies behind the Vietnam war and Watergate; the shocking revelation of President Nixon's criminal activity; the tension around the Cold War and the fear of the atom bomb – something that, unfortunately, has become relevant again. I realised that all that secrecy and fear confined inside the base could create a wonderfully paranoid and emotionally heightened atmosphere. And then I came across the true story of MK Ultra and the awful experiments conducted in the name of world peace. Everything came together, and I knew it could be the backdrop to an explosive family drama.

**Hedy is such a strong heroine, from childhood through to adulthood. Do you identify with parts of her character?**

As with all the characters I write, a part of me is woven into Hedy's DNA. I like the fact that she's practical, brave, determined, protective, and kind – but she's also vulnerable, awkward, and confused about her sexuality. Her character is tested when her family is destroyed around her, and it's tested again in a different way when she's trapped in the middle of nowhere. One similarity I definitely share with Hedy is impatience, so I felt for her during her years on the Norfolk farm, when her instinct to be proactive was thwarted; instead she had to be patient and wait for information and people to come to her, for the timing to be right.

**Can you talk about how the theme of identity is explored in the story?**

All the main characters struggle with their sense of identity. Todd's idea of himself as an all-American action hero is destroyed the minute he starts his new job on the base. As he crumbles, this impinges on Ruby, because she takes her sense of self from him. The old Ruby she left behind on the farm, along with the guilt she carries about her brother, is always there inside her, threatening to wreck her new and carefully constructed self. Hedy and Christopher have to contend with the prejudices of the time, and because of that it's almost impossible for them to discover their true sexuality, and therefore the foundation of who they really are. For Christopher, his disability and torturous brace stop people from seeing him. Instead, he creates a space for his true identity to thrive inside his stories. His self-portraits sketched in his notebook as the weird kid in the brace, then brave space explorer, highlight the discrepancy between how the world sees him and how he sees himself. A sense of self usually turns out to be a complex and fragile thing, yet it's at the centre of everything human beings do, driving their emotions, behaviour and actions.

**Twins appeared in your first book *The Twins* and you've written about twins again here. Why are twins so fascinating to you?**

I think twins are fascinating to most people. I am particularly interested as I have identical twin daughters. As an author, twins are good fictional fodder: the relationships between twins are more intense than between normal siblings. We tend to presume that they'll be born with similar abilities and almost identical opportunities; when this isn't the case, it throws up questions of loyalty, justice, jealousy, luck, duty and love.

**Was it difficult to write about a character with a physical disability and did it take a lot of research?**

It was difficult in that a lot of writing comes from experience. It's impossible for me to truly understand what it's like to be inside the body of someone like Ernest or Christopher, as I lack that experience. Fortunately for me, I've never known their particular kind of pain, suffering, loneliness, and indignity. In order to write their stories, all I could do was invest time in research, and then use my empathy in trying to imagine what these characters would feel – emotionally and physically. As I wrote, I felt grief for both of them.

**The end delivers a shocking twist. Did you always know how the story was going to end?**

What's happening under the bunkers on the base, and under the stones in the forest, was part of my premise from the beginning. I'd already researched MK Ultra and knew the part it was to play in the plot, and Hank's involvement in it. However, I remained unsure about how to do the 'reveal' until quite late on in the writing – I played around with various ideas, but in the end kept it simple with just one chapter where we enter Hank's point of view.

**What are you working on now?**

I'm right at the very beginning of the next novel, but I can tell you that it's a love story. I'm sticking to one genre for the first time ever. It'll be a love story that spans several decades and, naturally, is fraught with conflict and complications.

Read on for an excerpt from
Saskia Sarginson's exceptional debut novel,
and Richard and Judy Bestseller

# the •
# twins

'Outstandingly good. Part-thriller, part-love story, I
guarantee you will not be able to put it down' *Sun*

**Available now from Piatkus**

We weren't always twins. We used to be just one person.

The story of our conception was the ordinary kind they tell you about in biology lessons. You know how it goes: an athletic sperm hits the egg target and new life forms.

So there we were, a single ho-hum baby in the making. Then comes the extraordinary part, because that one egg split, tearing in half, and we became two babies. Two halves of a whole. That's why it's weird but true – we were one person first, even if only for a millisecond.

Mummy always said that having twins was the last thing she'd expected, except she knew there had to be a good reason why she couldn't fit through doors at four months, let alone do her jeans up. Mummy was beautiful. Everyone said so. She looked like an ice queen from the pages of a fairy tale. A queen who wore flip-flops and Indian skirts with tassels dangling down, and whose fingers were stained nicotine yellow. She wouldn't tell us who our father was. Not that it really mattered. We just pretended it did, because it felt exciting to try and guess who he might be, as if we could invent the story of our own birth.

There's a Greek myth that says if a woman sleeps with a god

and a mortal on the same day she'll have two babies: one child from each father. Even our mother wouldn't do anything as slutty as that. But when we climbed the branches of the lilac tree to sit on the roof of the shed, sharing an apple and discussing possible paternal options, the idea of being fathered by a god was satisfying.

The obvious choice was a rock god. Our mother played The Doors obsessively. She looked at Jim Morrison's picture on the album cover and sighed. The only thing we knew about our father was that our mother met him at a festival in California. Bingo. It had to be Morrison. We didn't want our dad to be one of the creeps and weirdos we lived with at the commune in Wales. Lanky Luke or smelly Eric. Mummy didn't love any of them. We wrote Mr Morrison a letter once, secretly, signing it from Viola and Isolte Love. We never got a reply.

On 3 July 1971 Jim Morrison was found dead in his bath in Paris. Cause of death: heart failure brought on by heavy drinking. He'd planned to stop being a rock god and become a poet. He'd been waiting for his contract to run out. The day the news broke we came home from school to find our mother playing 'Hello, I Love You' over and over and weeping into her glass of red wine. We cried too, up in our bedroom, howling into our pillows. At first it was a kind of show; but then fake turned to real. You know how sometimes when you laugh really hard you can trip some emotional switch and start crying instead? This was a bit like that. Except pretend crying tripped the real thing, and suddenly we were drowning in tears, taking shuddering gasps, snot smearing our cheeks. We had no idea what we were crying about. Later, when Mummy was sober and we were all hiccuping and squinting through swollen eyes, she told us that Jim Morrison definitely wasn't our dad. 'You nitwits,' she said wistfully, 'where on earth did you get that idea?'

We tried a few more times to discover who our father was.

But Mummy got irritated. Shrugging and rolling a cigarette slowly, she'd blow smoke spirals and look disappointed by our dull questions. 'I've started a new dynasty,' she explained. 'I want you to build your own future. You don't need a past.' We knew that she thought our desire for a father was petty and bourgeois. All the worst things in the world were petty and bourgeois.

It was the spring of 1972, and Mummy said that, what with the miners' strike and the three-day weeks, the country was going to hell. Ted Heath was a Tory fool. We had to be pre-pared for the worst. We needed to be self-sufficient. She dug up the weedy flowers and planted vegetables and bought two nanny goats: Tess and Bathsheba. One brown and the other black; they both had switchy tails and cloven feet like the devil. We wanted to love them, but they just chewed all day, grinding their long teeth. Even when we squatted to scratch their ears, they kept on chewing, marble eyes looking through us. The goats broke free of their tethers and trampled the vegetable patch, pulling up plants by the roots. Every morning, Mummy spent grim hours trying to replant limp broccoli and carrots before she sat with her head in a goat's flank, fingers working, swearing at their fidgeting, to emerge with thin milk as rancid as old cheese or stewed socks.

She had a book showing which wild foods were safe to eat and when and how to pick and cook them. That book was con-sulted constantly, pondered over, worn and stained from being taken along on walks and splattered from being propped next to the stove. Foraging became a new religion. Plucking berries and mushrooms and apples from the hedgerows – now, Mummy said, that was free-spirited and free. Two things she approved of.

We got scratched from pushing through brambles to get at the crab apples, our mother barefoot beside us. 'Higher, Viola. That's it.' Tossing her hair impatiently. 'Get the ones on the next branch up, Issy.' She made jelly and wine from those: tangy-tasting and pink as a tongue. Once we got terrible stomach cramps from some speckled mushrooms she'd put in a stew. But we got to like brain fungus fried in butter with salt and pepper and a little curry powder; a crinkly, rubbery, pale fungus that grew at the foot of pine trees – we tore up handfuls whenever we found it. And puffballs, picked when they were fat and white, rolling in the dewy grass on autumn mornings like misplaced snowballs. We had them sliced in batter for breakfast with crispy bacon.

Have you ever felt real hunger pangs? Not just a growl, the casual complaining of your stomach missing a meal, the inconvenient rumble and gurgle when lunch is late. I mean the deep birthing pain of true emptiness. The hollow ache of nothing. Fat is a human fault because it's only humans who are stupid with greed. Birds are light as a handful of leaves. I want the lightness of wings to enter me. I've learned to eat like a bird, not a human. In this place they try and trick me into eating, they play mind games, stick tubes down my throat.

Of course, it hurts to starve. But you can use those pangs like a knife to slice out the bad things inside you. Eventually you'll come to crave that feeling. Because hunger is a friend. With it you can get down to your bones quicker than you'd think. I feel them under my fingers, nudging up close below my skin, closer every day: smooth and flawless and hard. That's what everyone says about bones, don't they? That they're pure. Clean. I trace the lines of mine and they make a shape: the scaffold of myself.

It's all we are in the end anyway. Sometimes not even that. Sometimes there aren't even bones to show for a life – just molecules shifting in the air – and a few memories locked up in your head, yellowed as old photographs.

I'm tired now. I'd like to go back to sleep. I'm rambling. I know I am. Issy wouldn't like it. She told me to shut up when we had to sit in that little room with a man and a woman asking us the same questions over and over.

What did we do? What did we see? What time and when and where?

They thought we were wicked, you see. They thought we'd done something unforgivable. I cried and shifted on the hard chair, feeling a shameful warmth seep through my knickers. Wet dripped over plastic until there was a puddle on the floor, and a policeman came with a bucket and cloth. I closed my eyes, trying not to inhale the sharp stink of urine. My bare legs stung.

Those days were filled with listless waiting, people whispering about us behind their hands. We were trapped in that bleak room, while they stared at us and tapped their pencils and made notes. I noticed them looking at the scar on my face and I pulled my hair across, trying to hide it, scared that they would recognise the mark of Satan.

But I wasn't alone – my sister was next to me, like she always was, stronger, bolder. Her eyes were dry and there was no wet patch under her chair.

'Don't say anything, Viola,' Issy said. 'You don't have to say anything. They can't make you.'

And she holds my hand tight, her curled fingers squeezing hard, steely as a trap.